THE SERPENT CODE

AR STEVENS

LINGOCCINO INC.

Cover Design by Patrick Knowles

Spider Rock Carving created for cover photo: John Triano

Publisher: Lingoccino Inc.

First Edition: December 2023

Name: Stevens, AR

Title: The Serpent Code

Description: First edition | Ontario: Lingoccino Inc., 2023

Identifiers: ISBN (paperback 5.25 x 8): 978-1-7753705-1-2 | ISBN (paperback 5 x 8): 978-1-7753705-2-9 | ISBN (ebook): 978-1-7753705-3-6

ACKNOWLEDGMENTS

They say writing is a solitary affair—and while that statement is true for the times we authors sit alone in front of our keyboard, staring at a blank page, it is also false.

Creating a novel and bringing it into the world requires support. And I've been lucky enough to have a great deal of it.

To Peter Senftleben, my editor, many thanks for sticking with this project, from its most humble beginnings through to the result. This book is much improved because of your skill and expertise, and I hope I've done you proud.

As I live in Canada, this book was written in Canadian English. However, having spent a good number of my adult years in the USA, it was a bit of a challenge to remain consistent. A big shout out goes to Susan Helene Gottfried at West of Mars, whose sharp copy editor eyes made sure I didn't stray too far from accepted conventions.

My sincerest gratitude goes to my friend and fellow writer, Steve Bennett, who took the time to read endless emails and progress notes, and whose proof-of-concept experiment led to an important revelation in the story. Your persistent encouragement and thoughtful feedback helped more than you know.

Extra mention goes to Allan May who kindly acted as an ideal reader for decisions related to book packaging.

And then there are those who provided their expertise, and without whom inspiration in fiction cannot take flight:

To Steve Wilson who literally wrote the book on the Spider Rock Treasure, as the story unfolded in Texas at the turn of the 20th century, and also to Bill Townsley, who supplemented his published notes by responding to all questions asked about the Spider Rock and about Texas mysteries. I thank you both for your time.

I also owe a debt to Dr. Stephen Injeyan, who alerted me to strange tales regarding parasites, and directed me to the case study that inspired a portion of this book.

In addition, I remain grateful to Friar Jack Clark Robinson, who gave me a much needed appreciation for the historic churches in the Southwest. Through him I learned about the different orders of friars and the difference between the Vulgate translation by Jerome and the Septuagint translation by Jewish scholars, of the Christian Old Testament. Jack graciously encouraged me to continue asking questions—which, of course, I did.

In acknowledging the tremendous help received from these many people, I must also note that occasionally, either for the sake of the story, or simply due to some misunderstanding, I may not have taken the sage advice that was given. Thus, all errors remaining in this work are wholly and truly mine.

For Jay—because some loves are eternal.

PROLOGUE

Sweat cascaded from her temples, matting the dark curls at her cheeks. Hair stuck uncontrollably to her face even as she pushed the strands away with the back of her hand. Hot as hell, and she was running out of options fast.

Resigned to the story her messy features told, she faced the camera.

"Briel. I don't have much time... "

It was stupid to record her "just-in-case" video in the tunnels under Teotihuacan. As usual, she did it anyway. Dr. Persephone Gilbert, field archeologist, international explorer and adventurer, couldn't help herself. One of many mistakes. Just like she should have asked her best friend, her ultimate guide rail, to come along on this expedition into her family's archeological inheritance. The trouble was, even at the tender age of eight, Percy had talked the rule-following, instruction-reading Briel Payce out of her narrow comfort zone about as often as Briel had talked Percy out of trouble. If Briel were here now? That didn't bear thinking about.

Still, if they caught her, Percy would go to her grave, grateful for solving the Spider Rock's origin. And that's why she chose this spot—right in front of the cavity in the tunnel wall under Quetzalcoatl's pyramid—to tape her message. The Spider Rock had to have been carved from there. It was the perfect size. The next step was retrieving the rock and testing her theory. She needed to be sure. Then she could finally expose the truth.

The video was a big middle finger to her pursuers, and a hoorah to her best friend, in case she didn't make it. Percy only hoped she'd laid the clues out well enough for Briel to finish this without pissing off the merry band of crazies stalking her this past week.

Tires rumbled on the surface overhead and headlights winked through the hole left by the latest cave-in. Did they know she was there?

She focused the camera on the paper with the coded message. Another sound came from above and she clicked off the recording, replacing the note in her pocket.

Time to go.

Percy crawled to where the passage allowed a cell signal and attached the video file to the email she'd prepared for her lawyer. He'd hold on to it, pass it on only if necessary. But, if Percy lived to tell the tale, Briel need never know how bad it really got.

Percy hit send, deleted all evidence of what she'd done, and scrambled for the exit near where she'd hidden her vehicle, praying it wasn't too late.

It wasn't.

Her car remained alone, shrouded by brush and camouflaged in its dark blue paint. Heart pounding, Percy checked her surroundings and then dashed to the driver's side door.

Within seconds, the engine was running and she crept from the closed tourist grounds into a moonless night. She didn't dare turn lights on. Unfortunately, by the time she got to the south Teotihuacan exit, high beams burst into her rear-view mirror.

They'd found her.

Her best shot was to head back to the city, or at least some version of suburbia with street lights and witnesses. Whether anyone would come forward if she was caught, well, that was another matter.

God, she was thirsty. Not a drop left in the metal canister bumping atop the passenger seat. Probably for the best. Her camp water filter had strained its limits at the mucky, algae-infested pond she'd found in the Cuapiaxtla desert. How long since she last had water? She couldn't remember. But it was worth it. She had lost them on that wild goose chase.

At least until now.

Percy reached for the mebendazole she'd stored in a mint tin in the cupholder, popped a pill into her mouth, and choked as she tried in vain to gather enough saliva to swallow. Damn that old taco stand near the pig farm. First thing she ate upon arriving two weeks ago. A rookie mistake, easily dealt with, given the right meds. Unlike the situation now. She hit the accelerator and the little Japanese rental lurched.

Street lights came into view on the horizon and she willed the automobile to go faster. It did not obey. Served her right for insisting on economy. Actually, it was all she could afford. This trip was totally off the record and on her dime.

Headlights in the mirror grew bigger.

Why didn't she heed her great-uncle's warning?

"Now I ask you to... forego this as an empty search. You are the keeper, not the explorer."

She'd passed it off as an out-of-date caution meant only for her aunt Lydia. Surely any danger was long gone. Besides, unlike her aunt, Percy was a trained field archeologist and a professional explorer.

The lights turned red as she reached the intersection and traffic crowded the street in front of her. A quick check of the sidewalks revealed no one was there. The rear-view mirror, on the other hand, alerted her to how quickly the hunters were catching up.

She pulled out against the light and into a mayhem of crossing cars. A truck barrelled toward her and she hit the brakes, swerving to avoid a collision with only inches to spare. The opposing driver stopped his vehicle and blew his horn. Unapologetic, Percy darted past the crossroads, leaving those chasing her to navigate a mine-field of vehicles left in her wake.

Percy laughed and patted the steering wheel, but in her adrenaline buzz, she noticed too late the stop sign ahead. An oncoming pickup sideswiped her car and spun it out of control. Airbags deployed and she faded in and out of consciousness. In the distance, she heard a jumble of unintelligible Spanish and sirens.

IT WAS A TALL ORDER, quietly extracting the "Jane Doe" from the hospital. Though it cost him, he'd managed it. And she recovered nicely—or at least sufficiently. It wouldn't have been difficult to let her die there. Kill her and be done. Except for the real issue at stake, and his mentor's reminder:

"Will you allow the birth rate in our country to decrease by over ten percent? You dedicated your life to preserving the population! You, a man of 'science'. How long before our people are gone? And all because you did not fulfil your duty..."

The high priest placed his deerskin tool roll beside the altar and stroked the pre-Columbian greenstone beads that secured the opening. His mentor's unbidden remarks plagued him.

"She refuses to give up the stone," his mentor continued. "A sure path to our communal destruction. If you do not believe she is the one, test her! You have the means."

Sound advice. Now, here he was, and so was she.

Her strength surprised him. The concussion was significant, and though the hospital hadn't run tests for internal injuries, that possibility was ever-present. Then she regained consciousness and even tried unsuccessfully to overpower his guards. He almost smiled. Going back to Teotihuacan was her mistake. He always had people watching that site.

When she finally calmed, she declared she was thirsty and drank the offering with gusto. Probably dehydrated from her time in the desert. Perfect.

And then, nothing.

He waited an extra hour. Well past time for the genetically modified parasite eggs poisoning her milk to hatch, and for those tiny wriggling creatures to reach her lungs. Still, this woman fought back—again.

It was almost a pity to give up such an amazing specimen without studying what made her so strong. But his mentor was right. He'd tested her, and she had passed. Now it had to be done.

Flames slapped the air at the cave's core and cast an auburn glow over the wooden platform where Persephone Gilbert lay peacefully in a drug-induced sleep.

He wasn't a monster. While his predecessors viewed pain as purifying, he saw no need for that. Only the sacrifice mattered.

The high priest wiped sweat from his forehead. This new location at Cerro de la Estrella, in Iztapalapa, had links to everything they needed: ties to the ancient Cuicuilco culture, a historical haven for the original people of Teotihuacan, and even New Fire ceremonies held at the top of the hill in modern times. However, the rituals to be conducted in this chamber—the truly sacred appeasement of Quetzalcoatl, their God, their saviour, the Feathered Serpent to which the final pyramid in Teotihuacan was dedicated—needed to remain hidden.

Still, the cave was too small, with a shorter tunnel and fewer good air vents.

No choice, really. When archeologists breached their true sanctuary by finding the tunnels under Teotihuacan, they had to leave. He had enough connections to still manage the original site's engravings that recorded their work. How much longer was hard to say. This woman had come closest to replacing the keystone that gave away all their secrets. If she'd willingly given up the rock, they'd have hidden it with their other icons, protected until the day they finally emerged back into the light. Now the Spider Rock was lost again, and after taking care of Persephone Gilbert, it would never be found.

Two birds...

He inhaled, hungry for air in the hot, damp surroundings, and peered across at the alcove where the beautiful green-black obsidian statue of Quetzalcoatl watched over the proceedings. The high priest envisioned his god's approving nod.

Replacing his hood, he straightened his dusty, rust-coloured robe and pushed himself to standing. The woman's naked, dark skin glimmered as flecks of synchronized firelight danced around them. Despite the peaceful rise and fall of Gilbert's chest, beads of sweat crowded her forehead. Applying paint would be difficult. At least the feathers would stick well. Her eyelids fluttered. Dreaming? Regaining consciousness? He motioned to his men. Time to move things along.

Of his fifteen acolytes, only two were worthy of helping with the preparations. Emmanuel, who, like himself, came to Quetzalcoatl through an ancient family line, and Arturo, whose failed research on roundworms gave them "the test". In fact, Arturo created a biological weapon of sorts. Though the high priest and Arturo were bound by their god to save the population, not destroy it, if someday Quetzalcoatl demanded it...

He selected an extra thick brush from his tool roll and dipped it in the bowl of charcoal paint Emmanuel placed beside the woman's shoulder. The high priest started there, fashioning a drape of black across her chest. He moved to Gilbert's wrist, and Arturo hastened to take his place at the head of the altar, adding iridescent green quetzal feathers in a decorative line over the brush strokes. Emmanuel held a bowl of yellow, red, blue and white bird plumes, ready to complete the handiwork. They laboured until the skin at the woman's neck and upper chest, wrists, and ankles was no longer visible.

She stirred.

Just in time.

Two more hooded followers pulled Persephone Gilbert to her feet. As the congregation chanted, stomped and prayed, they marched the semi-conscious woman around the fire. Gilbert's eyes opened into slits. Her mouth moved and she mumbled.

"It's safe."

A healthy specimen indeed. Unexpected awareness.

The acolytes placed her back on the altar while the high priest selected a small and then a large scalpel from the tool roll.

A quick slice through each carotid should provide all the blood they needed. Then to harvest the skin. Draped in Gilbert's hulled casing, he would finish the dance and, finally, satisfy his god.

PERCY'S LIDS FLUTTERED OPEN. Grit lined her throat and she couldn't cry out. Flames. Uncomfortably close. She tried to focus. A blur of brown-hooded beings surrounded her. She was on her feet. Walking? How was that possible? No, marching. Propped on each side, held up by firm grips.

Nothing left to do apart from die. Except... Could she form words? Quiet, but they came.

"It's safe."

Then she was lying down again. A sharp pain glanced at each side of her neck and something oozed over her skin. As Persephone Gilbert's life drained, satisfaction overcame fear. And something else. Regret?

Briel... I'm sorry.

CHAPTER 1

F*ive Years Later*

"A FORTY-YEAR-OLD female presents to your clinic complaining of headache and neck pain."

Briel Payce, Doctor of Chiropractic, PhD in Epidemiology and Clinical Research, addressed the one hundred and fifty aspiring clinicians assembled at the Chiropractic College in Stephenville, Texas.

She hated teaching—especially groups of this size. She'd accepted the contract solely for the opportunity to conduct groundbreaking research in the care of back pain, and with that came the occasional return to the classroom, sometimes at the whim of the Vice President of Academics.

The phone buzzed inside her black suit coat pocket and she flicked away the wayward strand of blonde hair tickling her cheek. Briel ignored the cell signal and instead scanned the faces in the auditorium.

A full crowd. Surprising in this era of online learning.

Then she saw the two administrative assistants circulating attendance sheets. Her scoff almost made it to the microphone. Yet among the sea of bored, annoyed faces finding refuge in their laptops, cell phones and tablets, Briel could almost always count on about five attentive students. She found them and acknowledged each with a nod.

"Okay. What are you going to ask?" Briel continued.

"How long has it been going on?" replied the tall, clean-shaven young man in the middle row on the right.

"Where is it, exactly?" came a response from the left.

"How often do the headaches occur?"

"What causes them?"

Reasonable questions. Not bad for rookies.

Briel proceeded, hoping her next two slides would capture the attention of at least a few others.

Her cell buzzed again. She didn't want to disrupt the flow by taking it out and turning it off—something she should have done before getting on stage. She was rusty at this. Hopefully, the microphone didn't pick up the noise.

Briel continued.

"On observation, the patient is slightly flushed. She mentions a vague gastrointestinal discomfort and has a dry cough. The woman's temperature is recorded as 101.5 degrees Fahrenheit, and the clinician refers her back to her family physician for follow up and further testing."

Briel noted a restless shifting of bodies in their seats. Even her favourite five looked ready to abandon her. After all, if the case was simply referred out, of what interest was it to them?

She almost smiled.

Briel hadn't bothered to tell them that the case was actually her, from seven years ago, after the trek to Ecuador.

TRYING to convince Briel to take that trip, Briel's dearest friend, Percy Gilbert, began by chiding her over the phone.

"Oh, come on," Percy had said. "This one's right up your alley. And you need another expedition or they'll put you out to pasture this year."

"They" were the administrators for the International Explorer's Network (IEN), the bureaucratic arm of a worldwide club of scientist-adventurers dedicated to studying some of the most remote regions on earth. Sometimes they searched for new medicines in previously untapped biodiversity; sometimes they looked for materials and artifacts to validate or challenge historical theory.

It was easier for Percy. As an archeologist, documenting exploits that qualified for the IEN was her day job.

"I... Well, we... spent hundreds of hours this year with the code-breaking committee, mapping possible expedition locations. Can't I use that?"

Percy's silence said it all. Same modus operandi from when they were little. Percy pushed, and Briel relented. Without Percy, she'd probably be a hermit.

That call was for volunteers to accompany scientists into Cueva de los Tayos (Cave of the Oilbirds) in the rainforest of Ecuador. The cave achieved notoriety after tales of a metal library and suggestions of a previously unknown civilization made the mainstream press in the late 1960s and early 1970s. To date, explorations came back empty. From a scientific perspective, however, the environment remained exciting. That year, the native Shuar people finally gave permission to search for the endangered astroblepus pholeter—a beautiful light-pink cave dweller from the catfish family, with long fins and whiskers. Field observations in other regions suggested crossbreeding was occurring. The fish had yet to be found in Tayos, but discovering this rare species there could help sprotect the site from foreign mining interests.

Since an earlier exploration had also found an ancient burial site, if Percy documented a few artifacts along the way, so be it.

The only problem was that entering the cave required rappelling down a 200-foot cliff face into total darkness. After that, the ground was awash with bat guano and alive with tarantulas, roaches, and all variety of biting and nefarious organisms.

"Fine," Briel had said. "What could go wrong?"

Percy laughed. "That's just what Dean said."

Dean Leggatt, fellow IEN member, made his living as a forensic geologist. Convincing him was probably easy. The cave's reputed "gate", once believed to be masonry, was long ago identified as remarkably flat layers of sedimentary rock. Coupled with spectacular stalagmites and stalactites, the prospect of this trip would make any geologist drool.

As usual, Percy had come home from Ecuador unscathed. Dean and Briel had avoided infection from the various microorganisms in the caverns, but both contracted a fine case of ascaris lumbricoides (roundworms), probably from something they ate before heading into the jungle. And in true silver-lining form, Briel's subsequent headaches (physical and mental) became today's case study.

Her phone buzzed once more. Whoever the caller was, they were persistent.

Time to re-engage the class.

"Blood tests revealed eosinophilia."

Twenty more heads looked up from their cell phones.

One particularly bored student called out, "Eosiniphilic pneumonia."

A bright one. "Confirmed by?"

"X-rays. CT."

"Cause?"

Heads dropped. This time, thumbs inevitably searched the internet.

"Allergies."

"Might be toxins."

"Hmm." Briel paused for effect. She had most of the class with her now. "We didn't quite finish the history, did we? What if I told you the patient just returned from a trip through Ecuador?"

Yet another call on her cell. The lab? Some emergency? Briel chanced a look at the ID. Lydia. All four times. Why? She hadn't spoken with Percy's aunt in over a year. Ten minutes to the end of the lecture, or she could speed things along.

"Parasites," Briel said. "Presenting to the clinic with a headache and what appeared to be a virus. Next time, we'll review how parasites may affect your practice. Between now and my return, there are three online lessons about the impact of world travel on your role in health care. Please complete them all."

BRIEL HEADED for the parking lot, phone to her ear.

"I'm dying." Lydia's voice cracked.

The words sucker-punched Briel.

"Lydia. What are you talking about? What's happened?"

"It's cancer, Briel. Late stage. Nothing the doctors can do. But that's not why I called."

Briel remained silent. What else could there be?

"I can't die and leave Percy's case open. I'm having her declared dead." Lydia sobbed.

"When?"

"This afternoon."

"I'll be there."

CHAPTER 2

Briel let her fingertips absently tap the cardboard cup containing stale coffee and two packets of the white powder euphemistically referred to as creamer. Across the boardroom table, at the law offices of Pendington and Pendington, sat Lydia, stone-faced, yellow silk blouse loosely draped over her skeletal form. Briel regretted losing touch. She wished Lydia had told her about the cancer when she got the diagnosis. And she wished Percy hadn't disappeared five years ago.

Lydia's half-open eyes fixated on some imaginary point behind Briel. Her mouth hung slightly ajar and Percy's aunt took air in through her teeth. Unlikely Lydia would admit to pain, so Briel did her best to join the older woman's meditative state.

The door burst open and Drake Pendington, tall, with short, graying curly hair, burst through the door. Briel startled to attention. Lydia barely moved.

"Sorry to keep you ladies waiting," he said. The senior Pendington stopped the instant he laid eyes on Lydia. After an audible sigh, he softened his voice and continued.

"I heard you were ill, Lydia. I'm so sorry... And you must be Briel. Lydia's told me about you. Shall we get to it?"

Over the next hour, Briel alternated between holding Lydia's hand, resting her palm gently on the woman's shoulder, and fetching tissues, while the lawyer explained paperwork and pointed to spaces that required signatures. The job done, Pendington left the room and Briel collapsed into her own sobbing heap.

"God, I miss her. I'm sorry, Lydia."

Briel choked on the words. When Percy disappeared in Mexico, Briel had tried to find her friend. She'd taken a month's leave of absence. In the end, she'd failed to turn up even a single clue. Now, beside the frail woman who'd finally accepted her niece's demise, the impact of Briel's defeat hit with a vengeance she'd never known.

"I need your help," Lydia said. The words were barely audible.

"Anything."

"I want a proper funeral for my niece."

"Of course."

"No. I want you to find Percy and bring her home before I die."

The words hung in the air like thick, wet wool.

"But Lydia..."

"No buts. She's out there somewhere. You've got connections. Use whatever you need. Find her."

"Lydia, I tried. You know I did. I went to Mexico as soon as we lost contact. The US authorities told us there was nothing they could do, so I followed reports saying she'd been seen in Mexico City. I contacted the local police. It was a bust. No body, no crime, they said. Too many other priorities on their agenda."

"I don't know why you even bothered with them. We both knew they were a long shot. But people don't just disappear. Someone saw her."

"I agree. That's why I interviewed the locals. I searched every lead. I even tracked down a Jane Doe matching Percy's description that the paramedics brought to the hospital. I contacted a colleague, a medical director in one of the regional services, and asked for help, in case it was Percy. Despite both our efforts, we found nothing."

"Sweetheart." It was Lydia's turn to put her hand on Briel's arm. "I appreciate everything you did back then. I'm just saying somebody knows what happened. I'm asking you to try other avenues... I need this."

The older woman's deep brown eyes bore through Briel. Unable to take more, Briel squeezed her lids shut.

"Lydia. I'd give anything for another lead. Last time, I even went to Mexico's Secretariat of Travel, Culture and Tourism. All he said was that over the previous half decade, about three hundred American citizens had disappeared. Percy was just a number to him. The guy even insinuated that Percy must have gotten into drugs, done something wrong, hung out with a bad crowd..."

"You know that's not true."

"Of course. But we both know what Percy was like when she was on a quest."

"That damned Spider Rock. I should never have given it to her."

"It's not your fault."

"Yes, it is."

Pendington returned to the room, this time announcing his entrance with a gentle knock. A padded envelope in hand, he strode to Briel. "With the sad business officially concluded, I'm instructed to give this to you."

Inside, Briel found a thumb drive and a copy of an email from Percy that read: "Upon my death, please give this video file to Dr. Briel Payce. She'll know what to do."

"What's on the video?"

"I have no idea," Pendington replied. "We don't go through personal messages unless instructed. We transferred the file from that email to this drive, in accordance with the legal directives of our client."

Briel balled her hands into fists, fighting the water that filled her lower lids and threatened to blind her view of the ridiculous man before her. She blinked the tears back.

"It didn't occur to you, in all this time, that something on that recording might help find Percy?" Briel spit the words through a clenched jaw.

If Pendington was affected by Briel's change in demeanour, Briel couldn't tell by looking at him. His reply was calm.

"My duty as lawyer for the Gilbert family has been, and still is, to follow their wishes within the boundaries of the law. Ms. Gilbert's email was clear. It did not authorize anyone, including me, to view the contents of the file, until and/or unless she was legally declared dead. I was obligated to safeguard it until then."

"Do you think something in that video might help?" Lydia asked. Her voice quivered and her eyebrows knit with what Briel interpreted as anxious concern.

Though Pendington sighed, his expression remained placid. Briel kept her sights on the man, waiting, hoping he would come up with some kind of explanation. Something better. The pause extended into an uncomfortable silence, and Briel knew nothing would be forthcoming. Then she slammed her fists onto the lawyer's walnut conference table and directed the words that finally came to Percy's aunt.

"Lydia, I will scour this file the same way I would have when Percy disappeared... if it had been made available." A slight shuffle of feet came from where Pendington still stood beside her. "If there is something on it, you have my word. I'll go back for Percy."

Then Briel turned again to Pendington. "If this video could have made a difference to Percy's situation when we lost contact... this is not the last you'll hear from me."

OUTSIDE BRIEL PAYCE'S HOME, the prairie grasses bent to the winds that accompany May sunsets in Texas. Laptop fired up, Briel waited for her computer to acknowledge the flash drive. Percy's face sprang to life on the screen. Only it wasn't the energetic Persephone that Briel knew so well. Percy's normally full lips curled into a thin frown. Beads of sweat dotted her best friend's temples. Was she ill?

"Briel, I don't have much time." Percy's normally strong, quick cadence gave way to a hoarse whisper. "If you're seeing this, it means I didn't make it. I'm sorry. But, I figured out the Spider Rock's secret, and I've hidden it. Somewhere safe, like when we were kids. Just remember: 19.18370, -98.68019. You'll know it when you see it."

There was a pause, and then a slight rumbling sound. Percy looked up and then fished a note from her pocket. "You'll need this."

Percy focused the camera on a set of numbers.

33: 3. 8+25; 12. 2+7+6

44: 10. 19; 11. 17+1+6

58: 6. 5; 9. 12+1+2+9+8+7

A PAUSE, and then, "Oh. And thanks for the Alamo."

The recording ended.

Briel replayed her friend's message four more times, looking for anything that might reveal where the words had been recorded.

The wall behind Percy was dark. If Briel had to guess, it was some kind of rock face. She thought she noticed chisel marks over Percy's right shoulder, and maybe, an alcove? Perhaps there were crack lines extending down the wall. But nothing, absolutely nothing, Briel recognized.

She picked up the padded envelope and looked at the header in the email message.

Region: Mexico City. Date: March 21, 2018.

Why didn't Percy send it directly to her? Because Percy wanted to intercept the communication if she made it home safely? So much wasted time. If Briel had this five years ago... But no one wanted to admit Percy was really gone—least of all her. And she couldn't blame Lydia for holding out hope.

The GPS coordinates were easy enough to look up, and Google Maps told her everything she needed to know. Briel's hand trembled as she raised the phone to her ear.

"Lydia? I'm going back to Mexico."

The response was a muted weeping, and then, "Bring my baby home."

HER NEXT CALL was to Dean Leggatt.

"Of course I'll go," he said. "We should have searched together the first time."

"I'm sorry I didn't include you then. You just seemed too distraught when she didn't come back."

"It was my fault she went to Mexico."

"Why does everyone keep saying that?"

"In my case, it's true. Percy guessed the Spider Rock originated there. She told me about some sheepskin treasure map stolen from a small town near Mexico City. She said it led a guy by the name of Freddy Palmer to unearth the rock where the Double Mountain and Salt forks of the Brazos River meet in Texas. That was over 150 years ago. Palmer thought he was on the trail of Mexican gold and silver brought to Texas by the Spanish Conquistadors. He dug up the Spider Rock instead, and never found much else."

"So?" Briel asked.

"It came to Percy's family through Lydia's great-grandfather. He was a freedman servant to the Palmer family. After Freddy and his wife died, their daughter wanted nothing to do with the Spider Rock. She told Lydia's great-granddad it was cursed, but he was welcome to it. When Lydia finally gave it to Percy, the mystery got under her skin. She begged me to test the limestone plaster that covered the stone. So I measured the levels of calcium oxide and silicon dioxide, expecting a match for a quarry somewhere in Texas. Nada. Then I found a study looking at the same minerals around the Mexico City region. Researchers wanted to know where the lime plaster used in the Teotihuacan pyramid complex came from."

"You're saying you told Percy her rock came from Mexico City? Aren't there thousands of sources for lime? It could have come from anywhere."

"No, I'm saying that the ratio of minerals matched the most distinct quarry among those studied in the region. It had the same mineral content as the lime plaster in Teotihuacan, originating in a mine in Tula, a few hours north of Mexico City. Before I'd even hung up the phone with the news, Percy had her flight booked. It's my fault Percy went hunting for the Spider Rock's origin where she did."

Briel played the message Percy had left her, and Dean let out an audible groan.

"We'll find her, Briel. Together. This time, we'll find her."

CHAPTER 3

riel savoured the breeze that momentarily cooled the moist cotton shirt that clung to her back. Perched high on the cliff where the Cascada Congelada, Frozen Waterfall, began its descent down the side of the dormant Iztaccihuatl volcano, she wondered, not for the first time, why she hadn't cancelled today's hike.

Knocking on Dean's door at 4:30 in the morning, Briel had come face to face with the saddest case of Moctezuma's Revenge she'd ever seen. They'd been in Mexico City for only two days, and already Dean had eaten or drunk something that got him into trouble. Had to be a world record. At least this time, it didn't get her as well. In a moment of madness, or perhaps channeling Percy, Briel had headed off by herself to meet the guides they'd hired for the trek.

She sucked an extra long breath, trying to fill her lungs with the oxygen they craved. When had she last climbed a mountain? Too long ago to think about. They were 13,000 feet above sea level on the side of the dormant Iztaccihuatl volcano. At its highest peak, the mountain was just over 17,000 feet up. From where she stood, Briel laid eyes on the still active and even taller Popocatepetl volcano to the south and wondered how the Aztec myth about the two mountains came so close to Shakespeare's *Romeo and Juliet*.

Regional stories identified Popocatepetl as a soldier who went to war to earn the right to marry Iztaccihuatl. After some time, jealous warriors told Iztaccihuatl that the love of her life died in battle. At the news, the woman fell into a deep state of depression, finally dying of grief. When Popocatepetl returned to discover Iztaccihuatl dead, he took her body and placed it where she remains today. Then he knelt beside her and died as well. The gods took pity on the pair and turned them into snow-capped mountains. The plumes of smoke and flame that still spew from Popocatepetl are said to express the warrior's rage as he forever mourns his loss.

BRIEL STOPPED on the footpath and checked her GPS. They were close to the coordinates Percy had given her, so she motioned to her guides, Jose and Raphael, to halt.

"I'd like to take a break," she said.

Raphael, the more gregarious of the men, offered a toothy smile. "We are good to stop here, señora."

He signalled to Jose to remove his backpack and the two men pulled out a blanket and a small camp stove.

"I'm going into the brush," Briel said.

"Why?" Jose asked.

Raphael's head shot up and he turned to Jose, surprise evident on his face.

Jose instantly cast his eyes to the ground and mumbled, "I only ask because it is easy to get disoriented walking alone here. The mountain is unforgiving."

"Uhm. Thank you for your concern, Jose," Briel said. "Actually, I'm looking for a spot to manage a different call from nature... A private need."

Raphael elbowed Jose and said, "Of course, señora. Take your time. Jose and I will prepare a most beautiful lunch for you. And after that, we will climb to the bottom of the waterfall and take pictures of you beside it. To show your friends."

He slapped a seemingly reluctant Jose on the back and they got to work.

Alone at last, Briel looked around. The twenty-foot potential error radius of her phone's GPS posed a significant problem, particularly given the rugged terrain. And she didn't have time—especially if Jose and Raphael decided to worry about how long her "business" was taking.

Come back tomorrow with Dean? She knew the way now. They could probably manage without guides.

She looked at the rock face in front of her and pivoted ninety degrees to watch the water tumble down in multiple vigorous streams. How far was the drop? A couple hundred feet? The GPS registered the coordinates she was searching for, right at the edge. Just like Percy not to make it easy—or risk someone else finding what she had left.

Checking one last time that no one was nearby, Briel compared the surroundings to Percy's personality. Which formation made the most sense? Better question: What would Percy do?

After all, in their duo, Briel's role was safety manager: inspecting jump points, clearance levels and surrounding regions for all manner of hazard. At first, it was to avoid red ant hills and snakes. As teenagers, it was to avoid climbing down a trestle rail that looked like it reached the ground but actually ended in midair. As adults, Briel checked their mountain climbing gear—always twice, and the weather more often than that. Once, in New Zealand, it was Briel who had convinced the local team lead to force Percy to stand down when the winds picked up and snow started falling. Three climbers died that day and Percy had finally acknowledged that Briel's propensity for rules and safety saved them and at least a dozen others who had pulled back as well.

Hands on hips, Briel turned again to the steep, mud-brown rocky folds that embraced either side of the water at the cliff's pinnacle. How hard could it be? She and Percy had spent years geocaching throughout the world. This was just one more—unrecorded—cache.

Then she spotted it. A shelf about ten feet from the water's edge and about twenty feet off the ground. A recess. Briel would need to spider up a sheer rock wall to reach it. Nothing of interest to curious hikers and not worth the effort for proper free climbers.

Did she have enough time?

Briel found the first decent foothold and then reached for a vertical crack she could follow with her hands. Not exactly Yosemite's El Capitan, but Briel hadn't climbed in years and this was plenty big for her. She brought her foot to the next ripple in the wall and without warning, it gave way. Her shin scraped down the rock and she clenched her teeth to avoid crying out in pain.

Off balance, her other foot lost its hold and she hung by her arms. Her toes were only ten feet up, yet the jagged ground below did not invite a soft landing. In a burst of energy that made her want to shout, Briel pulled her legs back under control and refound her footing. Under her breath, she cursed Percy.

She pawed at the opening above her. Hoping to avoid more tentative footholds, Briel blindly reached her hand inside. Something touched her finger and she pulled away. Un-snagging a twig from a crevice, she explored the recess again. A daddy longlegs the size of a fist did a weaving dance as it crawled toward her.

"Ew!" escaped her mouth as she discarded the small branch and its occupant. Briel realized something much more harmful could have made its home in there. So much for her "safety first" reputation. Against her better judgement, Briel pulled herself higher and peered at the ledge. Nothing except for a now empty arachnid's den. A total waste of time.

As she withdrew her head, ready to descend, her eye caught something in the cavity's ceiling. A thin beige line of plastic sat wedged between two vertical slivers of rock. Moving higher again, she allowed her arms to rest on the shelf. Keeping one hand propped, she reached for the small switchblade in her front pocket.

"Señora Payce? Where are you?" she heard Raphael call.

"I'm fine," Briel responded, trying not to sound winded. "I'll be right there."

She swung the hook on the opposite side of the knife's sharp edge toward the plastic and popped a small zippered PVC bag from its home.

No time to look inside.

As Briel pocketed her prize, she lost her grip on the blade and it skittered away. Seconds later, a faint plop told her it was probably in one of Cascada's multiple streams and presumably lost.

"Enough already," Briel mumbled to an unresponsive sky before she scrambled back down the rock face.

The moment she got out of the brush and found the path, she faced Jose and Raphael. How long had they been standing there? From where she now stood, there was a clear view of her climb route.

Jose looked as sullen and unreadable as ever. Raphael was clearly concerned.

"Señora. Are you alright? Your leg is bleeding."

Briel looked down, and there was the evidence of her altercation with the cliff.

"I fell," she said. "Sorry. That's why it took me so long. I'm fine."

"Come," said Raphael. "We have first aid. And lunch has been ready for some time."

CHAPTER 4

Curious as she was about the contents of the beige pouch now seated in the pocket of her hiking shorts, Briel resisted the urge to inspect it. Instead, she sat on the grey, black, red, and white striped falsa blanket the guides had laid out and accepted their offering of cheese, chicken, and beef quesadillas that stayed warm over a small fire. A pot of fresh coffee perked happily to complete the simple, yet satisfying, meal and she ate her fill.

The men seemed willing to linger but Briel wanted to leave, and despite their protestations, she helped with cleanup and then made for the path heading down to the waterfall's plunge pool. Raphael jogged ahead, stopping on a picturesque, tiny plateau with a spectacular view of the cascading water.

"We take photos here." Sunlight beamed off Raphael's teeth as he gave Briel his widest smile yet. He extended his arm to the falls, emphasizing the treasure.

"No thank you," Briel said. All she wanted was to get back to the hotel. If she was right, she now held the key to Percy's message.

"Señora," Raphael said, "you've come all this way. You must have your picture taken beside the falls, if only to show the world how beautiful you look next to nature's power."

Briel considered her next move. She didn't want to raise suspicion about the reason for her trip. After all, something Percy had found had caused her to disappear, and that something might now be in her possession.

"Okay," she said, mustering a smile. "But no posting for the world to see. I only want to show my friends and family."

"Agreed."

Raphael forged ahead to move a branch from Briel's path. Behind her, Jose texted on his phone. Typical young man in his mid-twenties. Girl trouble? That would account for the sullen behaviour.

At the base of Cascada Congelada, Briel did her best to continue the tourist on an iconic hillside charade, while Raphael positioned her for the "best light".

FINALLY HEADED BACK down the slope, Briel realized something was amiss.

"Raphael? Why haven't we passed other hikers along the trail? It's such a beautiful day."

The guide shrugged. "Seems we are especially lucky."

The path narrowed and Briel followed Raphael while Jose positioned himself last in line. Whether it was maternal instinct or discomfort with being followed, twice Briel turned to check on the younger man. Both times, Jose was eyeing the clouds.

"Storm brewing?"

"No, señora."

Jose cast his eyes toward his boots.

A few hundred yards later, the footpath turned ninety degrees and they entered a rock gorge that eventually spilled them into an overgrown meadow. Raphael sipped from his water bottle and Briel took a moment to walk through the native grasses and explore the flatter terrain. Within seconds, she heard Raphael shout.

"Señora. Be careful. That treeline you approach hides a cleft in the rocks."

Briel waved her thank you and checked the boundary. Indeed, the roots of the tallest pines draped over one side of what looked like an excessively wide climber's chimney. The drop was about fifty feet. Not something to dare without proper gear.

She returned her attention to the guides and found Jose hunched over and pointing, animated for the first time in their excursion.

"Señora," he said. "Look!"

Scampering among the tussocks were tiny rabbits. From the recesses of Briel's mind, she drew back to a lecture on Mexican wildlife by a Fellow of the International Explorer's Network. The endangered teporingo. The volcano rabbit. Immediately, Briel pulled out her camera, marked the coordinates, and began counting and taking pictures of the furry creatures.

Enamoured, she forgot about the prize in her pocket until the slap, slap, slap of helicopter blades found her ears and interrupted the moment.

"Probably park authorities checking the region for hikers in trouble," Raphael said.

Jose said nothing, though he straightened from his crouched position. From her vantage, Briel noticed an increased speed to the rise and fall of his chest. The hairs on the back of her neck stiffened.

The noisy speck drew closer and the problem became clear. It was a shiny black military chopper with two long gun barrels, and the weapons were pointed at them.

"What the hell?" was all Briel could manage.

She turned to Raphael, who seemed stunned at the sight. He looked at Jose, and Briel couldn't read what passed between them.

Raphael returned his attention to Briel. "That cannot be for us. Perhaps there is trouble somewhere else on the mountain. I am sure they will pass…"

They didn't.

Instinctively, Briel and the guides ducked as the mechanical whirlwind closed in on their location. Arms by her side, Briel stretched her fingers, and they stiffened with anxiety. She worked her hands, pushing down what threatened to be an overwhelming panic.

Aequanimitas. Osler, the father of modern medicine, had titled the essay that commanded health care providers to be the cool, authoritative lead in a crisis. It was the mantra she'd adopted a long time ago. Briel took a deep breath, swallowed, and found her clinical bearing.

She scanned the horizon for anything that could shelter them while they assessed the intent of these newcomers. The patches of coarse grass were too short to get lost in, and going up the path wasn't an option. While she stood, frozen by the lack of alternatives, the strangers' intent became obvious.

Two armed men emerged, automatic rifles directed at Raphael and Jose. Black bullet-proof vests, outfitted in camo, these guys were ready for a fight. One man was thin, dark-skinned, with a long scar reaching from the side of his mouth all the way to his left eye. The other was heavyset and bald. The bald guy seemed in charge, and neither looked likely to leave an innocent bystander behind.

Raphael was already crying. Shaking, he dropped to his knees, pleading to stay alive for the sake of his wife and two small children. His five-year-old daughter and three-year-old son.

"They need their papa," he explained.

Jose trembled beside him.

While the guides occupied their attackers, Briel knew it was her only opportunity to act. Betting the black-vested assailants were unprepared for someone with climbing experience, she made for the pine tree edge and the sheer drop. Maybe there was a foothold or a crevice where she could take refuge and figure out what to do.

Almost there, Briel heard the crack of a gun. A bullet whizzed over her left shoulder and the scarred man shouted for her to stop.

She did as she was told.

Scarface headed toward her while his comrade held Jose and Raphael hostage. Briel backed closer to the edge, praying she'd estimated the distance correctly. The slight man put out an arm to grab her while the weapon in his other hand faced the ground.

Perfect.

Briel yanked at Scarface's forearm, ready to recreate the move she'd won medals for years ago in martial arts. Counting on whatever muscle memory was left in her body for the throw, she dropped to the ground, keeping a firm grip on the gunman's arm, and used his forward momentum to flip him... right over the edge. His AR-15 clanked down the sheer rock surface, sending random bullets ricocheting from side to side. Briel kept her head down and hoped for the best. The rifle finally clattered on the ground while she was still hanging on to Scarface. Her instinct was to let go.

From somewhere deep inside, a picture of Raphael and the little children who, within seconds, would be fatherless, bubbled to the surface.

So she held on while Scarface dangled over the precipice.

"I've got your buddy," she called to the bald man. "Not sure how long I can last. Let Raphael and Jose leave or your partner is dead."

CHAPTER 5

Vivaldi's *Four Seasons Concerto Number Four in F Minor*, "Winter," streamed through the sitting room's twelve speakers. Outside, it was 26 degrees Celsius and sunny. A perfect day.

The Conductor's fingers kept time, mentally bringing in the solo, then the first and second violin sections, followed by the violas, cellos, double bass and harpsichord, as necessary. The composer's shivering themes foreshadowed the Conductor's frenzied call to action. How would the others respond? Hard to tell.

He rose from his blue and beige floral print overstuffed couch, walked past the ten-foot-high French doors on the second floor of his mansion, and looked toward the forests of Parque Valle de Las Monjas. He'd recreated the Mexico City home of a prominent government official from the turn of the 20th century and made it his sanctuary. A cross between a house and a museum, he had built his palace of solitude in a location that guaranteed his family's safety, where payback and crime would not touch their souls.

The bribe for land rights had been substantial, but worth every peso. This oasis was less than thirty-five kilometres from Mexico City's airport. From where he stood, it was three kilometres to the historic town of San Mateo Tlaltenango, cited in the Quauhximalpan Codex as part of Hernán Cortés's estate. In 1571, the Franciscans had built the tiny village's church in honour of John the Baptist. A hundred years later, it was rededicated to San Mateo. Today, the townfolk appreciated the church. However, they revered, and occasionally feared, his family.

High stone walls surrounded his compound. One twenty-foot fortified steel and oak gate allowed visitors in and out as he chose.

The Conductor turned to the protected courtyard, where his eight-year-old twin grandsons, Leonel and Mauricio, eagerly engaged in one-on-one football. A net placed at each end of the legal-sized manicured field guaranteed they used their time away from school well. They were good boys, usual mischief notwithstanding. Last Christmas, they'd discovered they fit into the mansion's ventilation system and stole the maid's cookie offerings. He had raged at them, knowing the trouble such misbehaviour could cause him if they loitered about, unattended. Yet he couldn't help but admire their resourcefulness. Now he checked where they were before dealing with business.

The music stopped. As he rounded the corner of the marble circular staircase, his foot caught on a step and his knee buckled. He grabbed the walnut railing and cursed. He'd need that hip replacement eventually. However, balancing weakness from surgery with the risk of falling with a gun in his hand, that was difficult. Perhaps Pedro could organize a rifle-cane for him.

At the landing, he called to his daughter.

"Dorothea. I am going to the study for a meeting. No disturbances, you understand? Not from you; not from the boys. Total silence; and stay out of sight. Take the children to town for lunch and ice cream if you must, but do it now."

"Yes, Papa."

The slight dark-haired beauty in the kitchen looked so much like his wife that some days he couldn't stand the sight of her. Still, this was family, and he would protect his grandsons, no matter the cost. He'd proven that the first time Dorothea's late husband showed evidence of striking Mauricio. A flat note for which there was no harmony. So he had banned that musician from life's orchestra.

ALONE AT LAST, the Conductor opened the gate to Pedro Serrano. His first lieutenant. His trusted ally. They'd worked together for over twenty years. Friends? No. That was a luxury he could never afford.

"Ready?" The Conductor slapped Pedro on the back.

"Yes. Only, I have news. We should meet first."

"No time. Get to your post."

A minute later, the first limousine arrived. The lieutenant directed the driver to remain outside the gates while he escorted the First Violin through the metal detector, patted the man down, and sent him to the house. Pedro repeated the same steps as the Second Violin, Viola, Cello, and Bass arrived. The Strings.

"Let's get started," the Bass said, bursting through the Conductor's conference room door. "Only two hours left in my stopover from Heathrow to São Paulo."

The Conductor bristled at the outburst; the Bass noticed, frowned, and reflexively bowed his head. Message received.

"Gentlemen." The Conductor motioned to the mahogany shellback chairs, seats covered in gold pinstriped silk perched on hand-carved ball and claw legs, that surrounded the matching boardroom table, and the Strings found their places.

"As you must know by now," the Conductor began, "I've taken care of the pervasive virus that infected our global enterprise."

"You're sure he's dead?" the Viola asked. "My office in Miami—"

"It's done."

"Thank God." The Second Violin leaned back.

"Yes," the Conductor sneered. "A single ex-police officer you hired as an anti-money laundering agent, and not one of you could deal with him in Brussels."

The Second Violin blanched. "It is not our way. We discredited him. I had his superiors build a file on his infractions and create complaints. We were working to dismiss him."

"Dismiss him? That doesn't stop a zealot. You are lucky he took the bait and investigated the source of his allegations personally."

"Well," the Cello chimed in, "you're set up for it here. His disappearance would have made the media in Germany."

"And that is precisely why I called you here. The bribe to avoid 'investigation'. It was small compared to our accounts, but noteworthy."

The Conductor wrote the sum on a piece of paper, and it passed from person to person. The First Violin coughed. The Second gasped. A disgruntled titter rose from the rest.

"May I remind you that typical assassinations cost up to two-thirds this price? And if such a hit required damage control...?"

"Fine," said the Bass. "I move to approve the expenditure. Let's be done with this."

The vote carried unanimously, and as per tradition, the Conductor distributed his finest brandy, pleased at the consonance his power engendered.

The First Violin moved to adjourn.

"No," said the Conductor. "There is one more pressing matter that must be resolved. We agree that the operation here is 'set up' to enforce the safe conduct of our business."

The Second Violin's face paled again.

Another sip of his perfectly aged, distilled wine, and the Conductor continued. "I have received word of an additional threat. Not to the distribution of our worldwide funds. Rather, to the *protection protocol*."

"What threat?" the Cello asked.

"Two 'tourists' entered my country the night before last. One led a search five years ago for our female troublemaker. The other is a forensic geologist, known for his understanding of all things related to rocks, and... volcanoes."

"So feed the intruders false data," the Bass said. "Make everything consistent. With nothing to find, they'll leave satisfied."

"If it is so simple, why didn't false data work on our zealot in Brussels? Gentlemen. A data screen is already in place. However, I need approval to remove these foreigners if they persist."

"Another protection protocol? So soon?" The First Violin was skeptical.

"Only for the geologist. The other is currently hiking on the side of Iztaccihuatl. It can be a dangerous place, even with guides. I've already authorized our forces. However, as rules dictate, you must ratify the decision for both hits and agree to the expenses."

It took longer than the Conductor expected for the debate to subside. Ultimately, between the Conductor's power, the Bass's impatience, and the weak stomachs of the rest, the vote passed.

THE CONDUCTOR STOOD on the balcony that extended from the second-floor landing, brandy in hand, overlooking the gate. His lieutenant re-checked each musician, lest someone leave with a note or recording that could be traced. Finding nothing, one by one, the limousines left.

A few moments later, Pedro reported the successful departure.

"They agreed to the hits?" Pedro asked.

"As expected. What was it you wanted to see me about?"

The lieutenant's lips thinned. "Our informant on the mountain says there is trouble. The woman fought back. She may need to be shot."

CHAPTER 6

Detective Inspector Ricardo De La Cruz, División de Homicidios de la Ciudad de México por Delitos contra Turistas, the Violent Crime Against Tourists Unit for Mexico City, directed his attention to the unsavoury task of going through the stack of files relating to unsolved foreigner deaths that weighed down his desk, and his heart. He found the Helena Garvey-type cases the hardest. Late-twenties, on holiday with her husband, recapturing their honeymoon adventure from three years earlier, the couple had walked out of a bar in one of the better parts of town, no idea that the owner had gotten on the wrong side of the Dañinos. Caught in the crossfire of a drive-by execution, she took a bullet to the head. Meanwhile, both the gang and the shooter remained anonymous. Even the forensics team came up with nothing.

Probably too scared they were next.

He sighed. How was it he had ended up here?

The Unit was the novel brain-child of the attorney general. De La Cruz held the bastardized Detective Inspector moniker of some North American or British plainclothes officer to comfort both US and European foreigners with a label they understood. To solidify the post, he'd studied at the police academy in San

Diego on a government-sponsored exchange program. A lot of good that did. Once back in Mexico City, the resources he'd been taught to use were unavailable. He even had to buy his own gun.

De La Cruz lifted his head and his eyes fell on the portrait of his great-great-grandfather, Capitán Daniel Garza. Now there was a hero. The name synonymous with honour, duty, and absolute loyalty to Mexico. At the turn of the twentieth century, at the request of no less than the president, Garza had travelled to Texas to pursue justice for a small family burned to death in their village home in the dead of night. The authorities suspected a foreigner named Freddie Palmer of lighting the blaze. Palmer had been staying with the family. He disappeared and later turned up in Texas with the family's most prized possession, a mysterious sheep-skin map.

The map was presumed to link to pre-Hispanic treasure that rightfully belonged to Mexico. Garza tracked Palmer through the scrub and sand of West Central Texas, captured him, and arranged for Palmer to face justice. Betrayed by a double-agent in Palmer's camp, Garza died in the line of duty. No treasure was found, though there was talk that the sheepskin map actually led to a stone carving of historical significance to Mexico. Where the rock was now, no one knew.

Garza had lived to bring foreigners to justice, while De La Cruz found justice for those who did not belong to his country. Was he betraying Garza? Perhaps. However, today's tourist industry was critical to Mexico's economy. Unfortunately, for De La Cruz, like Sisyphus in punishment, critical success remained elusive.

"Your performance is disappointing," his boss had said during the previous month's review. "When you came back to us, everyone hoped that the knowledge you gained in America would help turn our reputation around. But these numbers..."

His boss threw out phrases like "international incident" and "Embassy pressure", citing how Mexico's policing challenges consumed worldwide tourist blogs. With every failure, foreign governments issued travel warnings about affected regions in his country.

In fact, his boss's math only told half the story. If the masses understood per capita data, Mexico, and especially Mexico City, came out okay.

To the officials, the truth didn't matter. Unsolved tourist murders even affected worldwide trade negotiations. Yet, without proper tools and a team to rely on—one that rose above corruption—how likely was a triumph?

The knock at the door was a welcome interruption.

"Come in."

"There is a telephone call, señor," Clara, the office's portly receptionist, said. "A cartel helicopter has made its way to the west side of Iztaccihuatl. I don't know who to direct the caller to."

Understandable. The site was a popular hiking ground, both for locals and tourists.

He looked again at the stack of unsolved murders. He needed a win.

"Thank you," he said with a polite bow of his head. "Please put the caller through."

DE LA CRUZ hung up the phone. An anonymous source, but the details were credible and easy enough to check, though how the man knew a tourist on the side of Iztaccihuatl was being threatened by the cartel, he couldn't imagine. What to do? As far as he could tell, no one else was at risk. Let it happen? After all, what was one more file in his caseload? And the only way to address the situation now would be to scramble an official chopper. Did one tourist really warrant that?

"Your performance is disappointing." The words echoed in his ears.

De La Cruz faced his computer and accessed the tourist's international records.

She'd entered Mexico five years earlier, searching for a missing friend. A few additional keystrokes confirmed the woman to be an upstanding citizen, and a healthcare professional with connections spanning the globe. The cartel had interest in a chiropractor? That was surprising.

He picked up the phone and keyed the number he rarely used.

"Sí, señor. It is the only way. We may already be too late, but if we do not try, well, the optics would be bad for us both."

CHAPTER 7

"No shots. The woman dies as planned. A fall from the cliff."

Practiced calm, clear resolve laced the Conductor's icy tone. It had to be a clean hit. No bullets to suggest murder. Nothing leading to the cartel... or to him.

"It seems she surprised everyone. She has climbing expertise, and she's strong." The lieutenant spoke to the horizon. No direct eye contact. A sign of respect and submission. "Our informant reports that Doctora Payce had a specific location in mind as she headed up Iztaccihuatl today. She needed to relieve herself and was left alone for several minutes. The informant did not see her retrieve anything, but she returned from the brush with an injury to her leg. She may have found something then. Our team is waiting for your orders."

"You believe she now holds the key?"

"Uncertain. It would be a shame to kill her and not find out."

"Have her searched and then dumped over the precipice."

Perspiration built in Briel's palms and her grip on Scarface slipped.

"Grab my wrist," she instructed.

His sweaty hand engulfed the joint, and for a moment, Briel worried her shoulder would displace from the pull.

Baldy fired a shot and Briel whipped her head toward the terrified face of Raphael, who held up a phone that he then carefully and slowly slipped into his pocket.

Briel called to Baldy, hoping to draw attention away from Raphael.

"I don't know how much longer I can hold him."

She stared at the armed man, who seemed to ponder his dilemma.

A second slip of her grip made Briel wince and then shudder. It was no idle threat. She was about to lose Scarface to the cliff, and if that happened, surely both she and the guides would be dead in seconds.

"Vete!" Baldy shouted. AR-15 raised in the air, he fired several rounds for good measure. Jose scurried away, but Raphael turned toward Briel as though unwilling to leave her behind. She managed a curt nod, hoping to reassure him, and he finally disappeared too.

The guides gone, Baldy laid his gun on the ground, reached over Briel's arm, and together they lifted his partner to safety.

Briel sat, dazed by exertion. The rescued man caught his breath nearby, while the AR-15 remained unattended at the edge of the cliff. Too good a chance to miss. Briel rolled and then grabbed for it. Baldy got there first and now she faced the barrel of the weapon.

Scarface got up and spat in her direction.

So much for the lion and the thorn.

The lieutenant placed his cell phone back into his pocket. His boss wasn't going to like this. How the hell did the authorities find out about the mission? Only a handful of people knew what was happening on Iztaccihuatl. Were suspicions raised when his men inflated the Popocatepetl hazard level after Briel's guides headed out? Is that what alerted the National Guard? His own stupid attempt to avoid bystander fallout? No. This had all the earmarks of some hijo de puta do-gooder rescue mission. And there was only one person in his midst likely to take such a stand. Dealing with that would not be easy.

He knocked on the Conductor's office door.

"Come in."

The lieutenant shivered, discarding excess energy. He turned the brass handle and faced the solid oak desk.

SCARFACE HEADED BACK to the helicopter and pulled out a radio. Did her "good deed" have a karmic benefit after all?

Baldy's automatic rifle, the one aimed at her head, never wavered.

Moments later, Scarface went to where Briel had cast down her backpack to document the teporingo.

"Hey!"

When she moved to protest, Baldy struck her side with his weapon and she fell to her knees, gasping for air as her rib muscles spasmed.

"With these bullets, I can strip flesh and bone until there is nothing left to identify you. Do you understand?"

My God, Briel thought, gritting her teeth and holding her chest to manage the pain. Is that what happened to Percy?

Briel remained kneeling while Scarface dumped the contents of her backpack on the ground. All this had to be a mistake. She tried again.

"What are you looking for?" The barrel of the AR-15 inched closer. "It might be easier if you tell me. I don't have anything of value, I promise. Drugs? Is that it? I don't have those either... Well, maybe an antihistamine or an aspirin in the first aid kit—"

"Shut up!" The weapon struck her again. This time, it connected with her glenohumeral joint. The blow sent a nauseating ripple through her body and momentarily paralyzed her thoughts.

She struggled to recover, and through the din, she heard something. Another slap, slap, slap coming from the sky.

No way these guys called for backup. Not while she was here alone.

Baldy glanced toward the sound. Scarface stopped rummaging through her things, looked up, ran for the helicopter, and got back on the radio. Briel's heart sank as the new chopper, another military machine, came into view.

❦

"Señor," the lieutenant began.

His phone buzzed and he paused to check the number. Another report from the mountain. Good news or bad? Maybe he wouldn't need to tell the Conductor about their "problem". He motioned to his boss and then stepped back into the hallway. The message made his stomach turn.

"Guardia helicopter in sight. Orders?"

CHAPTER 8

The Conductor leaned back in his oxblood leather, button-tufted executive office chair. Heat radiated around his mouth and through his cheeks. The imprint of his anger.

How could his lieutenant have been so careless? He should have accounted for a National Guard response to closing the volcano paths down. Of course someone would become suspicious. Could it lead to him? Pedro had assured him it wasn't possible and the situation would be contained. But was that true?

Removing the desk key from its hidden compartment inside his gold pocket watch, the Conductor opened the left bottom drawer of his desk and removed five files of handwritten sheet music, each measure coded to represent a sum of money. The simple act of counting funds while creating a score calmed his heart. Perfect harmony.

He flipped open the matchbook the lieutenant had given him earlier in the day and looked at the number. Inhaling deeply, he fondled the first file, the one labelled *Phrygian Mode*. As he turned his head from side to side, he released the tension from his shoulders. A preperformance exercise. In a ritual act, he withdrew his fifteen hundred dollar gold-coated fountain pen from its holder and leaned over the first empty measure on the staff. A self-satisfied smile crossed his lips.

Even if his place of solitude was inexplicably breached, his accounts of pre-laundered cartel earnings remained unreadable. A normal bystander would never understand what the music meant, and any musician would assume he had an interest in "speculative" work. Someday, perhaps, an actual composition might be based on these sheets. For today, he needed to input the week's yield from the Rabia Cartel—or in his language, the Phrygian Mode. A minor mode for a minor enterprise. His personal joke. That was the musical name he gave to the gang that called itself "Rage". The mode Aristotle had suggested inspired "enthusiasm". Rage certainly inspired that. For good or for evil.

Despite the diminutive label, Rabia still netted over half a billion dollars each year.

Using full notes, half notes, quarter notes, down to 1024th notes (anything smaller seemed rather silly, though such fractions would be used if necessary), up or down the scale, plus or minus sharps and flats, and pauses, he effectively recorded all earnings down to the peso.

Then it was a matter of pushing the music along to the Strings, where the notes were cleaned. That interchange was more complex. No one knew how hard he worked to maintain harmony among the five men who dominated banking throughout the world. What his orchestra achieved in wealth, power and influence, he'd never imagined as the aspiring leader of a band in his youth. He wondered, just for a moment, what his life would have been like if he'd been successful in that adolescent dream. If his family hadn't forced him to leave it behind.

With new resolve, he pulled his mind back to the present. His thoughts drifted then, to the current dilemma, the danger here and now, to his intricate system of controls and counter-controls.

The Conductor closed the file and reached into his centre desk drawer for the folded slip of paper that laid inside his African black wood trinket box lined with a cherry wood inlay. On the back side of the paper was the owner's name: B. Payce. On the front were three rows of numbers. Some with plus signs beside them; others were separated by periods, colons, or semicolons. Years of effort and he'd yet to crack the code. If this woman on the mountain was the key to their secret, then today it would die with her and he would be safe once more. Or had she already found something? He needed to know.

A soft tap at the door announced Dorothea's arrival.

"Papa," she said. "You've been working for a long time. I brought you tea. And I'll start preparing for dinner soon."

"Thank you."

Dorothea hesitated. "Have you seen the news?"

"No. I've been too busy."

"Journalists are reporting helicopters over the west side of Iztaccihuatl. Apparently, someone ordered the trails closed for the day, and the Guardia Nacional is there now. Probably just a camper in trouble... Maybe nothing important. I will leave you to it." And the office door clicked shut.

The Conductor's hand trembled with renewed anger. He clicked the remote and a 48-inch TV rose from the leather-wrapped trunk with antique brass buckles sitting in the far corner of the room. Immediately, he turned to the news. A reporter at the foot of the mountain pointed cameras to a chopper flying in from the south.

"One helicopter is already believed to be on the ground," a voice on the TV said.

"We expect authorities to comment within the hour," another voice chimed in.

BRIEL DIDN'T BELIEVE in an organized religion, but logically, there had to be something. Some kind of life force that inhabited every being on Earth. She was already kneeling, so why not? She closed her eyes in silent prayer.

An explosion of gunshots interrupted her meditation, and for a split second, Briel wondered why there was no pain. Opening her eyes, she saw her attackers scatter for cover.

New 'copter pilot, not a fan of Baldy and Scarface then?

What about her?

Unwilling to take chances, Briel ran back to the pines lining the cliff. Baldy spotted her retreat and started firing again. Another round of bullets, this one from the sky, cut Baldy off. He motioned to Scarface, and they climbed back into their mechanical bird and fired up the engine.

Detective Inspector De La Cruz eyed the television with disdain. He'd predicted a media circus. Today, it came faster than even he had expected.

"Must be a slow news day," he said to Clara, who came in with a headpiece connecting him to the action.

"Report," De La Cruz said into the microphone.

"Shots exchanged. No casualties so far. Gunmen taking to the air. Still fighting. Target on the ground. Orders?"

Still fighting. His opponents had come prepared. Then again, the cartel enjoyed firing their weapons. He had known the score going in. The question now was whether to continue this foolishness and risk the lives of two good men. Would it be enough to report to the world that they'd sent help but it was too late? He could turn the chopper around and they'd all be home by dinner.

The detective inspector glanced back at the TV. A drone was in the air, its zoom lens pointed at the two black helicopters, now circling each other like prize wrestlers. Even from their distance, it was obvious they were firing at each other. If he backed down, it would look like the Guardia was running from the cartels—again. His choice gone, De La Cruz repositioned his mic.

"Take down that chopper and get the woman out of there."

CHAPTER 9

D r. Miguel Lobo, Medical Director for Hospital Escuela de Medicina de la Universidad, pushed his large, square glasses back up his nose and shook his slightly overgrown, wavy brown hair back from his face. Adonis hair. That's what his ex-wife had called it when they met as teenagers. Now, with his close-cropped beard showing patches of grey, he wondered if a more mature cut was in order. No. His lion's mane balanced his slightly more angular than average face. And besides, the ladies still seemed to like it.

Miguel positioned his thousand-dollar loafers over the only dry spot in the dank alleyway. The scent of vomit and urine assaulted his nose. There were few alleys in Mexico City. This one, a half-hour drive south of the city's historic centre, accessed only through the rear doors of local businesses, was a private spot where the criminal underworld guaranteed no one would "hear" their voices. It was also a place where discipline was administered, which explained the bodily fluids.

The call to meet here meant trouble, and Miguel needed the chance to explain. A chance to re-charm the man who had served as a surrogate father for so much of his life. To do that, Miguel needed to be at his best. So he feigned a sudden illness at work and put his assistant medical director, Dr. Carlos Stanton, in charge of the hospital clinics. Stanton complained he had a full patient load of his own for the afternoon. Miguel didn't care. His uncle's command was far more important than dispensing a few pills to the chronically ill. Those decrepit souls could wait for one more day. And if not? Well, his hospital's emergency department would take care of the remaining patients. The staff could cope.

The current problem was the priority. What a mess.

Without a doubt, his uncle knew, or at least suspected, that Miguel had made the anonymous call to the Guardia Nacional. He'd told his uncle about Briel when she came to Mexico a few years ago and contacted him for help with the Jane Doe a regional hospital had taken in. The trail was already cold, but he had tried to assist. He couldn't help himself. The woman was special.

He'd first met Briel after reaching out to the US government in search of funding for a research project and finding this chiropractor had somehow become an influential decision-maker.

Briel was knowledgeable and beautiful—in an odd, makeup-free way. Not his usual type. In her black suit and sensible patent leather shoes, he could still tell her legs went on for miles. But most everyone, including him, considered Briel untouchable. All business in the business world. *A challenge.*

Then came the day they sat on an international panel together.

Something was different. She handled the debate on economic problems in healthcare delivery with typical expertise, but she seemed sad.

Identifying and exploiting vulnerability was Miguel's specialty, so he did not hesitate to invite Briel for dinner. It surprised him that she accepted; astonished him when he successfully coaxed her into his room.

The fire he experienced under the ice queen's façade was something he'd never known before, or after.

But when he awoke the next morning, she was gone, and he

panicked. Would she tell anyone? He had a wife and toddler at home. Was it a mistake? What price would he pay?

He caught up with her at a table in the breakfast bistro. Fork in hand, poking at a fried egg, her left thumb and forefinger turned the pages of an official-looking document.

"Looks important," he commented, flashing his signature Cheshire cat smile and taking the seat across from her.

A tired grin greeted him in return.

"My divorce papers," she said. "I intended to sign them last night and ship the package with an overnight service."

She pulled a pen from her briefcase and Miguel watched with solemn interest as she signed and dated the last page before slipping the agreement into a cardboard envelope.

"I hope our... encounter had nothing to do with this."

"Our... encounter had everything to do with it," Briel replied. Her wry smile made him uneasy, and as astute as Briel was, she caught his concern and chuckled. "I was unhappy, and foolishly searching for... an outlet. That was you."

"So, what now?" Miguel asked.

Briel stood from the table.

"There is no 'now'," she said. "And there never will be."

And so she had rejected him, never mentioning their night together again. The ice queen was back.

THE SQUEAL OF a door opening interrupted Miguel's thoughts.

GUN HOLSTERED, Pedro entered the alley through the rear door of the local candy store. His quarry stood fifty meters away.

Pedro drew his gun and advanced on his nephew.

"No!" Miguel lifted his palms in a pleading gesture. "Please. Uncle, hear me."

He'd expected so much more of Miguel.

"What the fuck could you possibly say? Huh? That you betrayed my confidence? That you betrayed me and everyone I work for? That you have no regard for anything that made you the man you are today? And why? To save a woman who is of absolutely no consequence to Mexico?"

Pedro slammed the pistol into the side of Miguel's head and the doctor went down. Miguel's outstretched hand landed in a puddle.

Probably urine. Good.

The doctor put his clean hand over his cheekbone and got up.

"Uncle, listen. I was saving you, whether or not you want to hear it. I told you the woman is someone of influence. If I did not raise the alarm and she died, more would come looking. Probably many more. I know the people who surround her. They would never let it rest. You prize anonymity above all else. Today is a mess —yes. But this story will go away. If she dies, the repercussions... There would be investigations, I assure you. Many."

Pedro narrowed his eyes and unclicked the safety on his weapon. Miguel looked back in horror and cowered into the back wall, his silk suit scratching against the rough, dirty brick that defined the alley's boundary. Suddenly Pedro saw before him the frightened child he had taken under his wing so long ago. Miguel's father had died when the boy was only fifteen. When Pedro took over full-time care, he paid for his nephew's education and offered Miguel an alternative worldview. One that appealed to the young man's desire to "save the world". One that could be used as needed.

And it had worked. Until today.

The seconds ticked by, and Pedro didn't move. Sometimes a boy needed discipline, and Pedro's point needed to be made clear.

Finally, the lieutenant lowered his gun.

"Perhaps you acted out of care for your family. But Miguel, hear my words: Never again make such a move without my approval, or I will find you where you sleep. And then you will wish I had pulled the trigger today."

Miguel's Adam's apple rose and fell. Pedro turned heel and left the way he had come.

Once back in his car, Pedro Serrano found his blue burner phone and turned it on.

"Sí. It is me. I need a tail. Sí. Twenty-four-seven. The name is Miguel Lobo."

CHAPTER 10

O ver the field, on the side of Iztaccihuatl, the two choppers spun toward each other, tails raised, vying for the optimal position from which to fight. So far, all shots fired had missed their targets.

The sun's reflection revealed ghost graphics on the side of the aircraft that had arrived second on the scene. Guardia Nacional. The National Guard?

Briel strained to see if the helicopter that had first attacked her guides had the same designation. Perhaps she'd gotten in the middle of a drug bust? If that was true, why the battle in the sky? None of this made sense. Based on her earlier experience with the police in Mexico City, and the force's media-based reputation for corruption, Briel was unwilling to presume that their arrival meant rescue. For now, it was good enough that the two birds above her kept themselves busy.

She ran for her backpack, its contents still strewn on the ground, and began flinging items into the main compartment, not knowing what she might need if she made it into the woods to lie low for who knew how long. As she placed the last item, her water bottle, back in its holder, a shot hit the ground nearby.

An errant bullet or something meant for her? No matter. She needed to run.

The rocky portion of the path that led to this field provided some cover against gunshots, so Briel headed back up Iztaccihuatl. She rounded a corner and moved behind a stone outcropping just as a loud metallic pop overwhelmed her ears. Above her, a cloud of black smoke billowed. One 'copter damaged. Okay. Which one? Or did it even matter?

Briel crouched and waited for the crash. None came. Instead, the wounded bird crossed over her, listing to one side. She pulled back into her hiding spot, worried someone would find her and fire again, but it was clear the shooters had other priorities. Her gaze followed the aircraft as it limped away, and she tried to focus on the tail. Unfortunately, any ghost writing was obscured by distance and smoke. She couldn't tell which team had won. Regardless, she planned to remain unseen.

A metallic, burning smell reached Briel's nostrils and caught in her throat. She pushed away the desire to cough, choosing instead to remain quiet and still. A full fifteen minutes later, long after the propeller sounds had faded, she deemed it safe to move on.

Deciding the whole thing could not possibly have been about her, Briel cautiously tracked back toward the clearing. At the turn into the exposed field, she stopped. The helicopter designated Guardia stood among the grasses, propellers silent. Two men outfitted in tactical gear faced away from her, looking around. Scarface and Baldy were no longer a problem, but what about the newcomers?

Friends or foe?

Briel ducked back around the corner. Carefully, she tilted her head out from her hiding place, trying to assess the situation. A few seconds later, the National Guard, or whoever they were, made their way toward the tree-lined precipice to search... for what? For her? Doubtful. To take down a drug ring? That didn't make sense. If that's what they were after, surely they'd have finished off the disabled 'copter or gone after Juan and Raphael.

She chanced another peek at the field just as one of the would-be officers turned in her direction. Briel pulled her head in, but it was too late. The man alerted his colleague and they took off after her.

Briel spun around and headed the way she had come, cursing as she found herself at the ledge where the rock face shot straight up and the cliff angled straight down. No way her climbing skills were good enough to manage a quick exit. Footsteps echoed nearby and Briel tried to calm her racing heart while she looked around.

A single oak tree stood precariously on the edge of the drop about twenty meters ahead, its roots exposed, clinging like suction cups to the stone, drawing in every morsel of nutrition. She scanned the trunk and saw a stable-looking branch within reach. Would it hold her? One way to find out.

Briel checked her back pocket, making sure the pouch Percy left for her was securely tucked. She shimmied up and flattened herself among the leaves, hoping for sufficient cover, just as her two pursuers came into view.

One of the two men stopped in the middle of the trail, hands on hips. He motioned for the other to check over the cliff's edge. Seemed they had more faith in her skill than she did. Briel almost smiled.

Then the contents in her backpack shifted.

Crap. If she didn't stabilize it, it would pull her down.

Briel checked to be sure both officers were occupied and wiggled her upper body, trying to balance the weight once more. Unfortunately, the movement also disturbed the branch supporting her and she heard a loud crack. The limb held and Briel heaved a silent sigh.

Then she turned her head toward where the men searched and found herself staring into the business end of a long range rifle.

CHAPTER 11

The ice cube clicked over Dean Leggatt's teeth while he waited for the stupid thing to melt. God, he wanted to suck down on it. He was so damned thirsty; but he knew better than to take a swig from the bottled water on the nightstand in his hotel room. His stomach was still fragile. Seriously fragile, if he was honest, and satisfying that craving for a big gulp would only send him back to the bathroom, where he'd already spent far too much time getting to know the porcelain bowl.

The hotel staff had assured him the ice was made from purified water, boasting that the cubes came from their automated double filtered refrigeration system. He hoped so. The thought of making his situation worse increased the already prominent taste of bile in his mouth.

Early in the morning, he had tried using television as a distraction. Unfortunately, the moving pictures and noise made his head hurt, so he had lain in silence until impending vomit forced him up. At least the rate of bathroom trips had gone down and any minute, he expected a delivery person with meds from the pharmacy.

He glanced at the chair by the bed where his robe lay in a lumpy heap. All he had on were pajama shorts. The old tatty yellow silk ones with hearts all over that Percy had given him. The ones he remained unwilling to throw out. He'd brought them as a way of connecting with her again. His personal, if foolish, good luck charm. What if the delivery person was a woman? He should get dressed.

As he rolled to put his legs on the floor, someone pounded on the door.

Okay. Whoever the courier, they'd have to take him as he was.

The knock came again.

"Coming."

Dean pushed off the bed, unfurled his robe, and slipped it on. Then, moaning a little, he shuffled to the door.

His hopes for relief were soon dashed. Instead of a medicine-toting, tip-demanding delivery person, two clean-shaven, dark-haired men with identical navy blue suits blocked his exit to the hallway.

"Señor Leggatt?" Suit Number One, the taller of the two, asked.

"Who wants to know?"

Suit Number Two flashed a badge and Dean mustered what energy he could to focus on the letters. The man pulled it away, but Dean grabbed his arm. Suit One stepped forward to block him.

"I want to examine the badge." His voice was weak. All they needed to do was push with a single finger and he'd fall over. Regardless, he levelled a stern, stony stare in their direction, wanting both these guys to know that, at the very least, he was serious.

Suit Two nodded, and the badge re-emerged.

"Office of the Secretariat of Travel, Culture and Tourism," Dean translated. "What kind of title is that? I'm sick. Go away."

Dean tried to close the door, but Suit Two blocked it with his foot.

"You need to come with us."

Dean considered his next move. Two against one.

On a normal day, he could probably take them. But this wasn't a normal day. In fact, he'd been standing long enough that he was seeing spots before his eyes as he worked to stay upright.

"Señor Leggatt. You must come with us," Suit One said.

Suit Two was already in the room and gathering clothes. "Put these on."

He had no reserves. So Dean obeyed and the Officers of the Secretariat of Travel, Culture and Tourism escorted him to their waiting limousine.

Suit Two got into the driver's seat as Suit One pushed his head down and tried to manhandle him into the automobile. Dean made one last effort to resist and spun on his heels, ready to take a swing at Suit One. Instead of connecting with his target, an attack of vertigo made him fall through the door.

Then, as he descended to the seat, he vomited onto the man's shoes.

CHAPTER 12

Though the handcuffs dug painfully into her wrists, Briel moulded her face into its stoniest form. Despite the façade, her heart raced and her throat went dry. In fact, her entire body wanted to shake. She successfully wrestled her muscles under control, except for the quiver in her jaw that refused to yield. In the end, she turned her head, hoping to hide the remaining evidence of her distress.

She'd never been in custody.

Sure, she and Percy had had the occasional brush with the law —usually because of Percy's recklessness—but they had always found a way out. Together.

Alone this time, she didn't even know if these guys were really Guardia. Deep breaths, she told herself. Slow, deep breaths.

Surreptitiously, Briel let the fingers of her bound right wrist touch the pocket holding Percy's cache. The pouch had worked its way out a little, and she had just enough reach to tuck it back.

Think, she told herself. If she was going to survive this, she needed a clear head, and she needed information.

"Who are you?" she asked. Then, summoning as much strength as she could muster, she added, "If I'm under arrest, then let me see your badges. As far as I know, I've done absolutely nothing wrong."

Instead of answering, the would-be officers stood on either side of her. One ran back to retrieve her backpack and he slung it over a shoulder. Then each grabbed an elbow, and led—or truthfully, dragged—her to the helicopter.

Briel's shaking jaw clenched as anger replaced fear. Being ignored was something she had never learned to tolerate. Red flag to a bull. How dare they? At the very least, she had the right to know who was abducting her. So she made things a little harder and dug her feet as far into the ground as they would go. In response, the men used more force on her arms. As they neared the chopper, Briel struggled. No way she was getting into that thing without a fight.

The officer nearest the open door narrowed his eyes. Briel responded with a scowl of her own. Without warning, he raised a fist. Instinctively, she dropped her head and pulled her shoulders in, ready to withdraw from the blow. Her eyes landed on the man's legs and the opportunity was too good to miss. She kicked him in the shins. Hard. A satisfying yowl erupted from her attacker. The man moved away and readied his arm again.

This time, the partner intervened and motioned for the officer to get into the cockpit. One hand on his holster, making sure Briel understood he meant business, the partner directed Briel to take a seat on the aircraft. There was no escape from the gun, so Briel complied. A moment later, they were airborne.

Bravado spent, Briel rethought her situation. At least the man guarding her had prevented his buddy's assault. Should she talk to him?

"Do you speak English?"

No response.

"What's your name?"

No response.

"Where are you taking me?"

Still no response.

So Briel gave up and sat quietly, looking out the window.

Before long, Mexico City came into view and Briel's stomach rolled as the chopper neared the ground. They were headed for a greenspace Briel recognized as Chapultepec Park, the largest, most well-known city park in all of Mexico, with a history dating back to prehistoric times. The helicopter found a remote wooded area, away from the main grounds. Nestled among the trees was a small clearing, and off to one side was a black limousine. Beside the car stood a heavyset man in a black suit. The bottom of his buttoned jacket flapped as they touched down, and still the man didn't move. Sunglasses covered his eyes, and his expression was unreadable.

The officer guarding her guided Briel from the chopper and removed her cuffs. Hands finally free, she tensed, ready for another fight; for an opportunity to dash into the woods. Her captor caught her eyes and shook his head, just a little. And then, as if to emphasize the point, he reached for his gun, again.

Got it.

They walked to the limousine in silence.

THE NEWS STATION played and replayed videos of the two helicopters leaving Iztaccihuatl. One bird, clearly disabled, black smoke cascading into the sky, limped away. The other reportedly plucked at least one person from the hillside. No names yet. No information about who the two choppers represented, though reporters tentatively identified one as having Guardia markings on its side.

Teeth clenched, the Conductor drew in a noisy breath. True, his lieutenant had used the Maldito cartel. A major gang that could afford the equipment. That one, he coded as the Ionian Mode.

Gratefully, the mob remained at least one step removed from his operation, so there was little chance of tracing this debacle back to him. Still, this kind of incompetence was intolerable. He'd need to order punishment. No doubt they had a traitor in their midst. Who?

The Conductor fondled Persephone Gilbert's coded message. The only thing of note on Gilbert's person after the Conductor had his people bring her things to him from the hospital. He practically had it memorized.

He draped his fingers around the note, giving in to the urge to squeeze the life out of the paper it was written on before putting the crumpled mass back in its hiding spot. If the protocol was to remain in place, he needed the code solved or the woman and her findings buried. Preferably both. Everything rested on getting answers. And so far, not even the Lady Einstein he'd held in reserve had sorted it. He pulled this week's red burner phone from his pocket and dialled the lieutenant. Depending on Pedro's report, he might pay the lady a visit.

THE BACK of the limousine was sparse, though the plush black leather seats were roomy. There was no wet bar, hidden or otherwise, that might contain glass Briel could break and use as a weapon. She considered discretely rolling out of the door as the car got moving, but pulling the door handle yielded only a click. Damned child locks.

The burly driver got behind the wheel and Briel toyed with thoughts of a choke hold from behind. She'd have to wait until they were away from the helicopter. It might work, though there'd surely be an accident. What was the alternative? Heading into the unknown didn't feel better.

Her ruminations were cut short as the car started and an acrylic divider slowly rose between the front and back. Lunge for the driver's throat? No doubt the thick riser would trap her arm and probably fracture it. No. The moment was gone. Best save her energy.

At least she wasn't blindfolded. Briel concentrated on the road.

They'd been travelling less than five minutes and she already had her bearings. After all, she knew where the helicopter had touched down. In fact, visitors to the park must have seen the landing. Would it matter? Probably not.

A few minutes later, they passed the famous Zócalo, Mexico City's historic main square. Prior to the Spanish invasion, it was known as the centre of the Aztec Empire. Browsing through the ancient ruins and post-conquest buildings was one of the rare pleasant memories she had of her previous trip to the area.

A short time after that, an even more familiar sight—one that filled her with anger rather than fear—came into view. They turned into the entrance of an underground parking lot, tucked slightly away from the main building. The garage doors for the offices of the Secretaria de Viajes, Cultura y Turismo, Mexico's Secretariat of Travel, Culture and Tourism. The man who had failed her at every turn when she had pleaded for help five years earlier. What the hell did he want with her now?

The car stopped and Briel prepared herself to make a run for it as soon as the opportunity arose. Unfortunately, her heavyset chauffer anticipated the move.

"Ouch," Briel said as the man grabbed hold of her arm and prevented her escape.

He opened the building door with his other hand and led her through while she continued to struggle.

"Let go!" she demanded.

Employees milled about, so Briel tried to get their attention. "I've been kidnapped!"

She flailed her free arm and kicked her legs. For a large man, the driver was surprisingly agile, and he sidestepped every intended hit.

"This man is forcing me here. Get some help. Please!"

No one responded except a lone cleaning woman who stared at the scene, wide-eyed. She took one look at Briel's captor and studied her mop again while they passed. Why didn't anyone help? Were they warned that some crazed woman would walk their halls under protest, or was this a normal occurrence for these offices?

The grip got tighter and Briel worried the force might dislocate her shoulder, so she finally gave in. Instead, she concentrated again on the locale. Third floor, back staircase, carpeted hallway, Aztec relief, left-hand turn. Always good to know where things led when contemplating a hasty exit.

Three doors away, the man led her to the opening of a large boardroom. An eight-person mahogany table with rolling leather chairs sat in the middle. Two men, one tall, pudgy, with a round face, moustache, and cropped dark hair, silver at the temples; the other, her height with chiseled features and short, spiky black hair, a hint of arrogance in his bearing that contrasted with his big brown naïve schoolboy eyes, turned from a coffee stand in the corner. The driver deposited Briel in the middle of the room and then assumed the position of a bouncer by the door.

"Ah, Señora Payce," the taller, rounder man said. "I am Señor Mateo Tomás, the Secretariat of Travel, Culture and Tourism for Mexico. This is Detective Inspector Ricardo De La Cruz, of the Violent Crimes Against Tourists Division of our city's Guardia Nacional. Please."

Tomás pulled a chair out from the midsection of the long table and motioned for her to sit. Briel didn't move.

"Doctora Payce," she corrected the man. "I met the Secretariat of Travel, Culture and Tourism five years ago. I remember him well. You are not him."

"No. Señor Impaca... retired. I was assigned to his post six months ago. Together with Inspector De La Cruz, we are creating new initiatives to combat both real and imagined challenges to our tourist industry."

"I didn't imagine the way I was treated today. I didn't imagine the disappearance of my best friend five years ago. And I didn't imagine the complete lack of interest of this office the last time I searched for her."

"No. Sen... Doctora. My deepest apologies for today's events, and for the failures of my predecessors."

De La Cruz handed Briel a coffee, silently placing two

powdered creamers, two sachets of sugar, and a stir stick at her designated place at the table.

"Please," said De La Cruz as he motioned for her to take a seat.

Briel considered the request. Years of administrative, academic, and healthcare politics were excellent teachers. She paused long enough to sense discomfort from both De La Cruz and Tomás while they awaited her decision. Then she scooped up the condiments and headed for the end seat. She knew the secretariat would choose the other head of the table, but at least she held one of the power positions. For now.

Mateo Tomás assumed his predicted place and cleared his throat. De La Cruz looked around and finally settled for the chair to the right of the secretariat.

"Once again, I apologize for how you have been treated. I am given to understand that in our attempt to rescue you, you resisted our help, and our men, therefore, restrained you. It was not my intention. However, Sen... Doctora Payce, because of your reckless behaviour on Iztaccihuatl, we now have a problem."

"Reckless behaviour?" Briel slammed her forearms on the table, but the secretariat was checking his phone and heading out of the room. She looked at the detective inspector, who also picked up a call and disappeared.

CHAPTER 13

Ricardo De La Cruz couldn't decide whether to be furious at the woman's hubris or admire her bravery. Regardless, for all the affect, he knew she was afraid. The slight tremor in her left ring and pinky fingers as he had handed her the coffee betrayed her. He wanted to smack the officers who had cuffed and manhandled her. They had insisted she wouldn't have come any other way. Seeing her now, assuming a chair at the head of the table? They were probably right.

He sighed and pulled out the chair to the right of the secretariat, grateful and just a little surprised by how easily Tomás's support had come. Something to do with the revelation that "we" have a problem? Perhaps. But the immediate concern was PR, and Ricardo assumed the call Tomás had received was a signal to address the media lining up at the building's front door.

Then the phone in his own pocket chimed, and he checked the caller ID. Enrique Torres, his boss. The short man with a quintessential handle-bar moustache and a serious Napoleon complex was Ricardo's daily reminder as to why he sought justice for vulnerable tourists rather than hit the streets protecting his fellow citizens. Everyone suspected Torres of having ties to the Maldito cartel. Bad luck for the good local cops trying to rid Mexico City of drug crime. They were fighting the real uphill battle.

Truthfully, it wasn't much better for De La Cruz. After all, it was Torres who remained "disappointed" in Ricardo's results, and Torres who would never have approved a helicopter to rescue a foreigner in need. This call wouldn't be to congratulate him. Best get it over with.

Ricardo excused himself and stepped into the hallway and away from the man guarding the door.

"Hello?"

"Since when is the Violent Crime Against Tourists Unit assigned to the secretariat?" Torres laced his words with sarcasm.

"Coordinator Torres. I asked for help to avoid a possible international incident..."

"It did not occur to you to go through proper channels?"

"Saving this tourist will reflect well on our Guardia Nacional. The helicopter was identified as having Guardia markings, so even though authorization came from..."

"One tourist! Do you have any fucking idea how much of our budget was just spent on that helicopter? On one tourist?"

"Señor, the secretariat agreed..."

"Your boss... your employer, did not. Idiota! You didn't use the secretariat. He used you and my budget to further his political aspirations..."

"I'm sure that's not..."

"No? Then why is the press gathering outside the Tourism building for an update? I'm heading there now, before this gets further out of control. Then I will deal with you. And those friends you think you have in high places? Do not be so fucking sure they will help you."

The line went dead.

Ricardo considered his next move. It would be smart to run. Torres was angrier than Ricardo had ever heard him, and a man like that could arrange most anything. He stood in front of the conference room door. His career, maybe even his life, was on the line.

Then he remembered the picture hanging on the wall in his office. Garza didn't run. If it had to be, Ricardo would go out like his esteemed great-great-grandfather—doing his job for the higher good of the country he loved.

CHAPTER 14

A woman wheeled a television into the boardroom, plugged it in, and found cable coverage of the morning's events.

"Reporters with cameras have gathered on the sidewalks outside this office. Please excuse the secretariat. He was called to deal with them," she said to Briel.

On the screen, the secretariat positioned himself in front of a pre-placed microphone and spoke to the crowd.

"Today's events illustrate to the world the lengths to which we in Mexico will go to assure the safety of our national parklands and the people who come to enjoy them. We must protect our country's treasures, and that includes our citizens and those who visit us from foreign lands. As Secretariat of Travel, Culture and Tourism, I ordered Mexico City's Guardia Nacional to intercept a threat to the peace and beauty of our Woman in White, our Iztaccihuatl. The success of that mission saved the lives of two of our citizens and a tourist in trouble. For those concerned about the costs, I ask you: What price would you have me pay to bring home a loved one? We must all..."

"He's an effective speaker, I'll give him that," Briel said aloud as

Detective Inspector De La Cruz re-entered the boardroom. "So, the secretariat ordered you to send the chopper?"

"Not exactly." The inspector's lips thinned and his face took on the pained expression of someone sipping vinegar. Briel wondered if she could use this momentary discomfort to get the man to talk.

"Why am I here? What did Tomás mean by 'we' have a problem?"

De La Cruz shifted focus from the television to Briel. "Why didn't you try to escape while you were in this room, and alone?"

"Your guard is still blocking the door—and you got my attention. So, I ask again: Why the fuss to save me? Don't get me wrong; I'm grateful. I'm here now. Tell me why."

"At the moment, Doctora Payce, all I know is that both you and I have attracted unwanted attention. Exactly what the issue is, I cannot say."

CHAPTER 15

It had never occurred to Dean what a brilliant weapon human vomit might be. Okay, probably not effective in the long run, but seeing his captor jump back in disgust as a projectile of undigested stomach remains hit its mark was, at the very least, entertaining. Pity he was too weak to take advantage of the moment and run. Of course, Suit One regained equilibrium relatively quickly and shoved Dean further in the car before escape was a real possibility. After that, Dean stared out the window while the man found a patch of grass and wiped down his black leather Oxfords.

"You missed a spot," Dean commented, pointing to a remaining dollop of yuck on the left heel as the man moved toward the seat across from him.

Suit One gave no comment but went back out and tried again. Then he opened the front passenger door and removed an empty white plastic shopping bag from the glove compartment. He shook it out, returned to the back and handed it to Dean, presumably to contain any further gastric eruptions. Dean considered telling the chap that he had to be getting close to the bile retching stage and then reconsidered. Why give up his only advantage? He accepted the offering in silence.

The car sped around several corners and Dean leaned back, willing the world to stand still. He was about to ask the driver to at least slow down and perhaps open a window—even halfway—when the automobile turned toward an underground parking garage. Dean focused on the intersection they'd avoided. Two cameramen crossed at the lights and several men and women with microphones ran ahead of them, and he wondered what newsworthy event was occurring so close to where his kidnappers were taking him.

One level down in the dim lighting of the garage, the limousine pulled in front of a sign that read: Secretaria de Viajes, Cultura y Turismo.

Suit One yanked him out of his seat.

"Hey. Where are we going?"

No answer.

Catch more bees with honey?

Suit One pushed him through the door and motioned for Dean to go up the stairs. Dean stopped and looked down. "Sorry about your shoes," he said as they took the steps.

Still nothing.

Dean considered pushing down the captor behind him and making a run for it. Then he stumbled on the next landing. He didn't have the energy for a real fight, so he pulled the plastic bag closer to his chest and moved on.

CHAPTER 16

The red burner phone vibrated in Pedro's hand. No question who was calling. He was well overdue with a report to the Conductor, and he still wasn't sure if sparing Miguel's life was the right play. And if he wasn't sure, what would the Conductor think? Time to face the music.

"Sí?"

"What happened?"

"The woman was saved because one of our own took it upon themselves to tip off the Guardia."

"You took care of them?"

Pedro let an audible breath slip through his teeth.

"Not in our usual way. The offender is a significant asset. He knows the woman and came to believe that because of her connections, her death at the hands of the cartel would lead to an investigation, and eventually, back to us."

"That asset acted without authority. He still needs to be punished."

"Yes. But with him alive, it remains possible for us to get what we want. He's been assigned to get close to Briel Payce."

"After what happened today, we cannot trust him."

"Be assured he is now under surveillance. At the first sign of trouble, asset or not, I will eliminate him. Of course, that would complicate other matters for us..."

"Pedro. I hold you responsible for today's mess. Do not believe for one moment that I will spare even my most honoured lieutenant if this gets any further out of hand. Do you understand?"

The knot already choking Pedro's throat grew larger.

CHAPTER 17

Briel sat with her elbows on the boardroom table, fingers massaging her forehead. Every muscle in her body was on fire and though she wanted to go home, something important was going on. Perhaps something related to Percy. It was time to listen.

The secretariat pushed through the doorway and Briel instantly brought her arms and hands down. She took hold of the coffee cup, straightened and leaned forward. An authoritative stance, but one she hoped signalled a willingness to cooperate. After all, Percy had stumbled into some kind of hive and never came home.

After everything that happened on Iztaccihuatl mountain today, Briel had to admit she'd lost every last sliver of hope of finding Percy alive. Lydia had given up on that in Texas, and now she had as well. Briel was hunting for a corpse, and for those responsible.

Poorly executed though it was, the two men at the table had saved her life and were probably the only way forward.

A series of muddled questions swam haphazardly through Briel's brain as she searched for the most efficient way to gather information relating both to her present situation and to Percy's past. The pouch in her back pocket poked uncomfortably at her spine. At least it was still there.

As she opened her mouth to speak, someone knocked at the door.

"Sí?" the secretariat asked.

A disheveled, pale Dean Leggatt, gripping a white plastic bag, lurched into the room, pushed from behind by two pudgy arms presumably attached to a body obscured behind the opening.

Dean wobbled, his effort to remain upright clear, and Briel jumped to his aid, guiding him to a chair near hers.

"What are you doing here?" she whispered as he took the seat.

"Damned if I know," Dean said loudly enough for everyone to hear. "What's going on?"

Briel put her hands on her hips and addressed the room. "It's a relevant question."

The secretariat pulled a small yellow-orange box from his pocket and slammed it on the table in front of Dean.

"For Moctezuma's curse," he said. "Chew one now and another every six to eight hours. It will make you better, I promise."

Briel picked up the box before Dean had the chance to open it. She examined the seals, noting they were intact. Then she checked the ingredients. The last thing she needed was Dean to end up tranquilized or, God forbid, poisoned. She'd had rudimentary training in pharmacology during her chiropractic education, and she'd worked her way through school as a dispensary assistant in a pharmacy. An antibiotic coupled with an antimotility agent. A decent formula. In the US, he'd have needed a prescription, but here in Mexico, it was an over-the-counter medication.

She nodded and Dean popped a tablet into his mouth. He struggled a little to get it down, so Briel got him a cup of ice chips from a container near the water bottles beside the coffeepot. Then she unfolded Dean's white bag and lined a nearby trash bin, inching it toward Dean's leg. A precaution. Finally, she addressed the other men in the room.

"If anything happens to him, I will hold both of you responsible. How dare you remove a sick man from his bed like that? Even if you don't care, I'll bet those reporters downstairs will."

"Both of you," the secretariat began, "please accept my apologies once again. I am very sorry for the way you have been treated in my country. It was not how I intended we meet. However, what you have gotten into... A sleeping giant has awakened, and it is not good."

Briel caught the momentary narrowing of Detective Inspector De La Cruz's eyes. So, the Guardia was equally in the dark.

CHAPTER 18

The Conductor scratched at the artificial beard he'd carefully pasted over his chin an hour earlier. Unmistakable name-brand sunglasses, wide-brim black fedora, and hand-sewn black leather gloves completed the disguise he used whenever traveling outside the compound. These luxuries were a "tell" to his lifestyle, yet, somehow, the Conductor couldn't bring himself to dress down, even for this kind of errand. And, he took the time to change his jewelry. On missions like this, he wore his ruby ring instead of the onyx. On each side of the stone, gold flowed in the pattern of a conductor's wand in 6/8 time. It pleased him that both Puccini's "O Mio Babbino Caro", and the "Mexican Hat Dance" required it. Perfect symbology. The ring told his extended staff that their mysterious employer and patron, the one who must be obeyed, was in the room.

He drove himself to the outpost he had created next to a poorly traveled highway, about one and a half kilometers east of the Sun Pyramid of Teotihuacan. Heat shimmered from the chalky surface of the unpaved road that led to an abandoned fruit and vegetable stall bordering rows of maturing agave plants. On his right, a deserted patch of land flanked a barbed-wire-lined cement brick fence labeled "Building Supplies". The barbed-wire didn't look out of place here. It was how merchants in this desolate region did their best to prevent the continuous loss of goods at the hands of desperate thieves.

Not his concern. His "store" never opened. The rickety building inside the grounds made everything appear abandoned. It was anything but. A perfect camouflage. At some point, the city would probably repair the highway and urban sprawl would force him to move. For now, it was the perfect place to house his "guest".

The Conductor flipped open a cracked and weathered lock box and turned down the false number keypad. He removed his right glove and placed his thumb over the indentation, allowing the fingerprint scanner to do its job. The gate opened without complaint. Two guards, each holding a machine gun, instantly approached his car from either side. The Conductor extended his right hand out the driver's side window, showing the ruby ring, and the guards stepped back, providing him and his automobile a wide berth. The Conductor replaced his glove and smiled. Any burglar seeking entry to this business would be in for quite a surprise. He'd stationed a cadre of well-armed custodians here, men trained to defend this prize at any cost.

It was a safe house, really. Though not the kind used by the Guardia Nacional, or Mexico's Intelligence Agency, Centro Nacional de Inteligencia—CNI. No. This place kept his possessions safe, and he was here to visit an important one today.

He turned to the sentry by the building's only door. "I trust she is well?"

"Sí, Señor. We present food three times a day and sometimes she eats. We made her shower today and change clothes so she is presentable for your visit."

"Thank you."

The Conductor motioned for the man to open the door. It took a moment for his eyes to adjust to the darkness. The room had only one window, and it was high up. Bars stood three inches apart, blocking any attempt at escape or rescue, though rescue was already unlikely. This woman's capture had come off without a hitch, unlike today's escapade at Iztaccihuatl.

In the far corner of the room was a small cot, and in the middle stood a simple wooden desk with a modest lamp. A pile of books sat in the corner opposite the light. Of the woman's many demands, these research materials could not be denied. Not if she needed them to get the job done. He had even approved the Bible she'd ordered two weeks ago, though how praying to her god might help, he did not know.

The woman sat in the office chair. She was thinner than when he had visited her last—and she looked older. Weary. Her jaw sagged and her black hair, the wiry, curly kind, was longer and fell askew. More like the Lady Einstein she was purported to be.

"Report," he said, stepping closer.

She shook her head. Then she turned her brown bloodshot eyes toward him. "Why do you keep me here?"

"I told you. You are a brilliant mathematician, Maria. Not an academic, perhaps, but in your home village, you are known as a master code breaker, and I have need of your services. That is all."

"You kidnapped me," she growled. "You took me from my home in the dark of night. You could have asked for my help. You could have paid a fair price for my services."

"Come now, Lady Einstein. You needed a quiet place to solve this mystery. A place to hear the music in your head. A place to translate what I need. Have you done the job? I told you. You will be free as soon as the work is finished."

The lamp cast an orange glow on the moisture that gathered at the woman's lower lids.

"It can't be done," she finally said. The woman thrust the sheet of paper that held a copy of Percy's coded message across the desk and into the Conductor's gloved hands.

"What do you mean, it 'can't' be done?" The Conductor's voice came out in a menacing andante pianissimo. The woman was a worker. A means to an end. How dare she tell him no?

"I believe it is a book cipher. The sender and receiver agree to use a specific book. These numbers can represent pages and then lines within those pages, and then words within those lines. Without the book—in fact, without the specific edition—there is no way to solve this. At one time, it was common to use the Bible. As you can see, I've tried that, hoping chapter and verse might generate the correct letters. They didn't. Not in Spanish, and not in English. Without the key, there is no way to decode this. Of that, I am certain."

"You're telling me that the only way to resolve this is by finding a single book among the millions that exist somewhere in this world?"

"Yes. Find it and translation is a simple matter."

The Conductor inhaled. His chest expanded, as did his sense of authority and his frustration. He replayed what bits of information he had from the morning's events. Persephone Gilbert's friend had requested guides to accompany her to Cascada Congelada on Iztaccihuatl. The lieutenant's informant said she took time alone. Longer than expected. And she may have discovered something. Of course.

"Can I go now?" The woman's words tore the Conductor from his thoughts.

Then his mouth settled into its most benevolent smile.

He said, "I will make sure you find the freedom you deserve."

With that, the Conductor met his sentry at the door, slammed it shut and turned the handle to be sure the lock was secured.

"Kill her," he said to the guard waiting by his car. "Do it now."

As the Conductor seated himself behind the wheel, a shot echoed from the shed-like safe house. A flock of grackles in a nearby tree took to the sky. The engine of his luxury black sedan turned over and, from the speakers, "Dance Macabre" by Camille Saint-Saëns Op.40 played on Mexico City's classical radio station. He set the volume to full and drove away.

CHAPTER 19

The secretariat swirled the contents of his styrofoam cup with a rhythmic, almost hypnotic motion. Only the din of TV cable news, now playing at its lowest volume, disturbed the silence. Tension crept higher in Briel's shoulders and she wondered if the man who'd gone to all the trouble of making sure she and Dean were in the room was ever going to open his mouth again.

Enough of this.

"Señor Tomás," Briel said. "I... we... have the right to know about your 'sleeping giant' or whatever it is. I'm tired. Exhausted, actually. And Dean is sick. Either tell us what's going on or we're leaving. And before you get your goons to stop us, we have enough energy left to give the reporters below these windows plenty to see."

The secretariat leaned in his chair. "I do not doubt that, Doctora Payce. It is simply difficult to explain the challenges I face while balancing the cultural differences between someone raised in the United States and our social systems, while still managing what must be kept private. Some information is intended for only those who need to know. Do you understand?"

"I understand you're stalling."

Her chair screeched along the floor as Briel got up, and she motioned for Dean to follow.

The secretariat nodded and then waved at them to sit down once more. They did.

Last chance, Briel thought.

"Let me try... Doctora Payce. Our computers flagged your re-entry to Mexico when you went through customs at the airport."

A flush of heat rose in Briel's cheeks and she fixed her iciest stare Tomás's way. The secretariat's eyebrows rose.

"No, please. You do not understand. As a matter of following up on foreigners missing in our country, we routinely identify the comings and goings of those associated with open cases. It was an initiative brought in by my predecessor, but one he never used. I take my job more seriously. Doctora Payce, as you said, your previous search for Señora Gilbert was unsuccessful. Why are you back in Mexico now?"

"It's Doctora Gilbert, and—"

A knock interrupted the moment and a new face spoke. "Apologies. There are visitors downstairs asking to see Detective Inspector De La Cruz."

De La Cruz drew a finger across his lips as though considering the summons.

"Our visitors specified that this is an urgent request," the stranger said.

The detective inspector's eyes met the secretariat's and then De La Cruz headed for the exit.

As the door closed again, Briel appraised Tomás. He hadn't answered her question. Instead, he had gone on the offensive. Another strategy she knew well. A cat-and-mouse game they could both play.

"I had a lovely time hiking Iztaccihuatl, for scientific reasons. Climbing expeditions to relatively remote regions are a way of maintaining my membership in the International Explorers Network. Today, after a tourist-type look at the Cascada Congelada, I documented your increasingly rare teporingos. I have pictures. Would you like to see?"

Storm clouds brewed behind the secretariat's eyes as he met Briel's innocent façade. "The cartels do not send their soldiers when someone searches for 'bunnies'."

CHAPTER 20

The detective inspector followed the bureau's administrative assistant down a flight of stairs and into a hallway where every door was labelled "Meeting Room". One visitor had to be his unit coordinator, Torres, but who else accompanied him? Almost at the end of the hall, far enough from the curious ears of front desk personnel, the assistant turned a knob and motioned for De La Cruz to enter.

"Of course," escaped De La Cruz's mouth when he walked in.

Enrique Torres stood, arms folded, feet shoulder width apart, moustache twitching. Beside him, Frederico Constanza, State Coordinator for the Guardia Nacional, leaned against a table, arms also folded, a scowl on the taller man's post-acne pockmarked face. Over the grapevine, De La Cruz had heard that some scars hid blade marks on Constanza's cheeks, but the detective inspector was unwilling to check. Regardless, it must have been a difficult beginning for this now powerful man. Constanza's reputation was that he had learned early in life to never, ever back down from a fight. Torres looked like a child trying to imitate his older and more formidable brother as he positioned himself beside the state coordinator.

De La Cruz readied himself to give up his badge. He'd keep the gun. He'd purchased it with his own money, after all—and who knew when it would come in handy?

"I warned you," Torres growled.

Constanza stepped in front of Torres. "Explain yourself."

"Señor?"

Torres peeked out from behind Constanza and answered before the state coordinator could open his mouth again.

"De La Cruz. You have failed us at every turn. No movement on the numbers of missing or dead foreigners in Mexico City. Nothing that affects our government reports. You are a disgrace. And today? This is a disaster. We look like pawns in some game the secretariat is playing, and for our trouble, we are paying the bill! I cannot figure you out, Ricardo. Are you so desperate to keep your job or are you trying to get a new one in this building? If the latter, they can have you!"

Constanza raised an arm and, like the obedient dog Torres was, De La Cruz's boss stopped talking.

"I intend to rescue us from this PR disaster," Constanza said. "Bring us the woman. We will interview her and then she will announce her gratitude to local and federal police for saving her life today. She will announce it publicly and to the same press the secretariat addressed. Bring her to us, and do it now."

De La Cruz remained silent. Another no-win situation. Comply and alienate the only ally he'd developed, or don't comply and he was finished. Either path led to the end for him.

Then something crept forward from the recesses of the detective inspector's frustrated brain. The secretariat's words: "A sleeping giant has awakened, and it is not good." What did it mean?

Give Briel to these men, and he'd never know. And what would be the consequence? They'd let her go, and then what? The media attention would lead her attackers straight to her and she'd be dead within hours, if for no other reason than the cartel tied up its loose ends.

"Well?" Constanza stepped forward, arms still crossed, chin arched a little higher.

De La Cruz sighed. He bowed slightly, hoping to signal contrite resignation.

"I understand and apologize for my actions. I miscalculated. It was a bad mistake, and now the forces I have dedicated my life to are paying the price. I am sorry, and I hope you will allow me to see this through. Unfortunately, where Doctora Payce goes now is out of my hands. Perhaps, Señor, if you speak with the secretariat personally..."

Torres, red-faced, erupted, closing in on De La Cruz with a speed that surprised the detective. He wagged his finger under De La Cruz's chin.

Again, Constanza interrupted the scene.

"Torres," he said, walking to the exit. "Now."

Torres looked from Constanza to De La Cruz.

"You really fucked up," Torres said into De La Cruz's ear. "This isn't over."

CHAPTER 21

By the time the Conductor reached his compound and exited the black sedan, he was so blinded by rage that he launched at his waiting lieutenant. The adrenaline that consumed him swamped the mild palsy in his right arm and leg, the disability that his family said excluded him from mastering the baton at a world class level and caused his right hip to ache as it prematurely degenerated. He summoned the power of a man whose sheer will could optimize physical prowess. His right hand trembled, but the force with which he grabbed Pedro's throat was sufficient.

"What is the meaning of this?"

Pedro sputtered, trying unsuccessfully to respond, pointing to the hand that impeded his breathing. Reluctantly, the Conductor let go. Pedro gasped, doubling over to regain himself, and the Conductor tried again.

"Why are they here... again?"

"No... choice," Pedro said between breaths. "They insisted. They said they wouldn't leave Mexico without talking to you. I followed our procedures to the letter. They came in separate limousines. They have been searched. I locked them in the board-room and now they wait for you."

Though it was a significant breach, at least Pedro had been thoughtful. The Conductor simply wasn't willing to give up his fury. Not yet.

"Dorothea? The boys?"

"Gone to a friend's home." Pedro straightened as he recovered.

"When I finish, you and I will speak again."

Adrenaline abating, the Conductor's hip pain returned and he limped away.

IN HIS BEDROOM, the Conductor found the speaker for the bug in the boardroom. Handy item. Something he had installed himself. Something no one, not even Pedro, knew about. Something he'd never needed until today.

"I can't go back to Brussels. I'm finished." The Second Violin's whiny voice assaulted the Conductor's ears.

"What about me?" the Viola asked. A lower tone, but moaning nonetheless. How in God's name did these men reach such heights in the financial world? Idiotas.

The Viola continued. "Horkos put them on to my office. I'm sure of it."

The Conductor removed the ruby ring from his finger and exchanged it for the onyx and diamond. Peeling red-brown hair from his chin, upper lip and eyebrows, he checked his face in the mirror. A few more lines. Nothing to be concerned about. Perhaps the next time he had cosmetic surgery in the Caribbean, he'd ask for a change. Some unique feature; a new nose, perhaps. He'd have to lose weight first.

The Conductor traced the silver hair at his temples. He needed it cut.

The two Strings blathered on, revelling in their combined fear.

Timothy Horkos. So, that was the problem. A retired official from Greece's National Intelligence services turned champion for a worldwide crackdown on money laundering. A man who spent his career making trouble for foreign actors working inside his country. The single reason none of his Strings came from Greece. How or why this man had entered the stage remained a mystery. But his arrival set fear into the heart of drug traffickers operating through Spanish banks when he followed the money back to sequential inflated sales of art in Italy. Money washed through galleries of competent but insignificant artists. The bankers involved were well paid to suppress suspicious activity reports, but dogged as ever, Horkos and his team had turned over every stone. It was a bloodbath.

Surely, Brussels and Miami had learned from that example. Or had they?

He'd heard enough.

The Conductor strode to the boardroom, unlocked the door, and burst in.

"Ours is the single most influential organization in the world. We rule the economy. Even in the United States, we can make or break industry and undermine the government. And anonymity remains our greatest treasure. Layers of security, or so I thought, have been based on meticulously hidden paper trails that lower bank executives should not recognize. Yet here you sit. Together. Both missing from your posts and as frightened as little mice. Why? Because of a single man in your midst?"

The Conductor slammed his hands on the table and watched with satisfaction as the two men stiffened.

"Horkos isn't just our problem. He's yours, too," the Viola shot back after a quick recovery. "The man is turning the Miami offices upside down as we speak. And the IRS also arrived at multiple branches while I've been gone."

"The US tax authorities already contacted my banks," said the Second Violin. "Brussels is no more lenient about governmental violations."

The Viola continued, "We can't go back. Ever. We need new passports, and we need passage to Switzerland. Our contacts there can take care of the rest."

"Why the hell should I help you? I told you years ago that your shell game was a risk. It's your own greed that got you here. Solve your own goddamned problems."

"You're telling us you've paid taxes all this time?" The Viola remained defiant.

"In one form or another," the Conductor replied. He reflected on the number of officials he had bribed, either to turn a blind eye or to remove a tenacious opponent. Sometimes he wondered if it might be just as costly to pay his due, but then again, he wouldn't tolerate the government telling him how to deal with his money. He dictated the rules.

"Besides," the Conductor added, hoping to twist the knife a little harder, "it's better than turning a foreign shell company into a bank, opening accounts in Switzerland under the shell's name, and then having US fund managers wire money there. Talk about a paper trail! Ridiculous. Pay taxes or pay bribes. It's of no matter to me."

"Those shells protected you too. You owe us," the Second Violin squeaked.

"I owe you nothing. You made billions as part of this enterprise. What happens now has nothing to do with me."

"Yes, it does," the Viola said, his voice laced with self-satisfaction. "Horkos is the one who tipped off the IRS. Money laundering is his thing. If he's found us, he's bound to come looking for you."

"Let him. As you said, we in Mexico are 'equipped' to handle such matters."

Inside, however, the name peppered the Conductor's tranquil music with sforzando effects. He filed the threat away for future consideration.

The Second Violin and Viola looked at one another. Their sheepish faces disgusted him. If he had a gun, he might have ended their misery. But that wasn't his job. The question was, what to do now?

CHAPTER 22

The secretariat and Briel locked eyes. Dean didn't know Mateo Tomás, but he knew Briel. Once she set her mind to something, there'd be no changing it. Percy was the only one who'd penetrated that shield. The only one to force Briel out of her comfort zone. And why not? Percy had done the same for him. God, he missed her.

Dean felt for the charm at the end of the chain around his neck. A heads-tails moose nickel Percy had gifted him to remember their first encounter. He had been in a strewn field in the Sonoran Desert, along with most every other rock hound in the country, looking for meteorites from a fresh fall. She was nearby when his metal detector screamed a hit, and watched while he dug, laughing when all that came up was this out-of-place decorative coin. He had handed it to her and silently moved on, surprised when she showed up at an IEN meeting a week later with the trinket in hand, hanging from a necklace. She gave it to him and he had worn it every day since.

"Enough," Tomás said.

Dean smiled. The secretariat blinked first. Score Briel.

"I will be blunt," Tomás continued. "And I ask the same in return."

Briel tilted her head, a pout on her lips and the smallest hint of a smile creasing her eyes. Her "maybe" face.

"It was someone from Mexico's NCB who flagged your arrival. Do you know the organization?"

Briel shook her head.

"Mexico's office for Interpol's National Central Bureau."

Briel's poker face slipped and her cheeks turned red. She was about to speak when Tomás raised his arm and continued. "It is normal procedure for them to be informed. As I have said, your friend remains an international traveller who went missing in Mexico. She and you—because your first excursion here involved our authorities—are on a list, waiting for sightings."

Briel eased back into her chair and nodded.

"What you need to understand, Sen... Doctora Payce, is that the NCB alerted me to a departmental leak at the airport. That list, with your name on it, was accessed and given to the Maldito cartel. We also know that at least one of your mountain guides from this morning works for that despicable group. Then a cartel helicopter showed up on the side of the mountain you were traversing. So, I ask: Why did that happen, Doctora Payce?"

Every muscle around Briel's mouth and eyes froze. Dean knew that face, too. Others called it "deer in headlights", but he knew better. Briel's emotional control pose. The look she assumed while gaining mastery over a rising panic.

Dean didn't feel any better. Briel had been attacked on that mountainside, and he wasn't there. He cursed himself again for getting sick and then for not convincing her to postpone. Useless. No wonder Briel hadn't told him she was going to Mexico the first time. No wonder Percy had left on her Spider Rock trek without him.

Briel opened her mouth, and when words came, they were calm and clear. She'd won her war on emotional overload.

"I have no idea, Señor," she said. "I thought it was your job to understand the criminal element in this jurisdiction and keep them under control, at least as it relates to those of us visiting your land."

It was the secretariat's turn to struggle with his feelings. Dean noticed the flash of rage that peeked from Tomás's eyes just before his poker face returned. Dean would have liked playing cards with these two. He'd win every hand.

"Every country, including yours, Doctora, has its challenges. But you are correct to point out that tourists everywhere should be protected... if they are innocently spending time and money in our great land."

Briel leaned forward, ready for the next salvo, but Tomás continued.

"Shortly after my appointment as secretariat, someone approached me at a local restaurant. The man came with an offer. He could 'handle' foreign problems for me. Tourists who were themselves corrupt. As a patriot, wanting to keep Mexico clean from unlawful outside influences, he could make such problems 'disappear'. Of course, I said no."

Briel pushed away from the table and Dean wondered if she intended to stand up. When she didn't, he looked back at Tomás.

"My next visitor was from the Centro Nacional de Inteligensia, someone reporting directly to the Secretariat of the Interior, asking about that visit. There was little I could tell him. However, I have friends in high places too. Through my connections, I discovered that the mystery visitor was linked to a shadow group targeting foreigners digging into the financial concerns of wealthy Mexicans..."

Briel could no longer hold back. "Percy had no reason to delve into Mexico's banks, and neither do I. What in the world does any of this have to do with Percy, Dean, or me?"

Taking his cue from Briel, Dean jumped in. "I can answer that. Nothing. You, me... Percy. She didn't and we don't care one wit about the money in this country, corrupt or otherwise. And I think, as secretariat, you've already looked into our backgrounds, so you know that. So, we're asking again, why did your thugs feel the need to force us into this room? What's this really about?"

Tomás did not hesitate.

"I 'forced' you here for your own protection. You are correct. I found nothing linking you to our financial institutions. Yet, somehow, Doctor Payce has—what is the expression—poked the bear. As the two of you are already a part of a problem I know too little about, I hope that if I foster your search for your friend, and try to protect you in the meantime, you both will return the favour."

CHAPTER 23

Ricardo De La Cruz stood as Torres stormed from the room.

That was easy. Too easy.

Constanza controlled Torres, but only to a point. A thousand thoughts rattled in Ricardo's mind. Family, the training it took to reach the position he now held, what life after being fired might be like.

Oddly, they could have sent him packing as soon as he refused them. Why didn't they?

He headed out the door, intending to rejoin the meeting with the secretariat. A second later, Ricardo changed directions. He needed to clear his head.

Across the street from Tomás's offices stood a small open-air café. Just what his muddled brain called for. An espresso to remove the taste of the swill the secretariat's staff passed off as coffee, and something to mask the aftertaste of his latest encounter with his boss.

The reporters were gone now. Nothing left for them to find. With Tomás's statement and all the footage from Iztaccíhuatl, the talking heads had plenty of material for their evening deadline.

Unwilling to walk to the traffic light at the corner, Ricardo stepped into the quiet street, reaching the opposite side just as a squeal of tires announced a dark SUV rounding the corner and speeding his way. Annoyed by the dangerous driver, he pulled out his phone to catch a picture of the plates. That's when he saw the gun pointing through the rear window—at him.

Ricardo hit the ground, his jaw meeting the sidewalk with a loud thud while a bullet careened past his left ear, landing at the bottom of the café's exterior wall. Fragments of exploding cement peppered the top of his head as he rolled over and pulled out his own weapon, ready to engage the attacker.

He pivoted to his knees, looking for a clean shot, but the automobile sped away, so he stood up and checked behind him for any bystander who may have been injured by the altercation. Satisfied no one was close by, he scanned the street for witnesses and clues. His gaze locked onto a short, suited figure entering a limousine about a block away. The man turned his head, just for a moment, before disappearing into the back seat, and Ricardo caught the unmistakable handlebar moustache that belonged to Enrique Torres.

Game on.

CHAPTER 24

Briel forced herself to cross her arms and lean back, hoping to assume a neutral, almost relaxed stance. She was glad her tee-shirt was loose-fitting, otherwise the thumping of her heart would surely be noticed by everyone in the room. What possible expertise did she, let alone Dean, have that would benefit Tomás?

"Doctora Payce. Your friend, Doctora Gilbert. It is suspected that she discovered a network connected to my mysterious visitor. I believe when she was taken, she was trying to expose them."

"Why would you say that?"

"When I spoke with my contacts at the Secretariat of the Interior's office, I was given a copy of a file. In it were the names of missing tourists, now presumed dead at the hands of a renegade group claiming to rid Mexico of foreign influences."

"Percy's name was on that list?"

"Not only Doctora Gilbert's name. Yours too."

"What?" The question came out simultaneously from both Briel and Dean.

The secretariat opened a manilla folder. Inside was a photocopy of an envelope with "B. Payce" scrawled on the front and a small square of paper. Briel recognized it instantly. On the sheet before her were three rows of numbers, separated by colons, dots, semicolons, and plus signs. Percy's message. The one from the video. Shock settled into the pit of Briel's stomach.

"How did you get that?" Dean said before Briel could form words.

Tomás looked from Dean to Briel and stammered for the first time.

"I... Please. You must understand; I am new to my position. I gained access to the files of my predecessor only recently. This was included in a paramedic's report about a Jane Doe from five years ago. I was unable to track down more. It seems the medical history was recorded separately. Why? I do not know. When I searched for your name, Doctora Payce, it appeared."

Briel cleared her throat. Leaning in once more, she spoke. The voice that emerged was hoarse, almost snarling.

"Are you telling me that when I asked for help five years ago, this was in your system? A keystroke away? And not one of your officials bothered to look when I asked for help?"

"No, no. I'm sorry. It takes time to record these logs. They are always behind. Up to a year, in fact. At the time, there simply may have been nothing to find."

"All down to 'slow recording'," Dean mumbled.

Briel pursed her lips. She pumped her fingers to loosen the cramp settling in them. The pouch, still in her pocket, poked uncomfortably at her spine.

Tomás began again.

"If that was the only problem, I would simply hand this over to you and be done with it. Unfortunately, as before, someone else accessed the same file, and we suspect it was the Maldito cartel again. It is possible, Doctora, that you are now a target for whatever forces our mysterious network and the cartel have identified as a threat. This note links you with Persephone Gilbert's agenda in Mexico. And that is why you are here."

CHAPTER 25

The Second Violin blanched, and the Conductor wondered if the man before him might faint, understanding that the threat in this room was not to his wealth, but to his life. Enough of this.

The Conductor walked to the boardroom exit, ready to leave his unwanted guests in the manure their greed had created. But he couldn't justify another protection protocol. Not when one was already in the making. A cartel hit? An accidental death? Yes. Except there were two of them, and their profiles were raised by the nonsense going on in their home countries. Their deaths would attract far too much attention. Someone might find their way to his doorstep. He needed to think. The Conductor turned the knob.

A thin voice spoke from behind him.

"You're not so perfect," the Second Violin said. "We asked Pedro about the mission we agreed to finance. Seems our money wasn't well spent."

"You failed," the Viola echoed. "Nothing to show for a simple accident on the side of a hill. Why? Because you can't always control your enemy. Same as us."

What in God's name had possessed Pedro to tell these hijos de puta about today's failure? Was he trying to curry favour from a snivelling idiot and a cowardly fool? Or was Pedro past his prime? Two mistakes in one day. Pedro was lucky his plan for Miguel had possible merit. But when this was over? Pedro Serrano had grown too comfortable with the job. Time the Conductor looked for a successor; one whose first order of business would be to remove the old lieutenant. An icy chill ran down his spine. The familiar adrenaline that came from making landmark decisions.

He stared back at the two men he used to do business with. For now, they would live. He had other matters to deal with.

"Your friend Pedro," he said, "will give you the contacts you need for new paperwork. Get out, and never come to me again."

CHAPTER 26

The air conditioner in Pedro's dark green high-end sports car kicked in and the perspiration at his hairline evaporated. His frustration did not.

Bad enough that Miguel had leaked Briel Payce's planned demise to the National Guard. Worse, the unexpected visit by two of the Strings and their goddamned revelation that they knew about the failed assassination on Iztaccíhuatl. He'd never seen the Conductor like that. By the time Pedro had left his boss, the brandy glass in the Conductor's hand was quaking. Precious drops of golden alcohol spilled to the floor, acknowledging his boss's undisguised rage. The Conductor gave Pedro a sinister warning in a tone that brooked no argument. A single toe out of line and their years of work were not the only thing to be over. He wondered for a moment exactly how the Conductor would do it. It was usually Pedro who took care of such problems.

Pedro checked the rear-view mirror. No evidence he was being followed.

The call came just before the Second Violin and the Viola ran from the Conductor's office, demanding the contacts necessary to create the Strings' new identities.

The Conductor was right about them. Greedy cowards. Both

were leaving families behind to deal with their mess. In Mexico, that would not be tolerated. Still, as ordered, he gave them what they needed. He'd have liked to say good riddance, but if he survived this latest debacle, it would be his job to find their replacements. Easy to uncover corrupt foreign officials. More difficult to find them in exactly the right place and avoid tipping off their colleagues. That hunt could take a while.

In the meantime, Pedro certainly wasn't going to tell the Conductor about their newest problem. No. He needed to take care of that himself.

The sports car's wheels squealed through the last sharp bend into the hospital parking lot and heads turned to watch his entrance. Unwanted attention. So, he parked carefully at the far end of the visitor's lot. When he exited and clicked the door shut, he smiled at the last little old lady whose eyes remained on him. Eventually, she turned and hobbled away and everyone went back to minding their own business.

The steel of Pedro's concealed handgun lay cold against his back as he walked through the hospital doors and headed for the administrative wing. He cursed when the elevator stopped and a flood of junior doctors entered, complaining about some seminar they'd just finished. They squeezed into the small space, smelling like fruity air freshener and antiseptic soap. He gagged after they got out on the next floor, glad to be alone once more and grateful there were no witnesses to where he intended to stop.

Pedro barged into Miguel's office without considering if someone might be there ahead of him, or if Miguel was even in the room, since the doctor's duties required regular supervision of the wards.

But Miguel was there. Alone.

Miguel's jaw fell and he jumped back from his desk so hard, his chair slammed into the bookcase behind him. Two of the man's favourite baubles, awards for good works, fell to the ground.

Pressing his advantage, Pedro thundered.

"How dare you? You fucking ingrate. How dare you move against our cause… again!"

"Uncle. I don't understand. What is this about?"

Pedro slammed the door shut and lowered his tone.

"Do you think me a fool? Did you honestly believe I wouldn't find out?"

"I don't know what you're talking about."

"The message found on the body. The one you diligently passed to me five years ago. You deny sending a copy to the Secretariat of Travel, Culture and Tourism?"

The colour drained from Miguel's face and his eyes slid to his laptop.

"Well?"

"I did." The words were barely audible. Pedro pulled the gun from behind his back.

"Uncle!" Miguel raised his palms. "Wait. You don't under-stand. The paramedics made a copy for their files and it got logged. I didn't know. The secretariat surprised my staff by accessing the database and ordering the release of information to his office. By the time it came to me for approval, the note had already been seen by too many people. I couldn't get rid of it."

Pedro lunged forward and pushed the barrel of his gun under Miguel's chin.

"No. Uncle, wait." Miguel gasped, his voice box half closed by the force of Pedro's weapon. "I've been working on a solution, and I've got some of it solved. Finding the Spider Rock is critical to me too. If anyone discovers the location of those bodies, it traces back to all of us."

Pedro eased the pressure on the gun, but only slightly. "What is the solution?"

"Not what, but how? I found a computer program that solves such problems. It's based on Germany's Enigma Machine from World War II. Very sophisticated, and very secret. I had to bribe someone on the dark web, but I've got the key. All we need to do is put the message into the program. If you have the code with you, we can do it now."

A pleading, naïve, little boy look washed over Miguel. Thick lips slightly ajar, big brown eyes wide with surprise, the point emphasized by large, squared, brown eyeglass frames. Once more, it was the face Pedro remembered from Miguel's teenage years. Like then, the question was whether to believe him. Miguel's mother, Pedro's sister, had taught Miguel to be a romantic do-gooder. Not a foul word ever left his mouth. What went on inside the man's head?

Still, Miguel mostly did as he was told.

Pedro relaxed his gun hand and reached for the computer. He instantly regretted the mistake. Miguel pushed the gun away, and something hard hit the side of Pedro's head. It wasn't Miguel's fist. The doctor was not a natural fighter.

As he crumpled to the ground, Pedro remembered the glass paperweight his nephew had picked up at a medical conference in Malta. Miguel must have tucked it inside his grip. Maybe there was more to this boy, after all.

Pedro struggled to recover, but the blow left him dizzy. He shook away the pain and nausea, and spotted Miguel speeding from the room, laptop under his arm.

CHAPTER 27

Ricardo's eyes traced the path made by his boss's tailpipe. He grabbed a napkin from a nearby stand and wiped the grit from his hands as a portly, red-faced man in a white chef's coat bounded from the café, moist towel in hand, asking if he should call the police or the paramedics.

"Thank you, señor, but no," Ricardo replied, pulling the badge from his back pocket.

The man looked aghast.

"Come in; come in to my shop." He beckoned Ricardo. "Please, what would you like? No charge. Some of our citizens... I do not understand how they can be so disrespectful."

"Thank you. A latte, please."

While the man busied himself with the coffee machine and the frothing hot milk, Ricardo checked his surroundings, eventually focusing on the two bistro tables set up on the sidewalks in front of the shop windows. One was now occupied and as Ricardo looked closely, recognition dawned, not from previous encounters, but from the publicity photos accompanying every change in important levels of investigative personnel. The man's features were handsome. Perfectly proportioned blue eyes, slightly angular nose, light skin, impeccably coiffed black hair. The lanky figure stretched his crossed legs out in a pose that would have made the cover of GQ. The black suit and white shirt? It took no time to recognize they were tailor made.

Amid the scuffle with what had to be his boss's hitman, the head of the Agencia Federal de Servicios de Investigación (AFSI), Luis Menendez slid onto the scene and seemed to wait for someone.

For him? Surely not.

Ricardo thanked the store owner again and took his to-go cup, intending to head straight back to his meeting with the secretariat, the indomitable Briel Payce, and her friend, Dean Leggatt. As he crossed the threshold back into the heat of the day, he noticed the agency's leader now had his head buried in a newspaper. As he stepped from the curb, Ricardo heard a voice from behind him.

"About time you came out. I wondered if you were going to have dinner with Raul."

Ricardo turned to see the head of the agency with his newspaper folded, looking at him with a broad smile. "Raul in there? He is one of mine. Nice guy. Makes a wonderful Turkish coffee. If you ask nicely… Detective Inspector, please join me. We have something to discuss."

Ricardo didn't move. In the last hour, he'd endured his boss's boss dressing him down, and then found Torres watching while a drive-by shooter got too close to Ricardo for comfort. The last thing he needed was the AFSI.

"You are about to discover that I have many 'resources' in unexpected places," Menendez continued.

What was it the English were so fond of saying? Knowledge is power? Perhaps something useful could come from listening to what the man had to say. Ricardo approached the table.

"Sit down," Menendez said. "You seem at odds with those above your station."

He raised a delicate pointer finger into the air, and Ricardo saw the café owner scurry from behind the counter of his shop.

Ricardo said nothing.

"I presume that bullet was a warning from Torres?"

Ricardo stayed quiet.

The café owner placed a porcelain espresso cup on the table in front of Menendez, added a teaspoon of sugar, stirred, and shared a nod with the head of the AFSI. Interesting.

Ricardo was still staring at the cup when Menendez broke the spell. "Sorry, De La Cruz. Did you want Raul here to change out your ... latte for an espresso?"

The detective inspector met Raul's eyes and shook his head. "No, señor. Thank you."

Raul scurried back into his shop without another word, and Menendez tapped a long first finger on the bistro table.

"You want to know why I am here?"

"Of course."

"I was briefed about your escapade with Tomás. A bold plan. I can see the logic, though if you had called me instead, I suspect my team would have been more... efficient."

Ricardo took a breath. He didn't know what "efficient" meant in Menendez's world, and he wasn't at all sure he wanted to find out. Those in the AFSI were a dangerous lot. It was assumed they were on the right side of the law, but Machiavelli had nothing on the tactics these people employed.

"I didn't know your agency was available to help. Thank you, señor. I'll keep that in mind for the future." Ricardo pushed his chair back, ready to stand and leave.

"Stay," Menendez said, and Ricardo wondered if the man treated everyone as though they were his dog.

"It is my understanding," Menendez continued, "that Tomás accessed a file from our national database and retrieved a coded message presumably left by someone named..." Menendez reached inside his jacket pocket and opened a folded sheet of paper. "Persephone Gilbert. I believe the woman you and Tomás rescued today was identified as the intended recipient of that message."

That was news to Ricardo, but would explain much of the secretariat's odd behaviour.

Menendez went on. "We have that file. If the woman now with Tomás knows how to read that message, I would be much obliged to receive a copy of the solution before it becomes public."

"What is the simple matter of one missing tourist's note to the AFSI?"

Half-curled pinky finger extended, Menendez lifted the tiny espresso cup to his lips and took a sip.

"Ah. Raul makes the best espresso in town. I'm so glad he's here." Menendez winked, but Ricardo didn't care; the conversation was quickly gathering dust, and he wanted to get back to the secretariat.

"Alright," said Menendez finally. "The AFSI received word some years ago that an underground group of religious zealots—a cult, if you will—may pose a threat to certain tourists who come to Mexico. They were active when this Persephone Gilbert disappeared. We believe they are responsible for a recent hit, and they appear to be gearing up once more. There may be a link between the cult and some of our leading cartels. Thus, your territory and mine now overlap."

"It sounds like you and our Secretariat of Travel, Culture and Tourism have much to discuss."

"I tried that. For reasons I cannot disclose, Tomás is unwilling to share information. That's why I need you."

"I can't help you."

"But you can. My request does not come without reward. After all, we know about your daughter. It must be very difficult to keep up with her medical needs, let alone your aspirations for special care in Germany. I believe we can help you make genuine progress towards that goal. Perhaps even make it a reality."

A hot rock settled deep in Ricardo's gut.

Lilly.

A million thoughts careened through his brain. Ricardo's wife, Valentina, had died of a hemorrhage immediately following the unexpected and rapid labour that brought Lilly into the world. And then his sweet baby girl began to struggle.

At first, they thought it was Lilly's heart. Her oxygen levels were too low. Then came the diagnosis. A giant malformation of blood vessels in her brain. And then the surgery to repair it. A surgery that left his precious daughter trapped in a body her brain couldn't make move. Hope lay with new technology being tested in Germany. But the cost...

Thank God for his mother. If not for her, Ricardo wouldn't have trained for the force, or held the position that was, at least for the moment, his. Lilly lived with her grandmother in a small town outside of Mexico City, and Ricardo spent as much time there as he could. But his mother was aging. How much longer before they were both at risk?

"I'm listening."

"Right now, Tomás is interviewing Briel Payce. We believe she holds the key to breaking open our investigation. Understand, Inspector, we are as interested in cleaning up our reputation in the world as you are. Perhaps more. We need to know what Tomás discovers. If what you bring to us helps, you will be paid handsomely."

Menendez wrote a figure on the napkin beside his espresso and passed it to Ricardo. It was more than Ricardo could have dreamed of. Enough to send Lilly to Germany, with some left over to supply his mother with the support she would soon need. Ricardo felt the heat rise in his cheeks. Was he willing to make a deal with the devil?

"I'll think about it," he said.

Menendez smiled broadly.

"Of course."

The head of the AFSI reached into his inside pocket again and produced a card. He circled the email address.

"When you have something we need, send it here."

CHAPTER 28

Pedro wrenched himself free from the vise formed by Miguel's desk and the heavy oak guest chair wedged into the bookcase by the force of his fall. His shoulder ached and his left foot, the one with an old bullet wound, throbbed from the assault. Given the awkward twist required from his back to manoeuvre into standing, he'd be stiff all over tomorrow. He was too old for this, but damned if he would let his nephew get away with a computer that held the key to keeping things together in Mexico. Once they had the Spider Rock, he'd end Miguel's privileged life and, family or not, it would be a pleasure.

Pedro caught movement as the door closed at the end of the hall. His bones begrudged him the chase, but he had no time to argue. He made it through the exit and heard the noise far below him. He knew Miguel. The man had little creative instinct and would head for his car. Pedro took the stairs two at a time but held onto the railing, cursing yet another lapsed gym membership.

When he made it to the bottom, he flung the door wide and spotted Miguel heading for the doctors' parking lot.

Fire his weapon? One glance at his surroundings told him it was a bad idea. Several meters away to his right, a woman wheeled a baby carriage toward the emergency department, a second child holding her hand, crying. To his left, doctors assembled for a break, some lighting cigarettes and perhaps something else. So much for Miguel's tight ship.

Not a good place for an open attack. Still, Pedro needed to stop Miguel before he made it to his car. An oak tree and a small hedge to the left offered the only protection from inquisitive eyes. He certainly wasn't going to catch up with Miguel on foot, so he ducked behind a trunk and crouched low, just as Miguel got two meters from his goal. Without hesitation, Pedro fired and missed.

Miguel made it to the driver's side and scrambled to get inside. When he lost his grip on the laptop and it fell to the ground, Miguel reached for the computer, but Pedro was ready and sent another bullet his way. This one hit the rear frame. Miguel didn't hesitate. He jumped behind the wheel, fired the engine, and sped to the exit.

Pedro could have shot out the tires and trapped his nephew, but the sound of slugs had already scattered those close to the hospital's entrance. Security and police could not be far behind.

He crab-walked the hedge until he reached the doctors' lot, kept out of the line of sight of the surveillance camera on the lamp-post, grabbed the laptop and disappeared again into the brush. When Pedro emerged, he was only a few steps away from his sports car. He brushed himself off and nonchalantly sauntered through the visitors' lot before opening his door. Hospital security cautiously approached the doctors' parking area as anxious onlookers pointed to where they heard the sounds of gunfire. Sirens in the distance grew louder.

Pedro put Miguel's computer on the passenger's seat, started the engine, and drove away.

CHAPTER 29

"Do you know what the numbers on the paper mean?" Tomás asked. He furrowed his brows, but Briel couldn't get a good read on the man. Was he worried? If so, was it for himself, for her, or for them all?

As though on cue, the small zippered pouch dug harder into her backside.

"I might," she said.

She turned to Dean, hoping he had noticed something that could help her decide whether to reveal what she'd found, but he only shrugged at her unasked question.

Tomás spoke again. "Doctora Payce. You have no reason to trust me. I understand. You were treated badly by my predecessor, and our attempt to rescue you, well-intentioned though it was, left you afraid and uncomfortable. Still, our government resources saved your life today. For that reason alone, I hope you will help me now."

He had a point. With Briel dead, whatever Percy had left her would be in the hands of the Maldito cartel by now. Not a pleasant thought.

She pulled the PVC bag from her back pocket and laid it on the table. All eyes were on her as she unzipped it for the first time.

Inside was a three-inch by four-inch children's book. The brightly decorated cover depicted two youngsters flying a kite in a field, one with dark skin, the other light. Just like Percy and Briel.

Briel drew her hand over the hardback's surface. A 1901 copy of *The Misdeeds of Mischievous and Disobedient Little Boys and Girls*. Percy had gotten two copies at a local used bookstore and had given one to Briel soon after they became friends. It was still in Briel's home library. Her friend called it their "code for life". It had never seemed to bother Percy that the world pegged her as mischievous. Briel was obedient, but Percy saw their misdeeds as a team effort, and this book was where it all started. If Briel could have tucked herself away for a good cry, she'd have done it.

The secretariat broke the spell.

"What is that?" he asked, tilting his head to get a better look.

"I know," Dean said as he covered Briel's outstretched hand with his own and squeezed it gently. "It's Percy's. It's what she wanted us to find."

Briel accepted Dean's touch, surprised by the vulnerability that surfaced. She bent her head, hoping no one noticed the tear that slid down her cheek. Inhaling deeply, she removed her hand from under Dean's grip and refocused on Tomás.

"I need a piece of paper and a pen," she said.

Without comment, Tomás took an expensive-looking burgundy and gold pen from his top pocket and tore a sheet from the pad in the brown leather portfolio on the table in front of him.

Dean passed the copy of Percy's note to her.

"Like when we were kids." Percy's words on the video. The cipher was easy now that she had the key.

First number: 33. She turned to the page. Second number: 3. Briel brought her finger down to the third line. 8 + 25. The eighth letter was a capital F, and the twenty-fifth was an r. Then down to the twelfth line...

Dean left her to it, though Briel knew he could as easily solve this puzzle. He'd spent enough time with Percy and the IEN to know it was her favourite, if arcane and slightly sluggish, means of creating a code. Percy had conceived of this variation of the book cipher at eleven years of age, right after she read her first adventure novel and the protagonist solved for the location of an Egyptian treasure using a particular version of the Bible. Ingenious, she called it. As long as the coder and receiver held the same edition of the same book, secret messages could be sent at will, with no one the wiser.

Briel cursed herself for not figuring it out when she was in Texas. "Like when we were kids." It was the clue. She could have used her copy and then she and Dean could have gone directly to where Percy wanted them to be, without... No. Mexican authorities would have flagged her entry regardless. Maybe it was better this way.

Decoding completed, Briel put down the pen. Dean was already on his phone, searching the web.

"Well?" asked Tomás, irritation clear in his tone.

Doesn't appreciate being the last to know, Briel thought. It was nice to be in control of the situation, at least for a while.

"Friar Hugh Suthons," Briel said. "Dean is looking him up, but perhaps you already know how we can reach him?"

CHAPTER 30

Ricardo flipped the small white card between his thumb and forefinger. It was empty save for a handwritten email address: pasadizo19@miamail.com. Passage 19. A code name for Menendez's mission. But to what end? Which side was good and which was bad?

Menendez offered a backup plan if Torres fired him. After everything Ricardo had endured, coming home to scarce resources and a corrupt boss; at least with this deal, he'd have something for Lilly, and his mother.

So why did it bother him?

He pulled out his phone and added the information to his contacts list before knocking on the meeting room door and rejoining Tomás and the others.

Tomás. The man had used his own political capital to free resources, based only on Ricardo's request. He owed the secretariat. Was he really willing to betray him now?

"Friar Hugh Suthons? I don't know this man," Tomás said. The secretariat was pacing, arms behind his back. Dean Leggatt and Briel Payce sat huddled in front of a phone screen.

"What did I miss?" Ricardo asked.

Tomás explained how Briel had solved Percy's code and

updated Ricardo regarding his suspicions about a criminal force targeting certain foreigners. Ricardo blew out an uncomfortable breath. By saving this single tourist, he'd pushed his boat toward an iceberg, with no awareness of which direction was safe.

"We can't find Friar Suthons," Briel said. "Maybe he's not in Mexico City. He's not listed."

Ricardo drew out his cell. The order this friar belonged to, whether it was Dominicans, Franciscans, Augustinians or any of the other additional seven mendicants, he didn't know. However, he'd spent his life in Mexico City and he'd gotten to know a few religious leaders. He still went to them for their prayers for Lilly. Ricardo sent a text message to every contact he had, asking about this foreign friar. Within seconds, he had a response.

"Hogar de Niños San Antonio de Padua," Ricardo said. "The friar is in charge of both the orphanage and the church, located outside the city, in the hills to the west. I'll send you the information, Señor Tomás."

While the secretariat reached for his phone and Briel leaned over hers with Dean, Ricardo copied the link and sent it, along with Friar Hugh Suthons' name, to Luis Menendez.

Tomás spread a map on the table. The detective inspector and Briel huddled over it. Dean, however, pushed his chair back and considered his situation. He was feeling better. Tomás's meds had helped. He'd have to remember those ingredients. Definitely worth carrying on every trek.

Now what? Should he join the fray?

Already too many cooks in the kitchen, and he could see both Tomás and De La Cruz getting annoyed at Briel's insistence that she was coming along, regardless of where the path to Friar Suthons led. He agreed with her. They had come to find out what happened to Percy, and he'd be damned if that took second place to anyone else's agenda.

"Excuse me," Dean said over the excited din. "Doctora Payce trusted you with something we could have held to ourselves. Thank you for your help to date, but we'll take it from here."

The smile on Briel's face said it all. They were a team, bound by their different, but equally important, connection to Percy.

"It would seem, señor... excuse me, it is also doctor. Yes? Doctor Leggatt, that we all have a role to play here. I give you both safe haven, the detective inspector provides his knowledge of the city. Doctora Payce resolves the puzzle your friend left us."

"And me?" Dean realized Tomás had assigned nothing to him.

"This insanity is complex. From you, Doctor Leggatt, I have a special request."

"And what might that be?"

"Tell me, Doctor Leggatt, what brought you to Mexico?"

"You already know that."

"No. Five years ago, you did not come. I checked. Why did you accompany Doctora Payce this time?"

Dean looked at Briel, and she nodded. They'd already given away their hand, so why not?

"Guilt."

"Pardon?" The secretariat looked surprised.

"Guilt," Dean repeated. "I couldn't face it the first time. I did an evaluation of a rock sample Percy had, and it led her to Mexico. I've blamed myself for her disappearance ever since."

"Ah. But it is for your geological skills that I need you now."

De La Cruz sipped from his coffee cup, and all eyes focused on the secretariat while they waited for him to continue.

"Our search for the connection between foreigners with a clean reputation and our underworld revealed a potential link to the Departamento Regional de Monitoreo de Desastres Naturales. Those monitoring our continually active volcanoes."

"I'm not a volcanologist."

"I know. And in this instance, that is a good thing. You understand geological data—yes? And you have explored the world. In and out of dangerous places. As I understand it, you are credited with saving lives in remote regions afflicted by natural disasters."

The man was well informed. Dean kept his volunteer work with rescue organizations close to his chest. He waited for the secretariat to continue.

"Then you are the perfect person. You will be underestimated when directed to undertake an analysis of our constantly smoking Popocatepetl."

CHAPTER 31

Angelica, Pedro's favourite server, put a gin and tonic in front of him and gave him her most delicious smile. Her requisite black leggings outlined a perfect figure and the silk shirt open one button past suggestive was a clear invitation. He wasn't in the mood. Even the orange corona surrounding the distant mountains at sunset didn't have their usual impact.

He sat, stone-faced, on the top floor of the Mirasuprano, his go-to rooftop bar, staring at the horizon. When he finally took a sip of his cocktail, he pursed his lips in disgust. He'd need another talk with the owner. The most expensive restaurant in the entire city and, once again, they had substituted his favourite top shelf water for some inferior tonic. Probably some new corporate hot shot trying to cut costs. No regard for their patrons.

Just like Miguel.

His nephew's laptop lay on the chair next to him. He hadn't opened it. Not yet. He needed to calm down. To think. If Miguel had found the solution to the code, maybe the man was worth saving after all? And what about the Conductor? Would a success like this put him back in his boss's good graces?

Perhaps.

He lay the computer beside the drink he wouldn't finish—or

pay for—and opened the lid. The screen lit up. Password protected. Of course. Three chances to get it right before being locked out, and he couldn't ask for help. The credit had to be his. Think.

Miguel's son's name and date of birth. When Sofia left Miguel, she hid herself and their boy, Robertito. Miguel spent all his free time searching for them both.

"Incorrect Password"

Two tries left.

It was Miguel's work computer. Could his password have something to do with the hospital? He typed in MLDirector and hovered his index finger over the enter key. No. Miguel would honour his son, somehow. He added the year of his son's birth.

"Incorrect Password"

Pedro released a growl, ready to fling the foul device from the rooftop. A couple at the next table turned to look his way. He regained control and tried to smile.

"Computers. They can be frustrating. Sí?"

And the man and woman went back to their dinner without a word.

Last chance.

Miguel's interests. History was important to him. Teotihuacan, in honour of the famous and ancient pyramids that lay to the northeast of the city? Perhaps. No. Not specific enough for his nitpicky nephew. Quetzalcoatl? Yes. And then the year Robertito was born.

Pedro returned to the keyboard, and this time, Miguel's home page sprang to life.

"Yes!" His chair scraped the cement floor as he jerked with excitement. Beside him, eyes turned his way again, this time brows raised with distinct disapproval.

"My granddaughter," he lied. "She sends me news of her good school grades."

The woman broke into a broad smile. The universal understanding of a grandfather's pleasure in a child's success bridged his gap in social decorum. Again, the couple went back to their meal.

Pedro focused on Miguel's files, searching for the program his nephew had promised was there. A half hour later, the last flicker of sunlight descending over the horizon, he gave up.

Nothing.

Miguel had lied to him.

CHAPTER 32

T *he Next Day*

CHIMES over the mantle announced precisely nine o'clock in the morning. The Conductor looked again at the phone. An hour and a half late. Did Pedro not understand the fragile position he was in, or was he already on the run?

The Conductor's index finger tapped rhythmically on the desk. It was important to keep perfect time for the Orchestra. He'd never failed in that regard, until now. Actually, it wasn't his failure. Goddamned Second Violin and Viola. Didn't know the difference between keeping what they were owed and greed. The government always took its due, one way or another.

He'd need to be more careful finding their replacements. Pedro should have dealt with his wayward musicians by now. New identities and tickets to Switzerland. If the risk of killing them was too great, then at least they would soon be an ocean away. Good riddance. And if Pedro did his job right, nothing would ever lead back to him.

Pedro. Where was the man? He'd done well for so long, but the time had come and the Conductor had already sourced a possible replacement. The guard who had killed his Lady Einstein followed orders without question, and without hesitation, and had arranged for the area to be cleaned without a trace. So far, no mistakes. A younger man looking to rise in the ranks. Yes. He was worth further consideration. Perhaps his next job would entail searching for and eliminating Pedro. A good test before he assumed the post as the Conductor's most trusted ally.

A shrill ringtone grated across his ears. He needed to learn how to fix that in the instrument's settings. His grandsons would know. He could ask them to help him when they finished their schoolwork.

The phone sounded again.

"About time, Pedro," he said.

"Sorry, señor," Pedro said. "I know I'm late, but I had to be sure. Miguel set me up. He told me he had the key to solving the code, so I took his computer and checked, but couldn't find anything. I took the laptop to an expert this morning. Miguel lied."

"So you failed... again. Where is Miguel now?"

"He is being followed. I will catch up with him soon enough. I didn't want to delay my report, so I called you first."

The Conductor hung up and cursed Persephone Gilbert. Every avenue to solving her riddle thwarted. Would the discovery of the Spider Rock finally be his demise? He used to be sure his tracks were well covered. Yesterday's altercation with the Strings and Pedro's failures now cast doubt.

His hand shook, just a little, as he picked up a different phone. It was time to call in a favour. Time to reach out to the man he hated most in this world. He tapped the digits that were burned in his memory.

"Hello? Yes, it's me. We need to talk."

The Conductor took in a sharp breath as the familiar voice of the only man on earth who knew his true identity answered the phone. The man's tone was more clipped than usual.

"What do you want?" the man said.

"You have something I need."

"What makes you think that?"

"Friends tell me you solved the code."

"That was not me."

"No. You had help. But you have the answer, and I would like to have it... please."

It galled the Conductor to ask, but he was well past Pedro's foibles and his own lame attempts. He needed this before anyone else ended up on his doorstep.

"Why should I help you?"

"You owe me. You would not be where you are now without my help."

"And you would not be leading the easy life you have without mine. We are even."

"Not in the least. Remember, if my connections are revealed to the public, not only will I go down, so will you. And our little feud? That could turn deadly."

The silence on the other side of the phone told the Conductor that he'd struck a chord.

Good.

CHAPTER 33

The parking lot for the Church of San Antonio de Padua was empty except for a rusty, teal-coloured 1980s vintage pickup truck under the carport a good fifty meters away, near a side door. Presumably, the vehicle belonged to the local priest. Vow of poverty, Ricardo supposed.

Tires crunched on the gravel surface as he pulled into a spot near the front entrance and turned off his unmarked car. Doctora Briel Payce had said almost nothing on their trip here. He'd only agreed to let her come along because he had the distinct impression she'd have gotten there with or without him. And she didn't even thank him for the ride.

Payce was an enigma. He'd met American women before and knew them to be stubborn and provocative. This one was different. No doubt she was stubborn, but she was also measured, calculating, and observant. Besides her physical prowess, those characteristics were probably why his helicopter hadn't found her dead. Still, this kind of investigation was no place for a female health care provider, let alone an academic.

Ricardo opened his car door and headed to the passenger side. His mother had taught him to treat women with respect. All women.

However, as he rounded the front end, Briel Payce was already pulling at the ten-foot oak church doors. Iron hinges groaned in complaint, but she persisted and was through the opening by the time he reached the threshold.

"Doctora Payce." He tried to keep his voice low, and it came out like a hiss.

The church was empty. Every hair on the back of his neck stood at attention. The instinct of a seasoned professional who wandered into dangerous situations too frequently. This woman was oblivious to the feel of the setting. Perhaps she wasn't so observant after all.

"Friar Suthons?" Payce called out. "Is anyone here?"

The only response was the echo of Briel's voice in the empty hall.

Ricardo pointed to the exit at the North Transept. It was wide open. Left that way in haste? He considered his next move. Simple enough to go through the open door, except for the doubt that little voice in his head kept raising. More prudent to turn around and call the Parish Office and book an appointment.

The decision was made for him when Payce headed outside. He followed, his detective's eyes darting in all directions. A shadow blinked in and out of sight around a side wall of the building, and he ran to check it out. By the time he reached the corner, only two black squirrels remained. They were chasing each other, and one held a nut in its mouth.

Had the hollow feeling of an empty church simply spooked him? Damn. He turned to catch up with the doctora.

They emerged onto a well-manicured green space surrounded by a tall hedge of Mexican Orange Blossoms. A distant sound of children playing rang through the air, and Payce headed into the shrubbery to follow it.

Ricardo cursed again. He couldn't shake the feeling that something was wrong, so he put a reassuring hand on his weapon and went after the unheeding woman who forged ahead.

BRIEL COULDN'T UNDERSTAND the inspector's hesitation. She'd been in empty churches hundreds of times. Surely the pastor was simply on the grounds. Why was De La Cruz hanging back? Was it possible she'd finally met someone more cautious than her?

She shook her head and plowed through the blossoming hedge. This must have been how Percy felt all those times Briel had held her friend back. But the danger was obvious then. This was a church, and if the noise from beyond the shrubs was any indication, the orphanage was close by. Hardly a reason for concern.

Something tugged at her from behind and she turned, heart suddenly beating faster, wondering if she'd made a mistake. When she pulled away, Briel realized the hedge branches had snagged her cotton crewneck t-shirt. As she untangled herself, a sweet, citrusy scent wafted from the clusters of small white flowers disturbed by her movements.

Emerging from the brush and into another clearing at the bottom of a hillside, Briel plucked a few remaining orange blossom leaves from her white running shoes and sniffed.

Great. Her hands smelled like she'd just eaten an orange, and there was nowhere to wash the cloying scent away.

A clanging sound came from up high and jolted Briel. Looking ahead, she watched as a man and a woman, each with a bell in hand, corralled the children playing inside a fenced yard. Recess was over. Nestled on the high ground was a low, long building, presumably the orphanage with an associated school. She refocused on her search for Friar Suthons.

Scanning the region above her, looking for the best place to climb, Briel spotted a stocky man in a dark brown habit standing near the side of the schoolhouse. He was gesticulating at a younger fellow in dirty jeans and a stained tee-shirt standing beside a wheelbarrow.

As the sound of playing children receded, she heard the man in the habit shout in Spanish, "How dare you!"

If that was Fray Suthons, then he had a temper.

Briel sensed movement behind her, followed by muffled cursing. Someone or someones were in the back of the church building. An administrator back from a break? Perhaps another member of the order?

She turned around, ready to go back, as De La Cruz popped out from the hedge, sporting a significant scratch to the back of his left hand.

"Ouch," the detective said, and he blew gently at the wound.

"Ah. It's you. I thought maybe you'd left. Spooked by schoolchildren playing on the orphanage grounds."

Briel pointed to the grey stone building above them.

De La Cruz's eyes narrowed and his mouth settled into a frown.

"I saw something. A shadow. I have learned to trust my instincts, so I checked the area. You would do well to proceed more cautiously, too. This is not your country and you have no feel for the dangers."

"Let me see that." Briel took the inspector's hand and examined the torn tissues. "When we find the friar, we'll need to clean this and get a bandage on it. In the meantime, you'll live."

"Thank you, Doctora Payce, but I already came to the same conclusion."

Briel's shoulders softened as her title rolled from the detective's mouth. The man was doing his job, and if she was honest, if someone other than Dean had to be with her, De La Cruz was the best choice. She took in his sturdy build and understated but fashionable haircut and bet that like her, people underestimated his abilities. Worth giving the man a chance?

"As we're stuck together for now, formality seems a little silly. Call me Briel."

De La Cruz nodded and grinned for the very first time. "And unless my colleagues are with me, you may call me Ricardo."

Briel furrowed her brow at the inspector's caveat but decided not to pry. After all, everyone's insecurities were their own. Instead, she asked, "Did you find anything?"

"No. That doesn't mean... "

But Briel turned her back before Ricardo could lecture her again and headed up the hill. The man with the wheelbarrow was gone. However, the friar still stood at the top, habit fluttering in the wind, staring down at them.

CHAPTER 34

Unlike the day before, Dean Leggatt sauntered into the Secretariat of Travel, Culture and Tourism offices in Mexico City by choice. He'd taken a taxi from the hotel, courtesy of Mateo Tomás himself. Dean still wasn't sure what he'd gotten himself into, but a good night's sleep, and the medication provided by the secretariat, had done their job. At least today, he felt ready to either go along with or oppose whatever Tomás thought might be worth investigating.

That's what he and Briel had agreed to. More information was better than less. He wasn't at all sure about Briel going off alone with that detective inspector guy, but after her adventure on the volcano, he suspected De La Cruz would respect her at the very least. And Briel knew how to take care of herself, maybe even better than Percy had.

He fingered the moose nickel pendant around his neck. Percy had insisted it was imbued with magic. Something to keep him out of trouble. In return for the necklace, Dean had given Percy golden trowel earrings to commemorate her passion for the past. Maybe the moose should have been hers.

Then again, he'd had it on for his escapade in the Cueva de los

Tayos when that weird case of worms got to his lungs. Didn't do him much good then.

The secretariat was waiting outside his office door by the time Dean made it to the second floor.

"Thank you for coming," he said.

"My options were pretty limited. I'm here to see if your problem and mine are headed in the same direction. If not, you're on your own and I'll be finding my way to Briel within the hour."

"Understood. Our Secretariat of Environmental Stability, Donata Rangal, is already upstairs and waiting. Please come with me."

On the third floor, Dean re-entered the meeting room he and Briel had occupied in yesterday's adventure. A slight wave of nausea interrupted the smooth entrance he'd intended. Funny, the imprint left by some locales.

Rangal rose to greet Dean and Tomás. She was a small woman, perhaps five feet tall in heels. Tight dark curls descended to her shoulders and framed pleasant brown eyes. Her nose was a bit too large and relatively flat, but her wide, toothy smile spoke of a relaxed, confident presence.

"I must return to my office," Tomás said. "This is not my expertise. Doctor Leggatt, I leave you in Secretariat Rangal's capable hands. Someone will fetch coffee for you shortly."

Papers lay strewn over the long table, so Dean remained standing, unsure exactly where Rangal wanted him to be.

"Apologies, Doctor Leggatt," Rangal began.

"Dean," he said. "Dean will be fine."

The woman smiled. "And I am Donata. Please sit here and we will get started.

"A few months ago," Donata continued, "my sister-in-law asked me to give her son a job. The young man is... not the most reliable soul. To keep peace in the family, I asked him to create a database of volcanic activity reports collected on Popocatepetl. Understand, our automated systems already generate such files for study, but I wanted my nephew to believe he was doing something important, while ensuring the factual information in our volcanic alert systems was not compromised."

Dean raised an eyebrow and Donata smiled. "You misunderstand. I paid him from my own pocket. He played the role of an outside contractor who reported only to me."

"So what's the problem?"

"I told my nephew to bring me the original log sheets and a copy of his file for each quarter. I thought it important to show the young man both that he was doing something of value and that he was being watched. Here is the raw data he worked from over the last two months."

Dean studied the data sheets and noted the rise and fall of volcanic activity. For the most part, nothing seemed out of place, especially given Popocatepetl's persistent rumblings throughout time. Then Dean spotted a two-week period of significantly higher values before the numbers fell again.

"Did this"—Dean pointed to the aberrant data—"activity... alert your experts to prepare for a response?"

"No. Neither was I informed of a change or an error. When I asked my nephew about it, he told me there were two records for that time. The one you are looking at now came from a file that was discarded. His computer search found it, anyway. You see, he was trying to be conscientious. He's good with technology, and because he hopes for a job, he wanted to be sure to give me a complete record. He didn't know what to do, so he sent me two files."

"Where's the other one?"

Donata reached for another page and Dean put the printouts side by side. The time stamps were identical, but for those fourteen days, the readings could not have been more different.

CHAPTER 35

Ricardo spat. Immediately after making peace, the bullheaded Briel Payce left him behind to march toward the figure of a friar at the top of the hill. Then again, Briel was just a member of the public.

He reminded himself once more that the job description of a health care researcher didn't include police-level observation. He was on edge. Too many brave souls in his homeland died at the hands of evildoers. Some were paid to fight crime, like his best friend Julian, a rookie on the force taken out early when he refused a bribe. Others were ordinary citizens trying to do the right thing, or in Briel's case, hoping to find answers. If he lost someone he cared about in America, he'd be the same as Briel, badge or no badge.

Ricardo glanced behind him again, huffed out a breath, and followed Briel. It was, after all, the only path forward.

When Ricardo caught up with her, Briel was introducing herself to the friar.

"And I am Padre Hugh," Suthons responded. "I noticed you by the hedges. You saw me chastising our gardener?"

"Yes," said Briel.

"I am sorry. A patron recommended him to us, hoping our

environment would provide valuable structure. So far, the limits we've set are proving difficult for everyone. How can I help you?"

"My name is Briel Payce. I'm looking for a friend who disappeared in Mexico a few years ago. A note I recently found from her led me here. Her name is Persephone Gilbert."

The priest took a step back and raised his bushy grey brows. The crow's feet bordering his eyes deepened and he turned toward Ricardo and smiled.

"Ah," he said, folding chubby hands over his abdomen. "I certainly misread the situation." Then he chuckled at them both. "When I saw you appear from the hedges, I sensed some frustration between you. I thought perhaps you were both here for marriage counselling."

Heat spread over Ricardo's cheeks, and when he opened his mouth, no words came.

Briel was faster to recover and assumed a Mona Lisa-like smirk. "No, Padre Hugh. Most definitely not. This is Detective Inspector Ricardo De La Cruz. He is... accompanying me in this endeavour."

And there it was. The woman honestly believed she was the leader in this pursuit. From the corner of his eye, Ricardo spotted the gardener standing, only half hidden, by the corner of the school's wall. The man pulled out a rag and patted his face, but Ricardo couldn't help wondering if it was an excuse to stay within earshot.

"Perhaps we could take this conversation to your office?" Ricardo asked.

The friar followed Ricardo's line of sight and nodded. "Of course."

The speed with which the older man rambled toward the church impressed Ricardo. As they squeezed back through the overgrown hedge hole, the friar mumbled another complaint about his errant groundskeeper.

• • •

Padre Hugh's office was a simple affair. The ivory-coloured painted plaster walls were bare except for a single oil painting of the Virgin Mary that hung behind the priest's leather wingback chair and oak escritoire. Two high backs already faced the desk.

"Now," Suthons said as he drew his seat closer and folded his hands on the writing surface. He turned his head toward Briel. "How can I help you?"

"How did you know Percy?"

"Your friend came to me for help to decipher what she thought might be religious symbols on a carving in a rock. I understood at the time that she was an archaeologist. But you say she disappeared?"

"Actually," Briel paused, and Ricardo noticed the woman's shoulders stiffen, "she's been declared dead."

Padre Hugh's cherubic countenance dissolved as his cheeks sagged and his jaw slackened. When his eyes widened, Ricardo couldn't decide if the man was shocked or afraid. In an instant, the priest regained his composure.

"I'm so sorry," Padre Hugh said. He reached across the desk to pat Briel's hand.

Then Suthons turned his attention to Ricardo. "But if that's the case, why do you want to see me?"

Before Ricardo could respond, a shot echoed through the church's nave.

CHAPTER 36

Silence continued from the other side of the phone, until even the Conductor was uncomfortable, but he'd been playing this game for a long time, so he held firm.

Finally, the voice on the phone broke their stalemate.

"Then I repeat, what do you want?"

"You solved the cipher. Tell me what it said."

"Why?"

"I have as much right to it as you do."

"Does the name Hugh Suthons mean anything to you?"

"Thank you."

The Conductor was about to hang up when the voice called to him again. "Wait!"

"What?"

"Do not force this."

"Excuse me?"

"I know you. It is a more delicate matter than you realize. A plan is already in place to deal with this. One that satisfies both our needs. If you move now, you risk destroying the very thing you're after."

"I trust my team."

"The fewer people who know of this, the better. Wait for my

signal. Then we can both have what we need. Your lifestyle and my reputation, intact."

It was the Conductor's turn to exercise silence. He knew the right decision. Still, it was important to make the man on the line sweat, at least a little.

The Conductor finally said, "Don't take too long."

And he hung up.

The Spanish bronze, jewel-encrusted sheath of the Conductor's letter opener lay at the far edge of his leather desk blotter. That the device had potential as a proper weapon was a bonus.

He fondled the instrument, turning it over and over, moving his hands across the surface, roughened by precious stones. A flash of light caught his eye as he removed the blade, and the sharp silver edge reflected a ray of sunlight from the window behind him.

Fools, he thought. I'm surrounded by fools.

The question was, how best to deal with them? He hated his dependence on the man he'd just hung up on, and hated more that he could no longer trust Pedro, his lieutenant, his closest ally of so many years.

His father had made the family rich by farming cocoa and producing cocaine. No question how his papa had managed doubt. He taught the Conductor to be tough... aggressive toward anyone who even remarked on the disability his mother had left him with when he finally emerged from the womb.

Today, his father would tell the Conductor to kill them all and be done with it.

But the Conductor had reached heights well above his father's station. If his father were in business today, the man would report to him. The Conductor ran a monopoly. All the cartels came to him. His was the only path in the entire country, to cleaning money raised from the spoils of sin.

So what should a conductor of his stature do in the face of an orchestra weak with fear, a lieutenant now prone to mistakes, and a man who may or may not keep his promise to make things right?

Time to play the big card. Time to find those dearest to his problem children and take them away for a while—perhaps even forever. Yes, that would motivate those around him to get in line and stay there.

The sharp edge of the opener nicked his finger, and a drop of blood pooled from the wound. The Conductor closed his hand over a tissue and picked up the phone.

"Pedro. No thanks to you, I have the solution to our puzzle. And I understand your family disappeared. For now. You need to redeem yourself, for me, and for them. Here is what you will do... "

CHAPTER 37

Briel ducked behind the desk with Padre Hugh while Ricardo, gun drawn, moved behind the door frame. A second shot screamed through the nave and the bullet lodged itself in the friar's desk. Ricardo returned fire.

The priest jumped into the open and addressed the attacker.

"This is a church! Whoever you are, reveal yourself. Speak to me peacefully. This is a place of mercy... of sanctuary and of safety. You will not be harmed. I give you my word."

A third bullet whizzed through the air and Ricardo yanked the friar behind him just in time.

"Keep him with you," Ricardo said, pushing the priest toward Briel.

"Another lost soul," the friar mumbled. "We have too many here. The church used to be sacred, even among those taken by evil. Not anymore."

He knit his brows and despite their precarious situation, Briel envisioned grey furry caterpillars on tree branches. The sound of wood crashing on cement broke the spell.

Ricardo took aim through the office entrance, fired and jumped behind a pew in the nave. The friar crept from Briel's side and headed the same way.

"No." Briel said, grabbing hold of his brown tunic. "The detective inspector asked us to stay here."

"This is my church, and I'm going to see what I can do. Come with me if you must, or let me go."

Briel stifled the word that threatened to trip from the tip of her tongue and let go.

As the friar belly-crawled to shelter in the pew behind Ricardo, she considered their situation. She couldn't tell how many assailants there were, but based on the rate of gunfire, there couldn't be more than one or two, and so far, it sounded like no one had automatic weapons. She sent a silent thanks to the friar's god for at least that bit of help.

Ricardo seemed to know what he was doing. Suthons, on the other hand, was an unknown. A bystander, like her. Someone who didn't belong in the melee. Someone who might distract the only skilled professional there to help them.

Reluctantly, Briel emerged from behind the desk, kept close to the floor and followed the priest. The least she could do was keep the man out of Ricardo's way, though based on his behaviour, it would be a challenge.

She reached Padre Hugh just as he poked his head into the aisle. Briel yanked him back and searched her mind for a plan. Anything to avoid getting them all killed. A hymnal rested on a small wooden shelf attached to the backside of the next pew.

Best choice available? Only choice.

She grabbed the book and sent it sailing across the floor, aiming for the floorboard on the opposite side of the church. A ruse. Something to make their attacker believe someone else was there. Someone far from them.

Briel hoped her move would also give Ricardo the break he needed to gain control. Unfortunately, the gunman wasn't fooled and the next bullet landed in the pew's wood directly above the friar's head.

Ricardo swore and fired another round. A second later, the detective inspector was running to the church's open front doors.

CHAPTER 38

Dean opened a binder of raw data, allegedly from one of the seismic collection boxes positioned around Popocatepetl. What he really wanted to do was call his buddy Carl, an expert in these matters.

Dean had learned about volcanology in school. He'd kept up a little, both out of interest and so he and Carl would have something to talk about when they went out for dinner. Dean knew what the wiggly lines meant, at least to a point. He was competent enough to see big changes, but anything subtle? That was out of his league.

He had tried to make that clear to Donata and asked her to bring a specialist on board.

"No," she had said. "I need to know if the problem is real. If Mexico City is at risk because someone suppressed that data with intent, then as soon as I begin an official investigation with outside expertise, everything you are looking at, and more, will disappear. It's happened before. With proof gone, my credibility will be ruined and I will be fired. I cannot afford that. Please. At least help me to the extent you can."

Thus, Dean sat, binders of raw and summarized data in front

of him, trying to make sense of Donata's nephew's unexpected discovery.

Someone cleared their throat behind him and Dean looked up. A young woman, pretty, with long wavy black hair, enormous eyes, and a shapely figure, stood with a tray of freshly made tacos, a cup of coffee, and two cans of soft drinks. Dean smiled, knowing his hosts were only trying to make him comfortable.

"Do you have bottled water?" he asked.

The server's eyes flitted from the sheets of graphs to Dean's face, and he got the distinct impression the woman was searching for something among his pages. Instinctively, Dean closed the binder and raised one eyebrow.

"Sí, señor," the woman said, her eyes now focused on the date on the outside header of the binder.

"Excuse me," Dean said, as he took another set of papers, turned them over, and placed them where they would interrupt her gaze.

The woman's cheeks turned red and she scurried from the room.

Did it matter that she was so obviously on a quest to understand his progress?

Probably not, Dean decided. The exposed pages and data were unrevealing, but he resolved to be more careful of further interruptions.

Dean paused before returning to work. He picked up a taco and then put it back down, unsure after yesterday's escapade if he should even take a bite.

By the time the Secretariat of Environmental Stability, Donata Rangal, re-entered the room, Dean had eaten his tacos and was on his second bottled water. So far, his stomach was holding out. Maybe the food was better, or maybe it was the pills. Regardless, he was grateful. He was back, brain in full gear, and that led him to some interesting thoughts.

"The raw sheets match the actual data recorded in all cases except in the week before two dates. The first is the most recent incident your nephew identified, and the second is from two years ago. It looks to me as though someone saw the data and checked it. Maybe because other seismometers read normal, they found some glitch in an errant instrument and moved on. It happens."

Donata's matronly brown eyes darkened. "Exactly what are the dates?"

"Pardon?"

"Which weeks are anomalous? When did it begin, and when did it end?"

It was a simple matter to match and recalculate the yearly records into weeks. A few minutes later, Dean handed Donata the answer.

This time, the secretariat sat down and stared out the window without making a sound.

"Did I make a mistake?" Dean asked. "I told you, I'm no expert."

"No mistake," Donata said, still not looking at him. "Your results confirm my findings."

"Or your quality control procedures did their job. The faulty data could have set off your disaster alert systems. Imagine the unnecessary panic and expense."

"Indeed," Donata said. "Except, after my talks with Mateo Tomás about how the data could impact both our citizens and the tourists who hike through the passages, I discovered that each of those weeks corresponds with a trip to Mexico City, and then the disappearance of a foreigner holding a position with an international anti-money laundering assessment and reporting centre."

"I'm sure it's a coincidence."

"In each case, Tomás discovered that the men were at risk of losing their jobs. They came here, possibly to investigate on their own, and were never seen or heard from again."

"What made Tomás take an interest in these particular

foreigners?"

"The most recent incident came on his watch. My nephew's report, confirmed now by your findings, speaks to a separate investigation that Tomás is undertaking. He uncovered the earlier incident last month and began asking questions. He and I spoke about the situation at a dinner, just a few days ago. Your arrival was fortuitous. A way to confirm this 'under the radar', as I think you Americans say."

"Still sounds like a coincidence to me."

"Perhaps. But if it is, the anomalous data and bad sensor should have triggered another kind of notification. After all, volcanic activity readings approached the alert threshold in both cases. My office should have been told and we should have been involved in the resolution. I called the Departamento Regional de Monitoreo de Desastres Naturales asking about their equipment, and if perhaps I needed to include new sensors in my next budget. I was told everything was working fine."

Dean rubbed his eyes. He didn't know what to say. Donata's concerns were reasonable enough, but his job was done.

Or was it?

The disappearance of two more "tourists" in Mexico City. He had no reason to connect Percy to bank investigations. It was a long shot. Still, Percy had a tendency to tread—well, stomp—into wherever curiosity led her, and that made her unpopular with anyone hiding their dirty laundry. The head of the department at Percy's last university, the one abusing beautiful, young new students, had found that out the hard way.

"How about I look into the equipment at the monitoring stations?" Dean offered.

"Would you?" Donata didn't hide her surprise.

"I don't know what to look for, but I'd be happy to try... provided you allow me to go back five years into their files."

"Why five years?"

"It may be nothing. It's just that I also have a question that needs answering."

CHAPTER 39

Through the wide open door, Ricardo saw their attacker bolt into the church's front gardens and duck into the six-foot-tall ornamental grasses. He couldn't tell if it was a man or a woman. The figure was slight in build, dressed in black jeans, a black t-shirt and black vest, hair covered by a black woolen cap and face covered with a black mask. It was at least 38 degrees Celsius in the shade. If he gave chase, surely whoever it was would collapse of heat exhaustion in short order.

He positioned himself behind the door casing and raised his gun, ready to burst out. Then he noticed a flash of movement near the parking lot. Ricardo jumped to the opposite side of the door and spotted a patch of black cloth as the wind swept through the nearby vegetation.

A trap.

Someone planned to lure him into the open and then gun him down.

Ricardo turned back to where Briel and the priest were sheltering.

"Padre Hugh," he said. "Is there another way out of here?"

"We came in through the north entrance. We could go back that way."

"No. I believe we have more than one assailant. I suspect both main exits are now covered. We need something else."

"All I can think of is the crypt. I planned on taking you there anyway." The friar turned to Briel. "I kept something there that your friend gave me."

Briel looked at Ricardo, who shook his head. "If we get into that crypt, we'll be trapped. We'll need to take our chances here. I...
"

"Show me," Briel said to the padre.

Anger flashed through Ricardo. The woman was hell-bent on defying his every word.

But an instant later, he quelled the feeling. Sticking these two civilians into the crypt would keep them out of the way while he dealt with this. But they had to hurry. Their attackers were bound to come looking for them when he didn't take the bait, and he still needed to call this in.

Ricardo nodded and the friar moved into the church's elaborately decorated sacristy. Peaceful greens and flowing reds adorned the stone walls, reminders of the early Spanish history of the building.

He helped Suthons move a trunk, and together they lifted the trap door hidden in the amber-coloured tiled floor.

A light clatter of metal told Ricardo that someone was nearby.

Padre Hugh stood on the steps leading to the crypt and reached out his hand to help Briel descend.

A crypt. A dark enclosed space. No windows. No permanent opening like the wide-mouthed caves she'd explored with the IEN. When the friar shut the trap door, there'd be no way out. What was she thinking?

Maybe Ricardo was right and they should turn around and fight. There had to be something around here they could use as a weapon. If each of them guarded an entrance...

Briel felt a push from behind and almost fell onto the friar. Ricardo urged her to get moving. Still hesitant, she took hold of the padre's hand. The man stretched his other arm to a shelf about halfway down and grabbed a flashlight, flicking it on.

Some light was better than no light.

Without warning, the hatch above them thudded shut. She was alone with the priest. Ricardo had closed them in.

Padre Hugh seemed unperturbed by the situation and motioned for Briel to follow him. She looked back at the closed door and crept toward it. She wanted, needed, to know what was going on.

The old metal plate was heavy, so she pushed hard at the opening. It didn't budge.

RICARDO FACED the exit from the sacristy, one foot on the latch that opened the crypt. He bet Briel would try to get out once she realized he wasn't behind them, and he was right.

He waited for the pushing to stop and then placed the friar's wheeled garment rack over the floor panel, hoping to disguise the trap door before he faced whoever was out there. Then he texted headquarters, an S.O.S. signalling that he was an officer in trouble. He just needed to hold these guys off until help arrived.

Ricardo crawled toward the nave, spotting the barrel of a gun encroaching on the front doors. Trouble was back.

He rolled toward the nearest pew, popped up and angled a shot into the door frame. Out of the corner of his eye, he noticed a second gunman coming in through the north side, checking on the shots, momentarily exposed. Ricardo rolled again and fired, catching the second assailant in the shoulder. At the front entrance, his first problem sent another round. Ricardo looked for a decent angle of attack, but found nothing.

THE CRACK of a single bullet echoing through the church reached the stairs where Briel stood frozen. She'd given up trying to release the hatch and was fighting the excess adrenaline that stiffened every muscle in her body, when a wave of nausea threatened to double her over. The resulting dizziness would have sent her head over keister down the remaining steps, but Briel was practiced at dealing with her feelings. She forced herself to sit down, put her arms over her knees, and stuck her head in her lap.

The only sounds from above now were footsteps. From who? Their attacker? Ricardo? She desperately wanted to blow her way out. What if Ricardo took a bullet? He'd need their help. She reached for her cell. At least she could call 911 or whatever the equivalent was in Mexico. The screen lit up and she hit the emergency button. Nothing. No signal. In the hills surrounding Mexico City, and in a crypt, they were completely cut off.

"Are you alright?" The padre whispered close to her ear.

"Fine," Briel said. She looked up at the friar and realized that there were lights on. The room was wider than she had expected. The rock walls looked solid and a hallway extended from where they stood, openings on either side. As though a switch turned off, her heartbeat slowed. She brushed the sweat from her forehead and bounced up, only to discover that her body hadn't caught up with her brain, and she collapsed again.

Padre Hugh grabbed hold of her arm, steadied her and sat her down once more.

"Give yourself a minute," he whispered.

"We need to get out of here," Briel said.

"Your detective inspector seems very capable. And he obviously wants us to stay put. When you're ready to walk, there's something I think you need to see."

Briel tried standing again. More carefully this time. When the room didn't spin, she planted a solid foot forward, exhaling her relief as she managed not to fall over.

"Let's go," she said.

The friar led her halfway down the long hall to another lighted room. She mumbled her thanks to his god for electricity and for the solid workmanship of those early church builders.

Every wall glowed amber, as though the lights were candles and the stone from a quarry of some prehistoric coral reef. She'd have said it was beautiful if she didn't know she was sealed in an underground chamber.

That's when she spotted the sarcophagus, directly across from a solid mahogany antique desk. The stone funerary box was the only place for a visitor to sit if anyone dared have a meeting with Padre Hugh down here.

Suthons noticed her staring.

"The resting place of Fray Marcos de Niza," he said. "A controversial figure by many accounts, from the time of Coronado and the conversion period. Believed to have been buried in Mexico City, yet here he rests to remind me of the challenges of the past, and of human sin and frailty. He keeps me company."

"I'd have thought you'd want the world to know of such a historic site."

"Some would say so. Others believe his history is best forgotten. Your friend Percy wanted very much to study this place. When she didn't come back, I thought she simply changed her mind. I am sorry. I wish I'd followed up."

Briel said nothing.

More footsteps scraped across the floor above them and Briel wondered how much sound travelled from where they stood to the church proper.

Suthons sighed, pulled a key ring from a pocket inside the folds of his tunic, and unlocked a desk drawer.

"As long as we whisper," he answered her unasked question, "no one will hear us."

Briel expected the friar to retrieve a file, or a letter, or some other set of notes in a folder-sized repository. Instead, he reached above the neatly arranged documents and unstuck a photo taped to the wood.

Briel glimpsed the picture before the padre tucked it away. She recognized the symbols.

Percy's Spider Rock.

CHAPTER 40

Miguel had hoped for the cover of night, but "needs must", as his British colleagues often told him. So there he stood on the tarmac, the bright, blistering sun already making him sweat through the shirt under his black silk suit jacket. Miguel replayed the scene at the hospital again. His uncle had actually shot at him. It was time to disappear.

He'd emptied his savings, booked this private jet to Texas. After that, he had a seat on a Lufthansa flight to Frankfurt. From there, he'd drive to Switzerland, get the cash he needed from his account, and fly to Thailand. He had enough money to live on until his credentials were approved, and he was pretty sure he could set up a comfortable living as a doctor there.

And what about Mexico? His beloved country, his duty, his family. His wife and son had disappeared a long time ago. Not because of the affairs. Sofia always forgave those. No. It was his secret life. Like today. The life with his uncle and those connections. That scared her, and he understood. He didn't challenge the custody agreement. No one knew where they were now, including him, and that was good, especially today.

But his country, his duty, tugged at his heart, even now as the captain finally arrived and began engine checks. He wondered if there was a way he could monitor things from abroad.

Miguel placed his overnight bag in the storage box of the plane's belly. As he grabbed the handle, ready to enter the cabin, he heard a voice very close to his ear.

"Did you really believe I wouldn't find out?"

Miguel's uncle stood inches away, gun ready. Again.

"I... I... A last-minute meeting came up in the United States. I will be back in a few days."

"Liar. Move away from the door."

Arms raised, Miguel complied.

"Did you think it would be so easy to run?"

"I told you. This was unexpected. Hospital administrators. In Dallas. Let me show you. On my phone."

"You must think me a great old fool. Miguel, I have been tracking your every movement. That is how I found you. By the way, I cancelled your flight to Frankfurt."

The fear that already welled in Miguel crescendoed.

Pedro continued. "Miguel. You are my flesh and blood. I do not want to kill you. I will if I have to, but I do not want to, despite you lying to me about the cipher's solution. It's been solved, by the way. Water under the bridge. What I need from you now, nephew, is to honour your commitment. You said you could deal with Briel Payce. She is on the move, and there is an officer with her. It is time for this to stop. Either you deal with the woman or I will deal with you. Quite simple, really."

Briel. So much time had passed. The woman he admired most in the world. The ice queen who'd melted in his arms, never to be touched again. He couldn't, wouldn't harm her.

Miguel faced his uncle, and the weapon pointed at his chest.

"If you solved the puzzle, then you have no use for Briel. Let her go. I will help in any other way I can."

"No, Miguel. She is getting too close. This time, with official help from Mexican authorities. I need her stopped before this goes any further. You are not the only one in trouble. And if I go down, your end will not be as simple as a single bullet."

"Uncle. I do not even know where she is."

Pedro handed Miguel a slip of paper.

Miguel read the address and his eyes flitted left and right in confusion. It was the link to Persephone Gilbert that he knew about. The single plan he had set into motion as his parting gift to his beloved Mexico. He debated telling Pedro that there was truly no need to worry, but another plan emerged.

Perhaps there was a way to save both himself and Briel.

Pedro cocked his head, as if considering Miguel's odd reaction to the location.

"A church is a strange place to find Briel. She is an atheist," Miguel explained. "I will take care of this. Uncle, you have my word."

"Which is worth nothing." Pedro spat. "See that you get this done."

And his uncle left.

Miguel considered returning to the airplane, but when he turned to board, his single bag was on the tarmac and the jet was gone.

CHAPTER 41

The white vintage convertible was a pleasant touch. Top down, Dean drove the rental Donata Rangal had arranged for him. The sun beat on his face, but the wind in his hair more than made up for the lack of air conditioning. The Secretariat of Environmental Stability had approved the budget, and to Dean's surprise, he had his pick of any car in the line. This beauty was too good to pass up. No GPS? No problem. He had his phone for that.

What a difference a day made. Decent food, good water, and here he was helping the very people who had kidnapped him.

Mild indigestion made his gut tingle. He knew it wasn't something he ate. It was guilt. Briel was out there, properly searching for the path to Percy's remains. All he had was a fragile thought about how the mountain's data from long ago might apply. Highly unlikely. Unless Percy had stumbled into some kind of financial corruption? Percy had trouble balancing her own cheque book, so it was a stretch. Still, getting access to what was going on back then at least made him feel like he was doing something useful.

He'd told Donata the issue was probably a simple mechanical problem, and that was true. He didn't mention that the odd numbers suggested a change in Popocatepetl's geometry. A blister bulging. Along with the increase in seismic activity, the data should have triggered evacuations, even before a sensor check. The secretariat knew enough to be concerned, regardless. Better safe than sorry and all that.

The question now was what to do. Should he be straight with the volcanologist he was about to meet, or play dumb? For the moment, he was just a visiting geologist. Taking on the role of a scientist in the country, curious about the famous volcano, someone who had contacted Donata Rangal, asking for a tour of the facilities. And she was kind enough to oblige.

So far, his plan was to lull the centre's volcanologist with compliments and appreciation. Then, he'd ask for a sample of really old data (five years old, to be exact) of no use to anyone (except him). He'd decide what to do after that.

Dean maneuvered the automobile off the highway, to the ever-present voice in his maps app. "Turn right at the light... Turn right now... Turn right."

Such a nag. He smiled, recognizing he shouldn't be rude to the technology. In fact, he was grateful he wasn't in some dead zone in the middle of nowhere. Paper maps were hard to find these days, and he didn't have a backup.

He turned the next corner and spotted the Departamento Regional de Monitoreo de Desastres Naturales perched above a rock wall, behind an iron fence. An imposing structure. He supposed it had to be. Natural disaster warnings and emergency plans came from this building. And if some of that aberrant data were right and a volcano destroyed the centre before fulfilling its mission? Well, that would just be embarrassing.

Another right turn, and Dean drove past the open iron gates, up to the wooden cantilever barrier and alongside the security booth.

"I'm here to see Alejandro Vargas," Dean said.

The security guard hopped off his stool and grabbed his clip-board. "Name?"

"Dean Leggatt."

The man pretended to peruse his list, but Dean had a decent view of the page and could see that his name was the only one on it.

Everyone needs to feel important, he mused.

"Yes," said the guard. "Here you are. I will ask Doctor Vargas to meet you at the front door. Parking is down the hill and to your left. But let me record your plate number first."

DEAN ROLLED down the winding driveway, past two stop signs where the crossroads were blocked and a big sign read "Sólo Vehículos Autorizados". Apparently, these people didn't like visitors. Not another car in sight, Dean parked under a large shade tree despite noticing the oak was shedding. He raised the hardtop. The last thing he needed was to come back to a car filled with stringy brown tassels.

The hike to the Centro building wasn't arduous, but Dean was huffing by the time he rounded the last corner and found the main entrance. Outside, a slight, wiry man with thinning, shoulder-length black hair, wearing jeans, expensive sneakers and a starched blue and white chequered dress shirt, paced. Periodically, he stopped to check his phone screen and then marched back and forth again. Vargas? Already agitated? Not a good sign.

"Doctor Vargas?" Dean said when he was close enough to be heard.

Alejandro Vargas turned to him and nodded.

"I'm Dean Leggatt. I really appreciate you taking the time to show me around today. As a fellow geologist, I know you guys have a lot on your hands. I don't know as much about volcanology as I'd like. Thanks for helping me out."

Alejandro didn't crack a welcoming smile.

"Why?" he said.

"Excuse me?"

"Why does a forensic geologist want a tour here?"

"Uhm."

"There is nothing to see. A few buildings, some data that are available online, and video that we make for the world to see. You are wasting your time."

Dean paused, his mind racing for some logical explanation.

"Disaster relief," he said finally.

Alejandro's dark brows knit together.

"I'm a member of the International Explorer's Network. We're sometimes asked to help with rescue operations in remote regions. Many of those areas are at or near volcanic islands. I'd really like to know more so I can understand threat levels better when I'm on the ground."

"Hmm," Alejandro replied. His phone pinged. He looked at it again and exhaled. "It's a very busy day. I'll do what I can, but I may need to cut this tour short."

Despite Alejandro's protestations, the volcanologist took Dean floor by floor through the monitoring centre, and Dean took it all in with unexpected interest. Mexico City had a sophisticated system in place. State-of-the art, in fact. And that made Dean's next question much easier.

"And what about errors?"

"What?"

"Data accuracy. How do you control for unexpected readings? How do you know when one of your monitoring devices is giving you bad information? Quality control and all that."

"It does not happen."

"But I've heard it does. I've heard that for the same day, you can end up with two sets of data, one reading status quo and one eliciting emergency procedures. How does that happen, and how do you decide what to do?"

Alejandro's cell beeped and as he plucked it from his pocket, his hands shook and the device fell near Dean's feet. As Dean reached to retrieve it, Alejandro darted and yanked it back, but not before Dean saw the message on the screen.

"I am pregnant, Alejandro. There will be questions."

Explains the mood, Dean thought.

"Disagreements between sources occur. We triangulate to manage that," Alejandro said, his eyes focused on the phone. Then he turned back to Dean. "But disparate data from one source? That is not possible. You have been misinformed."

Dean couldn't tell if the man intentionally misunderstood him or if the text simply distracted him.

Alejandro smiled, yellow teeth peeking through his unkempt moustache for the first time. "It does not matter, anyway. Everyone knows if Popocatepetl is going to blow, it will blow. Prediction is overrated. Just do not tell anyone. Everyone here would like to keep their job."

CHAPTER 42

The screeching of tires and a fading engine roar suggested an end to the attack. Ricardo knew to be cautious. Ambushes had been a way of life when he was a beat cop. Ducking behind every available barrier, he made his way to the church entrance and peered from the doorway in time to see a black SUV exiting the church grounds at speed.

At the far end of the parking lot, a masked man, dressed completely in black, scrambled into the driver's side of a two-door pickup. He counted three heads and caught C32 on the plate before the vehicle turned sharply and sped away. Ricardo took a shot, trying at least to blow out a tire, but it didn't work.

His car sat alone, less than ten meters from the church's narthex. Hoping the gang hadn't left anyone with a weapon behind, Ricardo chanced a run for the vehicle. With any luck, he'd at least catch up to complete the license number and order a chase.

That's when he saw his driver's side front tire. Slashed. He turned and pounded the roof, only then realizing it wasn't just one tire. All four were slit. An effective way of making sure he'd stay put for a while. The question now was, why?

Ricardo picked his way through the church, checking every pew, going through every room, gun ready. Nothing.

He exited to the back garden area and through the hedge. When he looked up the hill, the gardener, the same man from earlier, was by his wheelbarrow, looking down at him.

Ricardo's phone buzzed with a message: "Backup on the way". Typical. Late to the party. He almost laughed. His next best move was to question the groundskeeper who had upset the friar such a short time ago. But when he looked up again, the man and the wheelbarrow were gone.

Padre Hugh led Briel deeper into the crypt. She labored more with each step, searching in vain for a second exit, a crack of light, anything to signal a way to the outside world.

"We can speak more freely in the room at the end," he said.

By the time the friar turned into the final opening by the back wall, Briel's hands were on her knees again. Her head ached and the old shale floor, probably uneven with the passage of over five hundred years on sandy soil, made her feel adrift in the high seas. Padre Hugh brought her a chair.

"Your friend, Percy, didn't have a problem down here."

"And she became an archeologist. I didn't."

"Deep breaths." The friar patted her on the back. Briel closed her eyes, visualizing the light flickering over the stones as a cozy fireplace in a cottage with doors and windows. It helped.

"I'm fine."

Suthons made his way to a small filing cabinet in the back corner.

"Doctora Gilbert was a special visitor here. She came many times. While I was busy, she played football with the children. Such a joy. Then she and I would come here and discuss this picture." He handed her the photo of the Spider Rock.

"Why did she want to meet with you? What did you have to do with this?" Briel waved the photo.

"Percy wondered if some symbols on her rock meant anything to the church."

"And?"

"At first I thought it was a child's project, but no child I know would have scrawled the symbol for the Septuagint bible on a stone."

"The what?" Briel stared at the picture. No S; nothing that said bible to her.

"The LXX. Here." He pointed to three of the Roman numerals in a second row of carvings. "Seventy—the short form for the original translation of the Bible into Greek, completed somewhere around the third to first century BCE."

"The line actually reads 8LXX1 or i. What made you pick out the LXX?"

"Percy asked me that as well. And I told her it could be my bias. After all, 'if all you have is a hammer'. Do you see the i8xii above it?"

"Yes."

"I read that as Chapter 8 verses one through twelve. In my brain, I assumed the number before the LXX referred to Chapter 8 as well. I didn't originally see the last symbol on that line and eventually, Percy and I wondered if it was a scratch or an affirmation for starting at verse one."

"Is that all?"

"No. At our first meeting, I also told Percy about this symbol at the top of the picture. Right here." He pointed to a lozenge-shaped mark in the stone. "It reminded me of the vesica piscis often associated with Christian art, used to distinguish seals of the Catholic Church from royalty, all the way back to the 1300s."

"Possible, but it's all so general. Even if you're right about the vesica thing and the Septuagint, the Bible is filled with Chapter 8s. How did your interpretation help?"

"The goat."

"What?"

"Here." Suthons brought Briel's attention to what looked like a child's stick drawing of a desk. Except that from the midpoint of one leg, a diagonal line ran to the top inside corner of the table surface. From one outside angle, a short stroke twisted up. From the other, a longer track finished in a large downward curl.

"I don't see it."

The friar took a pen and added two eyes near the top of the shape, and there it was. The scrawl transformed into a goat, with one horn dramatically longer than the other.

"The Book of Daniel," Suthons said. "The ram and goat are metaphors for Persia and Greece, and the Bible verses speak to the author's vision of their conflict."

"Why specify the Septuagint? I thought there was only one Bible."

"Many translations exist. The first to transcribe the text to Latin, for example, was St. Jerome. His version, the Vulgate, was completed in 382 CE. It's what the Church used for official prayers for centuries."

Feet stomped above them. The sound of running. Briel stood to leave, but the padre took her hand.

"Please. Leave what is happening above us to God. Let me pass on what I know to you."

Briel's eyes flashed to the ceiling, torn between her urge to get involved in the immediate battle and her mission to discover why Percy had sent her to this man. She reminded herself that Ricardo had locked them in the crypt to keep them out of the way. Eventually, she sat back down.

"Over her next few visits, your friend wanted to talk about her research on the other letters and numbers scratched in the stone. See the F, G, and 4?"

"Yes."

"F was the Roman symbol for forty, in the Middle Ages."

"Fifth to fifteenth century?"

"Indeed."

"Percy's findings showed that the capital letter G represented the Arabic numeral five... a notation attributed to Roger Bacon."

"A thirteenth century Franciscan friar? Really?"

Suthons nodded. "You know your history."

"Percy and I learned from each other. As the years went by, I spoke history and she spoke healthcare. That's how we stayed close."

"I can see that. And your Percy was a wonderful teacher. For me too." The crinkles above the friar's cheeks deepened as his lips turned into a sad smile. He continued. "The number four could actually mean a six, depending on the age of the Spider Rock. But the number eight? That remained the same."

"Why is all that important?"

"Exactly what 40, 5, and 4 mean, I don't think Percy ever figured out. However, by looking at the way the numbers were written, believing the stone began life at or near Mexico City, and noticing that it carried distinct religious symbols founded on the other side of the Atlantic, Percy wondered if the Spider Rock was carved in the early 1500s, during the time of the Spanish Conquest."

"Was it?"

"I don't know if she ever found out. On her last visit, she and I pored over the Book of Daniel both in my copy of the Vulgate and in the Septuagint as she found it online. When we compared the texts, the key differences were in verses eleven and twelve. Only the Septuagint verse eleven spoke of 'the holy place made desolate' and verse twelve 'And a sin-offering was given for sacrifice.' We thought, in the context of the Spider Rock, that 'made desolate' could refer to the decimation of indigenous structures by the Spaniards, to make room for colonial buildings, and 'sin-offering' and 'sacrifice' could refer to the practice of human sacrifice so common to the Aztec and other regional communities prior to the invasion."

"Percy believed that?"

"It was the theory," the padre said, "that she came up with. I wondered if she ever learned more, and I worried about her. A woman travelling alone in Mexico. It can be a challenge. When I told her I was concerned, she only smiled at me and said she was fine. But I could see something troubled her. What? She didn't share. That's everything I know. I hope it helps."

Briel leaned back. The ruins of Aztec Tenochtitlan sitting under Mexico City were a visual record of the indigenous buildings' destruction. And the ritual death practices would be terribly sinful in the eyes of European missionaries. Each piece of the story made sense. Unfortunately, there was still no way to know how or why they fit together.

A lingering sense of discomfort from her claustrophobia remained, pushed to the background while she considered the flood of information. When she finally paused her thoughts and tried to clear her brain, the silence above her hit Briel like a thunderbolt. "The sounds are gone. We need to check the church."

The friar nodded and helped Briel to the stairs. She found the hatch and pushed. Wheels squeaked and she heard something roll. After that, the door opened a little and she breathed a sigh of relief.

"Stay here," she said to Padre Hugh.

"No," was the priest's firm response.

"Padre. Your flock here needs you. If you hear me shout, you'll be in a better position to surprise whoever might still be there. Otherwise, stay here and I'll come back as soon as I know it's safe."

CHAPTER 43

"I am not a traitor." Miguel slapped the steering wheel for the third time. Damn his uncle for always making him feel guilty. He'd carried the weight of the country on his shoulders from the day he had reached the inner circle. Once he learned the secret, there was no going back. It was his family heritage. His destiny. And he would have fulfilled that destiny, even from hiding. He certainly couldn't do it if he was dead. And what male blood relative was there to take over, anyway? His uncle didn't have any children. Miguel's son? No, Sofia had him well hidden.

"I am not a traitor." He said it out loud, but with less vigour. The job ahead required a cooler mind. After he was done, he and his uncle would talk.

Miguel couldn't believe his luck when he read the address his uncle had given him. It was the one residual from his original hunt for Persephone Gilbert. She was seen having meetings with a local friar, even playing games with the orphans. By the time he had checked on the lead, she was long gone, but Miguel had never stopped trying to figure out what had passed between her and the holy man. To stay close, he offered his services, pro bono, to the church and the orphanage, betting someone would say something about what had gone on. No one did. And once he started work there, it felt good to give to Mexico's poorest children, so he stayed.

And now? His uncle didn't know everything after all. He'd kept eyes on that place for a long time, and today, after his plane should have landed in Dallas, he'd expected that lingering source of knowledge to be gone too.

He wondered if it had already happened, and what he would find.

He wouldn't need to hurt Briel. His uncle would be pleased, regardless. And Miguel could legitimately take the credit.

Of course, Briel could end up caught in the crossfire. He pressed down on the gas pedal. Maybe he could get there in time to help her. And if her exploration uncovered something, he could coax it from her and find an even better way out of all this.

CHAPTER 44

Unable to find the gardener, Ricardo crept back into the church. The only sound drifting through the nave came from the open entrance. It was the shrill squawk of a nearby grackle.

He was about to holster his gun and relax when the squeak of a hinge and a rustle of activity assaulted his ears. With the echo inside the empty building, Ricardo couldn't be sure which direction the sound came from. The sacristy? Did someone find the entry to the crypt?

Chipped wood from bullets marked the pew beside the room under which Padre Hugh and Briel were hiding.

A crash. Had to be the wardrobe rack he'd placed over the floor panel. He ducked down, peeking at the opening, gun ready.

Footsteps gathered pace, drawing nearer. Heart racing, Ricardo jumped up, ready to attack.

BRIEL STOPPED in her tracks at the sight of Ricardo's semi-automatic pistol.

With her gasp, Ricardo looked at the weapon and instantly

holstered it.

"Sorry," he said. "I expected you to stay put until I came back to let you out. Where is the priest?"

"He's still down there. I asked him to wait until I checked if it was safe. And just so you know, trapping us in the crypt was a cheap trick."

Ricardo didn't even have the sense to look contrite.

"For the best," was all he said.

Then he added, "You're here now. Knocking over the clothes stand probably alerted everyone within a mile that someone was in the church, but I think the threat is gone. We can check the rest of the building together, if you like." Then he winked and continued. "It will be easier to keep my eye on you."

Briel let out the breath she was holding. So far, the detective inspector had not proven prone to comedic relief. His apparent ease suggested this search was a formality.

As they looked left and right and through every potential hiding space, Ricardo spoke again. "I don't trust the groundskeeper, and I don't think the friar does either. The gardener was up on the hill again when I went back out. Just standing there, watching. I was about to go and question him when he disappeared. Did Padre Hugh say anything more about the man?"

Briel shook her head.

"I'll ask him for the gardener's name. At least I can run a search. I also called for backup. They're supposed to be on the way. I'll check on their status after this sweep."

Briel wanted to ask if the delayed arrival of backup was status quo for Ricardo's department, but held her tongue.

They finished checking the church and, finding nothing, she said, "Do you think it's over? Should we get the friar?"

Ricardo nodded and they turned back to the trap door.

Suthons was waiting at the bottom step. Before either of them could say a word, he put a finger to his lips and motioned for them both to come down.

CHAPTER 45

"Look," Dean said. His lips thinned, and if he could have spit venom instead of words, he would have. Alejandro's cavalier attitude was exactly why he and other volunteers in the IEN ended up risking their lives to save the hapless, helpless citizens facing disaster at their doorstep. "Your Disaster Prevention Centre has a reputation as one of the finest in the world. It puts out daily status bulletins on Popocatepetl, to alert the hikers and guides, let alone urban populations. You're supposed to be using the most modern technology. I've seen the scientific talks online. Are you telling me it's all nonsense?"

"No, no." Alejandro focused on Dean, all hints of distraction and flippant arrogance gone. "I only meant that the data are fallible. You know this. Even with the best of equipment and expertise, Mother Nature can play us for fools."

"The data do matter."

"Of course."

Dean reached into the back pocket of his khaki pants, where proof of the disparate readings was hidden. After a second thought, he let go of the paperwork and removed his hand. There was something more important he needed to know.

"I'd like to see all the raw data for the full two weeks before March 21, 2018."

It was the day he had lost contact with Percy. The day his life changed forever. If what Rangal had given him was something other than bad recordings, that data should prove it. And the potential link to Percy was the reason he'd accepted her request to begin with.

Alejandro's eyes glazed over and his brows furrowed. Either the man was confused or angry, or both. Dean hoped he hadn't pushed things too far, too fast.

"I do not report to you."

"No." Dean softened his tone. "I'm sorry. It's a personal issue. I was hoping for your help."

Though Alejandro's expression didn't change, his shoulders dropped. "There is nothing I can do. I am sorry."

"Why?"

"We collect reams of information. Far too much to keep, even in today's cloud technology. Each day, we purge files from the same time five years earlier. Only processed summaries remain. It is May 26, 2023. We destroyed what you seek two months ago."

Dean's heart pounded in his chest and a new wave of nausea washed over him. No way to connect with Percy. Again. In one swift flick of his wrist, he brought the secretariat's pages forward.

"Then tell me what this means."

Alejandro studied the numbers. "Where did you get this?"

"Secretariat Rangal asked me to look into the disparity her nephew uncovered."

"Why did she not approach us herself?"

"She sent me. I'd like to assure her you simply have a faulty collection box and your redundancy procedures did their job, but I don't know that. I need to check the seismic monitoring collection equipment in this region."

"You are a forensic geologist, not a volcanologist. You will not understand what you are seeing."

"Try me."

CHAPTER 46

Briel's compliance surprised Ricardo. She'd yet to do anything asked of her without knowing why. What an odd trust she'd developed for the priest. He considered her behaviour and, curious, he followed her into the unknown.

The moment Ricardo clicked the latch shut, he heard footsteps cross the church floor. A few seconds later, someone walked into the sacristy. The padre must have heard the echoes of a newcomer's arrival. Interesting, the way sound travelled to the crypt. Something Briel must have learned while she was down there.

Ricardo drew his gun. Best he could tell, it was only one person. No problem.

From behind him, the friar touched his arm. Ricardo turned to find Suthons shaking his head.

❦

More footsteps clomped above them. Briel's anxiety over being back in the crypt fought with the adrenaline from not knowing what they were dealing with. The room spun and she sat on the floor, hoping to avoid a faint.

Then came a voice, muffled, but familiar.

"Go. Call the police."

Sounds of running and then walking receded.

Ricardo climbed back up the stairs and peeked through the hatch. A moment later, light flooded the crypt and he signalled for Briel and the friar to follow him.

Silently, Briel held the ladder steps for Padre Hugh and then headed out herself. She closed the latch. After taking two great gasps of air and letting the relief of being free wash over her, Briel helped the friar replace the trunk over the crypt entrance and pull the wardrobe rack back up and in place.

From behind, a voice made her jump.

"There you are, Father. I was worried. What happened here?"

"Doctor Lobo." In the church proper, Padre Hugh gave the man a mighty handshake. "It is so good to see you. I am sorry to say we've had what the British refer to as 'a spot of bother' here today."

The priest pointed to fresh bullet holes in the surrounding pews.

Briel, partially hidden by the wardrobe rack, did her best to compose herself. Surely to God it wasn't Miguel. She combed her fingers through her long blonde hair, meeting resistance as stress, sweat, and heat created a tangled mess close to her scalp. Ricardo cocked his head, one eyebrow raised. She didn't take the bait. Instead, she shook her head and took a breath, readying herself for what was to come. For the briefest moment, she thought Miguel had spotted her. But if so, he didn't give it away.

"My goodness. Padre. I saw the damage when I first came in. I did not know what it meant, so when I spotted your administrative assistant on her way to your office, I asked her to call the police. Does anyone need medical care?"

"No, no, my son." The friar patted Miguel's shoulder. "The police are on their way, and by God's grace, no one has been injured. What brings you all this way?"

"It seems silly now. I was excited and wanted to speak with you in person. Our latest group of pediatric residents has shown an interest in completing a rotation at the orphanage. For a while, at least, I can provide more consistent care, and even preventative measures for the little ones."

The friar's lips parted in a benevolent and sweet smile, but his eyes peered at Miguel with some other intention. As Suthons bent his head in a slight bow, Briel wondered if the priest had been promised things from Miguel before... things that did not come to pass.

"I have new friends here," Padre Hugh said. "They've been very helpful this morning. Please, let me introduce you."

The friar stepped closer to where Ricardo and Briel were standing and introduced the detective inspector.

Miguel broke in and reached his arms out to Briel. "It cannot be! Briel. What are you doing here?"

Long, wavy brown hair softened the angular features of Miguel's face. A bit too young a cut for a man reaching past middle age? He took Briel's right hand and clasped it with both his palms. Then he adjusted his glasses, poking at the dark frames that matched his brown eyes, and stared deeply, longingly, into Briel's soul. His thick, pouty lips, slightly parted, always ready.

Some men never change.

BRIEL'S BEHAVIOUR told Miguel everything he needed to know. He had caught her preening when she thought he couldn't see. Though he almost gave himself away by stealing that glance, he counselled himself to back off. Just the right amount of attention. Not too much. He wanted her to know he remembered. As he held her hand in his, he was certain she did.

Though she tried to pull away, he kept his hold for an extra few seconds. The revelation of their tryst was no longer an issue for him. His divorce had assured that. For Briel? Plated armour surrounded her personal life. At the very least, he could use their shared secret to get what he needed today.

And the detective inspector? Not a problem, if, as the friar said, the police were on their way. Plenty to distract everyone but him from the good doctora.

CHAPTER 47

Ricardo's hand remained extended when Padre Hugh introduced him to Doctor Miguel Lobo, but the doctor ignored the gesture and turned his full attention to Briel. He'd encountered many Lobos in his life, most of them clumsy in their manipulations. This one was more polished than average.

By Briel's reaction to Lobo's greeting, he didn't think she was fooled. She wanted to pull away, but the man held her gaze. Little doubt they had a past, though exactly how significant was hard to tell. And the friar? No good way to know for sure what the holy man thought of the doctor.

It didn't matter. Ricardo had a job to do.

"Excuse me," he said to Padre Hugh. "My colleagues should be here soon, and I need to interview your gardener. He may have seen something important."

Suthons nodded and Ricardo headed back to the hedges.

Both man and wheelbarrow were still missing from their hilltop post, so Ricardo climbed into the orphanage grounds. No sounds of children playing in the yard. He hoped they were all in class. Surely, if anyone had been outside, the sound of gunfire would have caused even more chaos.

From a discreet distance, Ricardo caught sight through a classroom window of ongoing lessons. Closed doors, locked windows and air conditioning meant nothing had alerted the school to the nearby attack. And praise God, the assault didn't extend beyond the church.

He took a moment to admire the exquisite stone work that framed the building. Someone had gone to a lot of trouble to be sure the structure was secure. Ricardo had visited several orphanages early in his years on the force. Comparatively, this one was a rich endeavour. The friar must have courted the very wealthy—which explained Miguel Lobo.

Ricardo headed for an outbuilding several meters away, close to a rose garden in want of pruning and wilted flowers desperate for water. The sign read: Oficina de Mantenimiento.

The place was a mess. Tools strewn across work tables, lawnmower parts on the floor, and the wheelbarrow tipped up against a side wall. At least he was in the right place. Unfortunately, no one was there, so he moved on.

On his way past the main entrance of the school, he spotted a man heading for the parking lot, and Ricardo jogged to meet him.

"Excuse me," he said.

The man stopped and turned. "Sí?"

Ricardo produced his Guardia Nacional badge.

"I am looking for your groundskeeper. Have you seen him?"

The stranger checked his watch and smiled. "You mean Naran Bravo? I am the administrator here, Inspector. At this hour, our fine friend has already gone. Probably to a tequila bar, but we try not to remind Padre Hugh of that. He maintains hope of redeeming this particular lost soul. Though why, I cannot say."

"Thank you."

Defeated again, Ricardo returned to the church. Inside, Briel was still standing beside the friar, who was inspecting damage and relaying details of the crime to his patron. Lobo frowned, his large dark eyes focused on some unseen force far away.

"Doctora Payce," Ricardo said. "I believe it is time for us to go.

It seems my team has been delayed and I need to find out why. I will take you back to your hotel first. On the way, there are questions I must ask related to what you remember from your vantage point."

Padre Hugh and Miguel Lobo followed them into the daylight. As they neared the parking lot, Ricardo looked again at his four flat tires.

Too close to his ear for comfort, Miguel said, "I don't think you're going anywhere, Detective Inspector."

CHAPTER 48

Briel stood with the others and stared at Ricardo's damaged vehicle.

"Easily solved," Padre Hugh said suddenly, in an almost singsong voice. His face was hard to read, but she liked the man. Despite the attack, despite the mayhem, he seemed at peace. She'd seen, well, felt it before in the occasional church. Not so much in the churchgoers, but the church itself. A sense of something sacred. Suthons embodied that spirit, and it was contagious.

"You may use my truck," he said.

Ricardo eyed the old, slightly rusty, teal-coloured vehicle.

"No, Father," he said.

"I would be happy to help," Miguel offered. "I need to get back to the hospital, but a brief delay poses no problem."

"I insist," the friar countered. "My way of repaying your help this morning. You were God sent and very brave. You made sure Doctora Payce and I remained protected and then went off on your own. Please, let me do this now."

Suthons patted the detective's arm, and Ricardo nodded his thanks.

Then the friar slid his hands into the pockets of his habit and turned to Briel. "And you, Doctora. It has been a pleasure. You reminded me of good times with our mutual friend. A wonderful person."

He surprised Briel by taking her hand in his. "Go with God."

As she smiled back at the holy man, Briel felt the slip of paper Padre Hugh passed her. Done in secret. Why? She locked eyes with him, hoping he'd transmit the purpose. Instead, he winked and let go. Silently, she eased his message into her pocket, leaving her hand there, hoping to portray a casual stance. Percy would have laughed. Briel was rarely casual, and her friend would have seen through the façade in an instant.

"Aaa...ve Mari...ia."

The delicate, tranquil melody captured Briel's senses as the friar's tenor voice hit pitch perfect notes on his way to retrieve their ride. Tears threatened their escape. An unexpected release of the day's tension, and what she'd pent up since the start of her trip. Just what Schubert had intended. A prayer for help.

Reluctantly, Briel fought for control. It wasn't the time. Alone, tonight, she promised herself, in her hotel room, she'd draw on this memory and give in.

RICARDO'S MIND RACED. Why was he still here, alone? Torres's cronies had probably intercepted his call for backup, and that meant his fool of a boss had endangered innocent members of the public. Inexcusable, regardless of whether those affected were foreigners. Maybe it was time to leave the Violent Crime Against Tourists Unit and let the experiment die. He could join the AFSI. Menendez, at least, appreciated his efforts. So far.

What a mess. What had his city come to, that thugs would desecrate a church like this? And there wouldn't be a forensic team. Not on his budget. No one was hurt, and he was the principal witness. He'd interview Briel, but in the end, there'd be more damned paperwork and nothing to show for it.

And what about the friar? Like Briel, he was in the crypt for almost all of it. Then again, he could help shed some light on the gardener. He made a mental note to interview Suthons after getting Briel out of the way.

SOMETHING, a twitch of insight, lifted the hairs on the back of Ricardo's neck as the father sang "Ave Maria" at the top of his lungs while heading to the carport to fetch the pickup.

He reviewed the gunmen's actions. Satisfied to shoot at the pews, playing cat and mouse, keeping him busy, hurting no one, stealing nothing. And then his tires were slashed. What was wrong with this picture?

Herding sheep.

The nip and noise of dogs at work came to mind and the veil lifted. Ricardo's heart grabbed hold of his throat and he struggled to cry out. They'd been set up.

He saw the friar, some meters away, turn the knob to enter his car. Arms waving, Ricardo ran. He shouted for Padre Hugh to stop. But Suthons was still singing, oblivious to the inspector's plea.

Ricardo could almost hear the click as the friar set the key to start the engine. He jumped aside, anger reaching every pore, regret at his own stupidity pushing him into a fetal position.

When Padre Hugh's car exploded, the resulting inferno reached for the heavens. Flames licked at least thirty feet high, engulfing the wooden carport frame in an instant.

CHAPTER 49

Alejandro's eyes flicked from side to side, and Dean wondered if the man would bolt.

"Look," Dean said, intending to bring down the temperature, "I'm not trying to make your life difficult. I can be helpful. Wouldn't you rather be the one finding the problem and taking credit for solving it? I can make sure that happens."

Alejandro considered Dean's words.

"You don't understand," he said. "Anything can set off the equipment. A small animal finding its way inside the box, or a larger one, curious, pushing the device around. Severe weather. Anything."

"All the more reason to check."

"You are searching for a ghost, and the trek through to the sites on Popocatepetl can be arduous."

"I'm always prepared for a hike."

Alejandro froze. The only sign of life was a persistent blinking of the man's eyes. Dean was about to ask to speak with someone else when the volcanologist finally said, "I'll get my things."

. . .

DESPITE HIS MISSION, Dean couldn't help but stop to appreciate the vistas, the changing geology and the wildlife. It was a perfect day for walking up the mountain and he wondered if Briel had felt the same way about the sights on Iztaccihuatl before the trip turned on its head.

Sadly, with the seismic readings from the time of Percy's disappearance gone, there was nothing to tie this adventure back to her. So why the hell was he still helping Mexico's Secretariat of Environmental Stability when he was supposed to be working with Briel? Because he always finished what he started. His mother had taught him that, and she was whispering to him now.

Okay, Mom, let's do this.

They'd taken Dean's convertible a good way up the winding path on the lower part of the mountain. When that ended, Dean slung his backpack over one shoulder and almost skipped along the trail. Despite the thin air, it was a chance to clear his head, let his brain rest, and for a little while not obsess over Percy while he finished with what was turning out to be a rather pleasant side mission.

He agreed with Alejandro. Most likely, the data were simply corrupt and corrected by triangulation before any harm could be done. A random mouse digging its den under the box and flipping it while going in and out.

Dean calculated how long it would take to check the three major seismic boxes in this region. A quick report to Rangal that there was no foul play, and then he'd meet back up with Briel. He didn't like the look of that detective inspector. It should only have been Briel and Dean, searching together for the sake of the most beautiful, crazy, inventive, hardworking, intelligent woman he'd ever met. His Persephone Gilbert.

"This way," Alejandro corrected as Dean started down a path he thought led to the nearest collection unit. Dutifully, Dean turned back. Alejandro explained, "We'll start at the top and work from there."

Dean shrugged. Order didn't really matter, did it?

It was another hour of uphill climbing. The wiry Alejandro was more fit than he looked, and much more accustomed to the sparse oxygen conditions. As they ascended, Dean gave in and gulped air while trying to keep up.

Eventually, they turned onto a poorly worn footpath and found a telltale solar panel acting as a remote power source. Nearby, under a plate, was a hole in the ground that hid the seismometer, its free weight attached to the spring that allowed even the most subtle ground movement to be transmitted to the magnetic recording device. Dean had a fondness for the simplicity and elegance of these systems.

Alejandro documented the time of their intrusion and called the departamento. "It is me. Sí. I am at station three. All is good. Ignore the readings until I say."

Dean leaned over the blue tub that held the instrument and, with his finger, drew the path the signal took from rocky ground to electric current and then to where the data left to be transcribed.

He spotted something odd. A short distance from the expected technology was a secondary setup; three interconnected black boxes, none much bigger than his open hand. Something Dean had never seen before.

"Alejandro. What's this?"

Dean pointed to the mysterious assembly, and Alejandro brought his head closer.

"That's not normal for a seismometer," Dean said. He kept his voice authoritative, as though he knew what he was talking about. If it belonged to the system, so be it, but he didn't want Alejandro to bamboozle him if it was an intruder.

Alejandro rested on his haunches. "No idea," he said.

The picture of innocence, but Dean wasn't so sure.

Dean snapped a photo and texted it to his friend Carl, stationed in a lab on the Big Island of Hawaii; a buddy who knew a lot more than him about volcanoes.

'Seen anything like this before?' the message read.

In an instant, the phone pinged back.

'Where are you?'

'Mexico. I'll explain later.'

'The long skinny box is a speaker with an amplifier. From the arrangement of the connectors, I'd say the smaller square box probably holds a single board computer, and the thing with the antennae—that's a cell phone modem. Someone playing a joke over there?'

'What's it for?'

'My guess is to control some kind of sound from a remote location.'

'How do you know?'

'Used the same set up when our old house was empty. Worked lights and stereo from our new place, so the old one would still seem lived in. My kid used it to make crazy sounds last Halloween. Drove everyone nuts. Eventually I crushed the board. Oops.'

'Thanks. I'll ring you later.'

'Hang loose, bro.'

A speaker that could be turned on and off from a distance. He turned to Alejandro.

"Who attends to this station?"

CHAPTER 50

As the fire's heat built, the heavy wood beams supporting each corner of the carport blew out, sending timber flying in every direction. Time stood still for an instant as the ceiling hovered, untethered, above the raging inferno that was once the friar's truck. When the roof collapsed, the added fuel sent flames licking even closer to the church's stone belfry.

When Suthons got behind the wheel, suddenly hell exploded on earth. At the sight of flying debris headed Ricardo's way, Briel raced to drag him out of the path of a ten-foot-long strut that crashed to the ground within inches of them both.

Miguel was right behind her and together they headed toward what was left of the padre's vehicle. She was desperate to help the priest, already aware there was nothing left to do. They stopped and Miguel put an arm over her and pulled her close when she shivered, her brain hijacked by shock and helplessness.

She felt another hand on her back.

"Briel?" It was Ricardo. "There's nothing you or Doctor Lobo can do. I know this is hard. Please. Could I speak with you for a few moments? Alone?"

Briel squeezed herself from Miguel's grasp. His reluctance to let her go was understandable. As a patron of the church and its orphanage, he'd just witnessed not only a tragedy, but the loss, she was sure, of a friend. She considered staying with Miguel, so they could comfort each other, but when she lifted her head and saw spectators gathering, she pulled herself together. Aequanimitas. It was the hallmark both she and Miguel lived by.

Sirens sounded in the distance.

"Briel," Ricardo said when they were alone. "The fire services, at least, will be here in a moment, and I must get more help to the premises as soon as possible."

A matronly older female, with a red and white headscarf wrapped around grey hair that peeked through in front and in back, pushed bystanders aside and stood wailing, alone, near Padre Hugh's car. Too near. The friar's administrative assistant?

Ricardo closed his eyes for a moment and then turned back to Briel. "I also need to manage the crowd... Briel. How well do you know Doctor Lobo?"

"I haven't seen him in a few years, but at one time, I knew him well."

"Is he trustworthy?"

"What do you mean?"

"He offered to drive you back to your hotel. There is a lot to do here, and I think it's a good idea for you and he to go. I can speak with each of you later. I just need to know if he's someone you trust enough."

"I think so. But why would you ask?"

Ricardo opened his mouth to answer just as Miguel arrived. "I need a drink. Briel, perhaps a stiff tequila cocktail? Then I can take you back to your hotel. In the meantime, the detective inspector looks to have his hands full... Unless, of course, we can be of some help here?"

"No," Ricardo said. "Both fire and ambulance have arrived. No one else was hurt. There is nothing for a doctor to do now, and I must take charge. I have questions, but they can wait."

THE DETECTIVE INSPECTOR grabbed a megaphone from his car, drew his shoulders back, and commanded the assembled onlookers to keep well away. He escorted the older woman from the fire and asked someone to find her a place to sit down. Then he picked out crime scene tape from his trunk.

Ricardo turned in time to see Miguel open his passenger door for Briel. There was something about that man. Something he didn't like.

Ricardo shook his head. It was probably nothing. Lobo looked like a fine, upstanding citizen. He volunteered his medical services at the orphanage and Briel, while not comfortable, didn't seem afraid of him. Though he didn't know Briel well, she impressed him as being authoritative, worthy of respect. If she trusted the man, that was good enough for him.

Still, his arrival was quite a coincidence.

Ricardo cursed. He should have figured out the ploy well before it happened. The bullets were a diversion. His slashed tires intended to corral them into taking the friar's offer of help.

That's when it hit him. Who was the target? The friar? Him? Briel? All of them.

He watched Lobo get into the driver's seat and turn the engine over. Should he stop them from leaving?

The captain of the fire crew called his name. He waved a response and when he turned back, Miguel and Briel were speeding away, so he dialled his office assistant.

"Clara. I need you to do a background check. Sí. Doctor Miguel Lobo. Oh, and Naran Bravo. Yes. That one's posing as a groundskeeper. Thank you."

The captain called again, and as Ricardo headed over, another set of sirens echoed in the valley. Had to be the backup he'd asked for. He wondered how much it had hurt Torres to finally send help.

THE CAR LURCHED FORWARD and Briel's body pressed into the seat back and headrest. Miguel seemed in a hurry to get moving. Despite professed equanimity, she recognized her own shock, and Miguel was probably feeling the same—especially since he'd known Padre Hugh longer. It made sense to follow Ricardo's instructions and get out of the way.

That drink was sounding better and better.

A golden afternoon sunlight lit the scrub grass, sand, and cactuses that covered the landscape outside the car window. Where orange tones flickered, Briel replayed the friar sauntering toward the carport and the subsequent explosion.

Tears threatened and her nose ran. She reached into her pocket for a tissue and felt the piece of paper the friar had tucked into her hand when they said goodbye. Gently, she wiped her nose and dabbed at her eyes, all the while keeping Suthon's message in her grip. More than ever, she wanted to know what it said.

Miguel had his sights on the road, so, carefully, she twisted her torso while putting the tissue away, and opened her hand to take a peek.

"What's that?" Miguel asked.

CHAPTER 51

A small gold-rimmed, green porcelain bowl filled with fresh nuts sat on the desk, just within reach of the Conductor's hand. He put the phone on speaker, ready for Pedro's report while he picked out a Brazil nut, a cashew, and an almond, popping the cashew into his mouth first, savouring the sweet buttery flavour of his favourite treat.

"I believe Miguel will do his job this time. He knows he's being watched. He's on his way now to pick up Doctora Briel Payce," Pedro said.

The Conductor bit through the almond and grimaced as the bitter taste of amygdalin streaked over his tongue. He removed the foul nut from his mouth by spitting it into a tissue before discarding it into the trash. He couldn't believe his ears. His lieutenant had allowed Miguel to go free.

Again.

"And what is it that makes you believe that nephew of yours will do the job this time?"

Pedro stammered at the sound of displeasure. "I... I genuinely surprised him at the airport... And... and he doesn't know how we're tracking him. He just knows we are."

Not enough. Not by a long shot. Pedro was definitely losing his edge. Time to lay a few cards on the table.

"And your youngest niece. The one in Guadalajara. She and the baby are well?"

Silence.

The Conductor continued. "Pedro. Do you agree that by working for me, you have been generously provided for?"

"Of course, señor."

"And you understand the rewards of a job well done?"

"Sí. You've been very generous. More than a poor soldier deserves."

"I do not want your platitudes. Only results. This has gotten out of hand. You have until the end of day to prove that that foolish nephew of yours still has some value in this organization. Otherwise, I will send someone else to deal with him and then find the family you cannot hide."

More silence as the Conductor's message hit its mark.

Pedro's wrist jerked and his cell phone slipped through his fingers as the Conductor hung up. Instead of landing on the table, the thing clattered to the floor and bounced twice before laying flat under a chair. He thought to let it stay there. Then he thought to stand up and crush it under the heel of his three-thousand-dollar crocodile skin boots.

Who did the boss think he was? Pedro had been faithful all these years. Worked hard. Did all the Conductor's bidding. Cleaned up after the Conductor's Strings. Even today.

Emelia. Little Emelia and her new baby. The only blood relative he adored. The one with the innocent but penetrating deep brown eyes who had looked up to him during her childhood. She saw him as an adventurer, an interesting man. He never wanted that image to change.

Emelia was the one he'd encouraged to move away. He wanted her safe.

As for the rest, he'd stayed away from most of his family for many years. It wasn't hard. His only other remaining connection was Miguel. Taking charge of his nephew and recruiting him to meet his needs was an unexpected bonus. Until now.

Pedro had just gotten the note about Emelia's baby's arrival early last week, yet the Conductor knew. Had the Conductor already found someone to replace him? Pedro picked up the phone and scrolled through his contacts. He was going to need someone on the ground he could trust. But who?

A shrill tone and a sudden vibration almost made Pedro drop the phone again. The incoming caller was his man on Miguel. Now what?

"Yes?"

"Lobo just left the church. And he was in a hurry. The woman is with him."

A ray of hope peeking through this mess?

"Where are they headed?"

"To get tequila cocktails. Apparently, they need a drink to deal with the trauma of the friar's death."

At least part of the plan was working. Maybe Miguel and his career were salvageable after all.

"Is Miguel's car still bugged?"

"Sí. Signal is coming in loud and clear. And it just got interesting."

CHAPTER 52

"What's what?" Briel asked, shifting again to tuck the paper away.

"The note in your hand. Latin?"

Miguel's eyes were sharper than she'd expected. Of course, observation, especially where it concerned women, was his trademark.

"Just a blessing Padre Hugh gave me," Briel said. "Something personal. Something to remember him by."

"We could both use a blessing right now," Miguel said.

Like always, Miguel hoped to cross her personal boundaries. First, it would be the blessing. When she refused, it would be drinks and then her hotel room. He was upset and on the prowl. She didn't want or need his particular version of self-satisfying comfort. But how to get out of this without burning a professional bridge? Miguel still had a lot of clout in the funding community.

"I can read it to you," Briel offered. Her glance told him the message was another mystery. Perhaps it would settle Miguel and help her slide away.

"Oh," Miguel said. "Okay."

She brought the folded sheet forward again and read. "13 –

Supercelestium detestari regnum superne maiestatis desyderio appetere contritionem fatui."

"Odd blessing for a priest," Miguel said.

"We'd been talking about my lack of faith. I guess it was his way of trying to honour my path, while still speaking to the consequences."

Briel hoped Miguel would buy the lie. They both knew enough Latin from their healthcare studies to get the gist of the verse.

To DETEST *the super celestial kingdom from above; to seek the destruction of a fool's longing for majesty.*

WHERE IT CAME from and what it really spoke to, she didn't know.

"I'm actually feeling a little queasy and my head is pounding," Briel said. "Miguel. Would you mind if I take a raincheck on the drink? I don't think I'd be good company right now."

The pause was long and Briel hoped she hadn't angered this man.

"I understand," he said eventually. "I'm not feeling all that well myself. I'll get you back to your hotel."

Then he added, "I'm sure we'll see each other again before you leave."

Briel hoped not, but she knew better than to disagree.

"WHAT DO YOU MEAN, INTERESTING?" Pedro was in no mood for riddles.

"Hold on."

Imbecile.

The tail was a relative newcomer, still at the stage where being part of the action was a thrill. Pedro had been there once, a very long time ago. A time when excitement overwhelmed sense. Either you learned, or you didn't live. Hard to know which way it would go for this one.

"Tell me now, you motherfucker, or move on."

"Here. Listen."

The man played a tape of Briel Payce reading a Latin verse, supposedly given to her by the padre before he died.

Now that was interesting.

Pedro hung up and immediately called the Conductor. Maybe, just maybe, this was the chance he needed to redeem himself.

His boss remained surly, but Pedro persisted with the news.

"It's code," Pedro said. "I'm sure of it. He gave this to the Payce woman. It has to be connected."

"And why is the friar dead now? Did anyone think of questioning him first?"

Another accusation of incompetence, and it smacked Pedro hard.

"Miguel believed that with the friar gone, there would be no secrets to tell. Unfortunately, the Payce woman got to Suthons first. Ideally, she and the inspector would have died too. That didn't happen, but at least we have what the padre gave her."

"Verse 13: To detest the super celestial kingdom from above; to seek the destruction of a fool's longing for majesty," the Conductor said.

"Excuse me?"

"The translation. The Latin itself is simple, at least for any learned man."

Pedro grimaced but let it go.

The Conductor continued. "How do you intend to find out what this so-called secret means?"

"I have contacts who can deal with this."

"You said that last time."

"I know better now."

"For your sake, I hope so." And the Conductor hung up.

CHAPTER 53

Alejandro cast his eyes over the landscape, acting as though Dean wasn't even there.

Stalling.

Dean wasn't in the mood. The man was fit and could probably outrun him, but Dean knew who'd win if they fought. Dean maintained his skills in case they were needed in some of the rougher, more remote regions of the world he visited for the IEN and for when the volunteer network sent him to help where catastrophe struck. Looters accompanied disaster and Dean was unwilling to allow that kind of indignity on top of whatever calamity had befallen the population.

Alejandro seemed to weigh his options.

"Who attends this station?" Dean asked again. He suspected the answer was Alejandro himself. The question was whether the man would fess up.

Alejandro pulled out a cigarette, lit the end, and took a deep but shaky drag. A grey-blue plume escaped skyward on his exhale.

"It's my station," Alejandro said finally.

"Look," Dean said. "We don't know each other, but you have a problem and I have to report it to your boss's boss's boss. That can't be good. Why don't you tell me your side of the story and I'll see what I can do."

Alejandro took another puff and then dropped the cigarette, grinding the butt into the ground.

"I'm a pawn in this game," Alejandro said quietly. "What you need to understand is that the cartels have infiltrated much of my country, and corrupt influences exist—even among those who should know better—like our scientific circles. No one's life is untouched."

"Mexico's not alone in that. Every country I've encountered, including my own, has exposed corruption at the highest levels. We all live with it. The question is what decision will each of us make when it faces us directly? I sense you had important reasons for agreeing to this?"

Alejandro nodded. "I've been here for three years. On my very first trip on this trail, my predecessor showed me that set up. He told me what it did and how to control it. He said I'd rarely need to use it, and that it never undermined the safety of the population, but that occasionally, a second set of data, one showing Popocate-petl was waking, would be needed. I would be required to process the information and pass it to someone who would come asking for it. Obviously, I was unhappy. I just wanted to do my job."

"Why would anyone want fake data pointing toward an impending eruption?"

"I have no idea."

"Yet you agreed."

"Not at first. My predecessor, a man who left the country as far as I know, he took me to lunch. There I met a stranger. A man who seemed to have great power. Definitely a man to be feared. He told me how important the job was. He also said the data would never be used to panic our people. It was for personal use only. These two dangerous men outnumbered me, and I knew their secret. I thought if I didn't cooperate, I'd be dead. Since they assured me no harm would befall the people of Mexico, I agreed." Alejandro scoffed. "It was also the day I met my girlfriend. She was outside the restaurant. A beautiful woman. Filled with innocence and kindness, but accompanied by these men. I should have walked away... "

"And now your girlfriend is pregnant."

Alejandro stared at him, cheeks flushed.

"I saw you were distressed and caught the message on your phone. Sorry."

"It should be good news. I love her. But I am afraid. Afraid of who she belongs to, afraid of who looks for this false data, and afraid of the government officials. There is no one I can trust. Perhaps I am better off gone from this world."

Dean rubbed his temples. If Alejandro was telling the truth, he was a tiny cog in a machine neither he nor Rangal knew anything about. And it probably had nothing to do with Percy.

He could see the suffering in Alejandro's eyes. Dean wondered what he'd have done if he found out Percy had run in corrupt circles. And then he realized. Nothing. If Percy had found out she was affiliated with a nefarious crowd, she'd have taken care of it herself. Boldly and publicly. No question about it. Consequences be damned. And that's why, even after losing her, he still loved her.

Dean put his hand on Alejandro's shoulder.

"I've got an idea," he said.

CHAPTER 54

Dean opened the mint tin he took from his pants pocket. The candy was long gone, but the container was the perfect size for an emergency stash of acetaminophen. A little trick Percy had taught him when they headed out on IEN treks. He was glad the sun was waning in the rear window as he pulled out of the Regional Department for Monitoring Natural Disasters headquarters.

The hike down the hillside was uneventful, but Alejandro's revelations, the thin air, and lack of food were getting to him. Or maybe it was time to acknowledge he was getting older and his system just wasn't as flexible as it used to be. Percy would have called him a wimp right before making him a cup of peppermint tea. He smiled at her memory. She'd have loved the climb, and she'd have pushed him to tell the Secretariat of Environmental Stability everything. The right thing to do? Probably.

He couldn't help but feel sorry for Alejandro. The guy was a mess, and definitely in over his head. Dean wasn't sure if the girlfriend was part of the scheme, but he sensed Alejandro loved her. And Dean was a sucker for that. If he couldn't have his love, he could at least understand it vicariously through others.

The phone buzzed and he put it on speaker. Donata Rangal.

"Hello, Secretariat. I was just about to call you."

"How did it go?"

"The official data showing Popocatepetl's rumblings within normal bounds is correct. There was never a risk to the population."

"Then why was there a second set?"

"That's... complicated."

"I can deal with complicated."

"Sure. I just meant that it would be better to go through what I found in person. I could meet you tomorrow."

The pause told Dean that Donata Rangal wasn't happy about waiting, so he added, "I've been up and down the side of your mountain, and I'm exhausted. I don't think I could give a coherent account right now."

"I understand," Rangal said, her voice sounding a little more sympathetic. "Tomorrow it is then."

He disconnected the call and a moment later, another came through. Hungry and fed up, he thought to let it go to voicemail. Then he saw it was from Briel.

"Hey," he said.

"Hey to you too. You sound tired."

"I am. Everything okay?"

"It's been a tough day on my side. Listen. I need a sounding board. I think I've got another lead. Only, it's confusing. Any chance you could come by and help?"

A new lead about Percy? Of course he'd help.

"Sure," he said. "But under two conditions."

"Shoot."

"First, after we deal with your discovery, I'm going to need to talk strategy about my own findings today. Second, I'm starving. You order the food."

PEPPERONI PIZZA with a side of Buffalo wings on the way, Briel went back to the slip of paper she'd laid on top of the desk and pressed out the creases as best she could, just in case something more hid in the folds. She wouldn't put it past Percy or the padre.

The note was in Percy's handwriting. That was easy enough to tell. And it was a detail she knew enough to keep from Miguel. None of his business. It was also the reason Percy had wanted her to see the friar. She was sure of it. Was it why someone had killed him?

God, Padre Hugh. The portly, cheerful man with a twinkle in his eye at the mention of her best friend's name. A man who looked as comfortable in his authority over the church and orphanage as he would have looked among Robin Hood's gang.

That's the way she wanted to remember him. But every time she closed her eyes, the image her brain recreated was the one where he sauntered to his death, singing "Ave Maria" at the top of his lungs.

"Ave Maria."

The song's last line: "Holy Mary, Mother of God, pray for us sinners, now and in our hour of death." The irony was not lost on her.

Briel rubbed her temples and willed herself to concentrate. She couldn't allow the friar's death to be in vain. There had to be something in that Latin verse. "Supercelestium detestari..."

And why "Ave Maria"?

The thought came to Briel in a flash. Did the priest know he was about to die? Unlikely. Then why burst out in song? Especially that one.

She picked up her phone and opened an internet page. In the search line, she typed: Ave Maria, code, Latin verse. Less than a second later, first on the list of possibilities, she had the answer.

The Trithemius cipher.

FIVE YEARS. Five years Miguel had spent cultivating a relationship with the priest. Pretending he had an affiliation with the friar's blasphemous beliefs, donating time to the wards of that church. Not once could he get the man to talk about his association with Persephone Gilbert, let alone a Latin verse that could have been a code between them.

Damn the man. If Miguel's team were but a few hours earlier, the secret would have gone to the grave with Suthons. And if it all had really gone right, that nosy detective inspector would also be dead, with Briel Payce none the wiser and on her way home.

He'd memorized the verse as Briel spoke it. A trick he'd learned during anatomy class many years ago. Latin names of body parts were the universal standard and his brain stretched to match logic with language.

"To detest the super celestial kingdom..."

It was easy enough to convert into either English or Spanish. What did it mean?

He pounded his fist on the desktop. What had Suthons been up to?

His mind flashed back to the look the friar had given Briel as he said his goodbye. Miguel had thought he had seen the man pass her something, and he was right.

Then the fool began singing. Loudly enough for the adjacent countryside to hear.

Singing.

Another thing the friar never did in his presence. Why?

It was a hymn. Which one?

"Ave Maria."

He brought his computer to life. In the search bar he typed: Ave Maria cipher Latin verse.

Immediately, the screen filled with choices. The first said: Ave Maria Code. The article spoke of a German abbot who used Latin words to encrypt secret messages. When strung together, the words took the form of a verse or prayer.

The Trithemius Cipher.

CHAPTER 55

Ricardo white-knuckled the steering wheel and the car jerked left, almost crossing into an oncoming lane. He counselled himself to take a breath.

It took ages to clean up the mess at the Iglesia San Antonio de Padua and get new tires on his car. Despite the late hour, he still couldn't eat.

What had he done?

The only person he had given the friar's name to was Luis Menendez, and now Suthons was dead. He'd been played.

Well, he had connections to deal with this; or at least his assistant Clara did. She'd come back to say that Miguel Lobo was clean. Naran Bravo was a dead end. A made-up name. When Ricardo spoke with the school's principal before she left, he was told that Naran, or whoever he really was, had called to quit. No surprise there.

Ricardo told Clara what he needed next, and she got her brother-in-law, a consultant HR administrator for the network of enforcement agencies in the region, to access the home address of the head of the AFSI. It was so easy, it actually worried him. He trusted Clara implicitly, and she him. They'd worked together for a long time and in some ways, she took on the role of a second mother. Still, if it was that simple for her to get the information, was anyone really safe? He supposed not.

Ricardo pulled into an upper-middle-class suburban neighbourhood. Pleasant homes, but not the gated mansions he expected of someone from Menendez's station. Maybe the address was fake? A cover to protect Menendez's anonymity.

He slowed down at the next corner, anticipating the street number to be represented by an empty lot, ready to call this ride a waste of time and find a beer. Instead, he spotted the house number ahead, in front of a modest building lit up on all sides as though inviting guests to a party. It was a two-story affair with a wide front porch lined with decorative planters. The stately border of three-foot yuccas on one side would have made the city's botanical gardens proud.

Still, it was hard to tell if he was in the right place, and the last thing he wanted to do was barge in on some innocent family.

He turned off his headlights and parked in front of a home a few doors up the road, aching to confront Menendez, wanting him to explain why. Or was it retribution Ricardo was really after? His clenched fists said yes, but his brain was cooling. Better to deal with this in the light of day.

He was about to start up the car and turn around when a limousine whizzed past, screeching to a halt in front of the AFSI director's house. The Secretariat of Travel, Culture and Tourism stepped from the vehicle, refastened the bottom button of his suit coat, and surveyed the surroundings.

Ricardo ducked, hoping he hadn't been spotted. When he tentatively raised his head again, Tomás was pounding on Menendez's front door.

Even as Luis Menendez cracked open his entry way, Mateo Tomás's angry shouts reached Ricardo's ears.

"Hijo de puta! You shit! What the hell are you doing in my affairs?"

Ricardo's jaw dropped when the AFSI director's response was to push the secretariat out of the way and look up and down the street. Knowing Menendez's reputation for being a ghost, "all-seeing" and "ever-present," Ricardo was sure he'd be discovered.

Did it matter? Not really.

Ricardo was ready for a fight. The only trouble was, he couldn't tell which side to be on. Did Tomás also blame Menendez for Padre Hugh's death? The wires were sure to have picked up the news as soon as Ricardo called for help. Did Tomás know Ricardo was the leak? Or was it Tomás who ordered the hit and Menendez found out?

Menendez grabbed the secretariat's jacket and yanked him into the house. Suddenly, all was quiet on the street once more.

Ricardo leaned back, palpitations pounding his chest. Was it possible he had no allies in this fight? He needed to know.

Now.

Slowly, Ricardo cracked open the driver's side door. He searched the street, including rooftops, for security, but found none. Either Menendez's men deserved their reputation or the man was here alone.

Tomás's limo driver remained facing forward and in the front seat outside the director's house, but one look in the rear-view mirror and Ricardo's presence would no longer be a secret.

Headlights from a car turning onto the street hit the windshield of the secretariat's car and Ricardo took that opportunity to dart across the road and hide behind the nearest tall tree.

Camouflaged by the landscape, Ricardo wound his way to the bromeliad border at Menendez's home. Muffled raised voices escaped the concrete and steel frame. He needed to get closer.

CHAPTER 56

Briel took another bite of pizza. Pepperoni, sausage, mozzarella cheese, tomato sauce, onion, and green pepper soothed her taste buds and her brain rewarded her with a solid shot of dopamine. Dean's arrival back at the hotel had relaxed Briel enough that she could finally eat. Comfort in the familiar, she supposed. It was nice not to be alone in this.

Dean picked up a morsel of sausage that fell from his slice, and eyed the container of salsa that had come, uninvited, in the box. Briel almost laughed out loud. He was thinking about it. She understood. Pizza was hard to mess up, but wherever in the world she ate it, some evidence of regional tastes came along. Once, in Japan, her pizza had arrived with a container of soy sauce.

Dean's inspection of the Mexican addition meant he was definitely feeling better—and he was hungry.

He took a swig of beer and she sipped her wine. They'd spoken little since he got to her room. Seemed like they both needed to calm down.

"So you went up Popocatepetl?"

Dean answered as best he could between bites. "Not all that high. No need. The local seismic stations solved the problem. Still a beautiful view, though. But never mind my side trip. It didn't get me closer to Percy, and I can ask for help with my problem later. You could have been killed today. Tell me."

They spent the next hour catching up, piecing together the bits of information they each had and trying as best they could to understand what they'd tumbled into.

"We need to stick together from here on," Dean said. "I'll give a report to the secretariat tomorrow morning, and then it's their problem."

"Perfect. Seems to me our next move is to find a copy of the *Polygraphia*."

"What's that?"

"It's the code book written by Johannes Trithemius in the late fifteenth or early sixteenth centuries. It's the only way to solve what Percy left. I already looked it up. The trouble is, the only known copy of the work is in the US Library of Congress. No scans, no pages on the internet. There's a notation beside the book's listing. Apparently, it's in really poor condition and it can't be photographed for fear of further degradation."

"So we're going home?"

"That doesn't make sense, does it?"

"Not really. How could Percy create the Latin verse without having Trithemius's text in hand? Her memory was excellent, but not photographic. And I can't see her preparing the text before leaving the US."

"Then there has to be something here. Something nearby."

Dean opened his phone browser and got to work, as did Briel. This time, Briel headed to the academic sites on the internet and specified Mexico in her search. Scrolling through on page four, a tiny article held promise. She clicked it.

"Got it!" she said.

Dean leaned over to look.

"There's another copy. It seems a French/German Dominican friar was assigned to a church in Tepoztlán in the early 1960s. He donated the book when he retired. That's got to be it."

"Where's Tepoztlán?" Dean asked.

That search was easy.

"About an hour and a half south of Mexico City. Seems to be a bit of a tourist attraction. And look... it's considered a spiritual place. A nearby stream is called the birthplace of the Serpent God, Quetzalcoatl. Isn't that the same name as a pyramid in Teotihuacan?"

Dean opened his mouth, but a knock at the door interrupted his answer.

"Room service!" someone called.

Briel and Dean froze. They'd ordered nothing.

Seconds ticked by and Briel was about to speak again when they heard the rustle of keys outside Briel's room.

CHAPTER 57

Alone in the dark, Pedro sat on the blue vinyl seat of the chair in front of his vintage aluminum kitchen table with the Formica top, one hand wrapped around a crystal tumbler filled with his favourite gin and quality imported tonic. His other hand felt the smooth table surface, following the fancy scrollwork that had enamoured the girl he had married when he was only eighteen years old. It took two years to pay off the debt, and by the time the table was theirs, Paloma already had her diagnosis. He prayed and prayed. And when the god of his ancestors didn't respond, he looked to other gods to take up the call. None did. That's when he saw his devotion for what it was, a tool, only for those in power. That's when he changed sides and devoted himself to worldly pursuits. If his God didn't exist, or didn't care, why not take what he could while he was on this earth?

Now?

He'd never been on this side of the Conductor's rage.

He'd sourced a Latin expert he had heard could help with the friar's verse, but he doubted it. He couldn't even be sure it was a code.

Pedro felt the hard steel of the gun in his hands as the street-light outside the kitchen window reflected off the barrel. It was loaded and ready. Surely if he was gone, the Conductor would have mercy on little Emelia and her new baby.

Or would he?

Damn Miguel. And damn the scheme he'd concocted so long ago to solve his ancestral obligation to feed Quetzalcoatl's needs. At first, he had considered himself lucky. The young doctor's naïvete knew no bounds. It was too easy to pass the baton, but at what cost?

Pedro took another sip and looked again at the gun. Make a choice. Fix this or take the coward's way out.

He pulled the pistol closer and fingered the trigger, and a new thought emerged. Like the sun peeking through storm clouds in an unsettled front.

Could Miguel still be the answer?

It galled him to still need his nephew. But he'd turned the man once. Surely he could do it again. Get what he needed and make things right.

Pedro gulped the rest of his drink and slammed the tumbler on the table. Weapon holstered, he grabbed his keys and headed for the door.

THE CONDUCTOR SAT ALONE in the dark. Remnants of a fajita dinner Dorothea had insisted on bringing to him sat on the trolley beside his desk. At least he'd prevented his maid from entering the office to tidy up. He needed the solitude.

The box that once held Persephone Gilbert's message was empty now. No need to keep a useless scrap of paper. Instead, he had the friar's misbegotten Latin verse. Was it a cipher or just the ramblings of an old, religious fool? Did it warrant replacing Gilbert's puzzle?

He tipped his head back, comforted by the leather headrest behind him. Not usually given to melancholy, on this day, when success only led to another enigma, he tumbled into the rare state of questioning his life's choices.

"Think of what you could do for all the performing arts if you were a patron and not a performer," his brother had said. That was during high school, and his parents had agreed. When the Conductor hadn't been sure how to amass sufficient wealth to become a patron, his father taught him to supply "pain medication" to students in need. He had found talent there too, and his path was set.

What if he'd kept hold of the baton instead? Would his life be better now? Simpler? Or would he have become another starving artist?

A phone on his desk buzzed. Unknown Caller. Only a handful of minions had that number—the one that bypassed the lieutenant and allowed the Conductor to talk directly to a lower level if needed. Like the guard at the compound where he'd had the cryptologist killed.

Who would dare call him?

"Hello."

"Hello, señor. I have information you need… "

"How did you get this number? Who are you?"

"I am Enrique Torres."

Torres, Unit Coordinator of the Guardia Nacional. How in the hell did the man find him?

Torres said again, "I have information you need. It would be in both our interests to meet."

The Conductor checked that his VPN was on. The device told him the caller would believe his location to be in Venezuela. Good.

"What could you possibly have that I would need?"

"I believe you know my friend, Sebastian Blanco."

Maldito. Sebastian had said he could hold the Guardia in line. Now the Conductor knew why.

"What do you want?"

"Your business is being threatened. I know from who and what is being planned. If we meet, I can show you. And I believe my talents are being wasted here. Perhaps I can be of greater help in the future."

The Conductor said nothing. But in the dark corners of his office, a glimmer of light arose.

"Alright, Torres. Let us see what you have. You will be sent instructions. Follow them to the letter."

Then he called Pedro.

"Secure a meeting site... Yes. Now."

CHAPTER 58

Dean placed himself in front of the closed hotel room door. The bolt was of no use if someone had the proper key, and only screw holes remained where the security chain was once attached. He positioned his hand to grab the knob and then put his foot on the threshold, ready to block any intruder.

Briel took up a position behind him, aluminum extendable walking stick poised like a baseball bat. Not likely to do much damage if they needed it, but it was all they had.

He heard the click of the door and felt the thud against his foot as someone tried to get in. Whoever was there backed off, and Dean waited. The second he felt resistance again, he yanked the door wide open.

A tall man, medium build with black hair and wearing a suit, spilled onto the hotel room floor. A shorter female in casual dress and running shoes, long blonde-streaked hair done up in a bun, followed the stranger in. She tripped over Dean's foot and landed on the ground next to her partner.

Dean grabbed Briel's hand and tried to exit the room, but Briel caught her foot on one of the sprawled legs and went down. Dean yanked her up as the man reached for Briel's leg. Instantly Briel came down on the man's hand with the walking stick.

Spanish curses accompanied the satisfying smack. Meanwhile, the woman untangled herself and as she rose, Dean kicked her in the shins.

They ran for the exit to the stairs. Just as they dove through the door, a shot rang out from behind them and hit the frame. As they bounded toward the street level, Briel motioned for Dean to follow her and they tucked into the hallway on the second floor.

It was unlikely the move would fool their pursuers, and Dean wanted to question her, but Briel was already bolting to the other side of the building. That's when he realized she was headed to the parking lot.

As he caught up with Briel, the man and woman chasing them leaped into the hallway and fired another round. They were too far away and the bullet missed, but the pair was at least as fit as Briel and Dean, and they were still too close for comfort. Briel and Dean took the next set of steps two at a time and jumped the last three, dashing into the night air.

Briel was about to head for their car, but Dean held her back.

"GPS," he gasped. Briel had to be rattled. Normally, she'd have been the one to think about a tracking device in the rental car—part of her "safety first" persona. Briel looked at him, wide-eyed. And then he realized she didn't have a Plan B.

He spotted a boulder and, with his strength waning, he rolled it to block the exit, knowing it would only hold for seconds.

Dean was looking around for other options when Briel tugged at his sleeve. Across the road was a side street devoid of lights. The pounding sound of metal against stone left them no choice. They ran toward the darkness.

Dean and Briel tucked into what appeared to be a complex of commercial and home addresses. Doors directly in front of the sidewalks and business fronts were shuttered for the night. Dean looked behind them and sure enough, the man and the woman had escaped the door and were looking in their direction.

Briel headed down the street, trying every door handle along the way. Dean took the other side and did the same.

"Here," Briel said. They were halfway down the block, and from his vantage, Dean could see their pursuers crossing the road toward them. He ran to Briel, and they jumped inside. Briel found the lock and twisted it shut. That's when Dean noticed the damage in the wall where the deadbolt should have entered the strike plate. No way to prevent intrusion.

Dean poked at Briel.

"I'm trying to find something to block the door, but it's too dark. Can you turn your cell screen on?" she said.

Immediately, a beam of soft amber light struck the surrounding floor.

"Nice," Briel whispered.

Dean poked her again.

"What?"

Briel looked up at Dean, eyes squinting with irritation. He pointed to his phone screen. It was dark. Then he directed Briel's attention to the stairs that extended from the door, and Briel followed his line of sight. At the top, in the shadow of light from an open door, stood a figure.

With a rifle.

Pointed at them.

CHAPTER 59

On hands and knees, Ricardo squeezed himself behind the thick sword-shaped leaves of the hedge plants and crouched under an open window near the front of Menendez's house. He peeked through the brush at the secretariat's limo, worried his maneuvering may have attracted attention, but the driver's head was back and his mouth hung open. He could imagine the man's snoring.

Menendez's low tones floated from the small opening above him, still unintelligible. Beginning to feel silly, Ricardo thought about making his way back to his car. He wouldn't like to be caught lurking around the property. Better to confront the head of the AFSI in daylight. After that? Well, he'd have one more enemy to add to the long list he was amassing in his life's work.

He was about to turn away from the house when the secretariat began shouting again.

"How dare you! I tell you again, you have no business in my affairs. None!"

The tone of Menendez's response was solemn but indiscernible to Ricardo. However, the unmistakable sound of smashing glass and the thuds of physical combat that followed left no doubt; the two men had descended into a physical fight.

Ricardo turned toward the limo driver and noticed that the man was awake, so he crouched back into the shadows. Then the door to Menendez's home flew open and the secretariat ran out. The driver jumped from the vehicle, ready to attend to his boss, but Tomás waved him away and dove into the back seat.

As quickly as the limo had arrived, it sped away.

Ricardo waited for Menendez to reach the threshold and step onto the front porch. Instead, the house turned eerily quiet.

"Señor Menendez?" Ricardo stepped cautiously through the frame and into the small greeting room.

Even in the dark, Ricardo could tell it was tastefully decorated. He picked up the vase perched on the wooden stand next to the door, surprised when he drew his hand across it and recognized it as a colourful but cheap offering from one of the local grocery store chains.

There was no answer to his call, so he headed into the sitting room. It was dark there, too. He stepped forward and something hard crunched underfoot. When he flicked on his cell phone flashlight, shards of glass strewn in a cone-shaped pattern sparkled back at him. He followed the trail to its apex and fingered the edge of the empty side table. The place where a lamp would normally have stood. Sure enough, under the table, a burgundy light shade lay on the floor, one side dented from its fall.

A moan came from behind the couch.

It was a familiar scene. One Ricardo knew all too well from his time with the force. He just didn't expect to find Menendez down, the victim of the secretariat's beating. In fact, if he hadn't heard the altercation and witnessed the secretariat coming and going, he'd never have believed it. The secretariat was older, rounder... definitely out of shape. Menendez seemed so fit, so capable. What had happened?

Ricardo stepped to where Menendez lay. The head of the AFSI was unconscious again, so he checked the man's pulse. Weak, but there.

He stood, contemplating the best course of action, when

suddenly Menendez's arms and legs shook, jerking the man's stiff body as though it was a marionette driven by a sadistic owner. The seizure lasted only seconds, but Ricardo felt each moment tick by as though it were an eternity.

When Menendez was finally still again, Ricardo knew his questions didn't matter anymore.

He dialled for an ambulance.

CHAPTER 60

Took her long enough, Dean thought when Briel let out a breath.

Dean slowly raised his arms in the air, and Briel followed his cue. The sound of a trash can being overturned outside made them jump. The couple from the hotel? Probably. And they were close.

Though the light in the room behind the man was soft, it was a direct hit into Dean's eyes, almost blinding him, and he couldn't help but feel the fear of a caged animal with nowhere safe to go.

He leaned a little into Briel, and she leaned back. Propping each other up, for Percy's sake, just like old times.

A second sound came from the street, even closer. Dean chanced turning his head toward the door, and when he looked back at the man with the rifle, the weapon was pointed at the ground and he was waving them up the stairs.

A third noise. Next door? It took no convincing. Dean and Briel vaulted toward the apartment. As the door shut behind them, they heard a squeal of metal on cement. Their pursuers had found the unlocked street level entrance.

Dean turned to the man with the rifle. Craggy lines dug deep into his leather-like cheeks and there were too many crow's feet in the corners of his eyes to count. Gray hair extended from a well-used cowboy hat. Cowboy boots decorated with metal stars were visible under his faded jeans, and the old man wore a fringe-lined leather vest. A real-life symbol of the Old West.

The man put his fingers over his lips and then waved at them to move to the other side of the room.

Dean caught the sound of someone, or someones, making their way up the steps.

The old man placed himself by the door, ear pressed into the wood. A second later, he was gone and the sound of gunfire shook the small building.

"Damn," spilled from Dean's mouth and he was up like a shot, heading for the door to the stairs.

BRIEL PULLED DEAN BACK. No additional gunfire followed. The only question was who won?

Either their pursuers were headed up the stairs, gunning for them, or the old man would be back. Something told her if the man who owned this home was injured, the intruders wouldn't care, and following him could only mean additional casualties. Theirs. And that wasn't good for anyone. Not them; not the old man.

They needed to wait long enough to see who entered the apartment.

The doorknob rattled and Briel grabbed a heavy glass ashtray from the coffee table and drew Dean behind the couch. The look on Dean's face told her he'd rather engage in the fight, but he followed her without complaint.

When the door cracked open, Briel flattened herself so she could peek from under the couch at whoever entered.

Cowboy boots, metal stars winking in the living room lights, appeared.

Briel heard the lock click behind the old man, and she heaved a sigh of relief. She popped up from their hiding place and yanked Dean up with her.

The old man's smile was broad, providing them a full view of his crooked teeth and gold crowns.

❧

BRIEL WAS RIGHT, as usual, Dean thought, pushing off stiffening knees to stand. The day's hike, age and the chase were all catching up with him. He'd need to consider that when he re-upped for the IEN. On the other hand, the satisfied smile on the old man who'd just dispelled the bad guys suggested one could have adventures well into—what? The guy had to be in his eighties.

"Problem. Gone," the man said. "All good. For now. You are in trouble with the police. Sí?"

"No," Dean and Briel said in unison.

"I'm Dean, and this is Briel. We're searching for a friend who went missing some time ago."

"Ah," said the man. But what did his eyes say? Amusement? Skepticism? "I am Gael. Please. Sit. Sit."

Gael pointed to the couch, waited until they complied, and then disappeared into the kitchen.

"We can't stay here," Dean said to Briel.

"I know. This is the logical place we'd be hiding. And they'll be back with reinforcements. We'll need to take Gael with us."

"I'll go talk to him."

Dean stepped toward the kitchen. A kettle boiled on the stove, the whistling obscuring Gael's voice as he spoke to someone on the phone.

Now what?

CHAPTER 61

The Conductor strolled to the bistro table, set up in Hangar 13 under the wing of a private jet at the tiny airport outside Mexico City's easternmost suburb. A bottle of champagne cooled in the wire stand next to the chairs, and a white tablecloth supported two place settings that included gold-rimmed dessert plates and gold forks. A basket of sweet cakes sat nestled beside a bud vase that held a single, perfect red rose. Mozart's "Eine Kleine Nachtmusik" played softly in the background.

What the hell did Pedro think this meeting was? Some kind of assignation?

The Conductor snapped the rose in half and turned the champagne on its head in the cooler. He waved a hand and the music stopped.

It had taken almost two hours for this site to be cleaned and cleared for the meeting. Because the Conductor no longer trusted Pedro, he'd asked the guard from his compound near Teotihuacan to spy on the arrangements. Perhaps this bistro nonsense was the brainchild of that man? Initiative bred from inexperience. He'd deal with the guard later.

The squat leader of the Guardia, handlebar moustache twitching, sauntered in from a side door. The Conductor didn't like the look of him. Torres was… unrefined, yet his manner was arrogant. The combination suggested a loose cannon. The worst type of informant.

"You were supposed to come alone," Torres complained. "We agreed."

"Then tell me why you have a man standing immediately outside that door?"

Torres's scowl made him look like a child playacting the part of a villain in an old Western.

The Conductor flicked his eyes to the left and gave a curt nod. Instantly, a bullet pealed through the air, landing on the floor at Torres's feet. Shards of cement kicked up by the projectile reached as high as the officer's waist.

In an instant, the side door opened and a pistol appeared. Another nod, and the Conductor's man covering the door fired. The pistol clattered to the floor, followed by the yelp of a wounded animal, and then a gasping "Fuck" as the entrance closed again.

The Conductor's eyes bore into Torres. "Say your piece."

Despite being visibly shaken, Torres took a breath, drew himself up and put his hands on his hips. More bravado than the Conductor had expected. Perhaps there was some use for the man, after all.

"I am here to warn you," Torres said. "One of my officers, working outside my authority and with the help of the AFSI, is looking into the ex-gardener your men had placed at Hogar de Niños San Antonio de Padua. From there, it is an easy jump to Pedro Serrano, and then to you."

At the mention of his lieutenant's name, the Conductor's gut lurched.

"Why are you telling me this?" The Conductor chose his most menacing tone. No better way to cover the inkling of fear brought about by this breach of his anonymity.

"Protection. No other organization is so well equipped to shield a soldier looking to move above the ranks of our cartel lords.

You know my affiliation with Maldito. It is not enough. I can do more."

"You want to be a Guardia Nacional mole? For me?"

"No. I can be of more use if I am on your team. I want to leave the force. I have built a lifetime of connections and I can use them all... for you."

PEDRO STOOD at the threshold of Miguel's high-end home and glanced at his watch.

Ridiculous. On the one hand, the Conductor had threatened not only his life, but that of his niece and her baby daughter. On the other, the man expected him to drop everything and arrange... what? A meeting; some kind of assignation? Assignation. That was a personal joke. One that wouldn't be well-received. Pedro didn't care. He'd blame someone else. Besides, what did his boss expect if he didn't share the details of the impending encounter?

The trust between them was razor-edge thin, but Pedro did his job. The private airport from Miguel's failed attempt to run was the perfect site to secure. At least something useful came from that confrontation. The location made it easy to hide the Conductor's support team. There would be no surprises, whoever the Conductor was meeting.

Why didn't the Conductor tell him? Because he was meeting with Pedro's replacement?

How had everything gotten so far out of hand that his best hope was bartering with his nephew in the middle of the night?

Pedro banged on Miguel's door. Hard.

When Pedro's demand to enter came to nothing, he hit the door again. Harder.

Lights finally turned on, but Miguel didn't let him in. Instead, the speaker from Miguel's security system crackled.

"What do you want?"

Pedro calmed himself. Disrespect from his junior wasn't to be tolerated, but the insolent fool would need to be placated if Pedro was to make headway.

"Miguel. I came to apologize. I behaved badly today. I should never have shot at you, or threatened you when you tried to leave. But nephew, you must know I report to those above even my station. I needed your help and you let me down."

"So you are here to kill me again?"

"No. I'm here to find out what happened. I know you fulfilled your mission at the church. Well done. I am here to talk this through. We've been a team for so many years. I'm in trouble. More than I can say. However, if I must go to my grave, I don't want to leave with such bad feelings between us."

The pause that followed lingered. Pedro stood perfectly still, his face in front of the camera, expression serious, hoping Miguel would interpret sincerity.

As seconds stretched to minutes, Pedro turned, ready to give up. Behind him, the door cracked open. Pedro pushed through before Miguel could change his mind. The manoeuvre landed him to the left of the entryway, directly into Miguel's home office.

On the computer screen, in bold letters, he read, "The Trithemius Cipher".

No music played on the Conductor's car radio as he drove home from his meeting with Enrique Torres. The man was a weasel. That was certain. And the low-life wanted a place in the Orchestra.

Could he be used? Perhaps. Even the lowly theremin had a place in some compositions. Could the man actually play? He'd need to know more before deciding.

And the leak that allowed Torres to find him? No doubt who orchestrated that. Sad, but not totally unexpected. He'd need to deal with that, too.

The Conductor's phone rang. Pedro. He really needed a

replacement for his lieutenant. The bud of a plan formed and the Conductor clicked the accept button on his cell. "Yes?"

"Señor," Pedro said. "I have good news. Our search for the rock, the protection protocol, the tail on Miguel. There is success. We have control again."

The Conductor straightened in his seat. "You found the rock?"

"Not yet. But Miguel knows how to decipher the Latin verse. His search for the key will be successful. We will have what we seek and then we can put everything back together."

Humpty-Dumpty.

No, thought the Conductor, too many pieces. All the great men... You've had a good run, Pedro, but this time, I fear we are at the end.

"Tomorrow morning," the Conductor said. "The boardroom."

And he hung up.

CHAPTER 62

"He's making tea," Dean said. "And he's on the phone."

"Who's he talking to?"

"Couldn't hear over the kettle."

"You don't think... "

"That he'd call the police, hoping to turn us in for some kind of reward?"

Briel nodded.

"Maybe. But I don't think that's his M.O. I'm pretty sure he thought that couple who were after us were some kind of police."

"Then we'll talk with him when he comes back in the room. He needs to understand the danger..."

A clatter of cups, saucers, and spoons announced Gael's arrival from the kitchen. Smiling widely, he put a tray on the coffee table in front of the couch. Briel couldn't help but notice the chips and cracks adorning the painted gold trim of what must have been an elegant and expensive tea setting when it was new, and she wondered what Gael's story was.

The old man looked so pleased with himself that when he finished pouring and gestured for them to add milk and sugar, Briel didn't have the heart to say no. She lifted her cup, tried to ignore the stains that lined the porcelain, sipped politely, and smiled.

Dean drank with gusto. No wonder he was always getting sick.

Gael pushed a plate of crumbly cookies in front of her, and she took one.

"Gael," Briel said. "Thank you for helping us, but Dean and I are worried. We shouldn't stay here. Those people. They may be back, and next time, it won't be so easy to fend them off. Please. Let's go. We'll take you with us. Somewhere we can all hide."

Gael took Briel's hand in his. His eyes were moist and the leathery lines on his old cowboy face deepened.

"You must stay," Gael said. "All will be well. Soon."

Briel turned to Dean, thinking perhaps he could get the point across. "Gael. What are you talking about? You made a call. In the kitchen. Tell us."

Gael pointed a gnarled finger at Dean and shook it.

"A surprise," he said. "For now, you stay."

Briel leaned back, trying to ease the muscles that stiffened between her shoulders. This was no time for surprises. Better to run. Far away.

Dean looked uncomfortable, too. She could almost read his mind. They certainly couldn't force the old man to go with them, but they couldn't, wouldn't, leave him behind.

Briel was about to try again when Dean cut in.

"Gael. What do you mean by 'surprise'? You can see that we brought trouble to your home. We don't want to bring more."

Gael opened his mouth to answer as a knock came from the other side of the apartment. Another exit? Leading where?

As Briel and Dean rose, Gael waved them away and headed toward the sound. Though Briel obeyed, she placed herself inside a nearby bathroom, ready to spring into action at the first sign of trouble. Dean stood around the corner, clearly with the same thought.

Gael looked through a peephole in the second door and

hopped back, clapping his hands. He opened it wide and smothered the newcomer with a firm, yet shaky, hug.

"Yolanda," Briel heard Gael murmur.

When Gael finally released his embrace, a young woman stepped inside. Briel crept forward and Dean emerged from his hiding place.

⁂

"Hello, I hear there's been trouble. I am Yolanda Ramirez," Yolanda said. "Grandfather tells me you need help. Please explain."

Dean eyed the petite blonde before him. Big brown eyes, and the smooth skin of youth. She was just a girl. What was Gael thinking to get her involved?

Briel verbalized Dean's thoughts before he could spit them out.

"I am so sorry. We don't want you or your grandfather involved in our problems. Please. We're happy to leave. Only... your grandfather could be in trouble for protecting us. Can you get him somewhere safe?"

Yolanda smiled, and the family resemblance became clear. She had Gael's kind, wide cheeks, though her toothy grin displayed perfect dental care.

"You don't need to worry for Grandfather. He will disappear when we're gone. He's... an expert at that."

She turned to Gael, and he hugged her again, kissing the top of her head. Something passed between them. A secret. The kind forged only through the best of relationships. Dean believed her.

"Then we need to get out of here," Dean said. "Without being seen."

Gael disappeared, and Briel spoke to Yolanda.

"Why is your grandfather helping us?" she asked. "He doesn't know us."

"He told me you had a 'hunted' look," Yolanda said. "He's seen it before. Not the look of betrayal, but of innocence. In this part of the city, we answer that kind of cry for help."

Gael returned, arms laden with multicoloured shawls, hats, and canes. He grabbed Briel by the elbow and pointed at the selection.

Obediently, Briel sorted through the pile, selecting the most neutral poncho available and a black baseball cap. Dean smirked. Even in her regular life, Briel did her best to blend in, to avoid public attention. Bright yellows, greens, and reds were not her thing. Especially all at the same time.

Dean chose a purple and white shawl, a Panama hat, and a walking stick covered in Aztec symbols.

They were ready.

"Are you sure you're going to be alright?" Briel said to Gael.

Dean grasped Gael's hand. "Please. Come with us."

Gael looked at the tea service and at Yolanda, water pooling at the corners of the old man's lower lids.

"Go," he said. "Come again to visit, sometime when it is safe. I will be here."

Dean hugged the man, and Briel, in a rare burst of emotion, kissed him on the cheek. When Gael rubbed his cheek, Dean read a mixture of sadness and mischief on his face. Definitely worth a return visit. This man had stories to tell.

Yolanda urged them out the door she'd entered. It led to a dimly lit common hallway outside Gael's apartment, and then to a set of rickety wooden stairs to the street level on the other side of the building.

As they exited, black shadows wove among the streetlights at the end of the road.

"That's got to be them," Briel whispered. "Yolanda, I'd never forgive myself if helping us got you in trouble."

Yolanda's smile radiated a calm intention. "You are in *our* neighbourhood, Señora Briel. We help each other here. Walk slowly and don't look back. Move as though you are old, like grandfather."

Dean hobbled with the help of his cane, and Briel took Yolanda's arm. Yolanda steered them to a small economy car parked alone in front of the local pharmacy.

Seconds later, explosions sounded behind them, followed by sounds of teenagers on a rampage.

The sky lit up with fireworks.

"Don't turn around," Yolanda said as they got into her vehicle.

Mines shot coloured stars high in the sky, in a non-stop, thunderous pyrotechnic display.

Settled in the rear seats, Dean chanced a look back. Amidst the lights and chaos, the man and woman chasing them flashed in and out of view. They were struggling to break free of the crowd.

"Tight community?" Dean asked.

"Very," Yolanda said. "And we have many young cousins. Grandfather's instincts for good versus bad have not failed us yet. You made good friends tonight."

CHAPTER 63

T *he Next Day*

PEDRO DRAGGED himself through the Conductor's mansion. Lack of sleep was catching up with him. His body ached, his head hurt, and he'd left home with too little time for coffee. Maybe Miguel's run to the airport was a good idea for them both.

In front of the heavy boardroom doors, Pedro steeled himself. He needed this meeting to go well. What he had was worthy of optimism, but was it enough?

He took a breath, gripped the door handle, and walked into the room, faintly hoping the Conductor's maid had put a coffee service somewhere he could access it. Unlikely.

And then Pedro froze.

Before him, standing casually by the window, was the Conductor, undisguised. One of Pedro's guards stood at his side, with none other than Enrique Torres. The short official twisted his handlebar moustache as though he were a character from a bad cartoon. Torres's lips curled into a sinister smile.

Pedro felt the colour rise in his cheeks and his heart pounded wildly.

The Conductor spoke first. "You once understood that 'on time' meant you were to be early. Now, you have five minutes to convince me you should not immediately be replaced."

Pedro considered his words. The Conductor couldn't possibly want him to provide confidential information so publicly, even if this was to be his last report.

"Señor. It would be best if we spoke privately. Perhaps we could step outside?"

"No, Pedro. If you have news, we all need to hear it. Here. Now. Four minutes remain."

Pedro clasped his hands together, hoping to stop his fingers from shaking, or at least to avoid anyone noticing the fear that threatened to overwhelm him.

"As you wish," he said with a slight bow. "My... contact... identified the cipher type as a Trithemius code. After significant research last night, I learned the key is a book. *Polygraphia*. With it, we will finally learn the whereabouts of the Spider Rock."

"And the location of this book?"

"Only two copies exist. One is in the United States. The other is in Tepoztlán. Quite a significant location."

"The birthplace of Quetzalcoatl," the Conductor murmured.

Pedro took the moment to glance at Torres. The man's forehead furrowed and his eyes narrowed. Confusion. Torres didn't know the significance, so Pedro pushed on.

"Indeed. I have tasked my contact with retrieving the tome from the Ex Convento Dominican Church. The appropriate 'donation' has already been made. As luck would have it, an earthquake damaged the house of the Christian God a few years ago. It needs repair. Our funds are particularly welcome. My contact leaves this morning. Everything should be settled by nightfall."

The Conductor's glare bore through Pedro. What was he searching for? Another mistake? In deference, Pedro cast his eyes at his feet.

"Shoot him," said the Conductor.

CHAPTER 64

Ricardo paced in front of the glass doors of the Secretaria de Viajes, Cultura y Turismo offices.

He'd left messages with the AFSI staff, letting them know Menendez was in the hospital after an altercation. There'd be an investigation, but for now, that was all anyone needed to know. Then he spent the night at the hospital, waiting by the head of the AFSI's bed, hoping the man would wake long enough to answer questions. Ricardo wanted—no, needed—information before facing the secretariat. Unfortunately, Menendez remained firmly unconscious, and with doctors unable to predict how his situation would progress, Ricardo left, still puzzling over who was friend and who was foe.

The secretariat had almost killed Menendez. If Ricardo hadn't arrived when he did, he might have awoken to a murder investigation. What he heard of the secretariat's shouts pertained to keeping out of Tomás's affairs. Did the affairs include Padre Hugh? Ricardo's name wasn't mentioned. Did that mean the secretariat didn't know Ricardo had leaked the friar's identity? Or were they arguing about something else entirely?

The pavement was mute to his questions. Still uncertain how to confront Tomás, Ricardo opened the door and took the stairs two at a time. Only one way forward. He needed answers. From whom? That almost didn't matter.

Ricardo stood alone in front of the long wooden table with its uncomfortable chairs. Instead of choosing a seat, he walked to the window. Hands behind his back, he surveyed his beloved Mexico City and renewed his promise to his great-great-grandfather Garza.

"Our people deserve the best, Great-great-grandpapa. I know. I'm trying."

A slam of the door brought Ricardo back to the present.

"De La Cruz. What business did you have with the head of the AFSI last night?"

That was fast. Obviously, links between the AFSI offices and those of the secretariat were closer than Ricardo had realized. How much more did Tomás know?

Before Ricardo could form words, Tomás continued.

"Menendez was taken to the hospital last night. What did you do?"

The accusation took Ricardo's breath away. His low station didn't matter. That the secretariat was a supposed ally—that didn't matter either. The words tumbled out, uncontrolled.

"How dare you? I was there last night when you and Menendez fought. I heard you. What business did you want him out of? I was there when the glass shattered, and when you ran back to your limousine. Given Menendez's state, be grateful I saved him—and I covered for you. Give me one good reason I should not shout all I know to anyone who will listen."

Tomás's face paled.

Good.

Ricardo readied himself to interview the Secretariat of Travel, Culture and Tourism. He'd threaten the man with arrest for assault or attempted murder, if necessary.

Then the door to the meeting room opened again.

Briel Payce and Dean Leggatt stepped inside. Dressed in dirt-stained ponchos and hats, they swayed, just a little, as they stood before him. Ricardo hadn't pegged the starchy Payce as the party type, and Leggatt seemed too sensible to go out on a bender so soon after being ill.

BRIEL BALLED her fists and her shoulders rose against the weight of the poncho. She and Dean had spent half the night being driven through the city streets by Yolanda and then by a cab driver friend of hers who ultimately delivered them to a van at a campsite in Chapultepec Park, where they had finally curled up for a few hours of sleep before taking public transportation to the secretariat's headquarters.

No shower; no coffee. They looked like homeless tourists coming off a pub crawl.

She was in no mood for attitude from the savvy, clean-shaven, fat-faced Tomás, or the awe-struck detective inspector who stood before them. So she went on the offensive.

"Who did you tell?" Briel demanded.

The secretariat actually had the decency to take a step back.

"What happened?" Ricardo asked, sincere concern written on his face. It was only then that Briel noticed the dark bags under the detective inspector's normally bright, big brown eyes. And he was wearing yesterday's clothes. A story worth asking about?

Dean cut her thoughts short. "One of you two big boys told someone you shouldn't have where Briel and I were staying."

"We ran for our lives last night," Briel added. "And possibly endangered the family who helped us get away."

Ricardo, at least, had the decency to seem shocked.

Decision made.

Folding her arms across her chest, she stepped within inches of the secretariat's face. Between clenched teeth, she said, "I ask again, who did you tell?"

As the secretariat tucked his chin and leaned away, the scent of expensive aftershave wafted into the void. She could only imagine what he smelled on her.

Tomás raised his left hand to his mouth, revealing a long, thin red scab. Relatively new but healing well without a bandage.

"I am so very sorry," Tomás said.

Dean didn't seem to notice the secretariat's wound.

"You said you were sorry two days ago," Dean said. "Been there. Done that. We've cooperated. Provided information. What the hell happened?"

Tomás sank into the nearest chair and rubbed his temple.

"I didn't think it would go this far," he said.

Briel raised her eyebrows. She kept her arms folded, this time to hide her shaking hands as her body once again acknowledged a lack of food.

Tomás stood up and paced.

"The AFSI," he said. "They are like your FBI. They have eyes and ears everywhere. I met with the head of that organization last night. I do not know their interest in this, nor their intentions. We should be on the same side. However, I discovered late yesterday that they orchestrated the unidentified access to Persephone Gilbert's medical file. The one that contained the note, Doctora Payce, with your name on it."

Tomás broke off and Briel turned to Dean. Behind him, Ricardo stood, pale, his square jaw slightly ajar. The involvement of the AFSI affected him somehow.

Tomás continued. "As I'm sure you understand from your experience on Iztaccihuatl, I have, and am willing, to spend resources to ensure your safety. Now that I understand the lengths to which the AFSI will go, I will be more diligent."

"Nope. That's your fight," Dean said. "It's time Briel and I went back to our own priorities. We'll take care of ourselves from here."

"How can you say that after the consequences of your first attempt to strike out on your own? What chance do you really have of finding your missing friend when both the cartels and the AFSI are against you?"

The man had a point, and even through her fury, Briel knew it.

"What do you suggest?" she asked.

"We continue working together. Your friend's note led you to a holy man. My informant suggests that the shadow group we are after may be a religious cult."

"What cult?"

"There is talk of a small group of worshippers who believe they descended from the peoples who built the pyramids at Teotihuacan. Do you know the history of the pyramids, northeast of the city?"

"No."

"The indigenous people built Teotihuacan after Popocatepetl's eruption in the first century CE. The native populations hallowed both Popocatepetl and Iztaccihuatl because rain clouds converged there. That persistent source of water was vital to their crops. The people revered the volcanoes for their role in sustaining life. Historians believe the survivors of Popocatepetl's first-century eruption moved to Teotihuacan and built the pyramids of the sun and the moon. Recognizing a need to appease the persistent rumbling of Popocatepetl in order to manage rainfall and avoid further disaster, they also built a pyramid to a god that is now called Quetzalcoatl, or the Feathered Serpent."

"That was over two thousand years ago," Dean interrupted. "How is that relevant now?"

The secretariat sighed. "Please, I am trying to explain."

He continued, "Recent research on the remains of sacrificial victims in Teotihuacan tells us they had a multiethnic background. Foreigners."

Briel tried to connect the dots. "Are you saying members of a current cult still believe they need to coax the volcano into providing life-giving water by sacrificing foreigners? That's nuts!"

"Indeed," said Tomás. "Our information is scant. However, unlikely as it is, our investigation into the relationship between money laundering and the deaths of foreign officials investigating bank fraud is leading us there."

"There's no way Percy would have involved herself in that kind of mess," Dean said.

"No? She is, or was, an archeologist. Sí? Interested in history? The pyramids? Why was she here, Doctor Leggatt?"

Dean sighed.

"Because a rock, passed down in her family, came from the same limestone quarry used to plaster walls in the Teotihuacan community."

It was Dean's turn to sit. He covered his face with his hands and added, "So you think Rangal's bad data from Popocatepetl is part of this?"

"I didn't. Until yesterday."

Briel put her hand on Dean's arm. He already felt responsible for Percy's quest taking her to Mexico City. She couldn't imagine what he was feeling now.

"Then it's the mountain we need to focus on," Briel said.

"Did your trip to the friar confirm that?" Tomás asked. Then he added, "I was sorry to hear of the tragedy."

Briel bristled at the still raw memory. "What does the friar have to do with this?"

Tomás flushed. "I know how upset you must be. But with the AFSI involved, I need information. It is the only way I have any chance of staying ahead of this. The only way I can protect you both."

Briel looked at Dean and waited. They were a team, after all. Dean returned her gaze and nodded.

She focused again on Tomás, suddenly realizing that Ricardo was still in the room, silent, having taken a corner seat. The man looked like a diminutive, lost child. Perhaps his night hadn't been any better than her own.

"Padre Hugh suggested there were symbols in what Percy studied, pointing to sacrifice. He gave me a message from Percy before he died," she said.

Briel explained the Latin verse, what information she had

about the Trithemius code and the possibility that a copy of Johannes Trithemius's 16th century book rested in Tepoztlán.

Ricardo straightened. His arrogant attitude partially restored. "We must go there."

"Why?" Tomás asked.

"Doctora Payce's friend wanted it to be so. Suthons gave his life passing that secret on. It must be important."

A gloomy silence followed and Briel looked again at Dean. He'd withdrawn. Much the same look as five years earlier. The expression that had caused her to go to Mexico alone in her initial search for Percy.

"Tepoztlán isn't far. Right?" she asked.

"About an hour and a half south of here," Ricardo said.

She needed to give Dean something productive to do, but she suspected he wouldn't be helpful to her in his current state.

"I'm going to Tepoztlán," she said to Dean. "How about you stay here and follow up on the Popocatepetl data? You promised Rangal a report, after all. Maybe there's more you can find out."

"You can't go to Tepoztlán alone," Dean mumbled.

"I'll go," Ricardo said. His cell phone binged with a message, and when he looked at it, he scowled. Turning again to Briel, he said, "I know the area. My family vacationed there when I was a child."

Tomás stepped in. "I will give what cover I can. But please, trust no one outside of this room."

CHAPTER 65

Pedro opened his hooded eyes wide in shock.

At his feet lay the body of Enrique Torres. Shot on the Conductor's command by the guard from the outpost compound. Pedro waited, shifting his weight over the old wound in his foot in order to stand at full attention. If he was to be next, he intended to take the punishment like a man.

The Conductor spoke. "Torres believed his association with the Guardia Nacional was an asset. It was not. He wanted your job, Pedro, and I considered his request. I have tolerated too many of your missteps."

A drop of perspiration found Pedro's right eye. He didn't blink, even as it stung.

"Sí. Señor," he said. Hands by his side, he stood at attention.

"You and Andre," the Conductor continued, pointing at the guard still holding a gun, "clean this up. Spotless, you understand? This is a cartel hit. Nothing more. No trouble comes here."

Pedro nodded.

"You have one last opportunity to make things right. Use it well."

As the Conductor walked from the room, he met Pedro's eyes. A rare occurrence. A slight tilt of his head and a nod toward

Andre. The signal was clear. *Kill the guard when you're done. No loose ends.*

Andre positioned himself over Torres's body. "I can carry him out," he said.

"No," Pedro said. "There is a carpet downstairs that needs to be taken for cleaning. Get it."

The guard left and Pedro stood stone still over Torres. Even if he regained the Conductor's favour, the time had come for him to leave. This. A killing at his boss's home turf was not the act of the genius who built an international money-laundering empire. It was the act of a frightened old man. A desperate man. And that was a problem.

Pedro wasn't the only one to make mistakes. The Conductor had let the Second Violin and Viola disappear without reprisal. True, they weren't ready for yet another protection protocol, and Pedro certainly couldn't accommodate two foreign banking power-brokers' bodies any other way. But the Conductor didn't even demand they stay in Mexico or send them to Argentina, where he or Pedro's contacts could monitor them.

Pedro still needed to figure out who could replace them. And when? Did the Conductor have a plan in the meantime?

And what was Torres doing here, anyway? Was it a double bluff? Yes, the man was ambitious, and he had connections with the Maldito, but which side was he really on?

And then the order to kill Andre. What kind of decision was that?

Cracks in the empire. How long before it all came toppling down? And when was the best time to escape the fall?

Pedro's foot ached. He'd been standing tall for too long. He leaned a little to the right to ease the burden.

Andre opened the door, carpet draped over one shoulder. Time to get this morning's mess cleaned up.

CHAPTER 66

Ricardo paid the toll to get on the 95D, hoping to make up lost time after driving Briel and Dean back to their hotel so they could shower and change.

There was no trace left of the break-in, and the assailants had worn gloves, so he didn't even try getting a forensics team to the scene.

Before Dean took the rental back to the secretariat's offices, he vowed to Briel that he'd get to the bottom of the mountain's association with their missing friend.

After that, Briel plopped herself into the passenger seat of Ricardo's vehicle and turned her head away to look out the window. They'd been travelling for close to half an hour and Briel hadn't uttered a word.

"Still thinking about last night?" Ricardo asked.

"Hm?" Briel turned toward him.

"Last night," Ricardo said. "It couldn't have been easy."

"No."

Briel's hands were in her lap. She squeezed her entwined fingers so tight, the tips turned red.

"You don't need to do this, you know," Ricardo said.

"Do what?"

"Stay in Mexico. If you're uncomfortable. Worried. I can drive you to the airport. No questions asked. The secretariat would understand."

Briel's words shot back at him with the staccato of rapid-fire darts.

"I am not leaving Mexico without finishing this. I don't care what your secretariat thinks or does. Someone, or someones, threatened my life last night—again. What I don't understand is why anyone actually lives here. It seems to me this country is riddled with corruption and violence."

Briel's face whipped back to the window, but not before her angry, reddening eyes found him.

Ricardo sank back in the driver's seat. When his response came, it was almost a whisper.

"You entered this country in search of someone close to you. I appreciate that. However, you chose, and still choose, to follow her path into some kind of criminal underworld. Do not blame my homeland for the dangers you face because of those actions."

"You deny Mexico's reputation for violence and corruption?"

"To the same extent you support the country you come from where corruption, sometimes at the highest levels, receives media attention daily. Where accusations of unwarranted police violence make the headlines and where the bodies of young people either caught up in gang wars or bystanders of such violence also pile up."

"It's different."

"No. It is not. The vast majority of people everywhere simply want to live their lives. Earn a decent living. Raise families as best they can. Life for some does not work that way, and what leads to a dangerous path can be complex. A world quick to judge rarely bothers to appreciate that."

The fingers in Briel's lap released and she stretched them as though finally aware of the pain she'd been holding onto.

"Sorry," she said. "During this trip, and in my last visit to Mexico, I've judged and been judged. The threats to my life and to Dean's haven't helped. And Padre Hugh's death was unconscionable. But, along with the bad, I've met good people. Without you and them…"

"You're welcome."

Another silence ensued. Ricardo allowed it to stretch until he was uncomfortable. He and this woman needed to form a team if they were going to come out of this unscathed. Though unschooled, Briel had skills, and if their quest, so far, was any indication, they were likely to need them. So, he tried again.

"The last time I went to the magical town of Tepoztlán, I was just a child."

"Magical town?"

"Yes. Pueblo Mágicos. A government program recognizing towns and villages across the country that offer unique cultural experiences and/or that are historically significant. There are over a hundred such places, and the designation is an honour for the citizens who live there."

"Do you remember much of this Pueblo Mágicos?"

"Sí. It is a vacation destination for many who live here. Few tourists discover it, but those who do are in for a treat."

"Then you know the Ex Convento Dominico de la Natividad? Where the book is?"

"I remember only a little. There are several churches of note there. The Ex Convento buildings, if I recall correctly, are imposing structures."

"Do you think they'll let us see the *Polygraphia*?"

Ricardo turned sharply onto the 115D, following the signs to the town he knew to be nestled in the shadow of the Tepozteco Mountain. The butterflies in his stomach should have spoken to the excitement of childhood memories. Instead, he feared they heralded something darker on the horizon. His mind shifted to Menendez. The lean, arrogant head of the AFSI, who still lay unconscious in the hospital.

"I don't know," he said.

The cell phone message he had received in the secretariat's office was from the hospital. Doctors were keeping Menendez in a drug-induced coma, waiting for the effects of trauma to calm enough to bring him around. There was unfinished business there.

CHAPTER 67

Dean sat alone, eyeing a sunbeam streaking across the boardroom table. Tomás had excused himself, saying he needed to meet the Secretaría de Estabilidad Ambiental, Donata Rangal, and escort her to the room. Dean hoped they never came back. Despite his promise to Briel, if he could have disappeared, to become nothing, he'd have done it. After all, he was nothing. Of what use was he to this world if he was stupid enough to let his girlfriend go alone to Mexico? If he'd gone with her. If he'd said no to the project his boss in the United States had said was so important that he couldn't leave five years ago. If... If...

His therapist had warned him about this kind of thinking. Told him the trip to Mexico might trigger a relapse. And here it was. She'd asked him if he'd really internalized the tools necessary to cope. Had he?

A loud bang as the door slammed into its stopper made Dean jump. Donata entered the room, followed by Tomás.

"But this is serious," Donata said to Tomás. "Surely we need to inform the Minister of the Interior."

"Let us meet with Doctor Leggatt first. We have only supposition. To do more, we need more."

With effort, Dean raised his head. 'Do. Find purpose. Be part of the solution.' The mantras that kept him alive during crises. The mantras that had pulled him from his stupor the last time he had reached this low. Dean shook his head and made for the sideboard, drawn by the smell of fresh coffee and pastries. When did breakfast arrive? Was he that far gone that he hadn't noticed?

He took a solid swig of the hot black brew and winced as the burn to his mouth and throat ignited an adrenaline push, kick-starting his return to the present.

Donata stared at him. "You look pale. Exhausted. Are you ill again?"

"Didn't the Secretariat of Travel, Culture and Tourism tell you of our little adventure last night?"

Donata looked at Tomás, who bent his head. "It was a troublesome business. But that is what we are here to deal with. Sí?"

"Sí," Dean said. He hadn't intended the sneer that came with his reply. Once it was out, he didn't regret it. He flipped the single board computer he'd confiscated from the monitoring station onto the table.

"This device. It is tiny," Donata said as she picked it up for closer examination.

"Small," Dean said, "and effective. The brains for a remote-controlled, sound vibration intrusion to a seismic box."

"To what end?" Donata asked.

"Good question. By itself, it means nothing. After all, data corruption from a single station can happen for many reasons, and whatever the problem, it's easily fixed. Such readings would never escalate the population alarm level; not without proper corroboration."

Donata returned her attention to Tomás. "And you believe this has something to do with some kind of cult?" Her voice was tinged with skepticism.

"I have no proof," Tomás said. "But it explains why someone would employ such a sabotage. From what Señor Leggatt has told us, the setup he found can generate information to be brought forward at will. The resultant data look official, while the implications of the readings remain under strict control."

"Could it be a prank?" she asked. "Is the timing related to foreign deaths simply a coincidence?"

"Of what value would this data be to a prankster?" Tomás said.

"Who else knows of this apparatus?" Donata directed the question to Dean.

"My contact at the Departamento Regional de Monitoreo de Desastres Naturales told me he'd been sworn to secrecy by the person who worked there before him, and some stranger he was afraid of. He said no one else that he works with had any idea."

"And you believe him?" Tomás asked.

"We just met. He was nervous. Upset. I think he told me the truth, but I don't know if he told me everything."

"With this device now removed, and your contact aware that we know of the false recordings, what is the risk?" Donata's political hat surfaced.

"Depends. It's a simple thing to mess with the instruments," Dean said.

"Then," Tomás interrupted, "with your permission, Secretariat Rangal, I would like Doctor Leggatt to continue with his fine investigation. If it bears fruit, we can both report the problem to our higher authorities. I can have someone look into who worked at the departamento before Doctor Leggatt's contact."

He broke into a wide, patronizing smile. Donata blinked back at him, stone-faced.

Finally, she spoke. "You will keep me informed?"

"Of course," Tomás said.

Donata huffed but eventually nodded. When she'd left, Tomás turned back to Dean.

"We need more. A link. A trail. Something that tells us not only how, but why the data were purposely corrupted. I need names. Will going back do any good?"

"Maybe. Alejandro is afraid. And there's something about his girlfriend. Something about how they came to be a couple."

"Then go. Please. Find out what you can."

Something positive to do. A way forward. For Percy. Dean stood and straightened to his full height.

"And Doctor Leggatt," Tomás said as he exited the room, "I've arranged a gun for you. You can pick it up from my assistant on your way out. After last night, I suggest you accept my gift and take it with you."

CHAPTER 68

Despite what Briel knew to be Ricardo's best effort at conversation, the drive to Tepoztlán was quiet. She wasn't in the mood; didn't see the value of being sociable.

The man was right, of course. If she'd been a proper tourist in Mexico City, her experience with its generous people would have been different. And even with the challenges of this trip, citizens like Gael and Yolanda had put themselves in danger to help her. The problem, as always, was figuring out how to distinguish who was who when everyone wore their sincerest faces.

Tomás was a case in point. His puffy eyes, round face and slightly crooked nose made him look like a mob boss. Yet he'd saved her life, and unlike her first search for Percy, this Secretariat of Travel, Culture and Tourism seemed interested. Almost too much. A shiver travelled down her spine. Her concerns coincided with a problem he had. Was his help Machiavellian? Perhaps.

Ricardo was another matter. Those big brown eyes. Little boy looks on a middle-aged man. It was hard to take him seriously. But he'd dealt with the attack and then murder of the friar like the pro he was supposed to be. He seemed the sincerest of all, or was he just a talented actor? She didn't doubt that he loved his country, but every once in a while, she caught sadness in those eyes. What was his story?

She pushed doubt aside. The man was her partner for the day, and they were headed to Quetzalcoatl's birthplace. That it all kept coming back to the Feathered Serpent God couldn't be a coincidence. Neither Percy nor Briel believed in those.

And Ricardo had a gun.

Ricardo turned at the exit marked Tepoztlán, and wound his way to a street labelled Avenida 5 de Mayo.

The scene before them stole Briel's breath. Quaint shops and cafés bordered a cobblestone street, nestled in the valley of the jagged Tepozteco mountain.

When she finally let out a gasp, Ricardo said, "Yes. Though I've seen it before, this view still touches me."

He turned onto a side road and parked his car in front of a closed governmental office.

"The secretariat arranged for us to use the spot," he explained.

As Briel exited the air-conditioned vehicle, the scorching sun bit at her bare arms.

"Sunscreen," she said. "We need to get some before we go too far."

"Glove compartment."

"Boy Scout."

"Excuse me?"

"Nothing," Briel said, rubbing SPF 50 over her bare skin.

Ricardo led them to an open-air market filled with vendors selling crafts, clothes, and kitchen wares, everything shaded by colourful canopies. The smell of fresh cooking, tacos, salsa, cheese and meat made her stomach growl.

No time. At least, not yet.

Ricardo marched through the crush as though he owned the place, but Briel had a harder time navigating her way around the throng of buyers and sellers, and she almost lost Ricardo, twice.

Midway through the market stalls, they spilled onto empty pavement. Briel's mouth fell open as she faced an intricately designed gateway. She bent her head back, searching for the top of the arch, where the artist had written "Ce Acatl Topiltzin". Above that was a figure that seemed to emanate directly from a pre-Hispanic codex. Then she moved closer to a side wall; to the image of an indigenous woman lying by an enormous agave plant, and a young man, seated on the ground nearby, knees drawn, hand covering his eyes, possibly in mourning. That's when she realized it was a mosaic, created entirely from dried seeds and beans in the widest range of colours she'd ever seen.

Ricardo stopped. With a broad smile, he acknowledged an old man sitting nearby on a folding chair. They spoke quietly for a few moments, and then Ricardo handed over a few pesos.

"A contribution for next year," he said. "Welcome to the Portada de Semillas, Briel. It has been a long time for me. This year's mural is spectacular. Yes? Our friend in the chair there tells me that Ce Acatl Topiltzin was actually Ce Acatl Topiltzin Quetzalcoatl. The son of a prominent king during the time of Teotihuacan. The prince was a religious renegade who advocated to use his own blood, or that of animals, in place of the human sacrifices to Quetzalcoatl that were usually demanded. His views were unpopular, and he may have been sent into exile. Possibly establishing a community at Chichen Itza."

Hands on his hips, Ricardo took in the sight. Then he added, "The Tepoztecan artisans have outdone themselves."

"Portal of Seeds," Briel translated. "Amazing."

She drew her fingers close to the wall, but not to where they would touch.

"The vendors organize and finance the creation of the Portada each year. It is a communal effort. Tens of thousands of seeds are glued, one by one, onto a plywood backing. Even the children help. The beautiful colours are all natural to the seed types. The designs always communicate Tepoztlán's culture and values."

There was a sheen to the surface, and when she questioned it, Ricardo explained that artisans coated the mural with varnish to prevent birds from eating their creation.

"Amazing," she said.

"Yes. And it leads to the Church of Our Lady of the Nativity. Where Trithemius's book awaits. Shall we?"

MIGUEL PARKED his rental in one of the paid lots on a side road from the main drag in Tepoztlán. He probably could have trusted the care of his luxury sedan to the attendants here, but he hoped to make this trip quick and quiet. No unnecessary attention.

Stepping from the nondescript four-door, he gazed at the beautiful mountainscape. The shadows outlining Tepozteco's jagged profile were striking today.

During his hiking days, Miguel had spent a lot of time here. A quick trip from Mexico City, the natural trails soothed his wounded soul while he endeavoured to protect his heart from the realities of being an intern in modern medicine.

He looked longingly to the east, wishing there was time for a day of pleasure. Droves of tourists invaded the Aztec ruins of Tepoztecatl, the Aztec god of pulque, these days, but the trail to the sacred pond, the birthplace of Quetzalcoatl, was rarely travelled. Brochures mistakenly billeted Tepoztlán as the site of the Feathered Serpent God's origin. In fact, the start of the trail was about a twenty-minute ride away in the ancient town of Amatlán. He always felt reenergized after visiting those hallowed waters, as though something spiritually significant remained. Others must have felt the same. The last time he was there, cut flowers lay strewn over the surrounding boulders.

Miguel shook off the call of the trails and headed through the market to the Portal of Seeds. The sooner he was done with this, the better. Briel's friend Percy had been a cloud over his head from the day he found out she existed. Once this puzzle was solved, he could leave his life in Mexico behind. And leave it he would. This time, with no regret.

As he entered the grounds to the Ex Convento Dominico de

La Navidad, he stopped short. The Cathedral, the magnificent 16th century church built by the hands of Mexico's indigenous peoples under the instruction of Dominican friars, was surrounded by a makeshift metal construction fence, a large red sign proclaiming "Danger: No Admittance".

What did that mean for Johannes Trithemius's text?

"Excuse me," Miguel said to a woman toting a small child through the grounds. He repositioned his prescription sunglasses on his nose. "I came from far away to see the church. Are we not allowed inside?"

"Sorry," the lady answered. "I hoped to go in there, too. The earthquake, 2017. It damaged the building. I thought it would be fixed by now, but progress has been slow. Of course, Tepoztlán is blessed with many churches. We are on our way to another one, just up the street. I can show you?"

"No," Miguel said, "But thank you. I will look at what I can while I am here."

The woman and child left the grounds, and he headed for the construction fence. He was halfway there when he saw a worker walk out of the building. The man pulled at a loose metal panel, swung it open and walked into the yard, settling under a tree, before unwrapping a package of cigarettes.

Yes. He could break in. Miguel looked down at his pressed white shirt and tailored black pants. Church garb. Not appropriate for burglary.

A hoodie and jeans. If a vendor asked why he was changing clothes, he'd tell them he'd come for the sights but decided on a hike up to El Tepozteco.

Miguel headed back to the market.

CHAPTER 69

Ricardo shouldn't have been shocked when Briel looked for a way through the fencing that surrounded the church. Every background search of this woman, and he had done several, suggested she was straight-laced, rule-following and safety conscious. If that was true, he had yet to see it. Was it desperation? Frustration? Perhaps. Her life had been threatened more than once. If he were in her shoes? Yes, he'd probably do the same, but most people wouldn't. Most people would run.

So, he stood and waited for her energy to dissipate and readied himself to step in if she actually found an opening. Though an earthquake had damaged the grand old building in the 1980s, it was the event in 2017 that was significant enough to prevent the public's entry to the church on this day. It was a setback, to be sure, but it hardly warranted breaking and entering.

It took only a few extra minutes to determine that the monastery portion of the complex and its museum were open. Surely the curator would have the information they needed. They might even gain official access to the church.

Briel kicked a fence post, wove her fingers through the metal grid holes and shook the barrier. Hard. Now she was creating a spectacle. Mindful of her state, Ricardo touched her arm.

"Briel," Ricardo said. "Briel. Stop."

He thought she would push away. Instead, he was met by tears streaming down her cheeks. That sadness was an emotion he understood. With his wife's death and Lilly's medical needs, he'd hit that wall many, many times.

He took a chance and embraced her. At first, she seemed to pull back, but as he thought to move away, concerned he'd overstepped, she leaned into his chest and wept. He lowered his head and allowed himself to sink into his own unhappiness. Two troubled people looking for something the world was unlikely to provide.

And as quickly as the moment came, it was gone. As though by mutual agreement, they each stepped back.

"Sorry," Briel said. Her running shoes scraped the ground.

"We're humans. We do best when we support each other."

"It's your job."

"Yes. But I am human too."

Briel fell silent, so Ricardo finally added, "I have an idea."

THEY MADE their way through the external archways of the historic monastery. The walls were richly decorated with red paint, intricate scrolls, decorative lines, and the faces of kings. The domed ceiling sported geometric shapes that seemed tattooed on the plaster. In some places, green vines with red flowers wound their way toward the ceiling, acting like crown molding.

A short woman with a slight build and grey hair greeted them at a podium in front of the museum entrance. The triple-wide, black leather wrist cuffs studded with skulls suggested more to this sixty-something-year-old female than met the eye.

"Can I help you?" she asked. Her voice was deep. The rasping sound of a long-time smoker.

Briel opened her mouth to answer but Ricardo stepped forward. The last thing he needed was Briel's conservative naïvete to prevent them from getting what they were after.

He flashed his badge.

"We are here on assignment from the Secretariat of Travel, Culture and Tourism. The church holds a book we have been asked to retrieve. Please have someone escort us inside."

The woman pursed her lips. Her eyes flicked to one side. "I am sorry you have come all this way. Our church is closed for repairs, as you can see. No one is allowed. It is too dangerous."

"Workers and engineers are already there. It will not take long. We simply need a book you house."

"What book?"

"Johannes Trithemius, *Polygraphia*."

The curator's lips thinned even more. When she spoke, the words came out with a hiss. "Trithemius was a magician, unworthy of this house of God. Nothing from the occult is here. Try the shops in town."

Briel pushed Ricardo out of the way. Attitude fully restored.

"Trithemius was an abbott of the St. James's Abbey, the Schottenkloster in Würzburg, until the day he died. The occult was commonly studied by many in the church during that era, all hoping to reach God while on this earth. That's history, not blasphemy. And we traced the book here."

Ricardo lifted a brow. Doctora Payce, Briel, had done her homework. He turned back to the curator, who reiterated that what they were looking for didn't exist in the church.

"You understand," Ricardo said, "that denying a request from the Secretariat of Travel, Culture and Tourism, and denying that Tepoztlán holds such a precious treasure, puts Tepoztlán's status as a Magical Town at risk."

The curator clicked her tongue, and Ricardo thought he might have reached the woman.

Then she met his eyes.

"Our resistance to outside pressure resulted in us losing that designation once before. We no longer fear it. If this is so important to the secretariat, why haven't I heard from him personally?"

Ricardo pulled the phone from his pocket, thumbed through

his contacts and read out the secretariat's number. "Please, call him yourself."

The curator stood motionless, eyes narrowed. Finally, slowly, she removed a cell phone from inside her podium.

As EXPECTED, Miguel needed to explain to the nosy woman who sold him the hoodie and jeans on such a hot day that he planned to go up Tepozteco because the church he'd originally hoped to visit was damaged. Of course, she waited until the sale was complete to let him know that the friar's quarters and the museum were open. Smart lady.

Miguel got changed, but rather than break in to the church proper, he decided it was worth speaking to the museum's curator first. If a woman was at the helm? Well, he could sweet talk his way in and out of most situations where ladies were concerned. Worth checking, regardless.

He padded through the decorated but empty passageways of the old monastery and stopped only steps away from the museum's entrance. His new fleece top, already damp from body heat, stuck to the back of his neck. Given that illegal entry to the church might not be necessary, he thought about taking it off.

Raised voices ahead of him made him stop. It couldn't be. Miguel tucked himself behind the nearest pillar. A poor hiding place, but at least the side of the arch obscured his presence from anyone already in the museum.

"You understand that denying a request from the Secretariat of Travel, Culture and Tourism, and denying that Tepoztlán holds such a precious treasure, puts Tepoztlán's status as a Magical Town at risk."

Detective Inspector De La Cruz? How?

Miguel chanced a peek from beyond the post that sheltered him just as Briel Payce repositioned herself in front of a displeased older woman at the podium that guarded the museum's entrance.

Was he too late?

Despite the suffocating temperatures, Miguel pulled his hood up. The curator's reply was muffled. Had she folded? He inched closer, hoping to hear more.

Without warning, his foot slid forward and he slapped his other shoe down to avoid falling into the streak of fresh bird guano that caused his misstep.

"Agh," spilled from his mouth as he dove back into his hiding place.

ONLY THE SOUND of grackles arguing loudly among the crape myrtles in the courtyard filled the silence as the curator pecked at numbers on the telephone's keypad.

Then there was something else. A scraping sound? A scuffle? Briel turned, expecting to find another patron or two behind them, waiting impatiently for her and Ricardo to move along. Instead, she caught a flash of jeans and a grey hoodie as someone tall, with a slight build, scampered through the arches and around the corner that led to the stairs.

Briel would have assumed it was a teenager out for mischief, except it was broad daylight and this place was hardly a worthy target.

And the shoes. Not runners. She'd only caught a glimpse. They were... out of place. Shiny brown wingtip loafers. The expensive kind. Definitely not a teenager.

Briel drew a finger to her lips as Ricardo cocked his head and narrowed his eyes. He'd heard it too. They didn't move. Their priority was the curator, and the woman didn't seem to care the least about the intrusion.

Instead, she hung up her call with Tomás's office.

"Fresa," the curator mumbled.

There were few slang expressions Briel knew in Spanish, but this one she'd heard before, long ago in the aftermath of an altercation she had witnessed between Miguel Lobo and an assistant. "Stuck up" the woman had called Miguel after he left the room. True, Briel thought. Mostly she considered Miguel's arrogance either a minor annoyance or vaguely humorous. Of course, she was at least on par with him professionally, and with her reputation as the ice queen, Briel wasn't one to cast stones.

The curator's upper lip twisted into a snarl that aged her well beyond the tough woman look her wristbands suggested. She finally returned her attention to the detective.

"The church elders moved some items. Artifacts, including books, were sent to our library for safekeeping. There is nothing here. Go."

Ricardo blinked. As his mouth opened, Briel pulled at his arm. The curator was a lost cause and they had a new lead. And there was something about the visitor in the hoodie. Those shoes. The kind favoured by Miguel Lobo.

Surely not here.

Miguel bounded from the Ex Convento, skidding around the corner and then stopping short at the realization that he'd landed back on the expansive public lawns in front of the church. Families with small children and old men and women milled about, appreciating the peace of the greenspace beyond the gates of the bustling open-air market.

He needed to calm down. To walk. He already looked suspicious in the hoodie, and after that run, he wanted nothing more than to rip the stifling fabric away. Could he?

No one was behind him. At least not yet.

Had Briel seen him?

How was it possible that she beat him here? And with the detective, no less.

Did they find the book? He needed to know.

His condensation-soaked sunglasses skittered down his perspiration-drenched nose, and he used the sleeve of his fleece to clean the lenses. The action left disgusting streaks, but he had nothing else. Then he wicked away the moisture on his face. He hated such plebeian actions. When this was over, he'd take a hot, soapy shower, clean his glasses with the proper solution, and wipe them down with his microfiber towel. And he'd throw away this awful sweatshirt.

Miguel checked behind him and spotted Briel and the detective leaving the museum building. Across the grounds, a large tent sheltered rows of pews. A temporary home for the broken church's faithful. For a split second, Miguel wondered if the earthquake's damage was a message. This was Quetzalcoatl's territory, after all.

No matter. The makeshift structure substituting for the church was his only option, and he sprinted toward it.

"Miguel?" Briel called from behind him.

He picked up his pace, not daring to look back. In a few swift steps, his long legs traversed the central aisle under the canopy. Without a pause, he passed through the sanctuary and back into the open air.

Several large trees lined the edge, and he chose the biggest to hide behind.

Within seconds, Briel called again. This time from the narthex under the tent. Too close for comfort.

"Miguel? Are you there?"

The detective's voice came next. "You believe that was Doctor Lobo?"

Miguel peeked from his hiding spot. Briel's shoulders dropped as she scanned the empty pews.

"The shoes," she said. "They reminded me of Miguel. And that man was the right height and build."

Briel tapped her fingers on the wooden edge of the nearest seat. A signature move when she was thinking, Miguel remembered. The ice queen was still an easy read.

The detective inspector walked up and down the nave, peering from side to side. "No one here," he said. "The shoes. That build. The description could fit anyone."

Briel took her time to reply.

"You're probably right," she said. "Let's go."

"Just so you know," Ricardo said as they turned around, "I had my assistant do a background check on the good doctor, as well as the groundskeeper at the friar's church."

"Why check on Miguel?" Briel asked.

"Just being thorough."

"What did you find?"

"As I'm sure you expected, Lobo was clean. The gardener? He doesn't exist. A dead end."

Miguel's heart raced at discovering that the detective inspector had searched his records. Thanks be to God that he had the foresight to keep a low profile where the law was concerned. And his plant, the groundskeeper? Good thing he'd insisted on the fake name.

He watched Briel and De La Cruz leave. Their hands were empty. No book.

He crept forward, waiting till they exited through the Portal of Seeds, and then Miguel headed back to the museum.

THE CURATOR STOOD at the entrance. Arms folded, a scowl on her face.

Miguel felt the gun in his waistband, moist with the sweat that dampened his body. He worried that if he needed to use the weapon, his fingers would slip.

It was a compact model from the 1980s. Not a big boy, and certainly not automatic, but it could do the job. His uncle Pedro had given it to him soon after Miguel's father died. Pedro had taken him into the desert, and they had spent many happy hours in target practice. Miguel idolized his uncle back then. The man had stepped up during a time Miguel was truly lost. No telling what would have happened to him without Pedro. Certainly not a career in medicine. Without his uncle's support, emotional and financial, he might not even have finished high school. What happened to that bond?

Two visitors exited the museum and the curator wished them a good day. Then the woman's head turned toward where he was hiding. He ducked farther into the corner, uncertain of his next move.

"You can come out now," the curator said. "Perhaps it is time we met?"

CHAPTER 70

Pedro headed west on the highway, summoned back to the Conductor's home compound. Second time in a single day. Not a good sign.

He and Andre had discarded Torres's body in the dump northwest of the city. The man's colleagues, Maldito, and police, would find him there—eventually.

Killing Andre was another matter. He was a fellow soldier. Not high in rank, but faithful. Pedro was tempted to let him go, to tell him to run. In the end, he obeyed the Conductor's order, like he had a million times before. While Andre looked over the edge of the thirty-foot drop that bordered the city's disposal centre, and surveyed Torres's corpse lying in a heap on top of the trash, Pedro shot him from behind. The bullet entered the back of the guard's head, the exit wound obliterating the top half of his face. Andre crumbled and Pedro had only an instant to pull the man's body back to avoid him falling into the pit beside Torres.

Recruited only for the Conductor, an investigation into Andre's murder would lead back to his boss. Pedro knew his job, even if the Conductor no longer had faith. So he used the Conductor's carpet a second time and dragged Andre's body to his car, drove the guard to the mass grave in the hills reserved for the Conductor's local hits, and buried him there. The mamas of Mexico's fallen boys relentlessly looked for such sites, desperate to find the remains of their loved ones. They hadn't found this grave pit. At least not yet.

The carpet was a bloody mess. It needed to be burned, so he stashed it in a storage unit kept for this kind of problem, and then called a cartel lord to have his men take care of it. Another fire in a coca field deep in the hills where no one would care.

He was exhausted. Pedro went home to shower and change, and then came the Conductor's summons. It gut punched him.

Pedro wanted to turn the car around. Head to the airport. Just like Miguel.

Of course, the outcome would be the same. Pedro could be headed to his death no matter what he chose.

IN ANOTHER STRANGE MOVE, the Conductor stood alone on his threshold, waiting for Pedro. Did he intend to hold their meeting outside in the front garden? True, towering stone walls surrounded the estate, and only a single gate allowed entry and exit. But Pedro knew how vulnerable the Conductor felt outside his sanctuary.

He'd seen the Conductor stumble occasionally, watched as pain spread across the Conductor's face when his disobedient fingers were forced to dart from one micro-movement to the next. The minor physical challenges that had disrupted the Conductor's early musical career were becoming more obvious. More problematic.

And nothing really prevented Pedro from pulling a gun on the Conductor, right here, right now, except, of course, whoever might be inside, watching.

Was that why they were walking the grounds?

Acting as though nothing had changed between them, the Conductor said, "There is a recent development that requires your attention. At the Departamento Regional de Monitoreo de Desastres Naturales."

"What is the problem?" Pedro asked.

"First, tell me how things went this morning."

Despite the years of practice, Pedro could not hide a shudder born from concern for what he'd done to Andre, and fear of what had become an unpredictable relationship with his boss.

The creases around the Conductor's eyes betrayed a smothered smile. The older man knew he'd gotten to his lieutenant.

"Torres will be found in the trash where he belongs. As he was loyal to no one, each of his affiliations will point fingers at the other. Nothing will come here. Andre's body is in the hills. Just another local cartel hit. The carpet is being burned as we speak."

"Pity about that. I liked the colours."

"And now?"

"The man our Strings approved a new protection protocol for removed the device from our monitoring station yesterday. Is there enough data to still carry that out?"

"There should be. I will need to check with Alejandro."

"Do that. And then remove him. He's become... a liability."

Had Pedro heard right? Another death. And Alejandro? The Conductor knew the scientist was Dorothea's lover. They'd been discrete, but Pedro had eyes stationed in many places. He had told the Conductor about their relationship over a year ago. Dorothea seemed enamoured with the man. Was the Conductor truly willing to isolate his daughter—again?

Pedro squinted as they turned, and the sun assaulted his face. A sideways glance at the Conductor's wrinkled forehead and stoic frown told him their meeting was over. No questions.

So Pedro left without a word.

CHAPTER 71

Briel and Ricardo rounded the corner back onto Tepoztlán's main drag and headed north toward Tepozteco. Nestled among the shops lining the east side of the street stood an unassuming building, the bottom half of its front façade painted a rust colour. A simple wrought iron fence bordered a miniature green space that led to the main door. Above the entrance, it read: Biblioteca Publica. The Public Library.

Inside, small rooms were filled with children crafting with coloured paper, glue, streamers, and sequins. Adults wandered through the tables, doing their best to instruct little fingers in their task.

Big or small, public or specialized, libraries were Briel's domain. Years of working in research taught her never to discount the wisdom of the ages, and much of that lesser-known wisdom was found in tomes that had not yet found digital footing.

She headed for the reference clerk. The woman looked to be in her mid-twenties, with long, straight black hair. Pudgy arms extended from her multicoloured blouse as she thumbed through a stack of papers on her desk. The eyeglass chain holding reading glasses to her chest made her seem matronly, and Briel wondered if that was something she intended. Much like a young adult male growing a beard to mask his youth.

Briel approached the desk.

"Can I help you?" the woman asked without looking up. The nameplate pinned to the wall behind her read Anita Rosas.

"We're looking for a book. It's among the artifacts the library is storing for the Ex Convento church while it's being repaired."

The young lady pulled her chin back and straightened in her seat. "We have nothing from Ex Convento. Who told you such a thing?"

"The curator of the museum."

"The curator is misinformed."

And Anita returned to the paperwork on her desk, evidently considering the matter dismissed.

Ricardo stepped in front of Briel.

"You have a lovely building here, Señora Rosas."

He flashed a toothy smile, cocked his head and blinked his dark, long lashes at the librarian. She raised her eyes toward his but did not look impressed.

"Only," Ricardo continued, "we have come such a long way. You do not have what we want, but if you could give us a tour of the facilities, perhaps our trip will not be in vain."

Not bad, Briel thought. Identify the storage areas and come back later to check them out.

Anita smacked her papers down, then shuffled them to realign the corners. She pressed a buzzer, huffed and stood.

"Come with me."

"I don't think she believed you," Briel whispered to Ricardo.

"No," Ricardo agreed. "But she knows her duty."

They caught up with Anita as she entered a main stairwell near the front doors, where a tall, sleek woman sporting shoulder-length dark brown hair, gentle curls perfectly placed, stood to greet them. Not a strand moved when the tall woman turned her head, and she wore her three-inch stilettos like a pro. Briel felt a little envy at that.

"I'm Fe Estrada." The older woman reached out her hand, and

they each shook it. "I'm the head librarian here. How can I help you?"

"We're looking for a book among the artifacts left here by the church for safekeeping," Briel said.

"We asked for a tour so that our time coming here might at least allow us to see your other fine collections," Ricardo added.

Fe Estrada twirled the cross that hung from a gold chain around her neck.

"Anita," she said, "you should get back to your post. Other patrons may need your services."

Anita blew out another disdainful breath and left.

"I will help you with your tour," Fe said. "Come with me."

They followed her up the stairs and past a set of glass doors leading to her office.

As Fe motioned for them to take a seat, the screech of something hard scraping across concrete sounded above them. That was followed by the clack and bang of a heavy object being dropped.

When they looked up, Fe explained.

"Please excuse the noise. I found out only this morning that our board organized roof repairs. Now, please, tell me about this book."

Briel opened her mouth to explain the history of the Trithemius manuscript and its travel to Tepoztlán, but the shrill blast of a fire alarm echoing through the library's loud speakers cut her words short.

CHAPTER 72

Dean Leggatt glanced at the passenger seat and the gun Tomás had handed him for protection. Unlikely he'd need it. He stuck the thing into the glove compartment before stopping at the security gate for the Departamento Regional de Monitoreo de Desastres Naturales. He hated guns. Even in the war-torn environments he'd encountered on aid missions, he'd managed without them, based on what he liked to think of as charm and good looks. More likely, the locals considered him useful, understanding that his efforts to save victims were unaffected by political persuasion.

Alejandro was no threat. Just a scared man looking for a way out. Today he'd dig deeper into this pregnant girlfriend issue, hoping the woman held the key to the volcano, the cult, and ultimately to Percy.

Once in the centre, Dean stopped at the front desk.

"I'm looking for Alejandro," he said to a receptionist. "He may be expecting me."

The woman disappeared into the back, returning a few moments later with a stack of files she dumped into her in tray.

"He's out," she said. "I'm told he's taking long-range photos of the volcano from one of our fields."

"Uhm. Thank you."

With no forthcoming details, Dean walked back to the parking lot and checked the posted map of the area. Only one field pointed toward Popocatepetl. Mature trees lined the path to where Alejandro was probably working, and it was a nice day for a walk. So he hopped the curb, ready to get answers.

Dean turned at the sound of another car approaching the visitor lot. From the shadows of a large oak, he watched as a man in a suit got out of a black SUV. Dean was about to move back to the path, assuming the guest was there for some kind of official meeting.

That's when he saw the newcomer adjust his side arm.

Dean waited for him to go into the building. Then he crept back to his car and retrieved the gun from the glove box.

As the Conductor's first lieutenant, Pedro had spent the last two decades believing he was the pulse of the older man's Orchestra. In the know—about everything. The last few days told a different story. The Conductor, a mastermind in moving money, a political powerhouse who owned much of the federal government, and a recluse, needed Pedro's arms and legs to carry out his plans. Yet Pedro knew little to nothing of the information system that underpinned the business. Case in point was the Conductor's sudden awareness that not only would he find Alejandro at the Departamento Regional de Monitoreo de Desastres Naturales, but Dean Leggatt as well.

The Conductor's call came right after he'd sent one of his best people to go after Alejandro. Now he was on his way to the centre too, another of the hired help with him. Taking both Dean and Alejandro down and getting it right was going to take some finesse. One needed to be captured, and one needed to be killed. And they both needed to disappear without a trace.

He rounded the corner into the centre's parking lot and found his man waiting.

"Target is on the grounds, reportedly taking distance photos of the mountain," he said.

"We have a second target," Pedro said. "We need this one alive. No telling where he is, but his name is Dean Leggatt, and he may also be searching for Alejandro. Here's a picture."

Then Pedro spread a map of the grounds on the hood of his car and pointed to the property's three green spaces.

"We will spread out. You two take the east side. One field each. I will take the west. My search will begin here." He pointed to the field closest to the entrance.

Pedro handed each of them a walkie-talkie. "Channel 13," he said. "Call when you find them. Either of them. Don't go in alone. This has to be done right."

When the men left, Pedro turned to the trailhead he'd assigned himself. His mumble fell quietly onto the dusty trail.

"I'm coming to get you, Dean Leggatt."

Alejandro stood fifty meters away, leaning over a fancy-looking camera perched atop a tripod. A perfect sitting duck in what was surely the most remote field on the grounds.

Standing at the mouth of the path, Dean had to wonder who had assigned Alejandro this task today, and why. There had to be a million photos of the famous Popocatepetl. Why would they send a volcanologist to take one more—and from what, a hundred kilometres away? Then again, when they were on the lower side of the mountain yesterday, Alejandro had said that given the distance, pollution, and weather, it was a rare and beautiful thing when Popocatepetl could be seen from the city. Perhaps this morning had presented an unusual opportunity.

Something crunched in the woods behind Dean. Javelina? No. The thump, thump, thump of footfalls that came next were definitely human. No time to figure out if the new arrival was friend or foe.

Dean darted across the field.

Less than ten seconds later, he reached Alejandro, grabbed him by the collar, and threw him into the brush.

"What the..." Alejandro said, shock written on his face as he tried to get up.

"Shhh! And stay down."

In one move, Dean uprooted the tripod and camera and jumped into the thicket beside Alejandro. Carefully, Dean wove the tripod through the shrubbery to keep it hidden, then he pulled Alejandro farther into the brush and peeked through the greenery toward the path that led back to the main building.

There stood the gunman from the parking lot, weapon drawn. No question what he was after, but had he seen them?

The man looked from side to side. He moved one leg, as if to turn around, when suddenly the brush where Alejandro was hiding shook, just a little. The foolish volcanologist was repositioning himself to see what was going on.

Dean knit his eyebrows and mouthed "No!"

All movement stopped.

The gunman turned back to the field and headed their way. He took a wide path, alternating his gaze from the grass to the surrounding brush, and then to the path behind him.

Eventually, he stopped. Right in front of where Dean and Alejandro were hiding.

CHAPTER 73

Every muscle in Briel's body tensed in response to the blast of high-pitched beeps, followed by clanging bells from the fire alarm. Her first sniff detected only a hint of moldy old books and stale office air, and though the noise was likely to trigger a headache in short order, she presumed it was all a test.

Seconds later, wisps of black smoke drifted from the ventilation grill near the ceiling behind Fe's desk, accompanied by an acidic, burning rubber odour that left no doubt. Not a drill. But the timing?

There was no time for questions.

Briel, Ricardo, and the head librarian leapt to their feet and catapulted toward the stairs.

"The children," Fe said as thickening clouds filled the stairwell.

On the ground floor, evacuation was well underway, adults from the small craft rooms filing coughing youngsters out the open front doors. Sirens sounded. Emergency vehicles weren't far away.

"Help with the children," Ricardo said to Briel. "I will do another sweep upstairs."

Briel nodded. She dashed from room to room, finding each empty except for one. A girl of perhaps eleven years sat huddled in a corner, frozen. The room's tutor was trying to drag her by the arms, but the child wouldn't budge. Briel dove behind the girl and brought one of the child's arms over her shoulder. The tutor instantly did the same on the other side, and they rushed from the building.

Outside, Fe counted heads and organized her personnel and their charges. Ricardo was nowhere to be found.

Briel took a deep breath, covered her nose and mouth with her cotton shirt, and ran inside.

She headed back to the library's stairs and found Ricardo sprawled over the bottom third of the steps. Too heavy to lift, she grabbed an arm and a leg and dragged him down to the ground floor, and then slid him to the exit. As she got close to the open air, Fe drew up next to her and together, coughing and spluttering, they pulled Ricardo through the iron gates and onto the sidewalk.

Parents and caregivers began converging on them, and Fe left to help them find their children.

Dropping to her knees, Briel faced Ricardo.

"Don't you dare die on me," she said. "We're not done. I still need your annoyingly kind help."

She felt for a pulse. It was there. Strong. Briel tried to bring Ricardo around by slapping his cheeks. Then she started coughing, suddenly aware of her own nausea and dizziness.

Searching around her, Briel realized for the first time that the scene was already awash with first responders. Between hacks, she called to a paramedic comforting an anxious but seemingly well child. The man left his patient with the closest adult and ran to Briel. Together, they lifted Ricardo onto a gurney. She was about to express her concern about cyanide poisoning when a second paramedic came to their aid, began an IV, and administered medication from a small vial. Briel checked the label. Hydroxo-cobalamin. A ragged breath of gratitude escaped her lips. Treatment would take about fifteen minutes, but Ricardo would be fine.

Impressive. This little magical town carried the latest in poisonous gases care.

THE FIRST PARAMEDIC continued to administer oxygen.

Ricardo's eyes opened and he began a spluttering cough, grabbing at the mask and pulling it away to free his mouth and nose. The paramedic struggled to keep the mask on, and once Ricardo's coughing ceased, he complied.

Briel smiled despite herself.

The fire department's ladders were up, hoses at the ready. But they spent no effort soaking the building. Briel moved across the street for a better view. On the rooftop, two firefighters wearing self-contained breathing masks and helmets moved a metal barrel billowing black smoke. They pushed it away from what had to be the intake air vent.

And then it hit her. She recognized the scent. The smell of burning tires.

More firefighters, also wearing self-contained breathing masks, entered the building, but Briel was betting they wouldn't find a thing.

MIGUEL ALLOWED his old 9mm to lead him around the corner, where he faced the older woman.

"Put that foolish toy away," she said.

The curator was alone. Miguel looked around him, wondering at the woman's bravado—and where the museum's patrons were.

"Same as when the others arrived this morning. I have someone stationed on the grounds, temporarily preventing entrance to these hallowed halls. I assure you, we are alone," she said to his unasked questions. "Now put that thing away before you hurt yourself."

The woman's defiance got under his skin. She should be afraid, not him. And she'd just admitted to being alone.

Miguel turned to the courtyard and fired a warning shot. Outraged grackles noisily formed an escaping black cloud.

Satisfied with his stunt, Miguel reset his focus to the curator, who now held a beast of a weapon, almost twice the size of his.

And she pointed it at him.

CHAPTER 74

The last thing the Conductor expected was another call from that goddamned ex-Second Violin. What did that sappy being want from him now? He'd already spared the man's life.

The Conductor thumbed the emergency phone. He should have changed the number the moment the Second Violin and Viola left his compound. He'd do that today.

The phone continued to ring.

Against his better judgement, the Conductor answered the call. "This is the last time. Do you understand? This number is no longer available to you."

A high-pitched voice trembled in return. "This is a courtesy call. You'll want to hear what I have to say."

"Then say it. I am busy."

"The Bass is in custody. London is compromised. The First Violin and Cello are on their way here to Switzerland. Extradition is still a risk, but so far, we're safe. Your Orchestra? It's finished. You need to close shop and run."

The Second Violin hung up.

The Conductor pitched the phone across the room. It flew over the floor like a flat stone thrown across the water. And the stupid thing remained intact. Damned protective plating. Damned Strings. He should never have trusted them. He should have cut them off. Some kind of termination clause. Real termination. In their own countries. Bodies to be found long before anything led back to Mexico.

Hijos de puta. So greedy, they didn't know to pay off the tax man.

And then the Conductor blinked.

The idea flew by so quickly, he almost missed it. A new Orchestra. Reborn so a Wind Instrument accompanied each String: an official from each of the federal tax offices. More of his music carried around the world.

But he was getting ahead of himself. The Second Violin was right, and the taste from that was sour. How long before these foreign authorities dug their way back to Mexico? The Bass would sell him out in a heartbeat if it would save his skin. Of course, the Conductor would get retribution. But that would take time.

First, he needed to secure his own funds and to do that he needed help. Those favours he'd done for officials on high? He was about to call every one of them in.

CHAPTER 75

Briel returned to Ricardo's side and found him pointing his badge at the paramedic who'd put in his IV.

"You should say thank you instead of flashing that," she said.

Briel smiled, more to herself than to the circumstances. It was good once again to see Ricardo's disgruntled face contrasting with those big, brown, naïve-looking eyes.

"There is no fire," Ricardo said when he saw her.

"I know," Briel said.

"We need to leave."

"I think they plan on taking you to the hospital." Briel pointed to the IV still in Ricardo's arm.

Ricardo remained resolute.

"We need to leave. Maybe this has something to do with the book. I do not know. But it cannot be allowed. We do not have time for the hospital."

Briel agreed.

FIREFIGHTERS DESCENDED from the roof toting a rusty steel drum filled with still smoldering rubber tire chips. The origin of the smoke that invaded the ventilation system. So much for the roofers Fe had expected. The scene nauseated Briel. Who would do such a disgusting thing?

A hoarse cough and a gag erupted from a small boy sitting on the curb. A slightly older youngster draped his arms over the little one's shoulders. A brother by birth or otherwise, doing what he could.

All critical needs seemed to be attended to, and parents were busily claiming their children, the healthy ones released to go home. Briel approached the paramedic who'd given Ricardo oxygen. He was examining a little girl complaining of nausea.

"My friend," she said. "He's doing well now. You need the gurney and room at the hospital for the little ones. Please. Let us leave."

The paramedic rose and surveyed the people that still needed to be triaged.

"You are alright?" he asked Briel.

"Just the expected sore throat. Nothing more. And I'm in healthcare. If things get worse for either of us, I promise we'll get help."

The young man went to Ricardo's side and spoke with his partner. A moment later, the IV was gone, a band-aid in its place.

"Thank you," Ricardo said.

But when he tried to jump from the gurney, Ricardo collapsed to the ground. The paramedic lifted an eyebrow and looked at Briel. Briel stifled a laugh at Ricardo's effort at machismo and waved the paramedics away. Then she grabbed hold of Ricardo's arm and hoisted him up. He wavered again, had to lean on her, but eventually stood upright.

CHAPTER 76

Finding his field empty and the bordering fence intact, Pedro tracked back through the trails, gun poised, as he wove around the thick undergrowth for his quarry. He checked each trailhead on his way to the farthest green space from the entrance. It was important his men knew he was monitoring their diligence.

In reality, this hunt was only for Leggatt. He was the real threat here.

True, he'd ordered them to shoot Alejandro, and if that happened, c'est la vie. But if he got there for Alejandro's capture? Pedro didn't know how, but he'd make sure Alejandro got away. The departamento's volcanologist was good. Asked no questions. Did as he was told. And despite his scruffy looks and foul teeth, Dorothea truly seemed to love him. If anyone deserved happiness, she did. The princess in the tower.

Pedro had had no trouble arranging Dorothea's ex-husband's demise. That man was a nasty piece of work. What kind of coward hurts a child?

So why did the Conductor suddenly want this boyfriend dead? Worried his daughter might finally move on with her life?

Pedro kept walking. He had one last man to check on, then

he'd double back and review everything again. If they still came up empty, he'd scrub the search and wait for better intel.

The path spit him out at the bottom of a shallow hillside. Like the other fields, this one was well mowed. His man stood in the far corner, scratching his head.

What the hell?

Pedro jogged over. In the building heat of the day, his shoes felt increasingly like lead, and he slowed his pace. The bullet-proof vest he had donned under his shirt didn't help. When he finally reached his target, he drew a huge intake of air and then had to stifle a cough.

"What?"

His man pointed to the ground, a self-satisfied smile on his face. Depressions. Three of them. An exact fit for tripod feet.

Evidence of Alejandro. Nothing on Leggatt. Pedro couldn't help his frown. No way to call off the search in front of his man. Especially given his strained relationship with the Conductor.

He motioned for a search of the surrounding shrubs and stepped closer to the trees to look for himself.

DEAN SAT ON HIS HAUNCHES, barely daring to breathe. Beside him, Alejandro remained rooted. The volcanologist finally seemed to understand the gravity of the situation.

A newcomer approached and the gunman pointed to the ground. Together, they examined where the tripod had stood. These guys were good.

When the newcomer turned his attention to the brush where Dean and Alejandro were hiding, the urge to run was overwhelming. But Dean knew if they even made a twig shake, they were dead.

Dean's heart pounded loudly in his chest as the newcomer and the gunman leaned into the underbrush.

The gunman's arms reached for the branches hiding Dean and Alejandro just as a shout sounded nearby.

The gunman withdrew.

Dean let out a breath and chanced a look through the thicket. A third man headed toward the other two.

Attention momentarily directed away from them, it was now or never. Dean tapped Alejandro's arm and pointed further into the undergrowth. They scampered through twisted blackberry bushes, thorny vines pulling their clothes and scratching their skin.

Dean felt something tear at his neck. Percy's moose nickel necklace was tangled among the prickly creepers. He sent a silent plea to the only woman he had ever truly loved. Any help you can manage... Instantly, the necklace popped loose. He removed it from his neck to prevent any further trouble and tucked it into his pocket. He'd raise a glass to thank Percy later.

Though neither Dean nor Alejandro vocalized their discomfort among the thorns, the ruckus their movements caused surely drew attention to their retreat.

"I have an idea," Alejandro whispered behind him. "This way."

Crab-crawling, Alejandro turned around, heading back to where Dean had spotted the three men returning to pursue the hunt. Dean was about to yank Alejandro back when he spotted a thin streak of bare earth. Probably the well-used path of javelina. Though Dean didn't want to disturb the pig-like creatures in their territory, the alternative was less appealing. He dove for the path, taking a persistent blackberry vine with him. Keeping behind Alejandro, he crept further into the thickets, making better headway by staying low to the ground.

Behind them, Dean heard cursing. The gunmen saw their movement. Would the attack of the blackberries be enough to slow the chase?

CHAPTER 77

Miguel froze as the curator's weapon fixed on his chest. He hadn't counted on someone else having a gun in this contest. Except, of course, for De La Cruz.

Sirens, not far away, broke the spell, and Miguel turned his head toward them. Pavlov's dog. Normally, that sound meant he and his staff had work to do.

"Ignore it," the curator said. "Our emergency services are busy... Not your business. Now. I will not ask again. Tell me who you are."

"Miguel."

The curator didn't move.

"Miguel Lobo."

A clatter rose behind him as a teenager with a bucket and tools headed their way. Oblivious to the scene, the young maintenance worker, earbuds in place, nodded to the beat of some unknown tune.

The bucket clanked to the ground and the young man raised his arms high when he finally took in his surroundings.

"Leave," the curator said to the intruder. "This does not concern you. And mind, Rubin, tell no one."

Wide-eyed, unblinking, the boy nodded, and crept away.

"Now. It seems, Doctor Miguel Lobo, you have friends in high places. Friends we have in common."

"Doctor". Miguel hadn't used his title. Did she know his uncle?

The curator still pointed her impressive firearm at him. If she was a friend to his cause, why hold him like this?

"I don't take kindly to being threatened," she said as though reading his mind. "So, while I am told we must do business today, we will do it my way. Put that toy of yours on the ground or you will find yourself in need of our hospital's care. And before you even think about pulling that trigger, I guarantee you my reaction time is better than yours."

Miguel laid his pistol down.

"Now, kick it over to me."

He did.

The curator picked it up and examined it, her weapon still trained on him.

Finally, she nodded.

"This plaything will do nicely for my twelve-year-old grandson. He needs something he can't do too much damage with."

Miguel wanted to protest. To defend the firepower of what he knew to be an excellent, if older, pistol. And certainly to argue for the return of the gift from his uncle. A reminder of happier times. Yet something told him to stay still.

Again, the curator seemed to know what Miguel was thinking.

"Your little gun? I'm keeping it as payment for the package you are about to receive. I'm owed at least that, and much more for the trouble our people had to go to for you and your kind."

What did that mean?

More sirens, close by. Something serious was happening along the main drag.

The curator smiled.

From behind the podium, she withdrew a small package,

wrapped as though it came from the museum's gift store. The right size and shape for a 16th century book.

The curator slammed the package onto the concrete, and the smack echoed throughout the arched hallway. With the toe of a blue suede ankle boot with black leather and studded straps, she kicked the parcel and sent it flying across the ground.

Miguel dove for it, reaching the prize just before it found the ledge to the courtyard below. His rough handling tore the bottom portion of the wrapping and exposed a crumpled, yellowed parchment book cover.

Miguel tucked the bounty under his arm.

"Go," the curator said. The steel casing of her gun danced as she emphasized her command. "Leave now and tell those who sent you that our debt is paid. In full."

"Juice," Briel said, shouldering Ricardo and then coughing. "We need juice."

Propping each other up as necessary, they lumbered down the street, away from the mountain pass that led to Tepoztlán's ancient Aztec pyramid and toward the open-air market around the Portal of Seeds.

Ricardo had to stop three times. In each case, there was no bench in sight, so they parked themselves at the curb that bordered the cobblestone street. Happy enough to catch her own breath, Briel waited until Ricardo could move along.

Each time, store vendors came out, asking if they needed help. The second shopkeeper was a plump, matronly figure who wrung her hands in a white apron with such fervour, Briel wondered if the woman was trying to wipe her worries away. She handed Briel a roll of cough drops, and when Briel dug into her pockets for the payment, the vendor refused, tilting her head at them and putting her palms to her cheeks.

Admittedly, Ricardo looked a fright. A thin sheet of soot darkened his naturally tanned skin and covered his clothes. Noticing for the first time the patches of black on her own legs, Briel realized she couldn't look much better.

She opened the packet of lozenges, handed Ricardo two and popped another two into her own mouth. As they dissolved, lemon and honey replaced the taste of burning tires. Whether from the sugar or from the flavourful potion itself, even Ricardo seemed to perk up after that, and Briel made a mental note to come by the woman's shop later, to buy something and repay her kindness. It seemed she owed many people on this trip.

At the market, under a tent, Briel dumped Ricardo onto the first stool she could find and ordered a tall strawberry-mango agua fresca for each of them. After a long swig of the cold, sweet liquid, Briel truly started feeling better. Except now she worried that their untidy appearance might put off nearby tourists. The last thing she wanted was to cost anyone their income.

But no one seemed to notice them. She turned back toward Ricardo, and out of the corner of her eye, Briel caught sight of the hooded figure she had seen at the museum. He was carrying a package, but she could tell from the wing-tipped shoes it was the same man. And his lips...

Wavy, slightly long hair protruded from the hood, covering the cheeks, but those full lips were unmistakable. It had to be Miguel.

She called to him as he went by, but he didn't stop. Instead, the figure picked up speed, weaving between vendors and jumping around corners.

It made no sense. Why was Miguel there, and why wouldn't he stop?

She gave chase and the hooded man ran, crossing the street and dashing around the corner. In his haste, a piece of paper flew from the package he carried and landed on the cobblestones.

Briel's lungs, still wounded from smoke, couldn't match the hooded figure's pace. Instead, she picked up the fallen paper and leaned against the nearest stone wall, gasping for air and giving in to another hacking fit.

When she finally regained control, she examined her find. Torn wrapping paper; and she'd seen the symbols before, in the museum where she and Ricardo had asked for help with Trithemius's book.

CHAPTER 78

"We need to hurry," Alejandro said. He drew Dean toward the tallest tree in a small clearing and pointed to a scattering of branches and leaves on the ground.

"What's that?" Dean asked.

"A disguise. It covers a hole. About three meters down and a meter and a half across. The javelina used to scratch themselves on this tree's heavy bark. You can see the damage here." Alejandro pointed to a low, wide patch of tree trunk worn almost to the cambium. He continued. "We once used this to trap the javelina. Their numbers were too high, and they wreaked havoc on the grounds. But those animals are smart and they know now to avoid the pit, so we have to pay others to manage them. Occasionally, we still use the hole to fool our newest recruits. A test."

Alejandro smiled.

Nasty, Dean thought.

Sounds of thrashing in the brush grew louder.

"We need to hide."

"Over here," Alejandro said. He pointed to a shaded area shielded by a thicket of six-foot-tall boxwoods on the other side of the tree. "It's where we sometimes waited for our new hires—to see if they could work out the problem, or if we needed to rescue them before they fell and broke a leg... or worse."

"Did someone play this game with you?"

"Yes," Alejandro said. He wasn't smiling now and didn't elaborate. Instead, he tucked himself behind the greenery. Dean decided not to press. Their pursuers were close and Alejandro's plan was all they had.

Dean grabbed a stick and did what he could to erase the tracks they'd made. Then he climbed in beside the volcanologist and prayed that whoever was chasing them wouldn't identify the hole before they were upon it.

The man Dean had seen adjust his gun in the parking lot was the first to climb out of the brush. He stopped at the edge of the clearing, alternating between picking vines from his suit and looking around him. The other two followed in short order. One younger, the other older. The young man took a few moments to help the older remove blackberry vines from his clothes.

The gunman and the younger man turned to the older. It seemed he was in charge.

"Well," the older man said. "Find them."

Alejandro brought his head close to the dirt, but Dean kept an eye in a peephole through the dense boxwood branches. If they were going to be caught, he at least wanted to know it was coming.

The man from the parking lot stepped quickly toward the tree while his colleague grabbed the stick Dean had used to mask their footsteps, and he started banging on the brush that bordered the clearing. It wasn't a gunshot, but if that stick got too close to where Dean and Alejandro hid, it would do some damage. Dean prayed the gunman by the tree would fall into the hole before that happened. They needed the distraction to help them get away.

Two more steps, Dean thought as the guy from the parking lot eased closer to the trap.

"Stop," the older man said.

Immediately, the gunman obeyed and loped back to where their leader stood.

"Marco, look at the ground over there." The older man pointed to the trap. "Where you were about to step? That disturbance on the ground. Smudges here and here. Something is wrong. You must learn to be more observant. Both of you. Uncover what's there, but be careful. You don't know what lies beneath."

While his men dug through the branches, the older man's squinting eyes peered at the surrounding landscape, giving Dean and Alejandro no chance to move.

The hair on the back of Dean's neck stood to attention as the older man drew a weapon, skirted the tree, and knelt down.

His sights fixed on the peephole and there he met Dean, eye to eye.

CHAPTER 79

Ricardo waved the server down and laid his pesos on the table, including a generous tip. Briel fleeing the juice stand couldn't have made a good impression.

And her leaving him in the dust. It was becoming a thing. The woman couldn't seem to grasp who was in charge. Something he needed to change.

His first steps out from under the food court canopy told him running wasn't an option. His chest hurt. Normal for smoke inhalation? He didn't know. What he knew was that dying in the middle of the street after insisting he leave the paramedic's capable hands was not the way he wanted to be remembered. And he still had Lilly to think about. She had been so happy to see him last weekend. Squeals of laughter. His mother had also looked happy, and maybe just a little relieved. She was tired.

Ricardo slowed his pace, stood up straight and headed in the direction Doctora Briel Payce had disappeared. He had a few choice words for her. If he ever caught up...

A burst of harsh coughing caused him to stop, lean over, and put his hands on his knees again.

On a hunch, Ricardo turned the corner, leading back to the main drag. There weren't that many streets in this town, and most led there. A half block away, he found Briel sitting at the curb, arms folded around her knees, head buried.

So, superwoman was human after all.

He ambled to her side and sat down.

"Please explain why you left like that."

Between gasping for air and trying to clear her throat, Briel said, "Miguel... hooded figure... here."

Then she handed Ricardo a torn piece of wrapping paper covered in museum gift store symbols.

"You really believe Doctor Miguel Lobo is here? The same Lobo from the orphanage?"

Briel lifted her head from her knees and nodded.

"I want..." Briel started. Then Ricardo saw concern fill her eyes. "You don't look good. Let's get you back to the juice bar."

"Too late. I'm not sure after seeing you run out, that our return would be welcomed. I think you may have scared a few customers from eating there."

"Oh."

"Come," he said. "Let us find a proper place to sit and snack. I know you want to find Lobo, but neither of us can do that right now. We'll heal ourselves as best we can and then I'll check on the library. I think the answer might still be there."

Miguel ran until he reached the street where he'd parked his car. He couldn't believe Briel had recognized him. He thought he'd lost her a block away, but he hid inside a door frame, just in case, and waited to see if she would turn the corner. She didn't.

It wasn't like Briel to give up. She'd always been more fit than him. Why did she stop the hunt?

He almost wanted to go back and look for her. For old times' sake.

Not going to happen, the rational side of his brain said. It was a close call, and he had the prize. No doubt the same prize Briel sought.

He sauntered the rest of the way to his car, periodically checking behind him. Still nothing.

The world spun, and Miguel realized the sun and the heat had finally taken their toll. He pulled open the car door, whipped off the hoodie, and took a swig of the water from the bottle he'd left in the car. It was hot. His vehicle had been there long enough to be a solar oven. No matter. Miguel splashed excess water on his face, sat down, turned the car on, and set the air conditioner to full.

When his body finally responded to the cooler temperature, he looked at the package from the curator. Open it, or just go home?

Immediate gratification was the theme of his life. No need to change that now.

Carefully, he unwrapped the curator's gift, cognizant that if it contained what he hoped for, his mission was a success.

Free of its packaging, Miguel gently turned over the fragile, yellowed cover of a book. *The Polygraphia*, by Johannes Trithemius.

Miguel leaned his head back. Alone in his air-conditioned car and away from prying eyes, he allowed himself to cry.

With the key to Persephone Gilbert's riddle in hand, he and his uncle could forge a path to the future. Not with the same trust. That bond was irretrievably broken. But at least they could have something—for the sake of family. After all, they only had each other left.

He called his uncle.

"Leave a message." Pedro Serrano's gruff, gravely voice left no room for niceties, and Miguel clipped his response.

"Parcel in hand. On my way home."

As he headed for the highway. Miguel considered the curator's final words. "... tell those who sent you that our debt is paid. In full."

His uncle. What had happened in Tepoztlán? What did the sirens mean? And what of Briel?

He pressed the button for the automobile's stereo and turned up the volume, pushing all bad thoughts away. At least for now.

"THANK YOU," Briel said as she settled into a cushioned bistro chair a half block from the library.

"You are welcome," Ricardo said. "You saved my life today. And as I am feeling a little better, I can express my appreciation."

"I owed you," Briel said. "Remember?"

"True." Ricardo smirked.

First time in a while.

And Briel returned a smile.

They'd positioned their seats so both had a full view of the comings and goings around the morning's crime. Most of the emergency vehicles were gone. Only a few uniforms remained out front, asking questions of the head librarian.

"It surprised me you didn't want to stay and help," Briel finally said.

"I was of no use to anyone an hour ago. You know that. But I thought the same of you. Why didn't you stay?"

"The entire of emergency services from the region were out in full force and parents were already arriving. Too many cooks... Honestly, now that I think about it, the whole scenario ran like a well-oiled machine. If I didn't know better, I'd have thought it was a simulation. A practice event for the teams in the area."

"Simulation. Yes." Ricardo bit his lower lip.

"Any chance you could get a report from the police over there? Officer to detective?"

"Too late."

The remaining officials started their vehicles and in an instant, they were gone.

Yellow crime tape blocked the entrance to the now empty library and the head librarian stood alone for a moment before turning to walk in their direction.

"We may yet have the chance to finish our meeting," Ricardo said.

FE ESTRADA AMBLED by their table, her eyes fixed on the horizon. She was deep in thought.

"Señora Estrada!" Briel reached for Fe's arm as she passed.

As though woken from a dream, Fe startled at Briel's touch.

"Please, join us," Briel said. "Let us buy you a drink. Take a moment and rest. You've been through so much."

Ricardo retrieved a chair from a neighbouring table and Fe accepted the invitation.

"Thank you," the head librarian said. "I hoped to see you again. If only to let you know how much I appreciated your bravery this morning. Few people would have willingly gone back into that blackness to find others in need. I am glad no one else was there, and very glad to see you both well."

"We're a little shaken," Briel said, "but with the excellent care from your paramedics, we're recovering nicely. How are you?"

"Also shaken. The firefighters said it was a hoax. Apparently, there was no actual order to fix the roof. The email alerting me was a fake. They found a barrel with smoldering rubber chips beside our intake vent. Someone with a sick mind. I am told that the search for who did this has begun."

"Everyone is alright?"

"Yes. By God's grace, we removed the children quickly enough from the building. Those few who showed signs of illness were taken to the hospital, and I am told they will recover fully. We are blessed."

"And the damage to the building?" Ricardo asked.

"Smoke, of course. But no fire and no water damage. It will take time to remove the smell. Tomorrow, I will meet with our insurers. Today, everyone simply gives thanks that it was not worse."

"What about the items you were storing for the church?" Briel asked.

Fe hesitated.

"Sí," she said finally. "We were instructed to tell no one about that. How did you find out?"

"The curator at the museum told us," Ricardo said. "Why is it a secret?"

"For exactly what happened today. Worry that important icons all in a single room would make stealing far too easy."

"Do you know if anything was stolen?" Briel felt a hitch in her throat as she asked.

"A book. Old and special."

"Trithemius's *Polygraphia*," Briel said.

"Yes." Fe seemed surprised that Briel knew.

"It's what we came here for," Ricardo said.

"Why?"

"I lost a friend," Briel said. "Here in Mexico. Five years ago. We recently found clues to what might have happened. I'm hoping to give closure to her aunt in Texas. Her aunt has cancer and doesn't have long. Those clues led us here, and to the book."

Fe placed a hand over Briel's. "I am so sorry."

And Briel thought perhaps she really was. The woman looked as though she knew loss.

Fe opened her mouth to speak again when a server came with the drink Fe had ordered. Briel tilted her head, hoping to encourage Fe to share whatever information she had.

Fe sighed and then asked, "Would a picture of the book help?"

CHAPTER 80

Fe Estrada's sage-coloured, three-inch stilettos clicked along the sidewalk. Ricardo and Briel fell in line behind her. Stylish woman, Ricardo mused, though his own feet ached at the thought of walking on cobblestones in that kind of footwear.

Despite being a trained observer, most of the time Ricardo only paid attention to facial features, walking patterns, and clothing styles and colours. Didn't all women wear high heels, and all men loafers? But Briel's observations of Miguel got him thinking. There was a lot you could tell from what someone wore on their feet.

Fe guided them to the home of the local woman she'd temporarily hired to take pictures of the inventory from Ex Convento. It was the precaution demanded by the church to be sure nothing went missing when they transferred items from one location to the next.

A block away from the main drag where they had eaten, Fe rapped on a yellow wooden door, its paint fading and peeling. A middle-aged woman in a blue and white apron answered the knock and lifted her eyes in surprise at the sight of the librarian.

"Señora Estrada," she said. "It is good to see you. Do you need my help again?"

The look was hungry. Hopeful. Something familiar to Ricardo. The face of someone who wanted… needed… to work.

Fe cast her eyes to the ground and shook her head.

"I am sorry, Delfina. Not right now. These visitors are asking about something that was moved from the church to our library. I told them you might know about it."

Delfina's features froze as her eyes bore into Fe's.

"They are friends," Fe said. "You heard of the trouble today?"

Delfina nodded.

"They helped. Risked their lives to be sure our people were safe."

"There were shots fired at the Ex Convento," Delfina said. "I don't want trouble."

Delfina moved to close the door but Ricardo stepped forward. If he read the situation right, the woman's need for money was stronger than her fear.

"Please," he said, taking out his wallet and bringing forward two 500 peso notes. "All we need is information. A few minutes of your time."

Delfina's brows knit together and her eyes never left the bills in Ricardo's hand.

"Come," she said finally.

DELFINA'S HOME was what Ricardo expected. A floral-patterned, well-worn couch stood behind an old, small table. The only significant decoration was a lavishly embellished silver Christian cross that hung inside a three-dimensional picture frame by the front door. A multicoloured candy bowl sat empty on the table. Family pictures were pasted to the wall, creating a collage that acted like wallpaper.

They settled on the couch and Delfina brought a chair from beside the kitchen table.

"Now," she said, pocketing the money in her apron. "What is it you want to know?"

"The pictures you took of the items from the church. Was there an ancient-looking book among them?" Ricardo asked.

"There were many old books."

"This one was unusual," Briel said. "Truly old. The writing would have been Latin. The author is Trithemius."

Delfina's cheeks flushed. No doubt she remembered the thing. But when she spoke, she turned to Fe.

"I'm so sorry," she said. "It was my only mistake, Señora Estrada. I promise. Just that one."

MIGUEL WAS MORE than halfway home, the rental providing a smooth and acceptable ride. If it weren't for needing to check his rear-view mirror every few minutes, he'd have said his trek north on the 95D was pleasant. Good sunshine, traffic-free roads, working air conditioner.

A single red compact rode behind him too long, so a test was in order. He alternated slowing down and speeding up and watched to see if he could frustrate the driver into changing lanes, but the vehicle tracked behind him, keeping a flawless pace.

He wished he still had his pistol, but he'd been unwilling to confront the curator once she'd decided to keep it. And now he was in trouble.

Enough.

Miguel took the next exit at speed. A dangerous move, but this was a dangerous time. Needing a place to tuck the car, he turned the next corner and spotted a taco stand beside an outdoor shed. Hoping there was a back parking lot near the shed, he screeched into the driveway and found a trash collection box on his left.

Good enough.

He backed his vehicle behind the wooden fence that blocked a street view of the metal bins. Letting the bumper kiss the backside of the box, only a few inches of the car's front remained in view.

He waited. Sweat lined his forehead despite the cool air coming from the outlets. The minutes ticked by.

Nothing.

More time spent watching, and still nothing.

Trithemius's *Polygraphia* sat on the passenger's seat beside him. Calling to him. Eventually, Miguel decided it couldn't hurt to have a look. He took a handkerchief from his pocket and carefully leafed through a few of its many pages. Each sheet contained the same columns of letters. The pages differed only by the Latin words assigned to each letter.

Miguel removed a slip of paper from his wallet. It was where he'd recorded Suthon's message.

Engrossed by the puzzle, the loud bang of something hard crashing into the wooden fence made Miguel jump.

Briel's teeth clenched as she braced herself for the worst. Delfina's apology to Estrada could only mean the book was gone. Her mind raced, searching for another path. Something. Anything to keep up the momentum toward finding out what had happened to Percy. She couldn't bear the thought of giving up now.

A trip to DC to the National Library, and then back to Mexico? She'd lose a week, if not more, but if it had to be done...

Fe draped an arm around Delfina. "Tell me. I know you. You are a careful and caring person. You wouldn't do anything wrong on purpose. Tell me. What happened to the book?"

Delfina used the back of her hand to brush away the wayward tears that wetted her cheeks.

"Our curator. She was so insistent. Everything. She said everything needed to be photographed. There were many books from the church, so I started with the one from Trithemius. It seemed the most fragile.

But when she saw me taking pictures of the pages, she got so angry! She shouted at me. Called me a stupid cow. Told me I was useless. That I understood nothing. I thought she would hit me. When she didn't, I was sure she would fire me. I begged her for a second chance. Checked everything with her. Made sure I was doing it right after that."

"You opened the book?" Briel asked.

"Yes. I am sorry."

"It is not a problem for us," Ricardo said. "What do you remember about it?"

"Not very much. Each page had letters of the alphabet. The same letters. Beside each letter was a word. I could not read those, but I could tell every page was different."

"I saw the file with your pictures," Fe said. "I don't remember any that showed the pages of a book."

"No Señora. I hid my mistake. I didn't want to remind the curator of my stupidity."

"So the pictures of the pages are gone." Briel's shoulders fell in resignation. Her heart ached. They'd gotten so close.

Delfina looked at the floor, her forefoot drawing circles in the dust that settled there.

"Are they gone?" Fe asked.

"They can be." Delfina's voice rose an octave and Briel noticed Delfina's tremble.

"You are not in trouble. Certainly not from us. But if you have a copy of the pages," Ricardo pulled out another 500 peso note, "we'd be very grateful to see them."

Delfina's eyes shifted to Fe, as though asking the librarian if the request was real. If she could truly take the money.

Fe nodded and Delfina rose, asking them to follow her up a set of banister-less, creaky stairs.

"Mierda. What are you doing there?" The driver of a rear-loader garbage truck gestured at Miguel. "Get out! You're not allowed to park by the bin. Can't you read?"

Miguel opened his window.

"Go to hell," Miguel said. "You are blocking my way out. If you want me to move, then back up."

Miguel should have been contrite. He was in the wrong. But he'd had enough of being pushed around. He was a medical director, after all. A learned man. And he was fulfilling an important mission. This pleb needed to know his place.

The truck driver slammed the door of his vehicle and noisily pulled back. Miguel took his time, but left. More angry words and he could end up in a fist fight, and that wouldn't be good for anyone, most especially him. Besides, the hiding place had done its job. Surely the little red car was gone by now.

Miguel pulled over again one street away, beside a field of agave plants. No one else on the road. Let the garbage man do his job. Miguel intended to solve the friar's puzzle. He'd do it now. Back in the city, he'd present his uncle Pedro with both the book and the solution.

Miguel scanned for the friar's words on each page. The arrangement of Latin words beside the letters was in no order he could see.

He stared at the note again. It started with the number 13. Unlucky for the friar.

Miguel checked the page numbers. *I wonder...*

He turned to page 13 and found "Supercelestium" beside the letter C. On page fourteen, he found "detestari" beside the letter V.

He was getting somewhere.

Eventually, he had nine letters: CVICVILCO

Miguel grabbed his cell and checked for an internet connection.

It had to be the city of Cuicuilco, but why the odd spelling?

His data plan kicked in and he managed a powerful signal. Then Miguel checked the age of Trithemius's text.

Of course. In the Middle Ages, U was still rarely used. The U and V were synonymous.

Location confirmed, there was only one question. Should he go there now, or speak with his uncle first and discuss exactly where to look?

Miguel started keying in Pedro's number. Halfway through, he stopped, put the phone away, and restarted the car. A conversation like this was better conducted in person. And this time, he didn't fear for his life.

CHAPTER 81

Dean reached for the revolver still tucked in his pants. Governed by panic, he pointed toward the man staring at him, and fired.

He and Alejandro jumped from their crouched position. Ten meters away, the older man lay on his back, his two buddies leaning over their fallen comrade.

Dean had never killed someone before. Guilt and relief flooded his system simultaneously. What had he done? He stood, rooted. Then, from somewhere far away, he felt a persistent pull. Alejandro wanted Dean to move.

The older man on the ground expelled a moan. Dean watched as the others helped their leader sit. Then the older man rubbed the back of his head. No blood. An opening in his shirt revealed the bullet-proof material that protected his chest. He'd killed no one.

A second wave of relief swept through Dean, and then… panic.

"Come!!" Alejandro was hopping up and down, yanking at Dean's shirt.

"After them!" Dean heard the older man call.

Dean's feet came alive, and he and Alejandro whipped through the next portion of the javelina trail. A few yards down the way,

Dean turned back and fired two more rounds from his gun, aiming up, hoping, at least, to delay their attackers.

Alejandro seemed to know where he was going, so Dean followed him deeper into the woods. Ahead of them, Dean saw a smooth, high wooden fence that marked a corner of the departamento's land.

No toe holds. No way to climb. A dead end.

Behind them, the older man's buddies rustled through low-lying branches, closing in.

Dean checked the revolver. They were cornered, and he needed more time to think. So Dean pointed the barrel and pulled the trigger. A sickening "click" wafted into the air. The chamber was empty. Three lousy bullets. What the hell was Tomás thinking, only giving him half the firing power?

He turned to tell Alejandro that they were finished and found the volcanologist pushing a boulder from in front of the fence.

It took a second before Dean got the message. The boulder covered a hole under the wooden barrier. More evidence of javelina damage. Handy creatures.

Dean joined Alejandro and pushed with all he had.

A thunder of footsteps told him their company was uncomfortably close.

PEDRO'S CHEST ACHED. How dare Leggatt shoot? Pushing past the pain, Pedro heard his quarry scurry away. The hunt was on. Moving carefully from tree trunk to tree trunk, he and his men followed. Pedro spotted the movement ahead first. Someone crouched near a boulder where the back and west side of the departamento's fence met.

Talk about his prey putting themselves into a no-win situation. About bloody time something went right.

As they neared their goal, Dean Leggatt stood up, gun in hand.

"Down!" Pedro ordered his men.

Thistles stuck again to his tailor-made silk suit as Pedro lightened the load from his old foot wound by leaning into the brush on his right. He really wanted to kill Dean Leggatt. No waiting. But there was another order in play. At least, for now, he still needed the Conductor to depend on him.

No sound exploded across the path. The man didn't take his shot. Or was he out of ammunition?

Pedro rose, just enough to see what was going on. Leggatt and Alejandro had pushed the boulder aside, exposing a hole under the fence. Alejandro was already shimmying through.

"Go!" Pedro commanded.

Without hesitation, his men dashed to where Alejandro's feet protruded and Dean cowered.

They reached the fence just as Leggatt was halfway through. Two of Pedro's henchmen each grabbed a leg and tugged. Leggatt fought back, kicking wildly, but there was no escape. Not this time.

Together, they overpowered the geologist. As they slid him back to their side of the fence, Leggatt shouted. "Run! Alejandro, run!"

Job done.

And Pedro had witnesses. Alejandro got away without his aid. If his boss still wanted Alejandro killed, Pedro would hire it out. At least then he could truthfully tell Dorothea he didn't do it.

Pedro aimed his weapon. "So, Señor Leggatt. Finally, we meet. Please, give me an excuse, any excuse, to shoot you here and now."

CHAPTER 82

The infamous sound of fingernails scratching a chalkboard. The bitter, terrifying sound of defeat. That was the music that played in the Conductor's head while he waited for his brother to say something. Anything. When no words came, he asked again.

"I need your help," the Conductor said.

"I already helped you. Your problem is in the hospital. And word has it the head of the AFSI may not make it."

"Yes. Thank you. I need more."

"There is no more, little brother. I have done all I can. Risked my career. Even now. Sources tell me De La Cruz made the emergency call that got Menendez help. I still do not know what De La Cruz saw. What he might have heard. This may be the end for me, too."

"Little brother". The Conductor hated that moniker. He was the younger by only four minutes. Identical twins, except for the cord that had wrapped itself around his neck during birth. The slight lapse in oxygen that caused "only minor damage". Enough to end his ambitions for the world stage. Enough for him to hide himself away.

In the end, he'd proven himself more than capable. He just

needed a way out of Mexico, for him and for his money. And only for a while. Until he could bring about his new Orchestra.

Dorothea could keep the compound. Sell it, for all he cared. If she ever found out that he had ordered a hit on her boyfriend, she wouldn't forgive him anyway.

"We can leave together," the Conductor said. "I have enough for both of us. Somewhere with immunity. I can use a new disguise. Then I will build again, from scratch. And you can work for me."

"Never."

The word came without hesitation, and the pause that followed lasted longer than it should have. But what was there to say? There would only be one survivor when the dust settled. The Conductor knew that now. Just like the doctors had planned at their births. He'd thwarted the odds then, and he would deal with them now.

CHAPTER 83

Delfina's computer was already on and set up with a computer game. Some kind of survival program, by the look of the screen.

"Sorry," she said. "I was checking something. For my neighbour's children."

Sure, Briel thought, looking at the extensive equipment. The technology in Delfina's computer room was more costly than all the other items in her home put together. Based on the woman's spending choices, Briel bet she was an addict, but she wasn't there to judge or to intervene. She needed the pictures.

Delfina opened a drawer full of flash drives and picked up one labelled sixteen gigabytes. They waited while the woman plugged it in and found the file with her photos of the items from the church.

"You kept this?" Fe asked.

Delfina turned her chair to face the head librarian. "The curator made no provision for a backup. I am sorry, but so many hands touched those sacred items. I thought of what might happen if the file became corrupted. I worried someone might say something was missing or stolen, and no one would know. I was trying to help."

She hung her head again, and Fe patted her back. "You did well, but if anyone else finds out about this… "

"Please," Delfina said. "Take it with you."

As she moved to close out the thumb drive, Briel put her hand over the USB port.

"No," Briel said. "We need to see the pages of the book first. Can you show us those? Then we're happy to leave you and Señora Estrada to whatever next steps must be taken."

Fe nodded, and Delfina went back to the file.

Briel took in a sharp breath as the computer screen flooded with the first pages of Trithemius's *Polygraphia*.

"How many pages are there?" Ricardo asked.

Delfina checked the number of photos in the subfile. "Fifty."

Most of the pictures contained either introductory material or were blank.

Finally, they reached a set of pages where letters of the alphabet were matched with Latin words.

"There," Briel said. "Supercelestium. It's beside the letter 'C.' Next page."

Delfina moved to the next photo, and then the one after that. They deciphered CVICVI, and then the photos stopped.

"This is when the curator found me and told me I was stupid," Delfina said. "It's all I have."

Briel bit back her anger. This timid woman didn't deserve the curator's wrath, nor her own displaced frustration. Still, it flared. She turned to Ricardo and, oddly, he was smiling.

"What?" she asked. "We don't have the rest of it."

His smile grew wider.

"Yes, we do."

CHAPTER 84

Pedro Serrano sat stone still on the farthest park bench from the tourist sites in Chapultepec Park. The designer coffee he'd picked up from the local bistro, flavoured with a hint of cinnamon, cooled beside him on the metal grate. Every breath reminded him that his chest was bruised. The back of his neck ached, and he still had a headache from when he had fallen over. Age had truly caught up with him. One day, he was fit for a fight, and the next, younger men helped him up from the ground.

At least he had Dean Leggatt in custody. Something to show for all the misadventure. He still needed to shut down Briel Payce, but one thing at a time.

A familiar pair of wingtipped loafers suddenly appeared in front of where he gazed at the ground. Pedro looked up, flicking his eyes left and right, making sure he was still within sight of the two guards who stood in the trees nearby.

Miguel followed Pedro's eyes and realized they were not alone. "Uncle?"

Pedro waved away Miguel's concern. He'd stationed the men in case Miguel suddenly developed the backbone to take him out, though it wasn't in the man's nature. He should have known. God, he was on edge.

"Don't worry about them," Pedro said. "Nothing to do with you. Tell me what you learned."

Miguel eyed the guards again, so Pedro added, "You can speak freely. They know their place."

The doctor finally sat beside Pedro on the bench. Almost whispering, he said, "The Spider Rock is in Cuicuilco."

"How do you know?"

"I decoded the friar's verse."

"The round pyramid. Why?"

"Xitli's eruption. The one that came late. Long after those of our kind already fled Popocatepetl's wrath. We'd built the Pyramid of the Sun, and we were finishing the Pyramid of the Moon, and we understood the volcano's needs. Our brothers in Cuicuilco didn't heed our warnings. Instead, they revered their round pyramid, adding tiers, believing it was enough."

"I taught you that when you were a child."

"And I remembered. Xitli drove the rest of our people to Teotihuacan. Everyone understood then. The temple of Quetzalcoatl was built with the labour of our Cuicuilco latecomers. Xitli went quiet, but Popocatepetl still threatened. With the help of those people, we finally achieved full devotion to our real god. Quetzalcoatl and, subsequently, Popocatepetl have remained satisfied for all this time. Cuicuilco is key. Persephone Gilbert must have known that. I should have guessed."

Pedro considered Miguel's words. Find the Spider Rock and eliminate Dean Leggatt. Two wins and the culmination of five years' work.

Perhaps there was something to be saved between them.

"I'm going to Cuicuilco now," Miguel said, breaking Pedro's train of thought.

"No," Pedro said.

Miguel shook his head. "Nothing pleases you anymore. Uncle, we have a chance to find the rock. To end all of this. And I don't need your permission."

"That's true," Pedro said. The surprised look on the doctor's face said it all. Miguel eased into a smile. "But. You have another priority. I've been busy as well." Pedro pulled out a sheet of numbers. "Popocatepetl is restless."

Miguel grabbed the paper and pushed his glasses back up the bridge of his nose. "This can't be. Not so soon. Why?"

Pedro shrugged. "Perhaps our mighty volcano feels the threat of strangers getting too close for comfort. It is not our place to question the gods."

"Quetzalcoatl. How can this be? No one is prepared. Why didn't you tell me?"

"The hunt for the Rock occupied us all. I only received the data yesterday."

"What can we do?"

"I have a candidate in custody. Persephone Gilbert's old boyfriend. The man who accompanied Briel Payce."

"How do we know he's worthy?"

"He's been sniffing around the monitoring department. A threat to our data. I had to smuggle this latest report out. He fits our needs. And, of course, you have the test. Let us see if Arturo's genetically enhanced roundworm infestation reaches Dean Leggatt's lungs. If not, we have our sacrifice. Otherwise, well, he is already a dead man walking. He knows too much."

Miguel swallowed. His appetite for outright murder was nonexistent. Fucking medical oath. Pedro added, "If Leggatt fails the test, I'll take care of the rest."

Pedro's nephew twitched and his long face turned pale, but the man finally nodded. His belief in Quetzalcoatl and his mission to keep Mexico's population safe from volcanic destruction held firm.

"What about the Rock?" Miguel asked.

"I'll go to Cuicuilco. You go to Plaza de Loreto. Our gift to Quetzalcoatl waits there."

CHAPTER 85

For the first time in the Conductor's life, there was absolute silence in his mind. Nothing. No plans. No music. It was gone. All of it.

He had thought at least his brother would consider the offer. Take a moment, even a day, to think it over. After all, though he was the younger of the twins, and oxygen deprivation had robbed him of his chosen career, Elpidio Tomás, the Conductor, was the wealthiest man on earth. And he'd used some of his substantial resources to foster his brother's bid for power, positioning his brother as the Secretariat of Travel, Culture and Tourism. One step closer to Mateo's goal to become president.

In return, Mateo kept him informed about threats to the Conductor's business. Foreigners poking their noses where they didn't belong. Like the anti-money-laundering agent he and the Strings had killed via the protection protocol, and the re-emergence of Briel Payce... and the surprise appearance of Dean Leggatt. Mateo had even orchestrated dividing the pair so they could more easily be picked off.

Sure, he had to play the game once the detective inspector got involved. Sure, there was greater risk once the AFSI took an interest. In fact, Mateo had almost killed Luis Menendez for his interference.

Even as they hated each other. A holdover from childhood bids for parental attention and jealousies born of each of their deficits. Clearly, they were both loyal to family.

Until now.

"Never," Mateo had said.

What did his brother think? That he still had a shot at the presidency? That he'd survive this? They were both at risk and they needed to disappear. Elpidio knew it, even as his brother rooted himself to his old dreams. Yes, there would be only one survivor.

A rustle sounded at the office door.

"Dorothea," the Conductor said. "I didn't see you there."

Her eyes were red and her jaw set in that same anguished look his wife used in the last years of her life, when his wife discovered what Elpidio's business was really all about.

"What's wrong?" the Conductor asked. He feigned innocence as best he could.

"How could you?" Dorothea asked. "Alejandro is good to me. Good to the boys. He ran for his life today. That was your doing."

Elpidio cocked his head. "Dorothea. You misunderstand. I needed to speak with him. That is all."

The Conductor stood and then strode to where Dorothea leaned on the frame at the threshold.

"I know you are close," he continued, his voice set to a slow tempo, projecting consonant harmony, "but Alejandro has a job to do. If that work is threatened, it affects us all."

He reached out to touch her arm, grab it if he had to. Perhaps it was time to lock away this woman and his beloved grandchildren. At least until he was gone.

Or maybe take Leonel and Mauricio away with him. On his trip. Leave Dorothea to the same fate as her beloved Alejandro. Other than the boys, she really didn't have much to offer. Too much like her mother.

Dorothea recoiled at his approach and ran. Did she sense his intention? The arthritis in his hips prevented a chase, but he had other means. So he watched her go.

CHAPTER 86

Briel hopped out of the car the moment Ricardo put his automobile in park at the lot for the round pyramid in Cuicuilco.

"Where are you going?" Ricardo asked. "You need to stop barging forward as though you own the land."

Briel stopped. She was too used to being in charge. In the classroom, in front of graduate students, and guiding teams of research assistants. She'd forgotten what it was like to follow in missions like those of the IEN. She was acting, well, more like Percy.

"Sorry," Briel said when Ricardo caught up.

His brows furrowed and he blew a puff of air from clenched teeth.

"Do you have any idea where we're supposed to look?" he asked. "This place is enormous. What Percy left could be anywhere. In fact, all she said was Cuicuilco, and this is a big city."

Briel faced the pyramid. Percy had told her about this place when they talked about the ancient buildings near and around Mexico City.

Construction on Cuicuilco's odd round-shaped structure had started about 1000 BCE. The ancients added tiers to it, creating an almost wedding cake effect. Percy believed the original people of this place were of the same race as those who had built Teotihuacan. The two cities had vied for dominance in pre-Columbian times. Only the top four tiers above the lava flow of the Xitli eruption remained for tourists to see. When Cuicuilco was destroyed, those that survived went to their brethren in Teotihuacan, searching for a safer community.

"Percy wouldn't have hidden it on the round pyramid."

"What?"

"Percy was a dedicated archeologist. She preserved these places. She'd never—and I mean never—deface such a place by either putting something in it or on it for us to find."

Ricardo scratched his head. "Then why are we here? Where else is there to go?"

Hands on hips, Briel did a slow turn, checking the region in a three hundred and sixty degree range from the path where they stood.

On her second pass, Briel mumbled, "What were you up to, Percy?"

On the third round, she stopped so she had a clear view of the museum. A fine structure conceived of by one of Mexico's renowned architects.

A low level stone barrier wall extended around the outside. From there, rock-bordered paths directed tourists throughout the grounds.

"I wonder," Briel said. And she headed toward it.

PEDRO EASED his sports car into the single spot left in the employee parking lot of the Cuicuilco archeological site. Always good to have connections.

Señora Persephone Gilbert was an archeologist. The round pyramid was the only logical place for her to have hidden either the next clue or the Spider Rock itself.

He was losing patience with the bitch. Even in death and so

many years later, she tormented him; caused every problem he had today. If she hadn't brought that relic home to Mexico. If that woman hadn't started asking questions and dug into the real meaning of the Rock, Briel Payce and Dean Leggatt wouldn't have come searching either.

He slammed his car door shut and headed for the stone stairs leading to the top of the pyramid.

No doubt the arrogant witch would have placed her prize at the top of their sacred site. Probably right in the middle of the ancient ceremonial space, on the shelf inside the alcove.

Pedro quickened his steps, acknowledging a fresh buzz of adrenaline.

A moment later, his body rebelled and he slowed again. Damn. Maybe getting back to the gym would help. Especially if he was going to stay in the field. If the Conductor...

Exiting to the platform, at the last step from the top, Pedro leaned over, hands on thighs, and worked to calm his breathing and slow his racing heart. He swiped a hand over his brow and straightened. A few steps down to the centre of the sacred space, he'd find his prize and maybe this hell would finally be over.

Pedro smiled at the barrier surrounding his target. A simple message for tourists to stay out. A message Gilbert should have heeded. He, on the other hand, had heritage on his side, and if that didn't persuade the powers that be, his pistol would do the trick.

He scanned the region, looking for any impediment to his intrusion, and noticed a man and a woman walking the path along the lower grounds. Pedro squinted, straining for a better look just as the woman turned her head toward the man and Pedro got a clear view of the face.

Doctor Briel Payce. How the hell did she figure it out?

CHAPTER 87

The room was barren save for the potted bamboo palm beside him, the wooden folding chairs occupied by two men with guns, and the chair facing them that Dean was strapped to.

He wasn't gagged. Didn't need to be. One gun pointed at him was enough to encourage his cooperation. Two guaranteed it.

And they hadn't blindfolded him. He could make out every landmark on the car ride over. He could see the faces of the men in front of him. Not a good sign.

Perhaps a little honey would get some answers?

"Excuse me," Dean said, his eyes floating from one guard to the next. "Exactly where am I? I mean, I know we're north of the Zocalo, but not by much, right?"

His captors' expressions didn't change. Guns remained trained on him.

Dean rethought his approach.

This had to have something to do with the fake Popocatepetl data. After all, they had chased Alejandro and him down at the detection site. God, he hoped Alejandro got away—and called for help. Though from whom, Dean couldn't imagine.

"So," Dean tried again. "You guys know about the scam data?

The little machine at the monitoring site that makes Popocatepetl look mad?"

The burly man to his left jumped up so fast that Dean's instinctive lean back almost tipped the chair to the floor.

Dean arched his neck as the barrel of the man's gun rested within millimetres of Dean's forehead.

The piercing brrring of the other guard's cell phone shattered the moment.

As the second guard left the room to answer his phone, Dean flipped his head under the first guard's gun and then pushed up and forward with everything he had.

If he was going to be shot anyway, he might as well go out fighting.

The guard fell over, and so did Dean. It was a stupid, desperate move. What was he thinking? He was in a room in some random building, up a flight of stairs, and tied to a goddamned chair.

Predictably, the second guard came running and Dean said a silent prayer to Percy, readying himself to join her in eternity.

MIGUEL CLOSED the door to his office in the upstairs apartment beside the Plaza de Loreto. He ignored the scuffle. Dean Leggatt was unarmed, tied up, and guarded by two of his most loyal followers. His men knew the score. Leggatt's destiny lay in Quetzalcoatl's powerful embrace. Of course, the man would never understand what a privilege it was. Most sacrifices didn't appreciate their status. Unlike pre-Colombian times.

Pedro's page of Popocatepetl data lay crumpled on the desk pad in front of him. As always, the numbers were irrefutable, but Miguel hated seeing them. Why was the volcano angry again so soon after they'd satisfied Quetzalcoatl's hunger? They hadn't tested the last sacrifice. There didn't seem to be a need. Was the man unworthy? Why?

Miguel pulled out the tablet he used only for religious

purposes. The one his acolyte had secured for his needs. A search for Popocatepetl's current status was predictable. The risk of violent eruption was low. The people of Mexico had no idea the lengths to which his small group of loyal supporters went to, to ensure their safety.

But time between ceremonies? It was so short. Perhaps an answer would come from Quetzalcoatl directly.

Miguel donned a robe and stepped to the tiny altar beside the small window to the right of his desk. Face shielded from the window by his brown hood, he took his place on the kneeling stool and offered his solemn prayer.

"Oh, glorious God of the wind and water, warring protector of this land and its people; Quetzalcoatl, hear the words of your most faithful servant..."

He remained kneeling, silent in his meditation. No answer came.

The previous sacrifice had to have been unworthy. Why? He couldn't know.

This time, there'd be no mistake. Thank Quetzalcoatl for the test.

He reached for the phone and called his ex-graduate student. "Arturo? Yes. I need a new test. We must be extra careful this time... No, come now."

Miguel hung up, tilting his head left and right, stretching the taut muscles until the stress-pain eased. He'd have a definitive answer soon.

And, one way or another, Dean Leggatt would be dead by the end of the day.

CHAPTER 88

The Conductor grabbed a cane from the circular teakwood walking stick stand that stood beside the door. The simple but functional mahogany number sat among the twenty-five he'd collected, always ready for when he chose not to pretend he didn't need one. Today was such a day.

With this added stability, the Conductor sped by the antique furnishings in the ornate upstairs hallway and headed for the weapons room. Family matters needed to be taken care of by family. But which to deal with first?

Mateo Tomás. The secretariat could not be allowed to live. Couldn't be left behind. If there was anyone capable of finding the Conductor wherever he went, it was his twin brother.

Mateo would never see the hit coming. Not from his "disabled" little brother.

His daughter was the easier hit. He'd leave that to last. Right before he disappeared and after he sorted someone to deliver his grandsons to the hiding place he finally chose.

Elpidio pulled keys from his pocket. It was time to unlock his stash of guns in the room around the corner.

The door was already open.

He stepped closer, and a body suddenly appeared beside him. Rifle pointed at his temple, Dorothea stood, tears still streaming down her cheeks.

"Not this time, Papa," she whispered. "You will not take away yet another father of a child of mine."

CHAPTER 89

Briel stood in front of the rocky landscape by the museum and scanned the stone half wall.

"Oh. And thanks for the Alamo."

The last words her best friend had said on the video. Briel had brushed it off as Percy's goodbye. Her way of remembering the day they met on a school trip to San Antonio.

Briel stood motionless, recalling the details of that fateful encounter. She'd wandered away from the school chaperones, distracted by the plants and rocks. When she'd passed a stone barrier, she found a rowdy gang of teenagers lined up in a semicircle facing the side wall of the historic church.

"What is it?" Ricardo touched Briel's arm, and she jumped.

"Sorry," Ricardo said. "You disappeared. I wondered if something caught your attention."

"The stone here. It reminds me of the Alamo. When Percy was little, a gang of teenagers forced her up against a mission wall. They didn't like that she was Black."

"What happened?" Ricardo's words were gentle. Kind. The man was practiced in speaking with witnesses to trauma.

"Percy fought back. Her screams and mine attracted a guard, but not before she got punched in the gut. When I found her, she was behind a three-foot barrier, like this one. She'd thrown up in the corner. I sat down beside her, gave her my water bottle. I wouldn't let anybody near her until she was good and ready. Percy insisted she could have taken care of things without me, and maybe that was true. But she appreciated the support and we became fast friends after that. Always looking out for each other."

Ricardo nodded, a sincere, slightly sad smile turning up the corners of his mouth.

"We should continue the search," he said.

"Everything on the tape she left me was there for a reason. We need to search every inch of the man-made rock wall in the area. And we need to check every loose stone."

"Done," Ricardo said. "Where do you want me to start?"

RICARDO FOLLOWED suit as Briel bent down and began picking through the low stone walls surrounding the museum grounds. A moment later, his back protested and he stood to stretch it. Briel, he noticed, bent from her knees as she crept forward.

Two things came to mind. First, she was a chiropractor. He figured she knew how to avoid the pain. Second, she was really flexible. He didn't think his knees would allow the movement she made.

He arched his back again before deciding exactly how to tackle the next few yards. Then he stretched his neck, as though preparing for one of his Guardia-run martial arts events. And that's when he noticed the man stepping carefully down the stairs of the circular pyramid.

Logic said it was another tourist, or a groundskeeper. Instinct told him something was wrong.

The Cuicuilco pyramid site was off the typical tourist path, though he was uncertain why. It was a spectacular sight. Still, visitors were far less frequent in this modest location than they were at the humongous Teotihuacan pyramids northeast of Mexico City.

He caught Briel's eye and motioned for her to get down. When she raised her brows with an unasked question, he pointed to the figure on the stairs and she obeyed.

Ricardo ducked behind the nearest tree and watched the man reach a lower rung of the pyramid circle and look their way. Then the stranger placed his hands on his hips and a burst of reflected sun exposed the weapon attached to his belt.

Instinct won again.

PEDRO PAUSED at the first landing on the stairs leading down from the altar. Briel Payce and the man were gone. The man with her couldn't be Dean Leggatt. Leggatt was tall and blond, and he was with Miguel. This was a shorter, dark-haired Mexican. This had to be Ricardo De La Cruz, Detective Inspector for the Violent Crimes Against Tourists Division for Mexico City's Guardia Nacional. Miguel had said the detective was with Payce in Tepoztlán. No doubt he had accompanied her here, and no doubt he'd have his firearm with him.

The question now was whether to pursue the pair. Surprise them and get them to tell him what they knew.

If he found the Spider Rock where he suspected it to be by the ceremonial center, just steps away, he wouldn't need either of them. He could take it and leave. Deal with Briel Payce when she finally came looking for Dean Leggatt. Pedro bet Payce didn't know the man was in danger. Best to keep it that way.

Pedro scanned the grounds one last time. Nothing. The pair probably had gone into the museum proper. A lot of good that would do them. He turned around and headed back up the stairs. More exercise than he wanted, but the prize was worth it.

RICARDO WATCHED the man with the gun turn back to the stairs. When the stranger put his hands on his knees to support himself and pushed off at the last step before the platform at the top, Ricardo estimated him to be older. In okay shape, but he could take him, if it was a fair fight. The weapon made them even.

A tiny puff of smoke showed that the man lit a cigarette. Not the best way of catching your breath, but Ricardo supposed it was how this guy relaxed.

"Psst."

The sound came from where Briel was still hiding. He signalled for her to stay down while he watched the man head for the sacred space in the sunken centre of the pyramid's top.

"Psst." The sound was louder this time. Insistent.

Ricardo turned and saw Briel crouched, only half hidden now, pointing. He followed her finger until his eyes rested on a flat cement-like rock, peeking out from the soil around a century plant inside a stone border.

CHAPTER 90

"Hijo de puta."

The abusive epithet came from down the hallway. It was the first signal that Miguel needed to get involved. This was a holy place, a place of preparation. His men knew better than to express profanity here.

When he reached the doorway to the room where Dean was being held, he found Dean Leggatt still tied to the chair but tipped over onto the floor. The geologist bent his knees, struggling against the ropes, scooting across the ground as though there was some place to escape to. Miguel's man, Eduardo, had his arms over Berna, who was lying on the ground, holding his nose. Blood oozed from between Berna's fingers.

"Eduardo, mind your language," Miguel said. "Attend to Señor Leggatt. I will take care of Berna."

Eduardo released his hold on Berna, eyes dark with emotion.

"Remember your oath," Miguel counselled.

It took a moment. Finally, Eduardo drew a deep breath, fixed his gaze on the potted palm and released at least some of his anger in a loud exhale. When Eduardo righted Leggatt's chair, he jostled it roughly, perhaps unnecessarily, but Miguel knew the outcome could have been much worse. Eduardo had learned a great deal since his initiation into Quetzalcoatl's arms.

Miguel pulled a handkerchief from his pocket, pinched Berna's nose, and then led him to a leather couch in the room next to his office.

"Lie down," Miguel said. "Lean your head back."

As Miguel made to leave, Berna tried to return the blood-stained white cloth.

"Keep it," Miguel said, wrinkling his nose.

Arturo was sitting in the chair in front of Miguel's desk when Miguel got back to his office.

"You have it?" Miguel asked.

"Of course." Arturo retrieved an envelope from his shirt pocket and shook it enough so the grains containing genetically modified roundworm eggs made the sound of sand moving in a child's toy.

"Administration?"

Arturo withdrew a small container of milk from a bag sitting at his feet. "Is the man lactose intolerant?"

Miguel only raised a brow. Hardly something to worry about now.

"Do you really think someday our God will ask us to test all of humankind?" Arturo asked. "I have sufficient stock now to infect the water supply in North America. Though this milk, or another foodborne route, would be more efficient. I am running new experiments."

A hungry look passed over Arturo's face, one that needed placating.

"It is possible. But we have a different priority. Go. Gather the congregation and prepare the site. I believe this man will pass the test."

As Arturo disappeared, Miguel poured parasite eggs into the milk, shaking the container slightly to be sure the embryos stayed afloat, ready for consumption.

By the time he re-entered the room where Dean Leggatt was

being held prisoner, Berna was back at his post. Miguel could see that Eduardo had not yet let go of his emotions after Leggatt's attempted escape. They would need to deal with that later.

"Who are you?" Leggatt asked.

"A doctor," Miguel said. "You need medicine, and I've brought it for you."

"Why?"

"You've been ill since you arrived in Mexico. We are here to help."

"By keeping me prisoner? Tying me up? Why am I here?"

"If your heart is pure, then all your questions will be answered in due time. Now. Take this medicine."

"No thank you."

"Señor Leggatt. We will administer this with or without your cooperation. Surely you are thirsty. It would be easier for everyone if you would simply comply."

"No."

Miguel slid his eyes to Eduardo and Berna, both all too happy to manhandle their prisoner. Eduardo leaned Leggatt's head back and Berna pried open his mouth. Leggatt fought back, kicking his feet and snapping his teeth at Berna.

Berna didn't waver. He peeled open Leggatt's lips and though the prisoner's teeth remained clenched, Miguel poured the liquid in.

Leggatt coughed, spat, and choked, but Miguel continued until he was certain that the man had swallowed an adequate dose.

When he left the room, Leggatt's chin was on his chest. Spilled milk streaked his lips and shirt, and some even covered the ground. His cleaning crew would need to be extra careful this week.

CHAPTER 91

"Dorothea," the Conductor said. "Please. My child. I only want what is best for you, and what is best for my grandchildren."

He felt the barrel of the rifle brush up and down on his temple as his daughter's body shook.

"And what about my unborn child?" Dorothea asked.

So, she admitted it. The whore got herself pregnant. Her voice was stronger than he expected.

"Dorothea. The news is good. Have the child. But the man. He is nothing. Still, if you want him so much, we can find a way. He can live here, with us."

The point of the gun eased slightly away. She wanted to believe his lies.

"Mommy!"

The shout came from the courtyard. Mauricio. God bless that child.

Dorothea turned her head and in that moment, the Conductor flipped his cane in the air and smacked the rifle away. As it hit the ground, a bullet ricocheted from the barrel, the loud bang momentarily stunning them both.

The Conductor's daughter recovered first and dove for the

weapon, but the Conductor woke in time to use his cane to draw the rifle toward him. Strengthened by rage, he grabbed the gun, aware that in less than a second, he could eliminate the mother of his grandchildren.

Her large, dark eyes met his. Instinct rather than skill or intention propelled him. He grabbed the barrel of the gun and struck his daughter with the butt end.

In the ten minutes it took him to go back to his office, retrieve the go-bag, make arrangements for his grandsons, and come back to point the gun at her head, she never stirred. The Conductor stood over his daughter's unconscious body, waiting for her to wake up.

She was still breathing, so he knew he hadn't killed her. At least not yet. But he was getting impatient. Perhaps a quick end would be better. Something he usually left to others. Since she was blood, something he should probably do himself.

As though on cue, Dorothea stirred, groaned, put her hands over her head. Awareness came slowly, but it did finally arrive. Eyes wide with terror looked into his.

"You would kill the mother of your grandsons?" she said. Her voice croaked.

"A last resort," the Conductor said.

He threw the pouch at her.

"What's this?"

"Money. Leave now and never come back. Find your lover, have your bastard child; I don't care. You no longer live here."

"I'll gather the boys," Dorothea said. She strained to get up, wobbled slightly, and placed a hand on the door frame for support.

"No," the Conductor said. "The boys stay here."

"What? No. Impossible."

"They are... insurance. A guarantee that you and your boyfriend will speak to no one about me or my business. I have trusted you for far too long. I can see you no longer put family first."

"The boys are innocent..."

"Yes. And they are safe. For now. Some time in the next few days, I will go on a... vacation. Once I have reached my destination, I will send word, and you may retrieve your sons. After that? I have no family."

Dorothea didn't move. The Conductor eyed the rise and fall of her thin chest. She was frightened. He could see her heart pounding. Still, she wanted to stand up to him. At least some of him remained in her. Perhaps he should reconsider? No. Too risky. She'd gone too far.

"Go," he whispered. And then, in a tone that brooked no argument, he added, "before your sons have no mother to think about."

CHAPTER 92

Searching the ceremonial centre of Cuicuilco's round pyramid took longer than Pedro expected.

It was easy enough to get under the flimsy caution tape that functioned as a barrier for tourists, and then jump down the few steps that led to the holy site. His search was relatively comfortable, thanks to the archeologists who he assumed had built the flimsy metal roof structure above him, to provide shade while they worked. It served the same purpose for him.

The problem was actually finding the Spider Rock. It was substantial enough that it should have been obvious to a keen observer. Over a third of a meter, an almost square piece of limestone. Pedro would have bet money it was turned over so none of the marks showed, and wedged, pride of place as the floor of the altar. It wasn't there.

In fact, he'd turned over rock after rock in his search through the sacred space he knew from childhood. Nothing.

One last look. Evidence of his foraging lay strewn about, and he left it that way. Something for the egghead archeologists to ponder and cry over. Pedro finally acknowledged that either someone else had found the prize, or it was never there to begin with. Had Persephone Gilbert sent them on yet another wild goose chase?

Pedro emerged back at the top of the pyramid, lit another cigarette, and considered his next move.

Perhaps Payce and the detective knew something after all?

He flicked the butt to the ground, watched it smoulder for a few seconds, and then crushed the lit end into the earth. No sense setting fire to the thing even if he was disgusted by the pyramid.

As he headed back to the stairs, he caught movement from the path near the museum. Briel Payce heading toward the visitor parking lot, accompanied by the detective inspector, who was carrying a large, square rock.

"It's the Spider Rock," Briel said. She kept her voice low while Ricardo's eyes tracked the stranger who'd climbed the round pyramid.

Ricardo's attention alternated between what was going on at the top of the monument and where Briel had already begun digging.

"Speed things up," Ricardo ordered.

"What?"

"That man up there? He's got a gun."

"Not here for the sights?"

"No."

As the stranger disappeared into the pyramid's top tier, Ricardo bent beside Briel and together they freed a large, flat chunk of limestone from its home. Ricardo tilted his head to the side and the corners of his mouth curved down as Briel brushed dirt from the empty backside of their prize. He went back to checking on their visitor.

Briel ignored him. If she was right, Ricardo's mood was about to change. She flipped the piece over. There, in all their glory, were the markings she'd seen in Padre Hugh's picture of the Spider Rock.

A low whistle blew beside her as Ricardo leaned close.

"Let's go," he said.

"What?"

"We need to leave. It isn't safe here."

"But the markings. If we stay hidden, just for a while longer, we can study it. That guy may be nobody. We can wait until he leaves."

"That guy is somebody. And it is not worth the risk. We have a chance right now. We need to take it."

Briel nodded, knowing Ricardo was right; wishing he wasn't. She hoisted the rock into her arms, surprised when Ricardo grabbed it from her and started speed walking toward the car.

Don't let that little boy face fool you, she reminded herself. The man obviously lifted weights.

They were halfway to the parking lot when Briel looked up. There on the stairs, gun in hand, was the stranger.

Ricardo pushed the Spider Rock into Briel's arms.

"Fast as you can," he said. "I will give you cover."

When she didn't move, he shouted, "Go! I'll meet you by the car."

A shot cracked nearby, and that was all the encouragement Briel needed. Ricardo was armed. She wasn't.

Hugging the Spider Rock to her chest, she took off.

RICARDO DUCKED behind the live oak tree in time to see the bullet kick up the dirt he'd been standing on. No question now whether the stranger meant them harm.

A new player, or was this guy responsible for what had happened at Hogar de Niños San Antonio de Padua?

Once Briel sorted out that this was serious, she hustled toward their car. Safely out of range for the gun pointed at them. Good thing she was in shape. The stone was heavy.

He, on the other hand, was too close to the man's weapon for comfort. Then again, his pistol's fire spanned about the same distance.

The man skipped down the pyramid stairs, probably looking for a better, closer position. Ricardo discharged his gun, stopping their attacker in his tracks. When the stranger flattened himself on a middle step, Ricardo kept him there, laying down bullet after bullet, trying to catch up with Briel as she made it to Ricardo's car.

Ricardo unlocked the vehicle, grabbed the Spider Rock and dumped it in the back seat.

"Get in!" he shouted, yanking open the driver's side door and starting the engine.

Their attacker was at the bottom rung of the pyramid now, close enough so his gun could do serious damage. Ricardo backed his car out with a screech and heard the snap and ping as lead found the metal on their back end.

CHAPTER 93

Ricardo felt the thud of a second bullet as he turned the car toward the street.

"Those shots didn't do much damage. The guy behind us isn't very good at this," Briel said.

In contrast to her words, Briel gripped her seat so hard, her pale fingers went white.

Ricardo had to admire the woman. This was the second time someone was firing at them and no matter how terrified, she didn't make things worse by descending into hysteria.

"Actually," Ricardo said, regaining control as the car veered to the right from the hit to his rear tire. "Whoever that is knows very well what he is doing. This is not the movies. He is saving his ammunition and has slowed us down."

Ricardo glanced in his rear-view mirror. "That move gave him the time he needed to get to his much faster vehicle and give chase. There will be no chance to get away on the main road."

Briel's cheeks reddened. Her eyes grew wide and she fixed her gaze on some unknown spot on the windshield. Maybe he was getting a read on this woman. It was the look of someone trying to control themselves.

"Of course," Ricardo said, "I am also well-trained."

Clutching the steering wheel harder, he yanked the car to the left and sped down a makeshift dirt road he'd spotted near the exit. He swerved left and right, kicking up as much dust as possible. Ahead, the road widened slightly. Enough room? It would have to do. He pulled the wheel hard and spun, forcing the car to stop when it faced the direction from which they'd come.

From within the cloud of debris in his wake, Ricardo heard the crunch of wheels on gravel as the dark green sports car approached.

TWO THOUGHTS DANCED through Pedro's mind when the cruiser pulled onto the primitive road inside the archeological site grounds. First, he'd trapped his quarry. This would all be over soon. Second, his beloved car was going to take a beating.

He gunned the accelerator, making the turn onto the dirt road. And then he knew. He'd underestimated the detective. A fog of dirt and dust blinded him and forced him to proceed slowly to avoid crashing into barriers on either side of the single lane. Still, there was nowhere for them to go. Payce and De La Cruz were only postponing the inevitable.

Fifty meters later, the dust thinned and Pedro caught sight of the detective's vehicle.

Facing him.

"GET DOWN."

It was the best Ricardo could do to protect Briel, and she didn't argue.

Their opponent's vehicle stopped short of their position and Ricardo didn't hesitate. He aimed for the driver and missed. His next shot put a bullet into the driver's side front tire.

Now what? His ammunition had to be running low. How many bullets left? He hadn't been counting. It would be embarrassing, let alone deadly, if he tried to shoot the driver and all that came from his gun was a click.

Safer to keep disabling the other vehicle if possible, and go. Not much of a plan. Then again, all he was running on was adrenaline and instinct.

Ricardo floored the accelerator but the sports car anticipated the move and repositioned, so he shot out the second front tire. It had the intended effect. Their pursuer's steering became clumsy and the man struggled to stay on the road.

Ricardo took full advantage. In the second before he was blocked, he sped onto the brush-lined shoulder that widened this section of the lane and flew by.

The gun that appeared from the sports car's driver's side window danced wildly as the driver tried to manage the sloppy grip of flattening tires on gravel. The attacker's first shot hit the top of Ricardo's window frame, and the next blew out the rear glass. A barrage of bullets followed that peppered the detective's trunk. The guy was seriously out of control.

In a moment's pause, just before getting away, Ricardo sent a slug into the sports car's back tire. Payback came to mind as Ricardo pictured the slashed rubber at the friar's church. He turned, again, intent on catching the last wheel.

No joy. Bullets gone.

Ricardo sped away, hoping he'd done enough.

CHAPTER 94

Dean's throat itched with the reminder that he'd aspirated milk during his struggle.

The man who assaulted him matched Briel's description of Miguel Lobo, the medical contact Briel had in Mexico City. The man who had supposedly helped her eliminate a Jane Doe as Percy five years earlier. Thick lips, Briel called them. Wavy hair framing a long face, and glasses. And he had told Dean he was a doctor.

If it was Lobo, the "doctor" wasn't a good guy. And whatever they had forced down Dean's throat, that couldn't be good either.

The question was, what to do about it now? The guard he'd given a bloody nose to stood by the door. Far enough away to avoid another encounter, and that was smart. Dean had enough fight left in him that the temptation to force another hit was high.

The other guard had disappeared. Gone with the doctor.

Distract the guy by the door long enough to vomit out whatever he'd consumed? Good idea, but where and how?

Dean inched his chair closer again to the potted palm, covering the moves by shaking his head wildly.

"Hey," Dean called to the guard. "Look. Sorry about your

nose. The spilled milk. It's attracting flies. Lots of them. And they're trying to land on my lips."

Dean spat for emphasis.

"Come on," Dean continued. "Can I at least have a moist cloth or something to clean up with? I'll bet it won't be long before the flies get to you, too. Maybe spread whatever I drank to both of us?"

The last bit was a risk, but the guard's sudden and sharp focus confirmed that Dean had consumed something his captor didn't want to get close to. In fact, there was a faint smell of bleach permeating the room from where the guy stood. He'd cleaned up before coming back to his post.

As though on cue, a fly buzzed past the guard. It was almost comical to watch the guy bat the thing away.

The guard eyed the ropes that bound Dean at the waist and legs. Dean helped with the inspection by lifting his arms and showing his captor that his wrists were still well secured.

As the man left, Dean instantly turned to the plant. He found a spot behind the potted palm where his head would be hard to see from the doorway, brought his bound wrists to his mouth, and stuck a finger down his throat and watered the plant with all the milk his gut would expel. Dean was all too practiced at emptying his stomach contents on this trip. He only hoped he got enough out to stay alive and figure out what was going on.

He took in a deep and haggard breath. It was too soon to vomit again, but there was no choice. He leaned his head forward and shoved his fingers as far back as they would go. The hard part was trying to keep the retching sounds to a minimum as his body responded with gusto.

Satisfied he'd done his best, Dean continued to scoot his chair, wave his bound hands and shake his head as more flies assembled around him. The mess on his clothes and face was worse but made of the same stuff, and he hoped his guard didn't notice the increase in insect activity around the plant.

By the time the man returned, Dean was perfectly positioned with his back to the palm, chair inching closer to the door.

"You thought to escape?" The guard's sneer was palpable.

Dean hadn't tried to leave the room. His policy was to look for at least a twenty per cent chance of success. Tied to the chair, multiple enemies in the building, his analytical mind estimated ten.

"No," Dean said. "But I was wondering if you'd ever get here. The flies are worse. Hand me the towel."

The guard took a step, looked at Dean's moist shirt, face, and hands, and retreated. Dean took a breath, waiting to see what the man would do next.

A second later, safely by the door again, the guard pitched the moist, grey cloth into Dean's lap. Dean bet the thing had been snowy white when it was new, but he was in no position to protest. He held the towel between his bound fingers and bent forward to wipe his face, paying extra attention to his mouth. The thing smelled of foul water. A dishcloth too old for good use.

His captor knit his brows, bemused interest written large on his round face.

"You should be very proud," the guard said finally.

"Why?"

"So far, you are a fine specimen. Perhaps you will prove worthy of our God after all."

CHAPTER 95

The blinding fury that burned in Pedro as his quarry whizzed by him seared his gut. He damned his knee-jerk decisions.

Pedro threw the steering wheel of his precious vehicle all the way to the left and put his foot down. The detective had proven himself a formidable foe, but Pedro couldn't afford this loss.

The automobile's tires screamed at his command. He didn't care. He pushed harder, and the car lurched. When he hit the accelerator again, the wheels spun, but the car didn't move.

Pedro jumped from the driver's seat only to discover his passenger side flat tire sunk deep in the soft chalky bank of the rough-cut road.

"Hijo de puta." Pedro kicked the tire. The last thing he wanted to do was call for help. Yet there was no other way.

He reached for his cell and then stopped. Call the Conductor with an update, or call someone in the network and try to hide this?

The Conductor would find out. He always did. So he traded cells. He'd explain the situation to the boss, assure the Conductor that he had his sights on the Spider Rock, and then get himself out of here.

"What is it now?" The Conductor's voice was rough, angry, and something else. Panicked?

BRIEL unfurled herself in the front seat and looked around. Gunfire no longer assaulted her ears. Their attacker was gone. Ricardo rattled down the pyramid site's primitive road, finally reaching asphalt at the main exit.

The sounds Briel attributed to the dirt track didn't stop. A clamorous thump, thump, thump persisted from the back end, and was made more evident by the lack of crunching gravel.

Seconds later, a scraping, metal-scratching sound replaced the rhythmic noises. Briel checked her side mirror, horrified to see a wide cone of streaking light coming from what should have been the rear passenger tire. Gunshots, possible fuel leak, sparks. It wasn't good, none of it.

"We're on the rim!" Briel shouted above the noise. "Flames. We need to get out of the car."

At the next corner, a sign directed motorists to a nearby mausoleum. Ricardo turned in, slowed down, and went in back behind the largest building on the premises. Well hidden from the main road, he stopped the car, jumped out and inspected the damage.

"You are right. The tire is completely gone," he reported to Briel. "But the gas tank was not hit. We are safe, for now. I will call for help."

Briel stepped from the cruiser and reached in back for the Spider Rock. So many acts of desperation, and for what? A flat piece of limestone with circles and lines?

Briel ran her fingers over the surface, removing bits of debris stuck from when they'd pulled the Spider Rock from the ground.

Beside her, she heard Ricardo's voice rise. "Dead? You are sure it is Torres? What was he doing near the dump?"

Ricardo hung up, his schoolboy face drawn. He looked older.

Briel thought perhaps Ricardo would let her know when help was on the way. Instead, he turned away, scrolled the phone and started a new call.

RICARDO SHOULDN'T HAVE BEEN SURPRISED by the news that his boss had been murdered. A professional hit, for sure. Bullet to the head, corpse thrown in the trash. Nothing good came from trying to play both ends toward the middle, and Enrique Torres had been suspected of doing that for a long, long time. That no one from the force had kicked him out wasn't a surprise, either. He had cartel-related friends in high places.

But the death signalled something else. A lot was happening fast, and he couldn't get a handle on which incidents were related. So he called the only person in the know he hoped was still trustworthy.

Secretariat Tomás picked up the call on the second ring. "Are you alright?"

Was he worried because he knew about Torres or because he already knew of the attack at the Cuicuilco site?

"We're alive. And we found the stone Persephone Gilbert left for Doctora Payce. My cruiser is wounded though. And we left our attacker on the grounds near the pyramid. With backup, I believe we have a chance of finding and apprehending the man chasing us."

A long, enigmatic breath came from the other end of the line, and the words that followed made the hair at the back of Ricardo's neck prickle.

"I am sorry. You understand, I too must report to my superior. My resources are not unlimited and it seems the rock you have found is more of a hot potato than even I realized. My driver will pick you up. No more searching for trouble. No stopping. You will come directly to me with the Spider Rock and with Doctora Payce."

"Sí," Ricardo said, and he hung up.

The tone of the call was wrong. What had happened to the secretariat's intention to clean up "the sleeping giant" that had been awakened? Now all he wanted was the Spider Rock?

Maybe it was best if they left before Tomás's driver found them. He'd go back to Tomás, but on his own terms.

Ricardo eyed the wounded wheel on his car. The rim damage didn't look too bad. The spare would hold at least until he got back. He just needed enough information to determine where "back" was.

He dialled again. This time, the call was to the hospital.

"Hello. This is Detective Inspector De La Cruz. I need to know the status of Luis Menendez."

CHAPTER 96

Dean hadn't moved in at least an hour—save, of course, for swatting flies and shuffling in his seat. His muscles were stiffening, and he fought to stay alert. His guard hadn't moved either. The man stood at the door, watching every move.

Dean didn't know what had happened to the second guard. He never came back. Someone assumed Dean wouldn't be a threat at this point.

Time to try a different tack.

"I need to go to the bathroom," Dean said. If they thought he wasn't a threat, maybe they'd let him up, and then he could surprise them.

His guard disappeared without a word. Probably needed help with the request. Dean looked around, deciding what to do. Maybe he could shift his chair to the window at the end of the room. The ledge was high on the wall, but even if he could pry it open a little, he could call for help. Surely someone on the street below would take notice.

The thought made him wince. He actually wasn't feeling all that great. Maybe enough of what was in the milk had gotten into his system to impair him. There was a tightness in his chest and a general sense of nausea. The nausea, he was all too used to since arriving in Mexico.

No. Not a time to spend precious energy on the window. He had a better shot in close quarters.

"So." The word came from the door. The "doctor" was back. "You are still with us. A fine specimen. Surprising, but fine."

"I need to go to the bathroom."

"It will have to wait."

"Not a good idea."

"Trust me. I have the means to take care of all such matters while you sleep."

And then Dean spotted the syringe resting at the doctor's side, in his right hand. A guard's head, the one whose nose Dean had bloodied, popped up from behind the doctor's shoulder. Dean didn't like the grin on the man's face.

Keep him talking. At least that's what they did in the movies until the hero was rescued. Right?

"I have a right to know what you gave me."

"You have no right!" the guard with the wounded nose said.

"Berna," the doctor said. "This one has proven his worth. What is it to answer his question? He will take it with him to eternity, and our God will still be pleased."

"You're Miguel Lobo, aren't you?"

The doctor's mouth dropped enough so Dean knew he'd struck a chord, and the man didn't deny the accusation.

"I'm Briel Payce's friend, and you're supposed to be that, too. What's this all about?"

Lobo crossed his arms, careful where the point of the syringe landed, and pursed his lips.

"You were given a significant dose of ascaris lumbricoides eggs."

"Roundworms?"

"Yes, and no. I had a graduate student some years ago whose studies... did not go as planned. The true God of the wind and rain, the One who speaks to us through the region's volcanic activity, led my student to genetically modify the parasite. Intending to render the species sterile, instead, he developed an extremely fast-growing worm that preferentially finds the lungs. Within only one hour, we know whether the suggested sacrifice is worthy of the ceremony that quells Quetzalcoatl's hunger."

"You're a man of science. A doctor, for God's sake! You can't possibly believe what you're saying."

"Some truths defy rational explanation, Doctor Leggatt. You are still alive. Popocatepetl is restless. What must be, must be."

Lobo uncrossed his arms and moved toward him, with Berna following close behind.

"Wait," Dean said. "The volcano data. It's fake. Double numbers. Donata Rangal had me looking into it."

"Your lies will not save you," Miguel said as he motioned to Berna. The big guard's gloved hands pushed Dean's bound fists down and pulled back his head.

"Not lies." Dean struggled to talk. "You've been fooled into becoming a killing machine."

The needle pricked his neck and Dean felt the room spin. He mouthed a brief prayer to his own god, figuring it would all be over soon. To his surprise, he didn't pass out. He couldn't fight, but he was aware.

"What did he mean by double numbers?" Berna asked.

"Never mind," the doctor said. "He passed the test. Quetzalcoatl will accept the gift. This man does not know what is real. We do."

CHAPTER 97

As Ricardo clicked off from his call, his frown suggested more trouble.

"Someone I need to get hold of," Ricardo said to Briel's unasked question. "Apparently, they will get back to me."

Then he rummaged through the car's trunk, dragging out the spare tire. Metal tools ricocheted off rocks as he threw them to the ground.

"I need you to close the door and step away," Ricardo said. "I am going to replace the tire so we can get out of here."

"Is there something I can do to help?"

Ricardo's eyebrows went up and his smirk suggested condescension.

"What? You think I can't change a tire?" Briel asked.

The grin disappeared. "No, no. I am sure you are capable."

"Then I ask again. Would you like some help?"

"It is a one-man job," Ricardo said.

As he turned his head, Briel caught another flash of amusement. He didn't believe her, and she thought to push it, but reconsidered. It was hot, and she was grateful.

Briel took the Spider Rock in her arms and stepped further from the car. With most of the debris removed, Briel realized for the first time how the slab had gotten its name. The friar's picture didn't do it justice. Lines extended from a central point, cutting the graphic into eight equal pie pieces. Also from the centre, concentric circles expanded outward. A spider's web. A simple one to be sure, but there it was.

And something else.

Briel traced the etchings: the numbers and letters Padre Hugh had translated, and then the strange sidewalk-like structure that extended from one side. The markings looked like a compass. North, south, east, west. But which was which?

An arrow in one quadrant caught Briel's attention. She oriented the stone so she faced it, pointing from right to left. Stepping back, she wondered.

A map?

Briel knew of locations and structures portrayed in stone, dating all the way back to the Bronze Age. In her meetings with the IEN code committee, they had studied the Saint-Bélec slab, an ancient stone construction depicting settlements, possibly along a river in France.

"What city is set up with this kind of circular shape?" Though the words were meant for her own reflection, she said them out loud.

Ricardo leaned over the spare tire he'd retrieved from the trunk, grabbed the tire iron, and on hearing Briel's words, looked over her shoulder.

"Most cities are circle-like," he said.

"True," Briel said. "It's just these other features. They almost look like bridges."

"Tenochtitlan," he said.

"What?"

"Historically, Mexico City was known as Tenochtitlan. Early Spanish artists often depicted it as a round island in Lake Texcoco. Cortez invaded by sending his army en masse down a causeway the Aztecs had built for exit and entry to their beloved place."

"I KNOW where the Spider Rock is," Pedro said.

Silence thundered on the other end of the line. He had told the Conductor the good news first, hoping it would buy him some measure of mercy when he had to explain that it was in Briel Payce's hands and she was gone.

"Well, get it and bring it here. What are you waiting for?" The tone was still angry. Abrupt. Not good.

"There are problems."

"What problems?"

"I'm still in Cuicuilco. My car is... disabled."

"Get it fixed. Why are you calling me?"

"And... Briel Payce and her Guardia Nacional escort got away with the stone. I promise, I can find them..."

The Conductor hung up.

Pedro stood for a long time. Too many failures. Too much stacked up against him, and his boss was unpredictable. More so than ever, it was time to run.

He threw the phone that led directly to his boss against the nearest boulder. After a satisfying crack, the shell opened and pieces flew in all directions. The battery hung by its wires, signalling the end of its life—and perhaps the end of his.

Pedro drew a hand over the hood of his dark green sports car, reminding himself of the pride he had felt on the day he bought his dream machine. A self-made man. In truth, the Conductor's man, but close enough.

Heat from the hood scorched his fingertips, prompting a swift withdrawal.

"Et tu?" he said to his beloved vehicle.

And Pedro began the long walk toward the main streets of Cuicuilco. He felt for the gun still in his pocket. Reloading was quick and easy. Whoever's car he hijacked would never see it coming.

BRIEL PULLED out her cell phone, opened a browser page and typed "Tenochtitlan and map".

The first image to come up was dated 1524. A multicoloured pictorial rendering of the city, published in Nuremberg. The features seemed close. Causeways extended from the old Zocalo. While it was hard to imagine a Mexico City surrounded by that much water, the picture still seemed wrong.

Briel expanded the map with her fingers and noticed something odd. The canoes and their paddlers were upside down. She checked other websites. In each case, the same drawing was positioned, to her eye, the wrong way around. No explanation.

"I like Bordone's wood cut best." The words came from behind. Ricardo had the shredded back wheel off. As he stood back and wiped his forehead, he'd checked what she was doing.

"Bordone?"

"Yes. We learned about it in school. The one you're looking at? It confuses me. I keep wanting to turn my head upside down to get the figures and houses right. The Bordone map is quite beautiful, and simpler to read."

Briel tapped in "Bordone, map, and Tenochtitlan".

From the offerings, she read that Benedetto Bordone was a cartographer who had created a wood-cut map of what he called "Temistitan" and published it in a "book of islands" in the 16th century. Looking at a picture of the work, Briel immediately saw the appeal. Although she was a foreigner in Mexico City, the current geographical locations of places like Iztapalapa made sense.

And then Briel had a thought.

CHAPTER 98

Ricardo was pleased Briel had found something to do while he busied himself getting their car ready to go. He had enough on his mind, and fixing his vehicle with minimal interruptions gave him the space to think.

The news that Menendez had regained consciousness should have provided Ricardo some satisfaction. He'd probably saved the man's life.

Unfortunately, Ricardo didn't have time to revel in his Good Samaritan status. He had left a message for the head of the AFSI to call him. What he needed now was information, and it was possible Menendez held the key.

He unwound the jack, allowing the replaced tire to bounce unceremoniously onto the asphalt. It looked diminutive. Out of place. A clear sign to everyone that his car had been in some kind of situation and lost. Of course, the bullet holes in the back end and the shattered windows already told them that.

Still, he was thankful. Unlike the incident at the friar's church, this time, he had the power to drive himself away. And that he would. Before the secretariat's man showed up.

He needed a better feel for what was really going on.

He took a cleaning wipe from the inside pocket of the front

door and did his best to remove the grime from his hands. It didn't work well.

Briel's head still leaned over her phone.

"All done," Ricardo said. "Let's get out of here."

Ricardo moved to pick up the Spider Rock and put it into the car.

"Wait," Briel said. "I just want to look at the rock again."

"We need to go," Ricardo repeated.

"Look." Briel pointed to the Bordone map that filled her cell phone screen and then traced the common features on the Spider Rock. The sidewalk-like detail on the etched stone matched the west side of Bordone's wood cutting. A dike-like marking on the east side appeared in both too. "This limestone slab is a 16th century map of Mexico City."

"Or some modern children's sketch of Bordone's art."

"I don't think so. When Padre Hugh met with Percy, they went over the symbols. He dated some of them from the Middle Ages. Not likely on a modern sketch."

"What does the arrow mean?"

"I don't know. But if it's a map of Mexico City at the time of the conquest, could it be pointing to some kind of feature on the Bordone? I've been looking from one to the other, but I can't get my bearing."

"Take a picture of the Spider Rock."

"What?"

"Take a picture and then give me your phone."

When Briel handed him her cell, he downloaded a blending app.

"Now," Ricardo said. "Superimpose one map over the other and see if the arrow lands on something. You can do that while we drive. We need to leave."

As Ricardo stepped toward the driver's side door, his phone buzzed. He considered not answering. He'd assumed, since no one had followed them to the mausoleum, that they were safe. But they'd stayed a long time, and he wanted more distance between them and their attacker. And he wanted to be gone before the secretariat's chauffeur showed up.

He opened the car door as the third buzz shook his pocket. Relenting, Ricardo looked at the screen. Menendez. A direct call. Not what he expected, and definitely not this quickly.

"Sí," Ricardo answered, his full focus on the phone.

"About time," Menendez said. "I'm leaving the hospital."

Background chatter suggested disagreement about the matter. Ricardo heard a door close, and then Menendez continued.

"I gather I have you to thank for my good health?"

"Uhm."

"You were there when the secretariat attacked me?"

"Sí."

"Did you know the secretariat has a twin brother?"

"No, señor."

"My office followed up on a tip about the brother, after I was attacked. The twins have been good at hiding each other—until now. Our analysts had to haul someone in from the records department. Under threat of being charged as an accessory to attempted murder, they gained access to all Tomás's information, including that little secret."

"Could you have made a charge like that stick?"

"No, but the records guy did not know that," Menendez said. "We believe the brother is the lead man for a conglomerate of cartel money being cleaned by foreign banks. It turns out one of the twin's partners has just been arrested in London, and that man has quite a tale to tell. We now suspect the brother is responsible for the disappearance recently of a money-laundering expert who came to Mexico in search of answers. My crew was busy while I was asleep."

"But the secretariat. Surely he is not involved."

"Maybe not directly, but you saw what happened when I started investigating his interest in the code Persephone Gilbert left."

The secretariat's admonishment for Menendez to stay out of

his "affairs". The twin brother. The cartels. The reason the secretariat wanted Ricardo and Briel to bring the Spider Rock only to him. Good God. How badly had he been played?

"There is more," Menendez went on. "The secretariat's brother, Elpidio Tomás, aka the Conductor, finally overstepped his bounds. We have Elpidio's daughter, Dorothea, and her boyfriend. The couple have interesting things to share, including the capture of a man by the name of Dean Leggatt, a cult group of volcano watchers, and the kidnapping of Dorothea's two young boys. I believe there is yet more to this story, and your investigation with Briel Payce may provide answers. We need to meet. Now."

RICARDO's brown face was ashen by the time he hung up the phone.

"What's wrong?" Briel asked.

"Official business," Ricardo said. "Something I need to take care of."

"What about me?"

"I will take you and your treasure somewhere safe."

"The hotel isn't safe."

"No."

"To the secretariat then?"

Ricardo's eyes narrowed. "The secretariat wants very much for us to take your Spider Rock directly to him. And we may go there in the end, but not right now."

"So what's going on?"

"It is a Guardia matter. Nothing for you to worry about."

"Excuse me? After everything I've... we've... been through, you can't say that. I can't stay safe if I don't know what's happening. Who do I trust? What kind of danger am I, or are we in? And what about Dean?"

"That's part of the problem."

"What is?"

"Doctor Dean Leggatt has been taken against his will. By whom and for what reason, I do not yet know. I need to do my job. Take care of another pressing problem. After that, I hope to get answers to your questions."

"Dean's been kidnapped?"

"We believe so."

"By whom?"

"As I said, I do not yet know."

Briel's heart thumped hard in her chest. She couldn't— wouldn't—lose another friend over that damned piece of limestone in the back seat of their car.

"Whoever they are, they're after the Spider Rock. Right? Let's just give it to them and get Dean back. None of this is worth people's lives." Her voice quivered.

She knew her tone was pleading, desperate. Ashamed, she drew herself up in the passenger seat. "I'm coming with you."

"No."

Ricardo turned at the next corner and pulled into a gated parking lot for what looked like a suburban condominium.

The swiftness with which Ricardo removed the slab from the back seat of the cruiser spoke volumes. It wasn't in Briel's nature to follow, but Ricardo's pace was frantic and Briel practically ran to keep up with him as he marched to the elevator. He hit the button for the third floor, and they went up without a word. They spilled out into a tastefully decorated hallway sporting gold and grey wallpaper. Murals depicting stylized ocean sunsets broke the monotony.

At the end of the corridor, Ricardo turned to a doorway, tried to adjust the rock in his arms and fumbled for the keys.

"Here," Briel said. She took the rock and gently placed it on the floor, only then realizing the map would leave a dirty outline on the beige carpet.

"There's a vacuum inside. I'll clean it up later," Ricardo said, successfully unlocking the door.

"Your house?" Briel asked.

"No."

"Safe house?"

"No."

"Where am I?"

"My sister's home. She has a different name, and she's not listed in my Human Resources record. She's away right now, helping my mother... with a different family matter. You'll be safe here. You can make tea in the kitchen. The bathroom is down the hall to the left, and the television works. Stay here and I'll be back for you and the Spider Rock later. Do not leave and do not answer the door."

Despite the air conditioning, beads of sweat lined Ricardo's hairline. They'd been through plenty together on this trip.

"Please find Dean," Briel said.

"I would like to. However, there is something urgent I must deal with first."

Ricardo opened the door and stopped. He looked again at the hallway carpet, grabbed the hand vacuum that stood near his sister's shoe stand, and quickly cleaned up the outline made by the Spider Rock. A moment later, he was gone.

Briel stood alone in the silence for a few seconds, not sure what to do next. Dean might not be Ricardo's priority, but he was definitely hers. She positioned her cheek between her teeth and chewed gently. A hold-over from when she felt helpless as a child.

But Briel wasn't a child anymore.

She went over what she knew. She was flagged coming into Mexico. The secretariat asked both of them to help, presumably to the same end. Find the Spider Rock and discover the link between it and the bad data from the volcano.

The Spider Rock sat on a towel on Ricardo's sister's coffee table. She approached it again.

Religious symbols speaking to sacrifices to God, dating possibly to the Middle Ages. Created to look like a map of Mexico City at the time of the conquest.

And the arrow.

That had to be significant.

Briel looked at the overlay she had created of the Bordone woodcut and the Spider Rock. The arrow definitely pointed to something. A building?

Checking the Bordone again, Briel located the nearest label. "Casa de li Solazzi del. s."

What the hell did that mean?

She tried Google translate, but the direct label yielded nothing. "Casa" was easy. In Spanish and in Italian, that simply meant home. "Solazzi?" When she entered the word alone, it translated to "solaces". Solace, another word for comfort.

Briel's researcher brain took over. With the help of the internet, she discovered Moctezuma had created "pleasure palaces". One, in particular, was never found in modern times.

Solace, comfort, pleasure. It made sense. But why did the arrow point there? And in today's world, where was "there"?

She searched the web for an image of modern Mexico City. Oriented it to match the direction of Iztapalapa and Atacuba. Then she focused on what she could see of the old Zocalo, and the boundaries of what would have been the man-made island created by the Aztecs. Finally, she blended a photo of that region over top of the Spider Rock and Bordone maps. Amidst the confusing interweaving of baffling lines, one thing was clear.

The arrow pointed to a very specific location.

Briel thought to call Ricardo and then realized he would only tell her to stay put—if he even answered the phone.

Should she wait? It was definitely safer.

But Dean was out there, and he needed help. With Ricardo prioritizing something else, she was his only hope, and this arrow was the only place she could think of to go.

Briel ordered a cab and headed for the apartment lobby. Maybe by the time Ricardo got back, she'd have something to help them find Dean.

CHAPTER 99

Miguel discarded the emptied syringe into the plastic safety container he kept locked in his left desk drawer. Not something he wanted the mail carrier to see. If it ever got full, he'd take it to the hospital and send it out with the usual trash there. So far, that hadn't been necessary.

He picked up his wallet and keys and found a sticky note from Arturo plastered to the middle of his desk pad.

"Preparation at Cerro de la Estrella, 19.3431,-99.0898 will be ready, 6:00pm."

His acolyte was always one step ahead of him. This man was a fine choice to take over the reins of Quetzalcoatl's followers. Perhaps he could abdicate to him sooner rather than later.

And what of his uncle? That relationship remained uncertain. Miguel was beholden to him for the true Popocatepetl data, and at least while Miguel remained in the city, he should inform his uncle that they were moving forward with the sacrifice.

The call to Pedro went to voicemail. Leave a message? Not protocol.

He tried again. Still no answer.

So Miguel left as cryptic a text as he could. "All good. Proceeding as planned."

He hung up and met Berna in the hallway. His guard had Dean Leggatt standing. Well-medicated, the man acted like a zombie. A child in their hands.

Miguel checked the time. They had just over an hour, though it might be less based on Dean Leggatt's behaviour. His ability to fight off what was inside him was remarkable. So similar to the woman from five years ago. What they had in common, he did not know. He'd have loved to do a proper autopsy on this one. Of course, that wouldn't be possible.

A shuffling sound came from the prayer room and Eduardo appeared at his door.

"Are you better now?" Miguel asked.

"Sí," Eduardo said.

"You are sure? We need purity at the site. No emotion. No pleasure at seeing our sacrifice die. That honour is for Quetzalcoatl, and for Quetzalcoatl alone."

"I know my duty. And the prayers helped."

"Good. Then go with Berna. Señor Leggatt is ready. Arturo points us to the old cave beneath Cerro de la Estrella. Do you remember it? The one we used five years ago. I have the GPS coordinates if you need them." Miguel lifted Arturo's note and waved it at Eduardo.

"No," Eduardo said. "I know the area well and remember the cave. The details are already programmed into my car."

"Then go. I will escort you downstairs and meet you for the ceremony."

Eduardo and Berna stood at attention, one on each side of Dean Leggatt, propping him up, guiding him down the hall. The steps were narrow and tricky. Berna's strength was particularly important there, but they'd done it before. And as this demand from their god came so soon after the last one, they were also well practiced.

Leggatt showed hesitation in his steps, as though somewhere inside, he willed his body to fight. When he began to struggle, Miguel considered giving their charge a second dose, but they needed Leggatt upright when he got into the street, and they needed him aware enough so they could manhandle him into the car. Berna's girth and his gun would be enough after that.

A clink, like metal against a hard surface, disrupted Miguel's thoughts.

"What was that?" Miguel asked.

"What?" Berna said between grunts.

"I heard a sound. Like metal dropping."

"Probably me," Eduardo said, jumping for a moment so Miguel could hear the tinkling of keys in his pocket.

Miguel wasn't sure it was the same noise. Still, Eduardo insisted, and they needed to leave.

At the landing that brought in the afternoon's daylight, Berna and Eduardo opened the door to their double-parked black SUV. Miguel ducked behind them and then slipped away. His car was two blocks up the road. If someone recognized him from the hospital? He was simply running an errand, or paying respects to the Carmelite nuns who had rescued the little plaza in the region from becoming a permanent garbage dump.

CHAPTER 100

On the modern map, the Spider Rock's arrow landed on the Plaza de Loreto, a few blocks northeast of the National Palace. Briel had no trouble making her way to the city park from Ricardo's sister's centrally based home.

The park was pretty. A tree-lined green space ran along one side, and a lovely cement-lined fountain on the other. People mingled, either stopping to rest on the cement benches by the water or walking through the park on their way from one city street to the other.

Briel sat and took some time to look at the bubbling water. A pleasure. Could this really be the lost site of Moctezuma's Pleasure Palace?

She shook her head. What did it matter? She was searching for Dean and there was nothing here. No clue. And what was she expecting? Some big sign that read "I'm here, save me, signed Dean"?

Briel thought about going back to Ricardo's sister's flat. The most logical place for her to stay. Wait until he came back with more information.

She got up as a black SUV drove by, and from the corner of her eye, she could have sworn a man in the back seat looked like Dean.

No signs of distress. No concern. A split second and the man was gone. Her mind wanted so badly to find Dean, she was hallucinating.

Foolish as she knew it was, with nothing better to do, Briel headed in the direction the SUV had come from. The turn from San Ildefonso Road.

Up one side of the city street, she found nothing of note. Nothing of value. She didn't even know how far to go. And if she really thought the man in the car was Dean, she'd have called Ricardo and asked for help. What she was doing now? Total waste of time. Damned Ricardo; he was absolutely right. Her best course of action was to sit tight and wait for his return.

Resolved to go back to the park and then to the apartment, Briel took to the other side of the road.

A few doors before reaching the corner of San Ildefonso and San Antonio Tomatlan, she noticed a sign by some open air steps leading to upper level offices.

Dr. Gio Mubello

Gio. Short for Giovanni? Italian? An immigrant from Italy setting up shop in Mexico City? Healthcare was good here, but surely the pay wasn't sufficient to prompt such a move. Of course, everyone had their reasons.

Mubello.

Odd name. Perhaps African? A quick internet search provided no worldwide results for the surname, at least not the way it was spelled here.

Briel looked more closely at the letters. If she ignored the Dr. moniker, the others were familiar. She played with them, much as a crossword enthusiast considered an anagram. Despite her love of ciphers, crosswords and anagrams weren't really her thing. In fact, the only man she'd ever met who really got into that area was Miguel Lobo. He pulled crosswords from the paper at every conference they'd been to together "for when the speakers were slow to come to their point".

Miguel Lobo.

Her heart raced as she counted the letters. Dr. Miguel Lobo, Dr. Gio Mubello. A perfect match. It couldn't be a coincidence.

Briel took to the stairs. What was the worst that could happen? Moth to a flame came to mind.

It didn't matter. For Percy; for Dean. The map led here, and possibly to Miguel Lobo. She needed to know.

The phone buzzed in Briel's pocket. Ricardo. She was about to answer it when a siren screamed from the road and a fire engine went by. The buzz came again, and the banging of a garbage truck echoed through the stairwell. Lots of street noise to accompany her response, and explaining that she'd left the safety of Ricardo's generous family home for the streets and a wild goose chase wouldn't help either of them. She let the call go to voicemail.

Briel was halfway up the stairs when something shiny caught her eye. She bent down and found a moose nickel pendant caught in the corner where the metal molding met the side wall.

A moose nickel? The only one she'd ever seen before hung around Dean's neck. A souvenir from when Percy had met Dean during a metal detecting event. She pocketed the token.

Her breath quickened as she found the door on the second floor. The sign beside the entrance read "Dr. Gio Mubello", and she turned the knob. Locked.

Briel examined the door and the latch. Could she break in? The old credit card to lift the bolt trick? No. This was a more modern mechanism, and she didn't have a key.

She turned around. Dean's charm tucked away, Briel knew she was on to something, and Miguel might be involved. At the very least, she could go to the authorities.

About to head downstairs, Briel came face to face with an older man.

"Can I help you? I am the landlord here," the man said.

What to do? Ask for Dr. Mubello? Pretend she was a patient? Push the man aside and run?

The right move came to her like lightening from heaven. Briel turned the corners of her lips into the most coy smile she could muster.

"I've lost my key," she said, pointing to the door. "Miguel Lobo and I... I'm meeting him here in an hour. I didn't want to wait in the heat."

She tilted her head and flipped her hair. It was a stupid move, and at her age, she wasn't at all sure she could sell it. But she'd already taken the chance that the man before her knew of Lobo's reputation, and as a landlord might know Mubello's real name.

A broad smile and hungry eyes filled the face in front of her. She'd guessed right.

"I have keys," he said, winking at her. "I'm sure he'll be pleased to see you."

The man took a long head-to-toe look at her, shrugged, and unlocked the door.

"Is there anything you need?" he asked.

"No," Briel said. "Thank you."

The man was close—too close. She worried he might come in, so she carefully shut the door in his face and waited until she heard footsteps descending the stairs. Safe for the moment, she let out a deep, ragged breath.

CHAPTER 101

Ricardo produced both his Guardia Nacional badge and the code word for the plainclothes AFSI agent posing as a gardener by the front door of Menendez's safe house.

Inside, a woman sat crying, hands folded almost in prayer, at a simple wooden kitchen table. Beside her, a scrawny man with a scruffy moustache and beard made comforting sounds. Menendez, head still bandaged, sat at the far end of the room, peering at his cell phone screen.

"You finally made it," Menendez said, not looking up when Ricardo cleared his throat.

"There is much to all this," Ricardo said. "As you say."

For the next half hour, between sounds of weeping and soothing, Dorothea and Alejandro reexplained their situation.

"Not only is the Conductor holding his grandchildren hostage, but he may also have Dean Leggatt at the compound," Menendez said.

"We were chased," Alejandro said. Dorothea's mournful eyes looked at him. "Leggatt saw the Conductor's men coming and warned me in time. I got away, but he was caught. Leggatt knows of the forged Popocatepetl data. He has proof of the scheme. And

Dorothea tells me her father feeds the false information to a cult that sacrifices foreigners whenever the volcano's rumbles grow."

Menendez pulled Ricardo into another room.

"How can I be of help?" Ricardo asked.

"Whatever move the Conductor has planned, it will happen soon. For the moment, the children are our priority. I don't think Leggatt is at the compound. Nothing in Elpidio's file suggests he would bring a hostage there."

"Agreed. But where do you think he is?"

"I don't know yet. Right now, we have an opportunity. Information. Regardless of the consequences, we must move on this. I'd like to save as many lives as possible. To do that, I need true cooperation between agencies. Can you get Torres to comply?"

"Torres is dead."

"When?"

"Last night, I think. He was found this morning. In the trash."

"A cartel hit."

"We believe so."

"Playing two sides has consequences. Eventually."

Ricardo said nothing. A career spent trying to determine who to trust, and he'd still been fooled by the secretariat.

"De La Cruz," Menendez said.

"Sorry. Sí. How can I help?"

"Remember that job I offered you?"

"Sí."

"It's time to decide."

Ricardo should have been pleased. The chance to jump ship. If everything Menendez said was true, then maybe he'd finally found the honourable force he longed for. But the Violent Crimes Against Tourists Unit was created with him in mind. Important work. And Clara risked much to supply him what information she could. She needed cover.

"I can't leave my people behind."

The silence between Ricardo and the head of the AFSI lengthened. Finally, Menendez said, "I can respect that. How about we consider you co-opted for now? We can try each other out."

"Done."

"Good. Let's move."

Before leaving the safe house, Ricardo tried calling Briel. It was possible, if unlikely, that Dean Leggatt would be found during this mission. Perhaps that hope would encourage her to wait quietly.

Three tries. No answer. What was the woman up to now?

CHAPTER 102

Briel faced the dark narrow hallway that extended from the door.

"Hello?" she said. "Anyone here? Miguel?"

As she headed down the corridor, the wood beneath her feet groaned with age. The place had the musty, earthy smell of an air conditioning unit that needed to be cleaned. And something else. Souring milk?

She followed the scent to the farthest room from the outside door. Two flies darted around her face as she stepped over the threshold, and she swatted them away. Guardians of spoiled remains.

The room was about three meters square, barren of all furniture save for a single chair placed near a potted palm, and something draped over the chair's seat. Closer inspection revealed a heavy rope, cut into pieces, knots evident between the ends. Easier to cut the rope away rather than untie. What? A prisoner?

Movement in the potted palm caught her eye. More flies, and something else. Larvae? Worms emerging from a milky scum that coated the soil.

Briel jumped back. An unintended shudder shook her from head to toe. Her hands flew to her face as a barrage of flies chose that moment to inspect the newcomer. Rushing out of the room, she shut the door behind her.

Retracing her steps, she found a small office near the front. On the utilitarian wooden desk she noticed a few bills labelled "Dr. Gio Mubello", along with a leather keychain sporting a single small key. In a clumsy hand, someone had scrawled "Papa" over the surface. Turning it over, the other side read "Miguel Lobo".

A banging sound made Briel jump. It took a second to realize it wasn't a knock on the door. Rather, someone using a hammer on a wall, somewhere nearby. Hanging a painting? Perhaps.

Briel tried the desk drawer on her right. Locked.

The key on the desk seemed about the right size, so she fit it into the tumbler button and turned it. With a satisfying groan, the drawer opened.

Inside, she found a Manila envelope, weathered and torn. It held a letter, addressed to Miguel, dated June 11, 1992:

"DEAR MIGUEL, Beloved Grandson,

"I AM TOLD that my time to enter Quetzalcoatl's domain nears. Sometime soon, by our God's good grace, I, his faithful servant, will become hummingbird.

"As your uncle was not blessed with a son, our family's mantel, the one that normally passes from a father to his eldest boy, becomes your burden to bear. When I am gone, learn from your uncle. Give him your attention. It will not be long before no less than the fate of the Mexican people will rest in your hands.

"It is so much to ask of a young man, and I am sorry for the weight you will carry, but it is our heritage, and the chain must not be broken.

"In this envelope, you will find the most precious item our family owns. It is a codex from the seventh century, written by our forefather, Ichtaca.

"Ichtaca, by Quetzalcoatl's command, became the high priest of the Teotihuacan people. These pages are for your eyes alone, and as knowledge of the language is long gone, I will tell you the story as it was passed down to me.

"Your ancestors, the Popopetl people, constructed Teotihuacan, guided by the Feathered Serpent God Quetzalcoatl after Popocatepetl's wrath forced them to leave their native soils. Our brothers from Cuicuilco fled there too. Led from the ashes of Xitle's catastrophic explosion, they helped finish the monument to our God that still stands today.

"For many years, life was idyllic. Quetzalcoatl gifted the population with the discovery of obsidian for making tools and weapons and for trade. Green obsidian, in particular, was highly prized. The region became rich and soon immigrants flooded our borders looking for peace and employment.

"At that time, Ichtaca was apprentice to the high priest, Meztli. Together, they worked to appease Quetzalcoatl's need for blood and grain.

"All was well until Quetzalcoatl sent a great test to the Popopetl people. The skies darkened, so that even in daylight, a grey-gold mist coated the sun's shine. Blood-red sunsets heralded no rain, and crops failed.

"Meztli understood that test and increased sacrificial quotas, but the local peasants grew angry. One day, a farmer named Milintica refused to contribute maize. He shouted for all to hear that there were too few crops and he had nothing to spare for the God that brought them drought.

"Meztli brought the man and his family to Quetzalcoatl's sacred chamber beyond the tunnel, under the Feathered Serpent's pyramid. The place where the great obsidian statue of our God was created and kept. There, Meztli gave Milintica a choice. Either provide the grain or become a blood sacrifice in place of a foreigner. Admiration would have come from choosing death. Quetzalcoatl's appeasement meant Milintica would have returned as hummingbird.

"Milintica refused, and in a fit of rage, he drew a sharp obsidian blade from his loincloth and slit Meztli's throat. Milintica's family escaped through the tunnels and incited an uprising.

"The peasant class surrounded the pyramids, armed with fire, spears and rocks, and during another blood-red sunset, killed many of the city's elite. Clouds of hummingbirds filled the sky in those days.

"Though Ichtaca stayed and fought valiantly, he was beaten and left for dead. By Quetzalcoatl's hand, families searching the burned Teotihuacan ruins some days later found Ichtaca and nursed him back to health. When he was once again able, Ichtaca retrieved Quetzalcoatl's obsidian image from the sacred space below the pyramids and assumed the role of high priest.

"Quetzalcoatl, angered by the disobedience of his followers, punished them with a mysterious fog that removed the sun's shine. Popocatepetl sent angry ash and rock up to a kilometre in the air, threatening anyone who dared come close. Ichtaca did all he could to calm the angry God, but few followers remained. It took ten years before the sacrifices and prayers finally took hold.

"Of course, sacrifice is not favoured in this modern world.

"Since that time, Miguel, we have practiced our religion in secret, keeping our people safe from the volcano by spilling blood, as necessary. The role of high priest has moved from father to son for the last 1500 years. It is a chain that must not be broken. Your uncle Pedro holds the key to our sacred sites, our God's obsidian icon, and our method of recording appeasements in our homeland. The honour of high priest will fall to you soon, my grandson. Do not let the Mexican people down."

BRIEL DOUBLED over as understanding and nausea gripped her simultaneously. Miguel Lobo, medical giant, researcher and consummate politician, was a cult monster.

She reached for her phone. Surely, what she'd just found out would cause Detective Inspector Ricardo De La Cruz to re-prioritize his concerns.

An unrelenting pain in her gut kept Briel bent at the waist, and she abandoned reaching for her back pocket. While she waited for the spasm to subside, she noticed a crumpled sticky note on the floor under the desk. Near enough to the trash bin, it had missed its mark.

"Preparation at Cerro de la Estrella, 19.3431,-99.0898 will be ready, 6:00pm."

Dean's moose necklace, evidence of a recent prisoner, and Miguel's cult. Briel looked at the time. Dean had less than an hour.

Note in hand, she ran from the apartment and, taking the stairs two at a time, called Ricardo, cursing when she got his voicemail. On the street, Briel hailed a cab. She couldn't live with herself if she didn't try to save Dean. No way she was going to lose a friend. Not again.

MIGUEL BROUGHT his luxury sedan to a stop in front of the rusted gate that barred entry to one of the several caves in the Cerro de la Estrella mountainside. This one was the favourite. It was directly beneath the temple that archeologists had finally identified as belonging to the Teotihuacan culture. Actually, it was a pity they'd figured it out. No doubt the place would crawl with scientists sometime soon.

Today, his followers had cleared the remains of the homeless who sheltered here, set up detection systems to prevent their untimely return, and warded off unlikely intruders while preparing the tunnel and cave for tonight's ceremony.

Miguel checked that no one was in sight, found the camera in the tree next to the gate, and lifted his palms to the viewer. Seconds later, two hooded men let him in and he found a spot for his car, hidden from view by thick brush a few meters from the asphalt road. He waited for the dust to clear before stepping outside. One look at his beautiful automobile told him he'd need to get the car detailed again tomorrow.

The acolytes who opened the gate waited at the tunnel entrance, ready with Miguel's robe. The one who positioned the brown cloak to fit Miguel's shoulders shook.

"What is it, Daniel?" Miguel asked.

"The sacrifice arrived with more awareness than usual."

"Indeed. He is a fine specimen. I will need to sedate him again."

"He says he has proof that the data from Popocatepetl is fake," the second acolyte said.

An involuntary twitch tilted Miguel's head. Would his uncle lie about something so important as their relationship with the volcano? A year ago, he'd have said no. Today?

His uncle had assured him this was necessary, had told Miguel to test the man lest there be doubts, and the test was clear. Still...

"What is Leggatt's proof?" Miguel asked.

"He tells us tales," Daniel said. "He is desperate. Maybe lying. We tied him up again. Everyone is waiting for you."

CHAPTER 103

Ricardo's car was the only one on the road. He passed the historic church of San Mateo Tlaltenango on his way to the location where he'd been directed by Menendez. Shuttered windows greeted him from homes on each side of Main Street. When he turned the corner, a curtain behind a closed window fluttered from the last house before the road turned.

Ricardo pulled up to a formidable stone wall and a closed, solid steel gate. Behind it lay a castle of a home.

Menendez stood to one side, surveying a map spread on the hood of a black SUV. Two armed men in tactical uniforms looked on as the head of the AFSI pointed at landmarks.

"Welcome to the team," Menendez said. The statement reeked of sarcasm.

"Trial by fire," Ricardo said.

"We have the compound surrounded. Surveillance tells us that at the very least, the Conductor and his two grandsons are inside. Elpidio's daughter contends her father put a gun to her head before allowing her to leave. She believes the old man will use his grandchildren as a shield if necessary."

"What about the secretariat?"

"Boarded a plane for Argentina an hour ago. We will get him, but that is tomorrow's job."

"What do you need me to do?"

"This siege prevents Elpidio from going on the run, but with every hour, as he gets more desperate, those children are in greater danger. Storming the castle would be foolish. The daughter tells us he has cameras installed everywhere. We need a better idea. Look around. Use what you know about the brother, talk with the men here. Find me a way in. That is what we are all here for."

Ricardo traced the boundaries of the compound with his fingers. A satellite image—and a good one at that—showed every tree and hole on the expansive grounds. The roof layout was complex, and entrances to the home were difficult to see. A lot of space to cover, and lots of room for error, but he could at least make out the balconies.

"Where did you get the map?" Ricardo asked.

"I have my sources," Menendez said.

Ricardo looked up. "I have an idea,"

THE CALL from Mateo had been short and unexpected.

"Get out," his twin brother had said. "The AFSI is on their way."

"Change of heart?" Elpidio asked.

"No. A parting gift. We will not see each other again."

And the man with whom he had shared a womb hung up.

Mateo was right. They'd never see each other again. Not on this earth. The question was which of them would reach the next life first.

It would be Mateo. He always wanted to be first at everything. And Mateo's network was filled with too many "honourable men". He'd be found. Sooner rather than later.

So, the AFSI was coming after him. Let them try. In thirty

years, no one had breached his fortress. They would not be successful now. Best turn to other priorities.

The Conductor phoned his so-called trusted lieutenant. A helicopter would solve his problem. But Pedro did not answer his phone. He'd already tried unsuccessfully to raise Pedro right after Dorothea left, and just before Mateo had interrupted his plans.

Where the hell was he? Ex-lieutenant, it would soon be.

The Conductor ambled to his balcony. He'd told Leonel and Mauricio to play there. Mauricio's call to his mother had probably saved the Conductor's life. The boy had been hungry, and the Conductor had promised him ice cream if the boys stayed outside until he called them. They'd been very good while Dorothea exited his life. Time for their reward.

And then? Perhaps a piano lesson. The boys needed more time with his music.

"Leonel, Mauricio? Come. Your ice cream is waiting."

CHAPTER 104

Ricardo's thumb hovered over the answer button when he saw Briel's name on his phone screen. His eyes met Menendez's. No time? Okay.

Briel was probably reaching her limit of patience, anyway, and talking with her now might prompt her to rebel and leave the safety of his sister's home. He hit the end button and watched as the call went to voicemail.

Crunching gravel announced several arriving cars. His buddies, Guardia members of Mexico City's Drone Club, stepped out of their vehicles, smiling, sunglasses on and birds in hand. He'd told them this was off the professional books. Strictly the public helping with eyes in the air, but if their extra training came in handy, so be it. These guys were up for most anything—and he'd promised replacement drones to anyone who lost one today. He knew several wanted to upgrade their technology. It was a decent bribe.

That was when the woman appeared. Probably in her mid-forties, she stepped from a bright yellow sports car. Flesh poking through torn jeans and tee-shirt hanging loose, she sized up the drone team and marched to Menendez, finger poking at his face.

"Are you loco?" the woman said.

Menendez stepped back. Chin tucked, he peered over his nose.

"Luis," she said. "Drones. Seriously? A fucking club of amateur pilots and you're asking them to surround the place?"

"Tábata," Menendez said. "The pilots will be safe. An armed AFSI agent will be assigned to each of them. And they have been briefed. They are here of their own free will. If you have a better idea, I am happy to hear it."

Ricardo decided it was a bad time to mention that while they were amateur pilots, they were not amateurs to this cause.

Tábata continued. "That hit on the head. It made you cuckoo. You are hanging your career on this, Luis. You had better be right."

Middle finger held high, Tábata stormed toward the men positioned along the compound walls. A good-sized semi-automatic pistol peeked out from the tee-shirt that hung over the small of her back.

Ricardo looked to Menendez for an explanation.

"We all have a boss," was the only response.

"Disculpe?"

It was Ignacio. Behind him, the other fourteen club members waited for instructions.

"What about interference?" Menendez asked.

"As long as the controllers stay at least ten feet from each other, they should be fine."

To the pilots, Ricardo said, "We need three of you on each side of the building. Señor Menendez's men will see that you are in the right location and stay with you should you need backup."

Twelve pilots left with their escorts.

To the remaining three, Ricardo said, "You will fly from here. Over the roof. Be as noisy as you can. We need the distraction while we look in windows to get the footage."

"And you will replace any drone that is damaged?" Fernando asked.

Ricardo smiled. Fernando's equipment was at least ten years old, and his bird was huge. Great for making noise, not so great for flying.

"Yes," Menendez said. "And thank you for your help."

As the assembled drone masters found their places, Menendez moved close to Ricardo's ear. "Brave people to answer such a call. Where did you find them?"

"Mexico City's Drone Club has a few hundred members. These fifteen are colleagues from the Guardia, interested in the sport."

"With that many Guardia involved, you probably alerted a cartel spy. If they come to rescue the head of the beast, we will need to be ready."

"Grandpapa." Mauricio's voice came out as almost a whisper. "Where is Mama?"

A weight settled on Elpidio Tomás's chest. The last of the family strings wound too tight. "You will see her soon, boy." He croaked the words, betraying his unhappiness.

Leonel finished the last spoonful of his ice cream. "Can we go back outside to play?"

The oblivious twin. Just like Mateo.

"Is there a bumblebee in the house?" Mauricio asked.

"What?"

Elpidio cocked an ear and caught a faint buzz overhead. A moment later, it was louder, and then louder again. As though a hive had exploded over his home.

"Come with me."

Elpidio took his grandchildren by the hand and led them to a windowless supply cupboard on the second floor.

"Stay in here and stay quiet. Your grandpapa will deal with... the bees."

"I'm scared," Leonel said.

Dorothea coddled the boys. That stopped now.

"Do as you are told!" He slammed the door shut and locked it.

Within seconds, sounds of whimpering children reached him. "Stop it! I said be quiet."

A more muffled crying continued. So many lessons he needed to teach those children when he took them on the run. Dorothea could keep the bastard child inside her. These boys were his. Heirs to his new Orchestra.

He walked away. His grandsons would figure out how to console themselves or exhaust themselves trying. It didn't really matter, as long as he couldn't hear it.

Elpidio grabbed his gun. As he neared his upstairs office, he covered his ears. The buzzing crescendoed. It was everywhere and nowhere.

He crept along the bookcases that filled the side wall and, gun raised, yanked back the curtain, only to jump back, horrified by the sight before him.

Three cockroach-like drones lined up at eye level, facing inside.

Without a second thought, he fired.

CHAPTER 105

Adorned in the rust-coloured robes of the ancients, Miguel followed Daniel into the ceremonial chamber. Only the crackle of the central fire broke the silence. Daniel was not alone with his concern.

Miguel greeted each of his acolytes with a nod, and then focused on Dean, hands and feet bound, a gag now covering his mouth.

"Let him speak," Miguel said.

"Why are you doing this?" The question wasn't asked with a tremble of fear. It was poised. One scholar to another.

"Our God demands sacrifice. Popocatepetl rumbles and Quetzalcoatl intercedes on our behalf to keep the Mexican people safe. It has been so over thousands of years."

"You have to know by now that the data you're seeing are faked. There's a machine. It disrupts the signals from the volcano. Makes it look bad. I removed the equipment. Let me show you. Popocatepetl isn't dangerous right now."

"Gag him," he said to Daniel.

Desperate struggles erupted from Leggatt, but his bindings held. With their prisoner's mouth covered, the chamber was quiet once more.

To Quetzalcoatl's followers, Miguel said, "Popocatepetl's call came from a reliable source. I too questioned the data and was told to conduct the test that, by our God's grace, came into Arturo's hands. I administered the eggs myself, and we can see the result. Quetzalcoatl has laid claim to this man's blood. The ceremony will proceed, as per our God's wishes, and not because of a trifling concern for a man's data."

"Let us not question the will of our God," Eduardo said.

"Hear, hear," Arturo added.

And the rest chimed in.

Miguel pulled the needle from his deerskin tool roll and filled the syringe. He leaned close while Daniel and Berna held Dean in place.

"You are a lucky man, Señor Leggatt. In past times, medicine was not as sophisticated as today. Your path to Quetzalcoatl will be easy. You must look at this as an honour."

As the needle penetrated Dean's upper arm, Dean shook enough of the gag free so he could speak. "This is wrong and you know it!"

The back of Miguel's hand struck Dean's face. Hard.

Immediately, Miguel bowed his head, asking for forgiveness. Defiling a sacrifice was never the way.

Leggatt's pupils grew large and dark. Through thick lips, and with great effort as the drug seeped throughout his system, Dean asked, "Is this what you did to Percy? Is this what happened? You owe me at least that before I die."

BRIEL'S CAB stopped in front of a derelict fence half hidden by overgrown brush.

"This can't be the place," Briel said to the cab driver.

"Señora," the cabbie replied, "check the GPS yourself. These are the coordinates. But you are right. It is not a good place here. Shall I take you back?"

"What do you mean 'not a good place'?"

"This area. It has a reputation. On the other side, tourists hike the ruins, and there is a good view of the city. But there are many caves here. Some inhabited by the poor, others used by dealers and addicts. Our police do what they can. They put up fences like this one. They put up cameras, like the one in the tree over there. They chase people away. But it is a never-ending battle. You should not come here, and you should not be alone."

"There's a cave here?"

"Probably. There is an opening in the rock over there. Those can lead to either tunnels or caves or both. Our archaeologists say that some openings were carved out, like those under the pyramids of Teotihuacan. When a tunnel leads to a hidden cave, it makes it harder for authorities to find squatters. Señora, there is nothing here for you. I will drive you back."

"No," Briel said. "Thank you, but I want to hike the area. I will be careful."

The young cabbie blinked at Briel, opened her mouth as if to protest, and then closed it again.

"You're sure?" the cabbie asked.

"Yes," Briel said, stepping out of the vehicle. She handed the cabbie a generous tip. "I appreciate your concern. I'll be fine."

Briel stepped close to the undergrowth, monitoring the camera. It was pointed at an old locked gate, the opening wide enough for a car to get through. She waited for the cab to turn around, a little surprised to see her cabbie was on the phone so quickly after taking her fare, and thought business must be good. However, as the woman drove by, driver's side window open, she heard the cabbie say, "Sí, Clara. You should..." Personal call.

ALONE AT LAST, Briel stepped into the brush, grabbed hold of the fence and climbed over, right under the nose of whoever had set up surveillance.

Arms already scraped by thistles, Briel considered turning back. What in the hell did she think she was doing? She wasn't some kind of superhero.

Briel reached for her cell, and as she leaned, reflected sunlight made her close her eyes. Changing angles, she checked ahead of her and noticed silver metal. Briel pushed the nearest branch back. It pricked her finger and she let it go, but not before she recognized the outline of Miguel's luxury automobile.

She checked her cell. Five-forty-five. Time was running out, and Ricardo hadn't returned her call.

Briel dialled 911.

DEAN LEGGATT's body slumped under the influence of Miguel's medicine. Good. Let the man rest.

"Persephone Gilbert was a blessing to us all, Señor Leggatt," Miguel said to the now quiet form. "Her gift to Quetzalcoatl was one that spread fertility and abundance to our worshippers, and to this land. Daniel here was childless before Señora Gilbert's donation secured his family. The police searched for us until Señora Gilbert gave her life. Now, we have influence at the highest level in this country. Like you, Persephone Gilbert was tested and passed. A worthy sacrifice. You should be proud. Your girlfriend fulfilled her role with an uncommon strength. And you will join her soon."

Satisfied with the rhythm of Dean's rising and falling chest, Miguel signalled Berna to remove Dean's bindings.

When Miguel turned to attend to his paints, a hand reached up and squeezed his throat.

THOUGH THE CABBIE had pointed to the opening in the side of Cerro de la Estrella near where she stood, finding it again from a new angle wasn't easy. The craggy rock face cast hundreds of shadows, especially as the sun began its slide toward the horizon.

Briel hung close to the hillside, creeping along the jagged edges until she met a deep, dark opening behind a narrow vertical ridge.

No sirens, nothing from Ricardo, and Dean was probably inside and in trouble.

Damn, Briel breathed.

Another hole to nowhere. But like Cueva de los Tayos, at least this one had an opening that couldn't be closed. She took a breath and slid inside.

It was a tunnel, much as the one described by the cabbie. Chisel marks in the walls indicated human construction. But how old were they? Percy would have known.

Some distance down the narrow passage, a faint light flickered, suggesting a fire and perhaps a cave. And there was a sound, like a swarm of hummingbirds all beating their wings at high speed.

A spot blocked the flickering light. Briel padded along the tunnel and narrowed her eyes for a better look, realizing too late that a dark figure was heading her way.

She pressed herself into the wall and leaned into what had to be a nook created for some kind of monument, now long gone. On the other side of the tunnel, a hooded figure, maybe one of the cult's acolytes, lit candle in one hand, entered an alcove and retrieved a wheelbarrow filled with something wrapped in a blanket.

The figure headed toward the light and in the wheelbarrow's squeak, Briel hid her steps as she followed.

Two more hooded people greeted the wheelbarrow where the tunnel extended into a large chamber. In the centre, a fire lit the walls, and together the acolytes unfurled the blanket to reveal a green-black glass-like statue. Half serpent, half bird, it could have decorated a pyramid at Teotihuacan.

The figures hoisted the statue into a cavity carved in the wall on the far side of the cave. Firelight shimmered over the obsidian lines, bringing the icon's snakelike nostrils and birdlike wings to life.

Off to one side, held down by outstretched arms, lay Dean, sprawled on a stone tablet. Long, dark curls and a hint of eyeglass frames peeked out from the hood of the person who hovered above him.

Miguel Lobo dipped a brush into a pot of black paint.

CHAPTER 106

Ricardo positioned his laptop on a fold-out stool he had grabbed from the trunk of his cruiser. All fifteen pilots input their video feeds via his hotspot, and Menendez cocked his head to look.

"Not bad," Menendez said.

Crashing glass and three shots interrupted their concentration. Two camera links went dark. A third on the same side of the wall showed an older man aiming a gun, and then a wild, haphazard collage of sky and ground scenes.

Menendez's phone pinged and Ricardo could hear Tábata shouting even from where he stood.

"What the hell was that?" Tábata asked.

"Looks like we found our man," Menendez said.

"Can you see the children?"

"No."

"Don't do anything until I get back to your position."

"Sí."

"We wait?" Ricardo asked.

"We wait," said Menendez. "The vice president doesn't trust the decision-making of a man with a head injury. A command from Tábata is a command from him."

"I wasn't given that command."

"But you work for me."

"No paperwork so far."

"What do you have in mind?"

RICARDO ORDERED two of his drone club buddies to cover the CCTV cameras at the four corners of the compound. Grabbing the tire iron from his car tool set, he took to the drainage pipe he had noticed at the bottom of the stone wall. He just needed to chip enough mortar away to squeeze through.

God knew how long the batteries on those drones would last. He couldn't afford to wait for Menendez's caretaker to decide. He needed every moment of distraction, every second of time, where he could stay hidden before rescuing those children.

They were innocent. Like Lilly.

Find and kill Elpidio Tomás, aka the Conductor? Bonus.

THE LATE DAY sun still packed a punch and sweat drooled down his forehead, stinging his eyes. Every time he thought he'd loosened a mortar joint, he kicked at the bricks, cursing when they didn't give way.

Ricardo just needed enough space for his medium frame. Good thing he'd stayed in shape.

A final hit, karate style, at the centre of the weakened mortar, and he burst through.

Ricardo strained to hear sounds of the Conductor's security force above the drones' hum echoing inside the fortress. Nothing. Did Elpidio Tomás believe his castle was impenetrable?

It was the old man's personal Titanic.

He called Menendez.

"Do the drones have eyes on guards?"

"No problem. I'm fine."

"What?"

The phone clicked off. Tábata, or had the cartels arrived? Either way, he was alone.

At least there was no more gunfire. Not so far.

Ricardo headed toward the main house, avoiding the side where the Conductor had shattered his window. The door to a downstairs kitchen was locked, but the one next to it opened with a single tug. He'd landed in a mudroom, multicoloured football gear hanging on hooks, running shoes in cubbyholes near the floor.

Ricardo rounded the corner and caught a whimpering sound coming from his left. The kitchen. Gun drawn, he peeked through the slat made by the open door hinges. An older woman sat trembling on a stool beside the sink, apron pressed to her red face. He angled his head, trying to see if she was alone.

No way to tell, and the drones had to be getting to their maximum flight time.

Ricardo swung into the room and drew a hand over the kitchen maid's mouth just in time to stifle her scream.

"Quiet," Ricardo said to the woman as her bloodshot eyes bulged out at him. "I'm here to help."

The woman nodded and Ricardo released his hold.

"Is there anyone else in the house?"

Between smothered sobs, the woman shook her head. "The master and his two grandsons. He fought with his daughter and she is gone. I do not know where the children are. Glass broke and there were gunshots. What are those things attacking us outside?"

"Is there a place you can hide?"

The maid returned a mournful look.

"A pantry perhaps? Until it is safe."

The maid allowed Ricardo to guide her to a small room under the stairs behind the kitchen. Among shelves of dry goods, Ricardo replaced the woman's stool, telling her to stay put.

A piano played above them.

"The master is practicing," the maid said. "It is 'Clair de Lune'. As the level of difficulty rises, he will make a mistake. His fingers. They do not always do as they are told. He will be angry soon."

"Are his grandsons with him?"

"I do not know."

He closed the door on the maid and followed the music. Pistol ready, Ricardo crept up the home's central staircase. The music was loud now, and the player accomplished. Perhaps a radio set to high volume or a recording. Was it meant to draw an intruder to a trap, or was the Conductor trying to drown out the sound of the drones? Most of the flying creatures were probably on the ground by now.

A wrong note surprised Ricardo when he got to the second floor landing. And the angry cursing that followed left no doubt it was a live concert, but for whose benefit?

Ricardo inched to the nearby open door. From his vantage, the backside of a black-lacquered concert grand piano was in perfect view.

The music stopped and the muttering sounds of an unsatisfied musician faded away. And then there was silence.

Ricardo inhaled, readying himself to breach the room. He took a step forward and heard a click behind him. The sound of a revolver being cocked, the feel of cold steel at his temple.

"I've been expecting you," said Elpidio Tomás.

CHAPTER 107

Miguel Lobo, high priest of the modern followers of Quetzalcoatl, secret protector of the people of Mexico, rubbed the front of his neck, where Dean Leggatt had launched his attack. A most powerful man.

By Quetzalcoatl's grace, the drugs already injected by Miguel's hand finally took proper hold and his assailant dropped away.

Miguel wished for a time when sacrifices understood that this was an honour, that each specimen served a higher purpose. He wished for a time when he and his followers could practice their religion in the light. Where the people of his country appreciated the gifts they were given.

He stroked the upper chest of Dean Leggatt's body with his paintbrush. Thick black paint covered the skin. Eduardo and Arturo took their places, bowls of feathers in hand, ready to decorate the form.

No more doubts. This man had proved himself worthy. The worms growing in his lungs would have killed him otherwise.

In Arturo's eyes, there was no question. Eduardo? Perhaps a little. They would have to deal with Leggatt's accusations again when this was over, and their next meeting would be spirited. Miguel would demand his uncle attend and explain himself.

Today? Quetzalcoatl had showed them he wanted this man. And so it would be.

The paint strokes grew uneven, the heat from the fire too close to the altar. Damned this site. There had to be a better one. He'd put that on the agenda, too.

But the feathers stuck, much the same way they did when they had sacrificed Persephone Gilbert all those years ago.

Leggatt moaned. So similar to his girlfriend.

Miguel motioned to his men, and the acolytes responsible for the march forced their captor to stand, and slowly, with loud thumps, they pounded the ground as they circled the fire.

BRIEL COUNTED eight members of Miguel's congregation. With Dean semi-conscious and Miguel heading the proceedings, her odds were nine to one. She didn't gamble when the numbers were more favourable and the stakes lower. No way she'd impetuously run in today.

Yet there had to be something she could do until the police arrived... if they answered her call at all. The experience at the friar's church left her uncertain. Surely, at some point, Ricardo would get the message and do something?

Think. What was there to work with?

Her hands followed the tunnel walls and found two additional shallow crevices. Large enough for more pre-Columbian statues long gone. Large enough for her. Then she eyed the wheelbarrow just outside the chamber and the rocks on the ground. Good enough.

While attention was focused on Dean circling the firepit, Briel turned the wheelbarrow point side down against the wall. Across from the target, she found three medium-sized hunks of dark rock. Taking shelter in one of the crevices, Briel threw the first rock at the metal bowl of the wheelbarrow. It smacked the target, emitting a satisfying metallic ring, and there was a momentary pause of the humming sounds from the chamber.

When they started up again, Briel let her second rock fly.

AT THE SOUND of two hard surfaces colliding, Miguel and his acolytes paused their activity. He signalled everyone to remain silent and they waited, in case there was more.

Damned ancient tunnels. This one had appeared well enough constructed, and the walls seemed stable, but they hadn't really inspected the surfaces in over a year. Their old subterranean passageway under Teotihuacan was notoriously treacherous. Archeologists had spent a good deal of time and money ensuring against collapse. That danger, and the scientific invasion, had driven the Followers of the Feathered Serpent from their true church. Was this second site at risk too?

Miguel motioned for the ceremony to resume. Best to get this thing over with quickly.

The second cracking sound heralded greater concern. It wasn't like a rockfall from the ceiling; more a metallic ring and then a crash.

An intruder? Surely not. Everyone here was trustworthy. All true believers, willing to give their own lives for the people of Mexico. They'd been together for years.

Nothing had shown up on CCTV. They'd have noticed that. Of course, there were ways of getting around cameras.

Miguel stopped the proceedings once more.

"Berna, Daniel, find out about those sounds. It may be a rock slip that we should be mindful of, but take your guns, just in case... Everyone. Let us rest for a few moments. We will resume shortly."

Miguel opened his leather pouch and set up a new syringe. Dean Leggatt would be awake again soon, and Miguel needed to be ready.

Two robed figures emerged from the light. Faces obscured by their hoods, light at their backs, Briel was blinded to their features. She couldn't tell if Miguel was one of the pair.

If he was, could she talk to him? Make this all stop? Make him see he was acting like a religious zealot, completely in contrast to his life as a clinician and scientist.

It must have been hard for them to see her, too.

One figure went directly to the wheelbarrow, examining its placement. The other passed right by where she was hiding. Briel pressed as far into the wall as she could. Whoever it was didn't seem to notice.

She picked up her last rock and waited. As the second figure came back from the tunnel entrance and passed by her again, Briel clocked the man in his temple. He crumpled below her, his robe askew, displaying the firearm at his belt.

The man's friend called out. "Daniel?"

Briel grabbed the weapon and squeezed the trigger.

CHAPTER 108

Rookie mistake. Well, deadly mistake.

Ricardo had misjudged the older man. The guy was on his own turf and hadn't reached his position by being stupid or fearful. The house, the empire, were all carefully constructed by a Conductor whose fingers didn't comply when piano notes became too difficult. It seemed they worked fine on a trigger.

Elpidio Tomás had a second exit from the room. Something Ricardo hadn't counted on.

He said a silent prayer for Lilly and for his mother. Ricardo's bravado was about to cost them both dearly.

As if an answer from God, a puff of dust floated past Ricardo, accompanied by a scraping sound above them. Rodents? Odd for the pristine surroundings.

THE CONDUCTOR'S weapon remained trained on the intruder's head, ready to fire

Movement stirred the air above him. Vent rats. He'd locked his grandchildren away, thinking they would be spared the inevitable bloodshed today would bring. He should have known after the cookie incident last Christmas that they could escape.

Which one was looking through the grate above them? Had to be Mauricio. His physically stronger brother would have boosted him up.

Well. The little boy would become a grown man today. He was about to watch an execution.

A second scraping sound came from behind him. Leonel too? God help him. This was not what he wanted for the boys.

No choice now. Today was the start of their training.

A click came from behind his right ear and something cold and hard penetrated his thinning hair and rested on his skull.

What the...?

THE SECOND CLICK made Ricardo squeeze his eyes shut. He'd expected a moment where his life flashed before him. Wasn't that what happened when you died?

Yet here he was. And the weapon still rested at his head. Was the Conductor out of ammunition?

"Elpidio Tomás. Drop your gun. You are under arrest."

Menendez?

"No."

The response was firm. Unlike the movies, neither he nor the Conductor was likely to make it out of this alive, and Elpidio Tomás knew it. If he was going out, he'd want to take Ricardo with him.

"Grandpapa!" A child's squeal came from above them.

It was the faintest of movement, the slightest hesitation and minute withdrawal of the gun barrel from his head that gave Ricardo his only chance. He was betting the Conductor would kill before being killed if he was given any time to recover.

Ricardo dipped low while simultaneously stomping on what he hoped were Elpidio's arthritic toes.

Two shots cracked almost in unison. The walls in the hallway shook and a barrage of screaming and crying came from the ceiling grate.

Ricardo flew across the floor and crashed into a door frame three meters away. His weapon slipped from his hand and skittered down the hall. Gasping for breath, Ricardo rolled toward the pistol. As he stretched his arm to reach it, a foot stepped on top and held it down.

Ricardo cocked his head and looked into Menendez's arrogant smile.

"Take a breath," Menendez said. "No need to traumatize the little ones further."

The sounds of weeping children penetrated Ricardo's heart where the bullet hadn't. He chanced a look behind him. The Conductor lay on the floor. What was left of his head was nestled in a pool of blood and fragmented bone.

A few seconds later he sat, inspecting his side where Elpidio's bullet had penetrated his bullet-proof vest, ripped a seam and grazed his torso.

"Need an ambulance, or just a hand?" Menendez asked.

"A hand," he said.

The beat of helicopter wings thudded above them, and wailing intensified from inside the vent. Ricardo held his side, holstered his gun and focused on the ceiling and the two young faces staring down at him.

"We will make sure you are safe," Ricardo said to the boys. "I promise. And we will take you to your mother soon, but you must calm down. I know it is hard. Help is on the way. Please. Move away from the opening and stay quiet."

Menendez was on the radio. "The Conductor is dead. We hear a chopper. What can we do to secure the site?"

Tábata's voice was all business. "We have word that the cartels are on their way. Chopper's ours. I am sending your drone hobby friends home. Reinforcements are coming. Prepare for war."

Ricardo pulled out his cell.

"What are you doing?" Menendez asked.

"Like you said, with so many Guardia here with drones, someone with connections may have alerted the cartels to rescue their own. What if I spread the news that their overlord is already dead?"

CHAPTER 109

A shot echoed in the tunnel and Miguel dropped the syringe. He cursed the woman at the museum in Tepoztlán. He hadn't yet replaced his gun.

Eduardo and Arturo already had pistols drawn. Hearing no additional shots, Miguel motioned for them to find out what was going on.

The rest peered at Miguel. The continuous fire had heated the chamber well past any reasonable temperature, and the robes Quetzalcoatl required stifled him. Miguel threw his hood back and shook the moist curls that stuck to his cheeks. Others did the same. Dean Leggatt lay supine on the rock beside him and moaned slightly.

"We have taken every precaution. The noise and shot are probably evidence of some persistent vermin. Rest now while our guardians complete their sweep on our behalf."

ONE MAN LAY UNCONSCIOUS, the other groaned, rolling back and forth on the tunnel floor, holding his gun arm. Briel had aimed for his leg, but good enough. Neither of the faces were Miguel's. That meant he was still in the chamber.

No doubt the noise had interrupted the proceedings. The humming had stopped. Briel took that as a good sign and, staying close to the shadows that kept the tunnel walls in darkness, she wove her way closer to the cave opening.

At the sight of two more hooded figures emerging from the light, she ducked back again, just in time to see another two men fly by her position, weapons drawn.

They seemed more interested in their fallen colleagues, and that was fine by her. The trouble was that she was still severely outnumbered and she could hear nothing from the tunnel opening to the road. Was she just too far away and help was coming, or were no sirens on the horizon?

The only way to save Dean and give herself some chance was to keep stalling. She'd be shot in an instant if she went in guns blazing. That, she knew.

Cat and mouse, however... Maybe she could extend the game. Big noise, more confusion?

Briel focused on the wheelbarrow behind her. It would be uncomfortable, even for her, but it was worth a try. Leaning into the side wall to protect at least one ear, Briel fired a round toward the metal bowl of the barrow.

The resounding clap of metallic thunder caused the conscious acolytes to slam their hands over their ears and sink to their knees. The ringing in Briel's unprotected ear was so bad, she couldn't tell if she'd perforated the drum. Too late to worry about that now.

Briel fired another shot, this time kicking up dirt in front of the wounded guards.

She reached the chamber but didn't go in. Instead, she tucked herself behind a small lip that extended on one side of the opening, hoping to pick off anyone who dared exit.

A loud bang shook Dean into awareness. Was he dreaming? More like a nightmare. From the misty depths of his drug-laced brain, Dean remembered Miguel Lobo, the syringe, and that he was in serious trouble.

The hooded beings around him seemed frozen in time. Each looking toward a dark opening in the wall that he hoped was an exit.

Desperation kicked up his adrenaline, and he drew himself up from the hard surface he'd been lying on. If he could get to the door...

His body slammed to the floor, his open mouth capturing a wad of dirt.

Briel peeked around the corner, gratified to see Dean stand. He was naked, black paint over his upper chest and at his wrists and ankles, feathers trailing across the paint, askew, tracking dark lines of sweat all over his body. The pleasure of seeing him still alive was short-lived, however. Miguel's hood was down and it was easy to see that her old colleague was in charge.

He pushed Dean over with the simple swipe of his arm and then called to his collective, trying to regain order.

Briel looked at the glassy serpent-bird icon in the alcove on the far wall. Resigned to the fate she and Dean were both likely to face amid overwhelming odds and with no help in sight, she resolved at least to go down fighting. She took aim at the obsidian statue.

As the gun went off, she felt a blow from behind and the lights went out.

CHAPTER 110

They needed to get Mauricio and Leonel out of the mansion before trouble arrived.

Ricardo didn't know if anyone in the drone club had become an agent for the cartel. No reason to consider it before now, and he did his best to stay out of a problem he couldn't fix. But if his phone call to tell his comrades that the Conductor was dead didn't do the job, then this place was about to become Armageddon.

He'd told Menendez where the maid was hiding. The head of the AFSI would take care of her. After all, she was also a vital witness to everything that had been going on in the house. With Dorothea, Alejandro, and the maid, the AFSI would have enough witness statements to keep them busy for a long time.

The young boys huddled together above him. He could see them shivering, probably terrified. If he had to manhandle them down, he would. He just didn't want to. They were about the same age as Lilly. His heart broke at the thought of Lilly being confronted by a situation like this.

"Mauricio, Leonel," he called up without looking at them. "I understand you are frightened. You have a right to be. Your mother told me about you both. That you are what she lives for. Did you know that?"

Slight pauses interrupted the boys' whimpering sounds.

"What happened here, it is a terrible thing. A tragedy. No one should see a family member die like that. I am sorry."

Whimpering changed to sniffing.

"We have a problem… It is possible that more trouble is coming. It is best if you are far away from here before that happens. There is someone outside ready to take you to your mama. Will you come down?"

"Why should we trust you?"

A child's voice, petulant and angry.

"That is an excellent question. After what you watched happen, I would not know who to trust either. But we have little time. You hear the helicopter above us? This situation may get worse. Please, let me get you out."

The boys went quiet and then Ricardo heard the scratching sounds of movement through the ducts. Damn. Where were they going?

"Mauricio, Leonel. Come back. We must leave. Now!"

He hoped his more authoritative tone would help.

"You promise you'll take us to our mama?"

The voice came from an intake grate by the floor at the end of the hall. Ricardo didn't move.

"Yes."

The grate flew out and a young foot appeared. A moment later, two tear-stained faces looked pleadingly in his direction. Ricardo's heart melted all over again. The little ones ran into his arms and he embraced them, allowing tears of his own, tears for his wife, and tears for Lilly.

Unfortunately, Ricardo's emotional indulgence had to be short-lived. He led the boys from the mansion, nodded, and winked when the twins sent him questioning eyes. An AFSI consultant escorted Leonel and Mauricio into an automobile bound for the safe house and Dorothea.

"They'll be fine," Menendez said when he reached the place where Ricardo stood.

"Yes," Ricardo said. Then he turned to the matter at hand. "What is the news?"

"So far, nothing, though Tábata remains on the warpath. Full preparations are underway to deal with whatever comes."

"She sounds like someone worth knowing."

Menendez heaved a sigh. "Yes. She is a remarkable woman."

There was a past in there somewhere. Not a line Ricardo would cross. Not now, and probably never.

Ricardo reached for his cell. Messages had accumulated and it was time to find out what else was going on before trouble arose again.

The first was from Briel. She'd be worried about Dean, and he didn't want to tell her he had nothing of help. Elpidio Tomas had died without providing a lead to Dean's whereabouts and the Secretariat of Travel, Culture and Tourism, a man supposedly on their side, had skipped the country in shame. No, that news could wait.

He picked up the second message. It was from Clara.

"Hello, Inspector De La Cruz. Please answer when you can. My friend, Yesenia, called me. She is a cab driver. She picked up a foreigner at Plaza Loreto, who asked to be dropped off at GPS coordinates on the side of Cerro de la Estrella. My friend thought it was strange. The woman wanted to be left in the middle of nowhere. Yesenia warned her, but she would not listen. The woman's name was on her credit card. It was Briel Payce. The same person you rescued from Iztaccihuatl. I thought you would want to know."

Ricardo dialled his office. "Clara. Any news?"

"Thank God. There was a 911 call from the same area. With Torres gone, there is confusion, but I understand they sent two officers to investigate."

Ricardo felt sick.

"How long ago?"

"A half hour."

"What about Dean Leggatt?"

"No word about him."

Ricardo clicked off the phone and almost bumped into Menendez.

"Bad news?" Menendez asked.

"Sí."

"Something you want to take care of?"

"Sí, but there is also trouble here."

"Go."

"But."

"Go. Take care of the trouble. Tábata has brought all our resources here, and if you do have a cartel spy among your drone club friends, they now know the Conductor is dead. Nothing may happen. At least we can hope. We have what we need. Fix your problem, and then be ready for work with the AFSI on Monday."

CHAPTER 111

Briel opened her eyes to a dim whirl of activity around her. Her ears felt thick, as though stuffed with cloth and she was trying to hear through it.

Shattered remains of the obsidian statue lay strewn in the dirt. Hooded acolytes hunched over the larger green-black, glassy pieces, raising them into the air and wailing. Smaller shards reached farther afield, a few scattering close to where she'd fallen.

Dean was on his stomach on the ground near the fire. She thought he was dead until she spotted the index finger on his right hand stretch forward as though he wanted to reach out for something.

A familiar scent wafted near her.

Miguel. He still wore the same cologne, though now it was mixed with the musty smell of sweat. He was kneeling over her, holding something.

Briel blinked. Miguel had a needle. A big one.

"You are lucky we have a past." Miguel pressed his thick lips close to her ears. "For old times' sake, your death will be painless. Just give me your arm..."

Briel's eyes grew wide as realization dawned. She'd gone in, guns blazing, after all. Desperate times...

"Don't do it, Miguel. I called the police. They'll be here any second. It's over."

Miguel laughed. "Do you think me so foolish? Enrique Torres? He has been an ally for years. He will recognize the call, and his men and women will stand down. And you willfully destroyed our sacred Quetzalcoatl icon. The twenty-five-hundred-year-old image that connects us with our God. You will die for this."

Briel tried to roll over and then rise to a stand but a dizzying head pain stopped her and she only made it to her knees. As she turned her head, she discovered one of the hooded figures pointing a pistol at her face.

"Believe me," Miguel said, "my way is better."

Briel felt the foundation under her. Soft. This section of the cave had either been ground down or never properly cleared. She dug her hands deep, waiting as Miguel approached again and the gunman watched. The moment her ex-lover drew close enough, she elbowed his arm and let the dirt that filled her hands fly.

DEAN OPENED HIS MOUTH, searching for a deep gulp of air. Instead, he hauled in another mouthful of gritty muck. He opened his eyes and realized he was lying face down on a cave floor. Flames danced nearby, sending flickering light up the walls. It was hot. His chest hurt. And breathing, even through his nose, was uncomfortable.

Looking away from the fire, he saw a vision. Briel. A hallucination? And something else. Miguel Lobo threatening her with a needle. He remembered that needle. That's what got him here.

He needed to get up. He didn't save Percy. He needed to save Briel.

Dean shifted in the dirt. The hooded figures around him seemed occupied. They were messing with shards of glass. Gathering them from the ground. He picked up a piece for himself, grabbing it with as much strength as he could muster. The sharp sides bit into his hand and he felt blood ooze from his palm. The stabs were painful, but cleared his fog, at least for the moment.

Were those sirens? Where were they coming from?

Dean looked around. No one was paying attention to him. He tried to get up. It was hard and he was wobbly, but he made it.

Dean looked Briel's way and saw a plume of dirt and dust. He took a step toward her, holding the glass blade in front of him like a dagger. And then the room started to spin. Miguel Lobo's face came into view and Dean dropped. With a final push, he sunk the obsidian shard deep into Miguel's belly.

Then the lights went out again.

BRIEL HIT the ground once more as the weight of a body, possibly two, piled on top of her.

The prick of a needle grazed her arm.

So, Miguel got her after all.

What did she expect? It was how many against the pair of them?

And then she felt something. Liquid. Thick and oozing. Pouring over her, not coming from her.

Briel wiggled her way out from under the mess of bodies.

Sirens screamed somewhere close. Hooded beings grabbed for Dean just as uniforms crowded into the small cavern and pulled them away. There were guns. Lots of them.

Dean's freed body went limp and he sailed, face first, to the ground. As the sounds of struggle receded, Briel pushed Dean over, praying he wasn't dead.

That's when she saw Miguel leaning against the cave wall, blood pouring from a wound to his abdomen. Eyes wide, glass shard embedded in his gut, Miguel's chest rose and fell with sickening speed. The man was alive. Miguel's weapon, his syringe, lay in his open palm. It was mostly full.

She went for it just as Miguel closed his hand around the syringe and gave out a loud cry.

He lunged for Dean.

Briel seized Miguel's clenched fist, pulled his arm down, and plunged the contents of the syringe into his leg.

Then she remembered Miguel's needle piercing her skin. The same medication killing him circulated in her own system.

Briel collapsed.

At least she'd gone down fighting.

CHAPTER 112

It was the light Briel noticed first. Wasn't that what everyone said dying would be like? She felt no pain. Miguel got his way after all. Was Dean here too?

As if on cue, she heard a male voice calling, "Briel. Briel. You're safe. Time to wake up."

And then Dean. It was definitely Dean. The voice was hoarse, thick even, but there was no doubt. "Briel. Wake up. Percy'd be pissed if she thought we were lounging in bed when there was work to do."

Work to do. Weren't they supposed to follow a tunnel or something?

She focused on the light in front of her and as her vision cleared, fluorescent bulbs came into view. Where was she?

"Hey." The man's voice was back again. "Doctora Payce. I am told you are going to be fine. Not enough of Lobo's drug to kill you. The reputed medical director, on the other hand..."

Briel turned toward the voice.

"Ricardo?" she croaked. "Where am I? What happened?"

Briel tried to get up.

"Not too fast," Ricardo said. "You're in the hospital."

"Dean?"

"Right here."

Briel turned her head and found Dean looking at her from a wheelchair on the other side of the bed. "I'm going to be fine, too. Turns out, we're both harder to kill than Miguel thought. Or Percy was looking out for us."

Ricardo raised an eyebrow.

"As were the Guardia Nacional," he said.

"The last thing I remember," Briel said as she slowly pushed to a sitting position, "is... oh my God. Miguel. Did I?"

"He's dead," Ricardo said. "Between the abdominal wound administered by Señor Leggatt here..."

"You're welcome," Dean said.

"... and the injection you gave him," Ricardo continued, "he was gone before we could get him out of the cave. We have ample evidence, including the witness of our officers who were first into the tunnel. It was self-defence. There is no blame. I know that at one time, you were friends. I'm sorry for that."

"Lobo was loco," Dean said. "He poisoned me twice."

"What?" Briel asked.

"The Followers of Quetzalcoatl, as we now know the group is called, were running the equivalent of your Salem witch trials. One of them developed a test. If you survived it, you were a worthy sacrifice. If you didn't... Dead either way," Ricardo said.

"Lobo forced milk down my throat. His graduate student developed a method of detecting gender in ascaris eggs. In doing so, he accidentally created a species that grew within hours to invade the lungs, cause pneumonia and then... Lung infection isn't all that unusual, but it typically happens over a much longer time. I threw up as much as I could, but some of those buggers still got to me. When I got here, my breathing was rough. The usual parasite meds still work wonders, though. I'll be fine."

The sour milk at Miguel's lair.

"I wonder how Percy passed the test five years ago," Briel said.

"Before we lost touch, she told me she was on mebendazole. Bad pork taco," Dean said.

"What about the drugs Miguel gave us?"

"Whatever potion Miguel stuck me with wore off before I even got to the hospital. You were a different story."

"He said killing me by injection would be kinder than a bullet," Briel said.

Ricardo nodded. "You shattered the cult's ancient icon. If he didn't kill you, one of his followers would have."

"I couldn't think of anything else to do."

"It worked. Caused total disarray while his acolytes panicked over the pieces," Ricardo said.

"And gave me a weapon," Dean said.

"And then the Guardia came? Miguel said he had some official in his pocket."

Ricardo's lips thinned. "Enrique Torres. He was found dead earlier in the day. Lobo obviously didn't know. Your call went through—and, as it turned out, my assistant and your cab driver are friends. She told us exactly how to find you. Though the GPS coordinates you gave dispatch helped, too."

"So it's over?"

"It's over."

"Except," Briel said to Dean, "we didn't find Percy."

"More like Percy found us. She helped. I'm sure of it."

Briel thought back to the moose nickel medallion she'd pocketed at Miguel Lobo's lair. "Yes. She did."

CHAPTER 113

T *he Next Morning*

"NOT EXACTLY STEAK AND EGGS," Dean commented as he and Briel tucked into their respective hospital breakfast trays.

"I've got an extra packet of salsa if it helps," Briel said.

"Humph," was the response. But there was the hint of a smile.

Dean released a long sigh and fingered the moose nickel securely around his neck once again. How it had stayed with Briel after all they'd been through, she couldn't imagine.

They hadn't called Lydia. It was too soon. Still too much to process.

Briel took out her phone and flipped to the blended picture of the Spider Rock. They had gotten close. Really close. Miguel had killed Percy. Another sacrifice. Had he lived, he could have told her where the remains were. Ricardo said the acolytes were tight-lipped—unwilling to be implicated in God knew how many murders.

Briel glanced at the television. The screen filled with the image of Popocatepetl spewing fire from its top. She turned up the volume.

"Due to falling ash, school is cancelled in the following towns..."

"What?" Dean turned to pay attention to the news.

"Two of Mexico City's airports have temporarily shut down and the Departamento Regional de Monitoreo de Desastres Naturales has upgraded their warning system to high alert. The mountain is closed to visitors within a sixteen kilometre radius of Popocatepetl's peak. Nearby residents are asked to remain vigilant in case the order comes to evacuate."

"Shit," Dean said. "You don't think...?"

"No. But I'm betting Miguel's followers will take it as a sign. And... I guess we're not going anywhere for a few days."

Briel muted the TV and took another sip of coffee.

"You never mentioned how you found me," Dean said.

Briel held up the blended photo. "The arrow. It pointed to what was probably Moctezuma's pleasure palace, or at least one of them, in the 16th century. It must have been a lair for Quetzalcoatl's followers even then."

"I'll bet every symbol on that rock means something important. Wish we could decipher more."

Briel leaned back on the pillows. She wanted to cry. They'd have to call Lydia soon.

As a nurse removed the breakfast tray, a doctor came in, followed by Ricardo.

"I imagine you are eager to go," the doctor said. "The detective inspector is here to take formal statements from you both. I will complete the paperwork for your release from the hospital, and then you are free to leave."

Ricardo took out a notepad and Briel put down the photo, murmuring a curse. "Damned Freddy Palmer."

"What?" Ricardo's face flushed.

"He was the original owner of the Spider Rock. His treasure hunt in Texas started all this. When Freddy Palmer's daughter gave the rock to Percy's great-great-grandad, it got passed down the family and Percy took up the quest."

Ricardo dropped his pen. "Did you say Freddy Palmer?"

"Yes. Why?"

"There is history in my family connected with that name. Palmer set a fire that killed a man and his wife and two small children here in Mexico. And he stole a sheepskin treasure map that took him back to Texas. My great-great-grandfather, Capitán Daniel Garza, went after him. Garza died in your country, a hero for his efforts."

"I'm sorry for your family's loss. And I wish I understood what it all means," Briel said, "for us both. Percy's message didn't give me much. When I was in the tunnel under Cerro de la Estrella, I thought maybe I'd see something there. Another symbol for what she was trying to tell me."

"Yes," Ricardo said. "It was strange to find them in that place. I'd have expected a cult related to Quetzalcoatl to position themselves under the pyramid dedicated to that god in Teotihuacan."

"It is from Teotihuacan," Dean said.

"What?" Briel asked.

"Remember the forensic evidence. The limestone is from the same mines that covered the walls in Teotihuacan. That's where the rock had to come from."

Briel turned to her photo. Her mind trailed to Padre Hugh and the Septuagint version of the book of Daniel.

The holy place made desolate.

And a sin-offering was given for sacrifice.

And then to the video Percy left her. The chisel marks over Percy's shoulders and the cracks behind her.

"Oh God," Briel said. "I think I've got it."

CHAPTER 114

It took two days for Detective Inspector Ricardo De La Cruz to get the special approval needed for Briel and Dean to go through the tunnel under the pyramid dedicated to Quetzalcoatl in Teotihuacan. Briel sat in the back of the cruiser, Percy's Spider Rock, retrieved from Ricardo's sister's apartment, on her lap.

She and Dean talked about calling Lydia with an update. In the end, they agreed it was better to find out if Briel was right before raising Lydia's hopes and then dashing them again if it turned out Briel was wrong. Lydia was in hospice now. On borrowed time and too fragile to upset.

Ricardo seemed in oddly good spirits, given what Briel suspected might turn into a sombre undertaking. Perhaps he was simply trying to keep things light?

"According to Lobo's family notes, the Quetzalcoatl pyramid was crafted, in part, by immigrants from Cuicuilco." Ricardo sounded like a tour guide. "And given that the area around Tepoztlán is considered the birthplace of Quetzalcoatl, it is clear your friend Doctora Gilbert was trying to tell you that the Feathered Serpent was the key. It makes sense that what we seek is under that monument." Then Ricardo added softly, "I would have liked to have met her."

Briel pursed her lips and steeled her shoulders, pushing down her thoughts.

She cleared her throat. "What ever happened to the parchment map your great-great-grandfather was after?"

"I do not know. Did your friend ever mention that it existed?"

"No," said Briel. "I don't think that part of the story came down to her."

"Then it is lost to history."

They rode the rest of the way in silence.

A REPRESENTATIVE from the team excavating the tunnel under the pyramid met them at the entrance.

"You need to understand," she said. "We found this tunnel, and the ceremonial cavity it leads to, because the ceiling collapsed in some parts. We have done our best to shore it up, to make it safe, but it is not meant for visitors. As I told my superiors, I would not advise this. You must be careful."

"We'll risk it," Dean said between his teeth.

Dean shimmied into the dark and reached back to Briel for the Spider Rock.

Briel took a breath, and then another.

More damned black holes.

The entrance can't be closed, she reminded herself. There's no way I could be shut in, the optimistic side of her brain said. A roof collapse would do the trick, the other side of her countered.

"It's okay, Briel," Dean said. "It gets wider down here. Plenty of room to walk, and the archaeologists put lights in. You can do it. But if you want to stay up there, I understand."

No, he didn't. She knew what was on Percy's video, knew what she was looking for. She jumped in, much like a swimmer on a lake in early spring, knowing the water would be cold but trusting she would acclimate.

Ricardo stepped in behind her.

Briel steadied herself by putting a hand on the wall.

"Please don't do that," their representative said from the opening. "You must avoid touching things. This area is still being investigated and the supports are minimal."

"Don't worry," Dean said. "We'll all be careful."

Ricardo said, "Briel should go first. She knows what we are looking for."

Obediently, Briel squeezed to the front of their line and headed deeper into the abyss. Every fibre in her body stood at attention and she reminded herself that the lights were helpful. Critical, if she was honest. God. How did Percy crawl through here five years ago?

They turned a corner and spotted daylight streaming through a hole in the tunnel ceiling. The archaeologists had added wooden planks to the sides and top, hoping to secure the walls in place and prevent further collapse.

Farther into the shaft, they found darkness. An area not yet touched by the experts.

"You must stop here," the representative said. "We have not studied this section, and it is not safe."

"I need a flashlight," Briel said.

Ricardo handed her one from his belt.

It was about three meters away, in the side wall. Lines, looking very much like the cracks Briel thought were visible on Percy's video. Extending from what? A black shadow on the wall.

"It's over there," Briel said.

"You can't go there," the representative repeated.

Ricardo flashed his badge. "This is now a Guardia Nacional matter. I understand the risk, but we must investigate. The responsibility is mine."

It took a moment, and then the representative relented.

Briel led Dean to the cracks in the wall. On closer inspection, as Briel suspected, they were carved lines extending from a Spider Rock-shaped hole.

"Do you want to do it, or should I?" Dean asked.

Briel motioned for Dean to continue.

Slowly, carefully, Dean hoisted the Spider Rock into its home underneath Quetzalcoatl's monument. A perfect fit.

The representative let out a gasp.

Briel followed the lines extending from the rock down the wall.

"There are more of them here than I expected," she said. "How are we going to figure it out?"

"The centre of skulls," Ricardo said, "in the Zocalo. That is here. Sí?"

He pointed to the circle in the middle of the Spider Rock.

"Yes," said Briel. "The oldest holding site for sacrificial remains. The Followers of the Feathered Serpent used this as a map of Tenochtitlan, the scattered circles telling each generation where the bones of those sacrifices are located. Sometimes in plain sight as part of Aztec rituals, and in modern times, the hidden murders of anyone getting too close either to the cult or to that international money-laundering empire you discovered."

"So these extending lines should tell us where all the remains of the modern day deaths are," Dean said.

"And without the Spider Rock in place, no one would ever know it documented burials. Forensic evidence, secreted away, but ripe for the taking for anyone seeking justice against the cult members and their protectors. No wonder they wanted it, or you, destroyed," Ricardo said.

"Yes," Briel said. "Even as archeologists moved to this part of the tunnel, how could they understand what the seemingly random lines and circles meant without the context of the map? Only the cult knew the landmarks these lines extended from."

"But there are many circles here. How can we know which is most modern, let alone where to look for your friend's remains?" Ricardo asked.

"Luckily," Dean said, "you know a forensic geologist. A few calls to my counterparts in your local university, and voila, I have sample bottles."

Dean took scrapings from the circles at the end of the furthest lines made in the limestone that covered the tunnel wall.

The representative looked aghast, but didn't protest. Perhaps because the detective inspector kept her at bay. Or maybe because the damage Dean did was minimal, and she'd been promised the Spider Rock for study when they were through. It didn't matter.

Briel snapped a photo of the wall. Once they had Dean's data, they'd blend it with a modern map and see where the latest circles lined up.

She took one last look at the place where she now knew Percy had taped her video from, five years earlier.

And as she turned to walk away, the walls shook.

As if getting out of the tunnel under Quetzalcoatl's pyramid wasn't difficult enough, Menendez buzzed Ricardo's phone, the surprise almost causing him to misstep.

He, Briel, Dean and the representative ran for the exit. Rocks shaken loose in the ceiling pelted them in a barrage sufficient to make anyone believe that they'd angered the deity to which the grounds were dedicated. The helmets their representative had insisted they wear protected their heads from the worst of it, but when they finally emerged, not one of them was uncut by the flying shards. Ricardo's arms and shoulders took a particular beating.

The representative lit into them with "I told you so" and "you were warned", but the information they had now? Invaluable to finding out what had happened to the so-called tourists who had come looking for evidence of international corruption.

His phone sounded again. Time to face the music, as the Americans would say.

"De La Cruz." Menendez's voice was stern. "Where the hell have you been?"

"Sorry, señor. I was... tying up loose ends."

"I am expecting you in my office tomorrow. Your new position has been approved. Your heroism did not go unnoticed."

"About that…"

Menendez continued as though he hadn't heard Ricardo. "Just so you know. We found Arturo Huerta's lab. Those toxic little worms. They are gone. God knows we do not need another biological weapon."

"Sí, señor…"

"Pedro Serrano, the Conductor's lieutenant? We picked up his corpse, abandoned on a dirt road just outside of Cuicuilco. Looks like another cartel hit."

"Señor…"

"And we got the secretariat. We had his plane to Argentina turned around. Mateo Tomas hated his brother, but he cried like a baby when he found out Elpidio was dead. Twins, eh? I guess they are forever connected. The boys are doing fine, by the way. With their mother and Alejandro. They make a nice family, though we had to put them in witness protection…"

"Señor." Ricardo's voice rose and Menendez finally stopped. "I have decided to remain with the Guardia…."

"What?"

"My place is here, señor. We have had a breakthrough with this case. It will make a difference. To us in Mexico, and to those who come to our land from around the world. I would like to see this through."

CHAPTER 115

Dean pulled every academic connection he had and finagled himself into a university lab where he conducted test after test on the samples he had retrieved from the tunnel. When he finally came up for air, he had an answer that made sense. Three of the circles were made in modern times. The bottom left one being the most recent.

"Probably within the last decade or so," he said.

Briel got to work, blending photos again, this time extending the perimeter well beyond that of the Spider Rock and its ancient depiction of Tenochtitlan.

The burial site was just outside the west boundary of the city, near a place called San Mateo Tlaltenango. When they brought the news to Detective Inspector Ricardo De La Cruz, Briel was surprised by his response.

"Show me again," Ricardo said. "Are you sure?"

"Very. Is there a problem?"

Ricardo hesitated.

"No," he said finally. "Only, the site is uncomfortably close to an emergency I dealt with recently."

And that was all he would say.

. . .

THEY HAD no difficulty finding diggers. The mothers of missing sons in Mexico were well organized. They understood Percy's Aunt Lydia's pain and offered all the help they could.

Ricardo supplied dogs trained to find human remains.

"Courtesy of Luis Menendez," he said. "Thank God the man does not hold a grudge."

Dean and Briel had pooled their resources and a bulldozer was on standby.

In less than half an hour, the dogs pinpointed a target near a tree line.

There was evidence of recently disturbed ground, but the soil was packed hard, so the dozer took off a first layer of dirt and clay. After that, the hand digging began.

Briel stood to the side. The dogs started barking, encouraging the team to dig deeper. Dean couldn't help himself. He grabbed a shovel and jumped in.

When bones appeared, all movement stopped. Briel lifted the back of her fist to her mouth, trying to quell a scream. Her shoulders shook.

Dean ran to her side and put an arm around her. His eyes were moist and he laid his cheek over her hair. Together, they stared at the ground, waiting for something that would tell them they'd finally found Percy.

Ricardo was on the phone the instant the burial site was revealed. He called an anthropologist who occasionally worked with the force and she came out to help.

In the end, there were three skeletons in the pit. Only one had remaining flesh. Muscle, no skin and no other distinguishing features. A few green quetzal feathers were scattered in the soil, but nothing else. Identification wasn't going to be easy.

The anthropologist pronounced two men and one woman. One man, she said, the one with flesh, was placed in the pit within the last year.

Briel looked at the skeletal frame of the woman. Perfect teeth. Except...

She elbowed past the anthropologist without apology.

"Excuse me?" The woman sounded offended, but Briel pushed on.

There, in the lower jaw, on the skeleton's left side, the first molar was covered in gold. The root canal Percy had had six months after coming back from Ecuador. Dean kneeled down beside Briel.

"Is it?" he asked.

Briel drew closer.

As a joke, Percy had asked the dentist to sign his work. He had refused, but did finally consent to inscribe a small "S" on the inside. The doctor's surname initial. That night, when Percy couldn't have the steak she wanted for dinner, she'd shown Briel her new "artwork".

The S was there.

Briel put her hands to her face and wept, and Dean leaned in and joined her.

Several minutes later, she felt another gentle hand on her shoulder. "We need to let the professionals do their job now," Ricardo said.

He escorted them to a nearby tree stump and had them sit.

"Will you be okay while I get this taken care of?"

Briel nodded and Ricardo left, already on his phone and shouting orders.

"Should we make the call?" Dean asked.

Briel pulled out her cell and punched the speakerphone button.

"Lydia," Briel said. "We found her. We'll bring her home."

It was a murmur that came to them from the other end of the line. The weak but coherent words of the dying.

"Thank the good Lord."

EPILOGUE

Light shimmered from the pavement in the parking lot of the cemetery in Granbury, Texas, near Percy's family home. Briel wished one more time that heat-absorbing black was not the traditional dress for funerals. The yuccas were in full bloom and the cicadas sang, letting Briel know that this year, summer would go on for a good long time.

She leaned into Dean while they stood alone in front of Lydia's headstone. Briel stooped down and placed a bouquet of flame-coloured calla lilies on the ground.

"A good woman," Briel said.

"Because of how she took care of Percy?" Dean asked.

"Because of how much she loved. Though her era didn't allow it, I think Lydia was an adventurer by heart. In some ways, I think she lived through Percy."

Dean nodded.

They turned to the next gravesite, where Percy had been laid to rest, and Dean placed a second bouquet.

Briel read the inscription on the headstone aloud.

"'The brave never die. Minot Savage.'…No, they don't, my friend. And we're glad to have you home," Briel whispered.

"No one left behind," Dean added. He put his fingers to his lips and then touched the granite headstone.

It wasn't until they were almost at the parking lot when Dean spoke again.

"I got a call from Ricardo."

"Really? How's he doing?"

"Pretty good. He asked if I'd consider being on his consultant list. Seems he's gone up in the world. He worked out some kind of deal where his Guardia unit is now cross-appointed to the AFSI. Bigger budget, more responsibility."

"Funny; he asked me to consult for him, too. Are you going to do it?"

"I'm considering it. What about you?"

"I think we owe him. If we can help... Don't you?"

"No question."

Dean revved the car engine and turned the air conditioning on full.

"Taco dinner before we get back to the real world?" he asked.

"Works for me," Briel said.

A tranquil smile crossed Dean's face, and Briel sent her own back. Not the outcome any of them wanted, but Lydia was right. With Percy home, they were at peace. All of them.

WRITER'S NOTE

I thoroughly enjoyed the few trips I've taken to Mexico.

Once, over thirty years ago, my husband and I trekked to the Yucatan Peninsula with our toddler. At a time when tourists could still climb the Temple of Kukulcan, the steps of the pyramid at Chichen Itza fascinated our little boy. Before we knew it he, and we, were at the top. Unfortunately, the ancient staircase was made for smaller feet than ours, so getting down was a challenge. We needed the help of a well-placed guide rope to maintain enough speed to keep up with a child who was sure he'd found the best place ever to practice his new climbing skills. I've never forgotten the beauty of the stone, the incredible views from the top, and the warmth of the people there and in the surrounding communities. It was a special trip.

Much of this book was written during the time of the covid pandemic. As a result, I relied on the internet for this portrayal of Mexico City and its surrounding regions.

As with so many works of fiction, the geographical locations are real, but details have been changed to suit the needs of the story.

For example, although tunnels and caves exist under the Cerro de la Estrella and Quetzalcoatl's pyramid, their specifications were reimagined in this writing.

The real tunnel under the pyramid dedicated to Quetzalcoatl in Teotihuacan was found by accident in 2003, when an exceedingly wet fall season and unstable grounds resulted in a sinkhole. For reasons unknown, the tunnel entrance had been blocked by large boulders in ancient times, so no one knew what lay beneath. The passageway actually ends in a chamber directly under the centre of the monument dedicated to the Feathered Serpent. Evidence suggests that the Teotihuacans decorated that space as though to recreate the underworld. It was the perfect spot for an origin story for Miguel's Quetzalcoatl heritage. However, the existence of the cult and the god's relationship with Popocatepetl are completely made up.

Real Feathered Serpent idolatry can be seen in structures originating in Teotihuacan, as well as those of the Mayan and Aztec peoples, who came after. The god's true purpose remains unknown and may have differed, dependent on time and which civilization portrayed its image. Quetzalcoatl has been associated with everything from fertility to culture, and more.

Teotihuacan as a whole was believed to be a thriving economic centre in Mesoamerica, as early as 200 BCE, when local farming communities banded together. As the city grew, it gained control over the region's obsidian mines, including a source of a rare green variation of the volcanic glass. It is the trade in obsidian for which the centre is best known. By controlling this commodity, the Teotihuacans controlled the supplies needed to create important implements such as knives and spears.

Thus, I chose to have the fictitious icon of Quetzalcoatl, used in Miguel's ceremony, chiseled from that most precious, clear green rock.

Evidence has also been found indicating that the indigenous

people of Teotihuacan conducted human sacrifice. In fact, it may have been a common practice.

The city, a once thriving metropolis, began its decline around 600 CE. The notion that an uprising led to Teotihuacan's collapse comes from scientific evidence of burned buildings and religious icons dating to around that time. It was the reimagining of such a battle that led to the creation of Ichtaca's story in Chapter 101.

Teotihuacan's deterioration is believed to come soon after the many historical reports in the world's northern hemisphere, of famine and climate change during the sixth century CE. These are attributed to significant volcanic activity around 536 CE. In a study published in the journal Geology, February 1, 2017 (42:2; p. 175-178), Kees Nooren and colleagues wrote an article titled: *Explosive eruption of El Chichón volcano (Mexico) disrupted 6th century Maya civilization and contributed to global cooling*. It is interesting to speculate on the role such events played in disrupting food supplies and creating general discontent among the Teotihuacans.

Arturo's use of genetically modified super-growing roundworms as some kind of test/weapon was inspired by two historical events.

The first was the well-known Salem witch trials, whereby passing the test to prove one was not a witch led to death, sealing the accused's fate from the start.

The second was a case series published in the New England Journal of Medicine, May 4, 1972, (286:18; p. 965-970) by James A. Phills and colleagues, entitled: *Pulmonary Infiltrates, Asthma and Eosinophilia due to Ascaris Suum Infestation in Man*. According to that article, four university students ate a celebratory meal deliberately contaminated with huge amounts of Ascaris eggs. Within two weeks, the students, presenting with respiratory distress and/or failure, sought help at a local hospital emergency centre. The details of the actual tainted foods were not provided, so for the sake of the story, I chose milk as a convenient carrier.

As stated in the Prologue, Percy, unbeknownst to Miguel, was already on a standard medication to treat a worm infection, and therefore managed to stave off the impact of Arturo's "test". In Dean's case, vomiting helped decrease the dose to the point where treatment could be successfully administered later.

The headache Briel lectured about, that came after returning from Ecuador, was not related to her ascaris infection. That detail didn't make it into the book, but I can explain it here. Her headache was due to the stress of being a busy professional and feeling poorly. The vague "poorly" part was because of the worms in her system. Her temperature and blood tests revealed an underlying condition that needed further study.

The locations in Texas were fun for me to write about. I lived in the state for quite some time and maintained land close to Lake Granbury. There is no Chiropractic College in nearby Stephenville, Texas. Rather, Stephenville is the home of Tarleton State University's main campus.

In *The Serpent Code*, I attributed the discovery of the Spider Rock to Freddy Palmer and connected him to both Percy and Ricardo's families. Freddy's story is a fictional retelling of an actual turn of the 20th century treasure hunter's quest for lost riches belonging to the Spanish conquistadors.

The real treasure hunter's name was David Arnold, and his search for riches is well described in a book entitled *The Spider Rock Treasure: A Texas Mystery of Lost Spanish Gold*, by Steve Wilson, published in 2004 by Eakin Press.

Arnold arrived in Haskell, Texas in 1902 with a mysterious sheepskin map that led him to unearth the original Spider Rock where the Double Mountain and Salt forks of the Brazos River meet. As Wilson describes, early in his book, no one knows how Arnold came by his parchment, but rumours suggest the treasure hunter saved it from a fire in a Mexican family home. There is also reference to the Mexican government being aware of Arnold, his map, and his hunt.

A published study looking for the origin of the limestone plaster used by the ancients at Teotihuacan and referred to by Dean in Chapter 2 actually exists. Results from that investigation are found in the article from Archaeometry, in 2009, (51:4; p. 525-545), *Provenance of the Limestone used in Teotihuacan (Mexico): A Methodological Approach*, by L. Barba and colleagues, and showed that the lime plaster came from outcrops in Tula.

However, the actual Spider Rock that was dug up in Texas in the early 1900s disappeared only a few years after it was uncovered, and therefore, the mineral content of that stone remains unknown.

For this book, I visited Haskell, Texas and nearby Rule, and then stood on the red earth, where the Salt and Double Mountain forks of the Brazos River meet. The puzzle of the Spider Rock has held interest in these regions for a long time. It captivated me too—so much so that it became the muse for this novel.

The Cueva de los Tayos, or Cave of the Oilbirds, in Ecuador, as referred to in Chapter 1, was made famous in a book called *Gold of the Gods*, from 1973 by Erich von Däniken, published by G. P. Putnam's Sons. In it, von Däniken suggested that a previous cave explorer found gold, a library of metal plates, and man-made structures the author believed were created with the help of extraterrestrials.

The entrance to this underground world is an amazing rift in the earth of the Amazon jungle—a two hundred-foot drop into a dark series of caverns that include unusual geological formations, waterfalls and, of course, oilbirds. The birds, like bats, go into the jungle at night, foraging for food and using echolocation to find their way. Given the region's biodiversity, the cave is an amazing treasure.

The number of Americans missing in Mexico that Briel refers to while speaking with Lydia in Chapter 2 is accurate and alarming. And the data have not gotten better. As of March 10, 2023, the

Washington Post reported that US citizens still missing rose from 324 in 2020 to 558 in 2023.

There are many references, especially early in this book, to Briel's climbing expertise. It was a joy to assign her that competence and watch her movements, and it is something she and I will never share. When searching for Percy's first coded message near Casada Congelada in Chapter 3, Briel mentions a free solo climb up Yosemite's El Capitan. That reference is to Alex Honnold's world-famous climb up the Freerider route in 2017, without ropes or other protective equipment. An amazing feat—and something the ever-cautious Briel Payce would be unlikely to try.

During Briel's visit to Iztaccihuatl, she encounters the teporingo. Also known as volcano rabbits, these tiny creatures live in the high altitudes surrounding Mexico City, and like so much unique wildlife in niche environments, their existence is threatened by habitat destruction. Briel's sighting of the teporingo would have been well worthy of her attention.

The Conductor's compound is completely fictional, but its location near the Parque Valle de las Monjas and the town of San Mateo Tlaltenango seemed like a prime spot. The park is known for its tall trees, beautiful springs and hiking trails—an oasis only a short drive from the action in Mexico City.

The Guardia Nacional in Mexico was established in 2019 by combining Federal, Military and Naval police. However, the División de Homicidios de la Ciudad de México por Delitos contra Turistas, or the Violent Crime Against Tourists Unit for Mexico City, proposed in this book as under Guardia control, is entirely my creation. The same is true of the Agencia Federal de Servicios de Investigación (AFSI), or Federal Investigation Services Agency. As a result, the fictitious Ricardo De La Cruz and Luis

Menendez were able to function entirely under the rules I developed for them.

There is also no Secretaria de Viajes, Cultura y Turismo, (Secretariat of Travel, Culture and Tourism), nor a Secretaría de Estabilidad Ambiental (Secretariat of Environmental Stability), nor a Departamento Regional de Monitoreo de Desastres Naturales (Regional Department for Monitoring Natural Disasters), in Mexico. Real governmental bodies deal with many, if not all, of these functions in most countries throughout the world, including Mexico. However, I adapted organizational concerns to meet the needs of the story.

Interestingly, on May 20, 2023, as I was finishing this book, Mexico's Centro Nacional de Prevención de Desastres (CENAPRED) reported three minor and one moderate explosion from Popocatepetl. Mexico City's Benito Juarez and the Felipe Ángeles International Airports temporarily shut down their operations due to spewing ash. The symbolism was too great an opportunity to miss, so I incorporated this detail as a way of delaying Briel and Dean's flights.

In *The Serpent Code*, I focused on only one of the many kinds of sensing devices used in volcanology to simplify the creation of Alejandro's false data set. It is true, however, that certain volcano sensor boxes can be tripped up by a variety of natural and unnatural causes.

Johannes Trithemius was a real German Benedictine Abbott who lived in the late 15th and early 16th century. He had a persistent interest in the occult, as did many religious leaders of the time, and is well known for his book *Polygraphia*, wherein he created the "Ave Maria" code described in *The Serpent Code*. In fact, photos of the actual pages of the book are available online from the Library of Congress, and I used those to create the Latin verse given to Briel by Padre Hugh.

Researching Mexico's Pueblo Mágicos, Tepoztlán was an absolute joy, and the town is now on my bucket list of must-see places. The Portada de Semillas, or Portal of Seeds project, began in 1991. As described in Chapter 68, each year, resident volunteers glue thousands upon thousands of naturally coloured seeds to a plywood board to create a gigantic mural depicting cultural or religious themes. And the nearby town of Amatlán actually does boast a sacred pond, said to be the birthplace of Quetzalcoatl.

Plaza de Loreto, first mentioned in Chapter 83, is a city park, about a ten or fifteen-minute walk north and east of Mexico City's historic centre. It is known today as the site of a fountain believed to be the creation of the early 19th century artist, architect and engineer, Manuel Tolsá—the man charged with managing Mexico City's drainage and water supplies at the time. His fountain, the one that now stands in Plaza de Loreto, began its life in the historic Bucareli corridor.

Discovering the Plaza de Loreto was a bit of an adventure.

I first went to Steve Wilson's book (*The Spider Rock Treasure: A Texas Mystery of Lost Spanish Gold*; 2004, Eakin Press), and found a picture of the blueprint of the Spider Rock carving provided by Doc Henderson. I was taken by how similar many of the features were to Bordone's 1528 woodcut of Tenochtitlan (Mexico City).

Like Briel, I lined up the two images and the arrow on the Spider Rock pointed to Bordone's Casa de li Solazzi del s. A "House of Solace".

The only thing I could think of as comparable for the time was Moctezuma's Pleasure Palace. At least one of them—apparently, there were many.

Next, I enhanced a map of the same region in modern day

Mexico City and added that to the other two layers. That arrow landed squarely on the Plaza de Loreto.

In a long and now deleted scene, I created a story of how the obsidian icon of Quetzalcoatl came to be housed in that park/pleasure palace grounds. In this iteration of the story, when I needed a place for Miguel's cult's headquarters, Plaza de Loreto became that spot.

Over the course of my research and in writing this book, I have come to believe that the original Spider Rock really was a hand-carved rendition of Tenochtitlan. A copy, if you will, of Bordone's rendering. How a parchment map from Mexico led to unearthing such a stone in Haskell, Texas, we'll probably never know. I'm satisfied, however, that the Rock doesn't, and never will, lead to treasure in Texas. Instead, I think it brings us to a greater understanding of history, geography and geology in both great lands.

Writing *The Serpent Code* and connecting Mexico City's history with a puzzle from Texas was a great pleasure for me. It is my sincerest hope that you, the reader, have found the result entertaining as well.

AR Stevens

ABOUT THE AUTHOR

AR Stevens was born and raised in Toronto. Growing up, the chilly waters of Lake Ontario held a special place in her heart, but she longed to spread her wings and explore the globe. Years spent conducting and presenting clinical research whisked her to almost every continent, and fed her need to write. Thirteen of those years were spent in the great state of Texas in the USA. Now, AR lives in the tranquil embrace of Lake Simcoe's shores, in Orillia, Ontario, with her husband and their remarkably articulate poodle. She's turned her full-time attention to crafting international, puzzle-thriller fiction. *The Serpent Code* is AR Stevens' first book.

She is currently working on her next novel.

Sign up for her Newsletter for updates, and receive a free short story by visiting her website at:

arstevenswriter.com